D0395377

DARK MIRROR

DARK MIRROR

A Brock and Kolla Mystery

BARRY MAITLAND

MINOTAUR BOOKS
NEW YORK

DARK MIRROR. Copyright © 2009 by Barry Maitland. All rights reserved. Printed in the United States of America. For information, address St. Martin's Press, 175 Fifth Avenue, New York, N.Y. 10010.

www.minotaurbooks.com

The Library of Congress has cataloged the hardcover edition as follows:

Maitland, Barry.
    Dark mirror : a Brock and Kolla mystery / Barry Maitland.—1st U.S. ed.
       p. cm.
    ISBN 978-0-312-38399-2
    1. Brock, David (Fictitious character)—Fiction. 2. Kolla, Kathy (Fictitious character)—Fiction. 3. Police—England—London—Fiction. 4. London (England)—Fiction. I. Title.
    PR9619.3.M2635D37 2009
    823'.914—dc22
                                                        2009012733

ISBN 978-0-312-65082-7 (trade paperback)

First published in Australia by Allen & Unwin

First Minotaur Books Paperback Edition: October 2011

10 9 8 7 6 5 4 3 2 1

[For Margaret]

With special thanks to Barry Sherringham and Dr. Tim Lyons, and to Alison Sproston and the London Library for their help.

ONE

NIGEL OGILVIE HURRIED UP the stairs to the Reading Room on the first floor, and made his way, panting slightly, to the big windows overlooking the square. It was a dazzling spring morning, the sun glistening on new foliage bursting from the trees in the central garden, so that it seemed as if King William on his bronze horse was prancing through a brilliant green cloud. Nigel spotted the familiar figure sitting on a bench not far from the statue, her head bent over a book, and watched as she wiped her mouth with a paper napkin, then slowly gathered up the wrapper and drink bottle by her side. He reached into his pocket for his mobile phone and took a picture, capturing the moment as Marion got to her feet and the sun caught her, setting her red hair alight. She began to walk towards the library, tossing her rubbish into a bin. Her coat was unbuttoned, and he watched the swell of her thighs beneath her dress as she strode, head up. *Lithe*, he thought, that was the word. He felt a small quickening of his heartbeat and turned away, making his way across the Reading Room to where he'd left his book earlier. Settling himself in the red leather armchair, he opened the heavy volume on his knee and waited, eyes unfocused on the text.

He was finding it hard to concentrate these days, his research not going well. The idea for the project, *Deadly Gardens*, had been dreamed up by his boss over a boozy lunch, and Nigel was convinced that it wasn't going to work. For the past week he'd been trying to make something of the gardens that Lucrezia Borgia would have known at Ferrara, Nepi, Spoleto and Foligno, but really, it was a waste of time—Lucrezia had had more pressing things on her mind than gardening. She too had red hair, if Veneziano's portrait was to be believed, and Nigel imagined that she and Marion might have other things in common—a dangerous attraction for one.

Deadly Gardens. He sighed with frustration. He detested Stephen, his boss, a philistine about half his age, who treated him with an amused contempt that made him feel as if he was back at school. But at least the project had provided him with an excuse to hide himself here in the library. He loved the place, a refuge where he could turn off his importuning mobile phone, bury himself in the womb of a million books, snuffle about on the steel grille floors among the stacks, do *The Times* crossword and—a particular satisfaction—observe the other patrons. Poking about in the memoirs of the dead was fascinating, of course, but there was a particular buzz, a special frisson, about the leisurely observation of lives in which passions were still unresolved, and suffering still to be endured.

And here she came at last, Marion Summers, making her entrance up the main stair and looking more Pre-Raphaelite than ever, with her long flowing skirt and that mane of thick red hair and complexion so pale—deathly pale this morning—that he could make out the faint blue line of the artery ticking in her throat. She too had her particular place in the Reading Room, at one of the tables, her pile of books next to the small vase of flowers she'd brought in the previous day. He wondered where they'd come from. They were white, and more like wild flowers than the sort of thing you'd find in a florist's, rather improbable in Central London. What had she been up to last weekend? Was there an admirer out there he didn't know about?

He watched her as she approached, trying to hide his eagerness, and wondered if she would glance at him and offer one of her knowing little smiles. They were at least at that stage, although in his imagination they were a good deal further. Stephen would be irate to learn that he had certainly spent more time studying her than the Borgias' gardens. He knew her borrowing record, her home address, her working timetable, her tastes in soft drinks and sandwiches. He could recall exactly the intonations of her voice when she was puzzled, amused, cajoling the librarians who helped her track down the things she needed. And he had many photographs of her, working here in the library, sitting outside in St. James's Square beneath William III on his prancing horse, and on the bus. And all this he had acquired in secret, without arousing the least suspicion.

Marion paused beside her table, splaying her fingers on its surface for support. There was a faint sheen of perspiration on her forehead, which was creased by a frown, as if she were trying to make sense of something. She grimaced suddenly, raising a hand abruptly to her mouth and reaching with the other for her chair. But before she could grasp it she staggered, and her hand knocked the vase of flowers to the floor. She doubled over with a moan and sank to her knees.

"Oh!" Her cry was cut off as she was abruptly sick, her body convulsing violently, sending the chair tumbling onto its back.

Consternation spread out in ripples across the Reading Room, people rising to their feet, craning to see what had happened. But Nigel remained where he was, eyes bright, phone in hand, fastidiously recording every detail. She was being sick again, poor thing, writhing in agony as she retched over the red carpet.

One of the librarians was running forward. "What is it?" she demanded. "What's wrong?"

A man who had been seated at her table said, "She . . . she's having some sort of attack," shrinking back with a look of horrified pity on his face. Last to respond, the two old codgers in the armchairs in front of the fireplace had belatedly risen to their feet.

Everyone's attention was focused on the epicentre of the drama, unaware of Nigel taking surreptitious pictures of Marion thrashing about helplessly on the floor, and of the shock on people's faces as they witnessed this awful scene, all of them struck by the same terrible realisation that such a thing, whatever it was, could happen to anyone, at any time, even *here* in this sanctuary.

"Is there a doctor here?" the librarian cried.

Actually there were six in the room, but none of them of the medical kind, and they were quite unable to help.

"Are you calling an ambulance?" she demanded, and Nigel froze, realising suddenly that she was staring straight at him.

"Yes, absolutely!" He dialled triple nine, feeling himself the focus of attention now as people thankfully averted their eyes from Marion. He spoke fast and clearly to the operator, feeling he was doing it rather well, and when they wanted to know his name he gave it with a little thrill of excitement—he would be on the official record.

"Airways," the librarian said. "We have to make sure she doesn't choke." But that was easier said than done, for Marion's body was racked by convulsive spasms. It was some minutes before they subsided enough for the librarian to bravely stick her fingers into the young woman's mouth to make sure she hadn't swallowed her tongue. Kneeling in the mess, she cradled Marion's head on her lap and stroked her hair soothingly, the wild flowers scattered on the carpet all around. Nigel got some good shots of that.

Someone was gathering up the contents of Marion's bag, which had spilled over the floor. Nigel stooped to help. He picked up a hairbrush, with strands of her red hair coiled around its bristles, and reluctantly put it back into the bag. But he palmed the computer memory stick lying beside it, slipping it into his pocket.

TWO

KATHY ROSE TO HER feet as the Crown solicitor came through the courtroom door and nodded at her.

"Looks like you won't be needed after all," he said. "We're pretty much wrapped up."

"Good." She felt some relief, tempered by a sense of frustration that this stupid business had gone on so long. The trial of the Fab Five—so called by the cops because of their sharp suits and hairstyles and breezy attitudes—had been endlessly prolonged by their individual windbag barristers, each intent on muddying the waters around their own client at the others' expense, as well as by the highly imaginative alibis provided by their various perjuring mothers, girlfriends and mates. They had gone to a house to recover a drug debt, not realising that the man they wanted had moved on weeks before, and the new tenant was too drunk to explain their mistake before they beat him to death. They had taken a life, and would certainly be found guilty, but any satisfaction was dulled by Kathy's calculation, made while waiting on the corridor benches day after day, that all the time the police, the lawyers, the gaolers, the administrators, the forensic staff, the court officials, the jury and the witnesses had spent in achieving this would amount to another human lifetime, a good part of it her own. All for one utterly stupid mistake. This was not what she'd been made up to inspector for. She badly wanted a case that would allow her to flex her newly promoted investigative muscle, a case that would, well, *mean* something.

As she made for the main doors she felt her phone buzz in her pocket. It was Brock, sounding rushed. "Kathy, still tied up?"

A crisis was gripping Queen Anne's Gate along with the rest of Homicide and Serious Crime Command, with the terrorist alert level newly raised to "severe specific" at a time when an epidemic of spring flu had cut through the ranks. It had made her own inactivity all the more galling.

"Just finished, hopefully for good. I'm leaving now."

"I've had a call from Sundeep, steamed up about something. Couldn't get much out of him, except that it's about an autopsy he's doing. He said it was urgent. I'd go myself, but I'm due at a meeting in Broadway in ten minutes. Could you look after him?"

"Sure."

"Good. I'll get Pip to come and pick you up, shall I?"

That was another source of irritation: DC Philippa Gallagher, known as Pip, also as Flippa, on temporary rotation through the team, for whom Kathy was supposed to be acting as mentor. Too pretty and fragile-looking to be a police officer, Pip seemed oblivious to the stares of the male members of the team. She was very eager and had an annoying habit of asking questions to which Kathy didn't know the answers, then staring with wide-eyed attentiveness as Kathy tried to improvise a reply. It was probably the same look she'd given her teachers in the school she hardly seemed old enough to have left.

But when Kathy stepped out into the fresh air, her mood lifted. It was a beautiful day, sunlight glittering on the golden figure of Justice on top of the dome of the Old Bailey against a brilliant blue sky. She made her way through the knots of the usual suspects huddled along the footpath, and bought a coffee across the road, then stood in the sun, waiting, wondering what Brock's favourite pathologist was in a panic about.

By the time the unmarked car slid to a stop at the kerb in front of her she felt ready even for DC Gallagher.

"Hi, boss!"

As a sergeant Kathy had occasionally been called "skip," but no one had ever called her "boss" before. She rather liked it. The girl gave her a big grin, and Kathy smiled back; maybe she'd been unfair to her. Pip was so keen, and Kathy had a sudden vivid memory of herself on her first murder case after making sergeant. That was when she'd first met Brock, and, come to think of it, Sundeep Mehta. It seemed a long time ago.

When they arrived at the mortuary they saw the little doctor waiting for them by the front desk, chatting up the receptionist with a kind of extravagant bonhomie that Kathy thought, as she caught sight of him, looked rather forced. The woman turned away to answer a phone call, Sundeep frowned, glanced furtively at his watch, then wheeled around to see Kathy and Pip approaching. He brightened, slipping on the cavalier persona he liked people to see.

"DS Kolla!" he beamed, teasingly formal. "How nice to see you again."

"DI," she corrected. "I've been promoted."

He raised his hands in mock horror at his gaffe. "Inspector! Of course, I did hear. And so very well deserved. I've told Brock often enough that you're the only one to be trusted to do a decent job in that place. I'm so pleased he sent you. And *who* is this?"

"Don't flirt, Sundeep. This is DC Gallagher—Pip."

"How do you do, Pip." He shook her hand delicately, as if it might bruise easily, then gave them both visitors' tags. "And why shouldn't I flirt? Am I too old? Wouldn't you call that discrimination, Pip?"

The usual patter, Kathy thought, but all the same she sensed his heart wasn't in it. He was worried about something.

He led them over to the stairs and they descended to a corridor and an overpowering smell of fresh paint. It was sharply cooler down there, and somewhere up ahead a radio was playing tinny

7

music. They reached a pair of double swing doors and Sundeep led the way into a brightly lit room in the centre of which was a series of stainless-steel tables. On the nearest a woman's body was stretched out, naked and recently dissected, but not yet reassembled. Kathy sensed Pip's stride falter at the sight. Her eyes moved from the woman's opened abdomen to her scalp pulled forward over her face, the top of her skull neatly severed, the brain removed.

Kathy turned her attention to Sundeep, who offered her a photograph of a young woman, head and shoulders. Even without the stainless steel on which her red hair fanned, Kathy would have known that she was dead. Her green eyes were open but sightless, her flesh like yellow wax.

"Her name is Marion Summers," Sundeep said. "She collapsed yesterday in the London Library in the West End. She was sick and passed out. When the ambulance arrived she was in a coma, from which she never woke. She was wearing a medical alert bracelet that said she suffered from type one diabetes, and a witness said she'd had fainting spells recently. The ambulance crew assumed this was the reason for her collapse, as did the doctor who treated her in A and E. They wondered if she might be in the early stages of a pregnancy, which can upset the insulin-sugar balance. She died ninety minutes after admission.

"I performed the autopsy a couple of hours ago. The toxicology results aren't back yet, of course, and I may be jumping the gun, but I'm sure I'm right. There were distinctive signs—severe haemorrhaging of the mucosa, for instance. Then when I opened her stomach I noticed the smell, quite faint, a bit like garlic. Here . . ."

He reached for a beaker containing some dark fluid and sniffed it like a connoisseur, wrinkling his nose, then offered it to Kathy. Reluctantly she did the same, then shook her head. "I don't know." She turned to Pip, whose eyebrows rose in consternation, and Kathy handed the flask back to Sundeep.

"No, well, anyone else probably wouldn't have noticed, because this is so unusual now, in this country—the first case I've come across, to tell the truth. But I remember that smell so well from my student days, in India. We opened up a number of victims—well, the stuff was readily available, you see, in herbicides and pesticides and industrial processes and God knows what. And they say now that the whole Bengal basin is sitting on a vast layer of it, and people are sinking their wells into it and drawing it up—my God, they say millions may die."

Kathy waited, but he seemed momentarily at a loss. "What are we talking about, Sundeep?" she asked gently.

"Arsenic, Kathy. I'm almost sure that she died of arsenic poisoning."

He saw the sceptical lift of her eyebrow and nodded quickly. "Yes, yes, I know, arsenic in the library, all very Agatha Christie. A hundred years ago arsenic was the height of fashion in England. You could buy it over the counter at the chemist, freshen your complexion with it, treat your syphilis, kill your rats, poison your husband . . . but not now. Where would you get hold of arsenic today?" He paused, then stressed, "It is *very* unusual, Kathy."

"It does seem unlikely, doesn't it, Sundeep? Shouldn't we wait for the test results?" She suspected there was some agenda here that Sundeep was holding back. She waited, he sighed.

"A dear friend of mine, a very distinguished surgeon, has a son, fresh from medical school, newly launched in his profession, working twenty-eight hours a day in accident and emergency. It was he who examined Marion when she was brought in yesterday. His initial tests supported the ambulance crew's assumption—there *was* a marked insulin imbalance. He treated this and decided to wait—there was so much else crying for his attention yesterday. That was perhaps a mistake, but an understandable one. If it was arsenic, you see, time was very short—in fact it was probably already too late. You only have about an hour to try to get the stuff out of the victim before it's absorbed. Once that happens there's no antidote."

"That's terrible . . ." Kathy hesitated, wondering how best to put this. "But it's not something we can . . . cover up."

"Good Lord, no!" Sundeep was shocked. "No one's suggesting such a thing. No, no. We . . . I just want to find out what really happened. If it was murder . . ."

"If?"

"Well, I suppose you'd have to consider suicide. I saw that too, in India, but only because the poison was available. And there are old self-harm scars on her wrists. But it would be a very unpleasant way to kill yourself. No, I was thinking, if it was a deliberate poisoning, how was it done, in a public place in the middle of the day?"

"Her food or drink?"

"Yes, a lethal drink-spiking, say. And then, was she deliberately targeted, or might it have been anyone? And if the latter, have there been other cases? It would be easy to misdiagnose, you see. Arsenic is not something one would normally test for, especially if the symptoms were masked, as here. And there might be no autopsy."

"A serial poisoner?"

"Or something else; India isn't the only country where arsenic wouldn't be hard to find."

The suggestion hung in the air for a moment.

"A terrorist? Surely we're getting ahead of ourselves, Sundeep?"

"Yes, yes. I'm not wanting to go off the deep end, but with all these terror warnings, and it being such an unusual poison these days . . . I've advised the National Poisons Information Service and started phoning around colleagues in other hospitals."

Kathy sighed inwardly. This was a babysitting job. Sundeep was having a panic attack. "All right. I'll check our sources. What do we know about Marion?"

"Not much. Age mid-twenties. I understand the hospital hasn't been able to trace her next of kin yet. They say she was a student. I have her things." He indicated a number of bagged items on the bench against the wall.

"And she collapsed in a library?"

"In the London Library—you know it? Just off Piccadilly. Apparently she's a regular there. They say she just returned from a lunch break and collapsed. I have a copy of the ambulance officer's report."

"If she was poisoned, how long would it have happened before she collapsed?"

"That depends on the concentration of the dose. She could have been feeling ill for hours, or it might have been more rapid, something in her lunch. I won't be able to make a time estimate until I get the lab results."

The pathologist's assistant came towards them carrying a blue plastic bag. She looked at Sundeep through her visor and he gave a brief nod, at which she began to pack the bag containing the remains of the soft organs back into Marion's belly.

"And were they right?" Kathy asked. "Was she pregnant?"

"No, she wasn't."

Kathy put on gloves and began to go through the woman's possessions. There was an elegant watch, Omega, and three rings, ruby, amethyst and diamond stones on generous gold bands. "Which fingers?"

He showed her. "Not engagement or wedding rings, I assume. I think the hospital established that she wasn't married."

"But nice things," Kathy said. "Not a penniless student. What about the clothes?"

She checked the labels. "Very nice."

Marion's wallet contained sixty-five pounds in cash, a credit card, a driver's licence with an address in Stamford Street, SE1 and some receipts, as well as a number of identity and membership cards, including a student card for London University. Her bag contained makeup, keys, a phone and a thick notebook with handwritten entries that might have related to her studies. There was also a bag of sweets.

"If their blood-sugar balance is unsteady," Sundeep said, "diabetics sometimes carry sugary sweets to help them adjust it. Maybe the same with the lunchtime drink. The sweetness would tend to disguise the taste of arsenic."

"Okay. I'll make some calls, Sundeep."

"Use my office across the corridor, Kathy." He started to take off his jacket. "I have autopsies to perform. But thank you for coming so quickly. I'm sorry if I'm wasting your time. You'll let me know?"

"Of course. And ring me as soon as you get the test results."

"They've promised to do a Marsh test straight away. I may be completely wrong. Let's hope I am, eh?"

Kathy led the way to Sundeep's office. Pip's face was very pale against her dark lipstick and eye shadow.

"You okay?"

She took a deep breath. "Yes, yes . . ." She swallowed.

"You're not going to be sick?"

"No."

"Just sit down for a bit."

Kathy took the big chair behind Sundeep's desk and began by putting a call through to the antiterrorist hotline, reporting Sundeep's fears. They promised to get back to her. Then she ran a check on Marion Summers, quickly establishing that she wasn't known to the police. She got the number for the student administration office at the university, giving them Marion's name and student number, and was told that she was enrolled as a PhD student in the Department of European Literature. Their computer had no record of her next of kin. Kathy followed with a call to the London Library, arranging to meet the librarian mentioned on the ambulance officer's report, and requesting contact details for the other person mentioned, a Mr. Nigel Ogilvie. Apparently Mr. Ogilvie, a regular, was at the library and would be asked to make himself available. Kathy thanked them and said she was on her way.

"I've never seen that before," Pip said as she hung up. Kathy thought she was referring to the autopsy, but then saw that she was staring at Marion's mobile, whose buttons she'd been working. "No call log, no phone book—no numbers listed at all."

"Maybe it's brand new."

Pip held it up for her to see the scuffed surface of the cover. "She must have wiped the memory."

"We'll have to check the phone records."

Kathy drove them back to the Scotland Yard annexe at Queen Anne's Gate where Brock's team was housed, and dropped Pip outside. "I want you to get on to the PNC. You're looking for reported cases of suspected poisonings, drink spikings leading to illness or death, unexplained deaths that could have been down to poison, anything like that. Use your imagination. If Sundeep's right it's possible that other cases may have been misdiagnosed. Start with the London area in the past seven days. Also any mention of arsenic."

Pip looked downcast. "You're not sending me back to the office as a punishment for feeling dodgy back there, are you?"

"Of course not. We all feel like that the first few times."

She managed a pale grin. "All right, boss, I'm on it."

THREE

THE LIBRARIAN APPROVED OF the detective as soon as she introduced herself in the entrance hall. They were physically similar for a start, both women lean in build, with blond hair cut short. The inspector's name, Kolla, was intriguing, and she wondered where it came from. It made her think of the Kola Peninsula in Russia, and she imagined it having some Nordic source. Her own name, Rayner, was originally Danish. She identified with the police officer's manner too—friendly, brisk and searching, she felt, for nuances in the replies she gave. And perhaps that was to be expected, for the professions of librarian and detective were not so dissimilar, were they? Both processing information, seeking cross-references, patterns of order in the blizzard of data.

"I phoned the hospital first thing this morning and got the terrible news that Marion had died," the librarian said. "I was appalled of course, we all were, although we realised that something was very seriously wrong. I've never seen anything like that before." She shook her head sadly.

"Did you know her well, Ms. Rayner?"

"Gael, please. She'd been a member here for over a year now, and we often exchanged a few words when she came in, which was fairly frequently in recent months—I'd say two or three times a week. We had a sandwich together once, when we bumped into each other in a café nearby."

"She didn't eat here?"

"There are no facilities for food or drink in the library at present, although we are in the process of expanding—you'll probably hear the builders before you go. But there are several coffee shops within a few blocks of here." She hesitated. "Is that relevant? It wasn't food poisoning was it?"

Kathy said, "It seems to be a possibility, yes. I understand she was returning from lunch when she collapsed. Do you have any idea where she'd been?"

"No, but I can give you a few names of places to try. Only she had been feeling a bit unwell lately, and she was a diabetic. I told the ambulance officer. I just assumed . . ."

"They're still doing tests. We haven't been able to trace her next of kin yet. Can you help? Do you know of a partner, relatives?"

Gael thought. "Well, she was Scots—she had a rather attractive soft accent. She didn't talk much to me about herself, just her work. I'm pretty sure she wasn't married, but I think there was a boyfriend, though I don't know how serious. I noticed a new ring one day, and she said it was a present. It looked expensive, but it wasn't an engagement ring. Have you tried the university?"

Kathy nodded. "We have an address in Southwark."

"Really? I thought . . . She mentioned a traffic hold-up at Swiss Cottage one day, and I just assumed she lived up there. Let me check our records." She went to a computer and typed, then looked up. "No, you're right. Stamford Street. Unless she moved recently and didn't tell us."

"Did she have any particular friends here, people she might have spoken to?"

The librarian shook her head. "Not that I'm aware of. She just came here to do her work. She was writing a thesis on the Pre-Raphaelite painters and poets; Dante Gabriel Rossetti mainly, I gathered, and William Morris—she was particularly interested in him—and their wives and lovers."

Kathy looked around, at the classical columns, the leather furniture, the other visitors. "Do you get many students here? It's not an ordinary public library, is it?"

"No, no, this is a private library, the largest independent lending library in the world. It was started by Thomas Carlyle, who got fed up with conditions at the library at the British Museum, and with not being able to borrow their books. Gladstone and Dickens and others agreed with him, and they established the London Library. You'll find more students at the British Library, now that they've opened their reading rooms to undergraduates, and at the university libraries of course, but we get a few PhD students here wanting to access the specialised areas of our collection, although they have to pay our membership fee. People in need can apply for a grant of up to half of that from our Trust, but I don't know if Marion did. Do you want me to check?"

"Yes, that might be a good idea."

"You're interested in her finances?" Gael's eyes grew sharp with interest.

"Just curious. I get the impression she wasn't hard up—for a student, I mean."

"Yes, I agree. She had very nice shoes. I couldn't help noticing."

She gave a rueful smile, and Kathy said, "When she collapsed, what happened to her bag, do you remember?"

"It fell on the floor I think. Yes, in fact her things spilled out. We gathered them up and gave them to the ambulance officer."

"Is it possible that anyone tampered with her phone?"

Gael shook her head. "I couldn't say."

"Well, I'd better have a word with Mr. Ogilvie."

"He's waiting up in the Reading Room, where it happened. I'll take you."

They climbed the carpeted stairs to the next floor, and entered a double-height galleried space, its walls lined with books. Several dozen readers were working on long tables or consulting periodicals racks and catalogue consoles. Gael took Kathy across the room towards a middle-aged man sitting in one of the armchairs with a heavy volume on his knees. He struggled to his feet as he saw them approach.

"Nigel, this is Detective Inspector Kolla."

They shook hands. The man was plump, with pink chubby hands and face, glossy black hair swept flat, a dark suit and tie. His eyes sparkled at her through large glasses. Like a mole, she thought. The librarian left them to get the information on membership grants, and Ogilvie led Kathy over to the spot where Marion had collapsed, describing, with some relish she thought, exactly what he'd witnessed.

"So she was just returning from a lunch break?"

"That's right."

"Any idea where she took it?"

"Well," the pink tip of his tongue flicked across his lower lip, "as a matter of fact I think I do, yes. Let me show you." He led the way to the large windows on one side of the room overlooking St. James's Square. Kathy stood at his side, seeing the gardens, the trees in bud and the equestrian statue.

"I was stretching my legs, and came to the window and happened to notice her out there, in that seat to the left of the statue. See?" He pointed. "She was reading, and there were paper wrappings at her side, as if she'd been eating a sandwich."

"Did you notice a drink?"

"I think . . . yes, I'm fairly sure she had a soft-drink bottle." He nodded eagerly at Kathy, very pleased with himself. "She got to her feet and dropped her rubbish in that bin down there before coming back into the library. A few moments later she was writhing in agony on the floor."

He's enjoying this, Kathy thought. "Did you see anyone else in the square?"

Ogilvie pondered, shook his head. "No, I can't say I did."

"Would you happen to know if she bought her lunch from around here?"

"I'm afraid not. Is that significant? About her lunch?"

"I'm just trying to get a picture of her last movements, Mr. Ogilvie."

"Oh, come, Inspector! There may be something I've seen that could help you, if only I knew what you're looking for. You must tell me."

"Anything you remember may be useful. Did you see her using her mobile phone yesterday?"

"I don't think so."

Kathy got him to describe exactly what happened when Marion reached the Reading Room.

"Who gathered up her belongings?"

"Oh, I can't remember."

"If you think of anything else just contact me on this number, will you? Thanks for your help."

She gave him her card, and then as she turned away he gave an odd little skip and leapt after her to say in an intimate whisper, as if he didn't want any of the other readers, who were trying to listen in to their conversation, to hear, "She was interested in poisons, you know."

Kathy spun around. "What?"

"Ah!" He stepped back quickly, eyes bright, perhaps just a little alarmed by the look on Kathy's face.

She looked past him at the others watching them, and drew him over to an empty table in the corner of the room. They both sat and she pulled out her notebook. "What about poisons?"

"Oh," he said, back-pedalling now, "it was probably nothing. It's just that one day I happened to notice her reading a book called *Famous Victorian Poisoners*, something like that. You see, I'm doing research on Lucrezia Borgia myself, for my company. We publish coffee table books mostly." He wrinkled his nose and handed her his card. "Anyway, I made some sort of a joke with Marion and she said it was to do with her doctorate."

"So you were on first-name terms?"

"Well, yes. This is a friendly place."

"Do you know anything about her circumstances? Partner, family, home?"

"Oh no, nothing like that."

Kathy nodded. She felt that there was something here, something beneath the surface, but wasn't sure what. "All right. Well, thanks again, Mr. Ogilvie. And do get in touch if you think of anything else."

Kathy rejoined Gael, who told her that Marion had never applied for any financial help. They walked together to the front door, and Gael pointed to a small bunch of white flowers standing in a tiny glass vase.

"A little memorial," she said. "Marion brought these in the day before it happened, and knocked them over when she collapsed. Afterwards I retrieved a few of them and put them in water for her."

"I'm sorry, this must be the last thing you'd expect to happen in a place like this."

"Not recently certainly, but we have had our dramas. Leigh Hunt's nephew shot himself here, you know."

From the way she said it, Kathy assumed she should know who Leigh Hunt was. She looked more closely at the flowers. "They're unusual, aren't they? From her boyfriend?"

"Not the faintest. She never said."

Kathy walked out into the bright day, warming up now, and crossed the street into the central gardens. She checked the rubbish bin—empty—and went to the seat that Ogilvie had pointed out. From there she could be seen from many of the buildings surrounding the square. They would all have to be door-knocked. Lunchtime was approaching, and a few people were making their way into the garden clutching newspapers and packets of food, coatless today. Kathy spoke to them, showing them Marion's picture. One thought she'd seen the young woman there, but not that week. All this would have to be done more systematically, Kathy realised and moved off to check the cafés that Gael had mentioned. On the way she noticed brass nameplates with the titles of venerable clubs as well as international companies—the East India Club, BP, Rio Tinto, the Naval and Military Club—which occupied the Georgian and Victorian mansions that lined the square and surrounding streets. She also paused at the small memorial set up in one corner of the square to Yvonne Fletcher, the policewoman who had been shot dead there in April 1984, during a demonstration outside the Libyan Embassy. It made her think again about Sundeep's fear of a political motive.

No one she spoke to in the cafés remembered serving Marion Summers, nor could recall anything unusual happening the previous day. There was a florist's a couple of streets away, but she couldn't see any flowers like those in Marion's vase, and the assistant had no idea where they might have come from. Kathy rang Gael and established that someone in the library had a digital camera, and asked her to send pictures of the flowers to an email address she gave her.

She drove across the river to Southwark, near Waterloo station, bustling and noisy with the sound of roadwork after the patrician calm of St. James's Square, and in Stamford Street found Marion's address, a converted block of self-catering student apartments. There was no sign of the name Summers on any of the mailboxes in the entrance hall, and the woman at the front desk confirmed they had no resident of that name. After a search of her computer she found that Marion had lived there for two years, but had moved on three months previously. The forwarding address she'd given them was the office of the university department in which she was enrolled, at the Strand campus on the other side of the river.

Kathy rang Pip.

"No, boss, I can't find anything on the PNC." She said it with a sigh.

"See what you can find out about Marion, will you?" Kathy gave her the credit card and driver's licence numbers. "I want to know where she's been living for the past three months. Possibly somewhere out past Swiss Cottage. Maybe we can find where those keys in her bag were cut. And find her parents too. And check Missing Persons, see if anyone's reported her absence last night or this morning."

"Okay. Er . . . someone called Rayner just sent me some flowers—pictures, on my email."

"Ah yes. I'd like you to find out what they are, Pip."

"Pardon?" She sounded incredulous.

"Marion brought them in to the library the day before yesterday. Maybe a boyfriend gave them to her."

"Oh. Anything else?"

"Yes, the first thing to do: phone Westminster Council and get them to try to trace the contents of a waste bin in St. James's Square. Marion dropped the remains of her lunch there yesterday."

"Ah."

"Just do your best, Pip. I'll get us some help."

THE SECRETARY AT THE Department of European Literature was eager to find out how Marion had died, and why the police were involved.

"We're trying to contact her next of kin and get her home address," Kathy explained. "So far we're not having much luck. I've just been over to Stamford Street, where she used to live, and they told me they've been forwarding her mail here."

"That's right." The woman reached for the glasses hanging from a fluorescent green plastic chain around her neck and raised them to her nose. She waved Kathy in through the flap in the counter.

A distraught student appeared at her back. "Karen, the student photocopier's broken down again. Can I use the office one? *Please?*"

"Certainly not," the secretary snapped. "Go and talk to Agu."

"Shit."

"Language!" She took Kathy to a bank of pigeon holes on the

wall, and pointed to POST-GRAD STUDENTS M-Z, from which she retrieved a thick wad of envelopes and began sorting. When she finished she had formed one large pile, many with overseas stamps, and another small one, of letters addressed to Marion.

Kathy began opening them: an overdue book notice from the university library; a bank statement showing a balance of £386.54; a jeweller's valuation of a diamond ring, given as £2400; a notice of expiry of a reader's ticket to the National Archives; and a letter from a Dr. Grace Pontius at Cornell University in the United States confirming her attendance at a conference in August.

The secretary didn't seem to know anything about Marion's family circumstances, and after checking with a couple of her colleagues in the office, couldn't find anyone else who did either.

"Maybe her supervisor would know," she offered. His name was Dr. da Silva, but it appeared that he wasn't in the department that day.

Kathy took down his contact details and suggested that surely the university would have some kind of record of an original home address or next of kin. The woman phoned through to student records, and after some time they rang back with the details that Marion had given on her original undergraduate enrolment form, six years before. Her home address was in Ayr, Scotland, with a phone number listed.

When she got back to the car, Kathy tried the Scottish number. It rang and rang, and she was on the point of giving up when a woman's voice answered, quavering and hesitant.

"Ye-es?"

"Hello," Kathy said, "I wonder if you can help me. I'm trying to trace friends or relatives of Marion Summers."

"Oh aye? Well, I'm her auntie, but if you're selling something—"

"No, nothing like that. My name's Kathy Kolla, and I'm a police inspector from London. Could I ask your name, madam?"

"Bessie, Bessie Wardlaw. Did you say the polis?"

"Yes. Are Marion's parents available, Mrs. Wardlaw?"

"Available? Well, her mother's living in London."

"Can you give me her name and address and phone number?"

There was a pause, then a plaintive objection. "I have no idea who you are, do I? I mean, you phone me out of the blue . . ."

"You're right. I can give you a number of the Metropolitan Police for you to ring back. It *is* important."

"Och, can you no' just tell me what this is all about?"

"I'm afraid I have some bad news, Bessie, about Marion. I'm trying to contact her nearest relatives."

"Oh no!" Kathy heard the woman's hoarse breathing on the other end of the line and hoped she wasn't going to faint. She was regretting this call, catching the frailty of the woman at the other end, and thinking she should have handed this over to the Ayr police to deal with. "Do you have someone there with you, Bessie?"

"Aye, the minister, Mr. Fotheringham."

"Would you mind letting me speak to him?"

There was a clunk as Bessie dropped the phone. Finally a man came on. Kathy repeated who she was.

"I'm very sorry to have to give Bessie some sad news, Mr. Fotheringham. I'm afraid Marion Summers, her niece, died in hospital yesterday."

"That's shocking news indeed. How did it happen?"

"She collapsed in the library where she was working. She went into a coma and I'm afraid they weren't able to revive her."

"Och, poor lassie. Was it the diabetes?"

"We're carrying out a post-mortem to establish the cause. You obviously know her well."

"Oh aye. She lived with Bessie for several years before she went down to London, to the university."

"Bessie said that Marion's mother lives in London, is that right?"

"Aye, she moved down a couple of years ago, I believe."

"Was Marion living with her?"

"Hang on, I'll ask Bessie."

After a moment he came back. "No, they had separate addresses. I have them here." Kathy heard the pages of a notebook turning, then he read out the entries. Marion's mother was Sheena Rafferty, with a home address in Ealing in West London. However the address for Marion was her old one in the student apartments in Stamford Street.

"You wouldn't know if she had a partner, a regular boyfriend?"

There was a muffled discussion, then, "I'm afraid we can't help you there. Bessie hasn't had much contact with Marion of late." Then he added, voice cautious, "There's nothing suspicious, is there, in Marion's death?"

"We're not ruling anything out at this stage, Mr. Fotheringham. Why? Is there something we should know?"

"No, no. Bessie hasn't spoken to her sister—Marion's mother— for over a year. She doesn't really know what's been going on down there. What was your name again?"

Kathy repeated it, and her phone number, and took a note of the minister's number, promising to get in touch when she had more information.

She rang Dr. da Silva's home number next. He too sounded shocked by the news of Marion's death, to the point of becoming almost monosyllabic. To each of her questions he returned a series of abrupt negatives. No, he didn't know where she lived, nor if she had a boyfriend, nor what other close friends she might have had.

Kathy snapped her phone shut and stared out of the car window, tapping her hand impatiently on the steering wheel. It was beginning to look very much as if Marion Summers had been covering her tracks.

FOUR

MARION'S MOTHER LIVED ON the second floor of a council block which had seen better days, its brickwork stained, concrete flaking. There was no reply to Kathy's knock at the front door. A small dark woman rugged up with headscarf and quilted parka approached along the deck carrying bags of shopping.

"Excuse me, do you know Mrs. Rafferty?" Kathy asked.

The woman looked at her warily and made to move on.

"Sheena?" Kathy persisted. "Mrs. Sheena Rafferty?"

The woman nodded back over her shoulder. "Supermarket."

Kathy followed her glance and saw the grey concrete box in a gap between two blocks of flats. "She's shopping?"

"She work there." The woman shuffled on.

"Thanks."

The supermarket was of the cut-price variety, bare concrete floors, industrial shelving and battered trolleys. Kathy found the manager, and saw the look on his face when she showed her identity and said she wanted to speak to Mrs. Rafferty.

He pointed to one of the checkouts. "What's she been up to now then?"

"It's nothing like that. I have some bad news about her daughter. Is there somewhere quiet I can talk to her?"

The man nodded and turned to speak to a woman stocking shelves, then led Kathy to a small office. Behind them Kathy saw the woman taking Sheena's place behind her till.

"Has she been in trouble?" Kathy asked.

"Nothing too serious, as far as I know. Borrowing from the other women and not paying back. We think she and another girl have a quiet line in writing off items at the end of the day and taking them home." He sounded bored. "Ah, Sheena, come in, close the door. This is a police officer."

Kathy suspected he knew exactly the reaction that would provoke. A look of panic crossed Sheena's face. If she had once had red hair like her daughter it was a desperate blond now, and Kathy could make out no resemblance to Marion in the worn face.

"I'm DI Kathy Kolla, Sheena. Please take a seat." She turned to the manager. "I'd like to speak to Mrs. Rafferty in private, if you don't mind."

He shrugged and left.

Everyone responds to the first impact of shocking news in their own way, Kathy thought. Sheena Rafferty blinked wildly, shook her head and looked bewildered. Kathy suspected this was a learned response, her way of postponing a blow by pretending she couldn't understand what was going on. Eventually there were tears. Kathy always carried a small packet of tissues in her pocket for just such moments. She had no idea how many she'd gone through over the years.

"She was such a darlin'." It was a Scottish voice all right, but not the attractive soft accent the librarian had described in Marion; this one had a smoker's rasp. "Such a treasure."

"Is there someone I can call to be with you, Sheena? A friend, perhaps?"

"Well, there's ma husband, Keith . . ." She said it with a doubtful frown. "But he's at work. I don't know if he'll get away."

Keith was a driver for a company on the nearby industrial estate, she explained. Kathy called them and they said Keith was out on a delivery, and that they'd contact him and send him home.

The packet of tissues was exhausted before they reached Sheena's flat, scattered in damp shreds along the route of their walk back together. By the time they sat down in the kitchen and the kettle was plugged in and a second cigarette on the go, an element of realism had crept into Sheena's account.

"Och, we didnae always see eye to eye, ye ken. In fact she could be a stubborn wee bitch, but I loved her aw the same."

Kathy wondered if she was displacing her memories to an early time, because Marion was a good bit taller than her mother, and could hardly be described as "wee."

"We had our fights, but deep down we were so close."

"Can you give me Marion's latest address, Sheena?"

"Aye, sure. It's a student flat in Southwark. I've got it somewhere."

"Would that be Stamford Street?"

"Aye, that's it."

"I believe she moved from there three months ago."

"Oh." Sheena Rafferty looked confused. "You may be right. Somebody said somethin' about that."

"Was it Marion? Did she give you her new address?"

"No, I was goin' tae ask her."

"When did you last see her?"

"Um, that would have been Christmas." Sheena shrugged. "We had a wee blue. Nothin' serious. Her complainin' about me drinkin' too much, I think. She could be . . ." A memory came back to her, and her face crinkled, tears welling.

Kathy waited, then said, "How about her friends? Do you know their names?"

Sheena looked vague and shook her head.

"A boyfriend maybe?"

The woman's mood lifted. "Oh no, Marion was never one for the boys." She gave a raffish smile—*Unlike me*, it implied. "She always had her nose buried in her books."

"Just for the record, Sheena," Kathy said, "I'm sorry, but I have to ask you—this is Marion, your daughter, yes?"

27

She showed her the picture Sundeep had given her and her mother nodded, weeping again. "Such a lovely lassie." Then she looked alarmed. "I don't have to see the body just now, do I? I don't think, without Keith . . ."

"Plenty of time for that," Kathy reassured her.

Later, as they sipped tea, waiting for Keith in a fug of smoke, Sheena tentatively raised the possibility of compensation for her loss. Kathy was saved from replying by the arrival of Keith.

It was clear that he didn't know what was going on and was prepared to make someone pay for the inconvenience this was causing him. He had a shaved head and a tattoo creeping out of his shirt collar. He glared at Kathy belligerently and said, "Who's this, then?"

Kathy watched Sheena's manner change, becoming pliant and eager to soothe him. "Oh, Keithy darlin', somethin' terrible's happened."

"What now?" he growled.

"It's Marion. She's deed."

The abrupt words must have hurt to speak, but Kathy also sensed the underlying message: *Now, be nice to me, please.*

They certainly had an impact. Keith frowned uncertainly. Finally he muttered, "I don't believe it. Who is this?"

"I'm a police officer, Mr. Rafferty—DI Kathy Kolla. I'm so sorry to bring this news." Again the bland explanation. She felt like a nurse tucking a shocking deformity up in neat white sheets.

She left them with what advice and contact numbers she could, and returned to her car. As she reached to turn on the ignition her phone went. It was Sundeep Mehta, sounding out of breath.

"Hi, Sundeep. Any news?"

"Yes, Kathy. I was right. It was definitely arsenic. Marion Summers died of a massive dose of arsenic poisoning."

Kathy felt her heart give a jump, and realised that all this time she'd been half convinced that Sundeep's suspicions were wrong, that some much more mundane and innocent explanation would emerge.

"I can hardly believe it myself," he was going on, "even though I saw the signs. To strike someone down in that way, in public, in the middle of the day . . ."

"You know the timing then?"

"Oh, the dose was so large it would have happened quickly, certainly no more than an hour before her collapse. Do you know her movements?"

"The librarian saw her leave the library for a lunch break at around twelve thirty, and the triple-nine call was logged at one thirty-eight."

"Well then. Do you know what she did during that time?"

"We have just one sighting of her so far, sitting in the gardens in the square outside the library, possibly eating a sandwich. She threw the remains into a rubbish bin which has now been emptied. We're trying to trace it."

"Her stomach contents weren't much help—she lost most of her lunch on the library floor, all cleaned up and gone now. What about a drink?"

"The witness thought he saw a soft-drink bottle."

"Hm. An open cup would be easier. The arsenic could have been in powder form, or possibly dissolved in a liquid. If a powder, it would have to be stirred in . . . I'm sorry, Kathy, I'm just thinking aloud. I daresay a hundred years ago my predecessors would have known all the tricks with arsenic. I'm going to have to do some research on this, try some experiments."

"We haven't been able to find any recent comparable cases, Sundeep. What about you? Have your medical friends got back to you?"

"No, nothing yet, thank God."

BROCK SAT HALFWAY DOWN the long table, irritably scratching his cropped white beard, trying to make sense of the point at issue. He was sitting in for Commander Sharpe, away at a conference in Strasbourg, and had a hundred other things to do. As far as he could see the last two graphs in the PowerPoint presentation they'd all been subjected to had blatantly contradicted each other. But then, his mind on other things, he may have missed something. Across the other side of the table Superintendent Dick "Cheery" Chivers was sitting with his habitual glum expression. His copy of the management report was impressively embellished with slashes of coloured marker pens, but so far he'd said even less than Brock.

Brock's phone trembled silently against his thigh, and he slipped it out and checked the screen, then put it to his ear, turning away from the table. "Yes?"

"Brock? It's Kathy. Are you busy?"

"Go on."

"I can ring back."

"No, tell me."

He listened in silence for a minute, then murmured, "Brief me at the office." He rang off and got to his feet. The droning voice of the senior manager at the head of the table paused and they all looked at Brock. "Sorry," he said. "Emergency. I think you know Commander Sharpe's position on the proposal. Dick will fill me in." He glanced at Cheery, who stared back with a look of profound envy on his face.

He made his way down to the ground floor and out into the sunshine, breathing a sigh of relief. Hesitating under the rotating New Scotland Yard sign, he watched a cluster of underdressed office girls dodge between the cars and thought with a shiver, *It's not that bloody warm.* But even as one part of his mind started working out his priorities, another was responding to a breath of pollen in the air, and his eye caught a flash of bright green foliage on a plane tree further down the street. He took a few deep breaths and turned towards Queen Anne's Gate, feeling the sun on his head, and his frustration easing away.

WHEN KATHY ARRIVED AT the office she found it almost deserted, the few occupants looking harassed. All except Pip Gallagher, who sat alone in the room she shared with Kathy and three other detectives, staring disconsolately at the screen in front of her, face cupped in her hands.

"Anything?" Kathy asked.

Pip shook her head. "Everyone's got her address down as Stamford Street. She probably moved in with some bloke, don't you reckon? How did you go?"

"Dr. Mehta got back to me. She was definitely murdered—big slug of arsenic in her lunch."

"Wow." Pip sat up, instantly revived.

"We've got to find out how it got there. I'm going upstairs to brief Brock. Want to come?"

In the outer office Brock's secretary, Dot, rolled her eyes as they came in. They could hear Brock's voice barking impatiently through his open door. Dot said, "Go on in."

He waved them to seats when he saw them, phone held to his ear, talking to Bren Gurney, one of the other DIs in Brock's team. "Well tell them, Bren. Make sure they understand that."

They sat. Brock's office was more of a mess than usual, files everywhere, resistant to Dot's attempts to keep things tidy.

Brock rammed down the phone. "I turn my back for ten minutes . . . All right, tell me about Sundeep's little mystery."

Kathy quickly summarised the ground they had covered, then went on to the next steps, which would involve much more manpower. All of the offices around St. James's Square and the surrounding streets would have to be canvassed, cafés and other shops visited, statements taken from everyone who was in the library, CCTV tapes scanned. The list went on, Brock listening in silence, occasionally nodding his approval, while Pip paid close attention, making notes. Finally Kathy came to her own requirements for the murder team. Three more detectives as a start, she thought, plus one additional to work with the City of Westminster police to organise the teams of uniforms, plus an Action Manager, Exhibits Officer and Statement Reader, plus a Rainbow Coordinator for the CCTV stuff.

When she was finished, Brock said, "You're right, that is what you need, plus someone to press your suit, because the media are going to be very interested in this one. But unfortunately I haven't got anyone. No one at all. It's just you and Pip, Kathy, I'm sorry. You're on your own, at least till the end of the week. I'll speak to Westminster police and make sure they do what they can for you. They can take care of the CCTV. And you can borrow Phil, part time, as Action Manager, to keep on top of your admin."

Kathy, taken aback, bit off the retort that came into her mind—that without a team there wouldn't be any admin. Brock read her expression and nodded sympathetically. "Now, what about this boyfriend, if that's where she's been living? Why didn't she want anyone to know? And why hasn't he come forward? You've checked Missing Persons, I take it?"

A small choking sound came from Pip's corner of the desk. She darted a glance at Kathy. "Sorry, boss. Not yet."

Kathy bit her lip, then raised an eyebrow at Brock, meaning, *You see? I need people.*

Brock appeared not to notice. "Surely there must have been someone, a student friend, a priest, a doctor, someone she would have confided in?"

Kathy said, "I'd like to release her picture to the press, and a statement saying forensic tests indicate she was poisoned, and giving a general warning to the public to be alert. But I don't want to say anything about arsenic at this stage, not until we find its source."

"What do we know about it? Does it taste? What does it look like?"

"According to Sundeep it depends on the particular compound, but in general arsenic has very little taste, just a mild sweetness, comes as a white powder and can be made in a soluble form. It used to be deliberately contaminated with taste and colouring to stop it being taken accidentally."

"Used to be?"

"In the days when it was publicly available. But now . . . well, I suppose we'd have to be looking at a laboratory of some kind, or as part of some industrial process. Sundeep's first thought was that it might have been brought in from overseas."

"The terrorist angle."

"Yes. I haven't had anything back on that yet."

They waited while Brock made the call to Westminster Borough Command, setting up a meeting for Kathy at West End Central police station, not far from St. James's Square. "They'll take care of you, Kathy. They understand the situation. Get over there and get them organised."

She left Pip checking Missing Persons. "And I want her phone records, Pip," she said on her way out, not bothering to hide the irritation in her voice. "I want to know everyone she phoned in the past six months."

She decided to cut through St. James's Park, and had turned the car into Birdcage Walk when her phone rang. It was her friend Nicole Palmer from Criminal Records.

"Hi, Kathy. Just wanted to tell you I've confirmed our bookings for this weekend."

"This weekend?" Kathy groaned. "Oh no, I thought it was the one after." She'd completely forgotten about the trip they'd been planning to Prague. Nicole's brother, a jazz guitarist, was appearing in a club there and had persuaded them to go. "It's impossible, Nicole. I've got this case just blown up . . ."

"You've always got some case just blown up. It's only the weekend for God's sake. You can take the weekend off."

"Yes, normally, but there's this crisis."

Nicole's voice became firm. "Kathy, Rusty'll be devastated if I don't go, and I'm not going on my own. I've paid for the flights, and the hotel room. You were so keen."

"Sorry I can't talk now, Nicole. I'm due somewhere. I'll call you tonight, okay?"

She rang off, feeling a tightness across her chest. It was still there when she arrived at West End Central where, it was rapidly made plain to her, Brock's assessment of their ability to help was wildly optimistic.

"I can let you have one PC and a couple of PCSOs for the best part of tomorrow," the inspector said. "That's about it."

After prolonged haggling, he promised to see if the West End and Chinatown Team could spare another constable and a police community support officer.

She felt as if she were running in soft sand, making no progress. It was dark when she emerged from West End Central, a light rain falling, and she drove back to Queen Anne's Gate with the swish of windscreen wipers and the glitter of lights on raindrops. When she got to her office she found Pip looking fiercely busy at her desk. There had been no missing person reports for Marion, she said, and someone from the media unit had left a draft press release on her desk for her urgent attention. Kathy checked it and rang them back with a couple of amendments, then forced herself to sit down with a cup of coffee and think.

Towards seven, typing up a report, she became aware of Pip checking her watch and looking edgy.

"Time you went home," Kathy said.

"Will that be all right? Only I'm supposed to be going out."

"Of course. Have a good evening."

"Thanks."

Kathy watched her go with a touch of envy. Pip had a private life, it seemed.

A little later she took a call from an officer in the Counter Terrorism Command. They were inclined to discount a terrorist angle to Marion's death, he said. It didn't fit with anything else they had, but they'd be pleased to hear if anything new cropped up. She also heard from someone in the Environment and Planning department of Westminster City Council. They had collected over a thousand tonnes of rubbish on the third of April, and whatever Kathy was interested in had almost certainly been incinerated by now.

She rubbed her eyes, feeling suddenly exhausted. This was not going well. She stared at the picture of Marion Summers that she'd propped up beside her phone. "Why does nobody know where you live?" she murmured. "Why is your phone blank? Where is your boyfriend?"

She was distracted by a smell of food and looked up, puzzled. She had thought she was the last one left in the building. The door of the office opened, and Brock stood there holding a cardboard pizza box. "Hungry?"

She realised she was—very, and he nodded and said, "Let's go down to the pub."

In the basement of the Queen Anne's Gate offices was a small Victorian bar, the Bride of Denmark, assembled by earlier owners of the building, and it was there that Brock would go when he needed a quiet retreat, or inspiration. He got a couple of bottles of beer from behind the bar, and they sat at one of the tables and ate and drank in silence for a while, overlooked by the large salmon and stuffed lion from the glass cases mounted on the walls.

Finally Brock wiped his mouth and asked Kathy about her day. He nodded sympathetically and said, "Tell you what, why don't we just get West End Central to take over the whole case? There's plenty of other things you could be doing. I'll square it with Sundeep."

"No." Kathy surprised herself with the firmness of her decision. "No, I'll run with it."

He gave her a little smile. "You're intrigued."

"Yes, well, it is different."

"And the victim, Marion, she interests you."

Kathy shrugged. He was right of course, perceptive as always.

"Okay." He yawned and stretched the muscles of his shoulders, and she decided to change the subject.

"How's Suzanne?" Kathy wasn't quite sure what the appropriate word was to describe Brock's friend. *Lover* seemed intrusive, *companion* made her sound like an elderly helper. They were a couple, their relationship recently recovered from a shaky patch, and not helped, in Kathy's opinion, by the fact that they lived fifty miles apart; Suzanne ran an antiques business in Battle, near the Channel coast. Kathy sometimes wondered if Brock, on the other hand, believed the distance was the reason their relationship had survived.

"Very well. Very busy of course, with the shop and the grandchildren."

"She's still looking after them?"

"Oh yes. There's Ginny in the shop, of course, and she does a bit of babysitting, but we don't see enough of each other. Hopefully we'll get together this weekend. The kids are great though, growing up fast."

He gave a little smile to himself, scratching the side of his beard as he recalled some memory, and Kathy thought what an excellent grandfather he would have made.

"Do you mind if I ask you something?" she said.

He raised a quizzical eyebrow.

"When we were stuck in that cottage with Spider Roach . . ."

Brock nodded, remembering the climax of their last big case.

". . . he said that he'd been responsible for your wife leaving you, to protect the baby she was carrying, because she was afraid of what he might do."

"Yes."

"And when we first worked together, you mentioned you had a son in Canada."

"Maybe."

"You haven't kept in touch?"

He drew in a deep breath. "I'm still here, in the same place, doing the same job as when she left. If he wanted to find me it wouldn't be difficult. I've left it to him."

"So you don't know if he's married? If he has a family of his own?"

Brock frowned, looked down at the remains of pizza on the table, and Kathy realised she'd gone too far and felt sad. She shivered. "Sorry. It's cold down here."

"Mm, and since we're in a ruminative mood, have you been keeping tabs on Tom Reeves?"

She fiddled with her empty bottle. "I heard he's living in France somewhere. Calvi, wherever that is."

"How is he, do you know?"

DI Tom Reeves, Special Branch, had also been involved in their last case, and, more personally, with Kathy.

She shook her head. "No, we're not in contact."

"He resigned of course. A clean break, according to HR. I imagine that's how he wants it. Well . . ." He got stiffly to his feet. "Time to go home."

FIVE

THINGS LOOKED A LITTLE brighter the following day. When Kathy got to West End Central she found that the inspector had rustled up another five people from different teams within the borough, and the group that he and Kathy briefed that morning looked almost adequate. They shuffled out armed with clipboards, photographs and report sheets, and the inspector took Pip away to work with the local Rainbow Coordinator on the CCTV footage, while Kathy headed back to the London Library, where she'd arranged to interview everyone that Gael Rayner had been able to track down as having been there on Tuesday when Marion had collapsed.

It was a slow job. One of the regular readers, a Mr. Vujkovic, said that he had picked up Marion's belongings from the floor, including her phone, which he insisted no one had opened. The others had little to add, and no one apart from Nigel Ogilvie had seen Marion eating her lunch in the square. But several had noticed her out there on other days, and one woman had sat with her for a while, on the same bench, about a week beforehand. She was certain that Marion had been drinking a bottle of juice, because Marion had commented that she usually carried one with her, in case she needed a sugar fix for her diabetes. The woman described the orange bottle and yellow plastic cap, but had no idea where Marion might have bought it. Kathy immediately phoned the information to Brock's office, thinking of other cases of industrial sabotage and tampering with supermarket foodstuffs that had been in the news lately.

From time to time she got up and stretched her legs, going over to the big windows and looking out at the uniforms working their way around the square. She knew they'd phone her if they discovered anything interesting, but by mid-afternoon she'd heard nothing from them or from Pip. She had interviewed thirty-six people, not one of whom had a clue where Marion had lived. None had seen anyone tampering with her bag.

As the streetlights came on and dusk began to fall, she collected Pip and they returned to Queen Anne's Gate carrying sheafs of interview sheets to process. On Kathy's desk was a stack of reports from the police hotline detailing phone calls from the public following the newspaper and TV coverage that morning of Marion's death, and on Pip's was a computer printout of Marion's phone records. Kathy had a sense of the overwhelming tide of information which so often bogged down murder investigations that didn't make the breakthrough in the first couple of days.

Brock came in and pulled up a chair beside them. "How's it looking?"

Kathy pointed to the pile of phone messages. "It's touched a nerve—the anonymous poisoner, the hidden assassin, striking you down where you're most vulnerable, inside your stomach, without you even knowing it's been done. People convinced they've seen someone putting something in the sugar bowls of the local café, sticking syringes into pastries, adulterating milk."

Brock said, "We've alerted soft-drink manufacturers and distributors and supermarket chains. They say they haven't received any recent threats. They also point out that they all have tamper-proof caps. Wouldn't the sandwich be more likely?"

"Maybe. I'd be more inclined to accept it was a random act if

Marion wasn't so damn mysterious. None of the people phoning in have any information on her, and nobody's reported her missing. But somebody knows, and they're keeping quiet."

The duty officer appeared with a message for Brock. He scanned it and said, "I have to go. Good luck." He headed off, looking as weary and frustrated as she felt, Kathy thought.

She looked across at Pip and said, "Why wouldn't you tell your mother where you live?"

Pip laughed. "Lots of reasons. You don't know my mum."

Kathy shook her head, trying to clear the cotton wool that seemed to have accumulated there during her mind-numbing day. "But you'd still tell her, unless . . ."

"What?"

"Unless she'd tell someone else who's giving you grief."

"Her husband? What's he like, the stepfather?"

"Looked a bit of a thug. Why don't you see what you can find out about him?" She checked her notebook. "His name's Keith Rafferty. He looked younger than Marion's mother, maybe late thirties. Address in Ealing: Flat 3, 37 Bradshaw Street. Works as a driver for an outfit called Brentford Pyrotechnics. They sell fireworks."

Ten minutes later Pip came over to her desk with a printout from her computer. "Assault, actual bodily harm, three years ago. He got four months. The previous year he was charged under the Sexual Offences Act, section 30, living off the earnings, and section 32, soliciting. That case didn't get to court."

"Aha . . ." Kathy looked up at Pip's expression. There was more. "Go on."

"And Brentford Pyrotechnics don't just sell fireworks, they also manufacture them."

"So?"

"You know that brilliant blue light they have in star shells? Apparently it's almost impossible to get it without using arsenic."

"Seriously? How did you find that out?"

"Google." Pip shrugged, as if to say, *What else?*
Kathy checked the time. "Got their number?"

THE MANAGER AT BRENTFORD Pyrotechnics seemed unsurprised by her request to pay him a visit; apparently it had happened before. "Just last month," he said. "It's the terrorist thing, I know, but really, you've got no need to worry about us. You'll see." They were working late that night on an order, and he'd be available whenever they called.

The industrial estate lay within a curve of the Grand Union Canal, beyond which the elevated M4 emitted a low traffic roar into the night. Kathy pulled the car into a parking bay in front of the doors of the offices and showrooms, whose windows were lit from within. Pip looked down the darkened flank of the big sheds to their left and gave a pout of disappointment.

"Aw, I thought they'd have a few sparklers going, at least."

Mr. Pigeon bustled out in answer to their ding on the counter bell. He looked as if they'd caught him in the middle of a crisis, and he spoke quickly, the glow of perspiration on his bald head. He barely glanced at their ID. "We've got a lot on this month, and several big productions next weekend."

"Really? I thought it'd be a quiet time for you—away from November the fifth, I mean."

"Oh no!" Mr. Pigeon chuckled at her ignorance. "It's not just Guy Fawkes night for us, you know. We're doing functions all the year round—weddings, public events, garden parties, funerals, celebrations of all kinds." He handed Kathy several brochures from the desk.

"Funerals?"

"Oh indeed. What better way to go than in a blaze of glory in the night sky above your assembled friends."

"You mean you pack their ashes into . . . ?"

"Rockets, Roman candles, giant catherine-wheels. Some want

lots of whizzes and bangs, and others prefer a quieter, more contemplative presentation."

"I didn't know that. And you manufacture these special fireworks to order?"

"That's right. Our run-of-the-mill stuff all comes from China now. Well, that's the way of things these days, isn't it? The great days of British fireworks are past, I'm afraid—Brock's, Phoenix, Britannia. You have to specialise now."

"Did you say Brock's? My boss's name is Brock."

"Really? Well, maybe he's related to the fireworks family. Theirs was the oldest fireworks company in Britain. They dazzled Queen Victoria at the Crystal Palace."

"But now you specialise?"

"Quite. We have our own design studio, our own laboratory for devising precisely the right mixtures, and our own specialty fabrication workshop. It's all top quality, and highly secure, believe me. We've had Special Branch, MI5, you name it—and Workplace Health and Safety, of course, all the time. They've picked this place apart. Well, it's only to be expected nowadays. When I was a boy I could pop down to my local chemist and buy concentrated acids, fuse wire, any kind of chemical compound I wanted. Why, when I was a lad, the sight of a schoolboy marching down the street carrying a .303 wouldn't raise a murmur, unless he had long hair—then, outrage! But now, the slightest hint of anything that goes bang . . ."

"Yes. Actually we're taking a different line. It's not the things that go bang that we're interested in, Mr. Pigeon. It's more the things that make you sick—poisons. Do you carry any of them?"

"Poisons? Oh, well." He thought for a moment. "Yes, of course we do. Acids, phosphorus compounds, copper salts . . ."

"Arsenic?"

"Yes, we have that too. But all those chemicals are subject to the same security procedures as the explosives. I mean, short of a full-blown assault on the place, there's no way anyone could get at our stocks of either raw materials or finished product. I told you, your people have been over the place with a fine-tooth comb. If you like I can show you the protocols, the security cameras, the locks and alarms, the inventory audits . . ."

He took them into his office and offered them the reports prepared by security consultants, compliance certificates from the local authority, fire brigade and health and safety inspectors. "Your counterterrorism officers didn't give me any documentation as such, but I can tell you who was here and when. You can easily check with them for yourself."

"Where do your chemicals come from?"

"All over. Mostly locally, in the south of England, some from up north, some from overseas. But all carefully tracked and accounted for."

"Thanks," Kathy said. "It sounds as if we're wasting your time."

Pigeon relaxed a little, wiping his pink brow. "Oh, I know you have to be careful about these things. It's the kind of business we do, and the times we live in."

"What about your staff? Do they get any security clearance?"

"Eh? Well, most of the senior people have been with us for years. Otherwise we get extensive references. We took on a new research chemist recently, most impressive CV, all checked out."

"What about support staff—cleaners, drivers and so on?"

"Well, it depends. Some are supplied by contractors. Our own people I interview personally."

"Do you do a criminal record check?"

"Well, no, probably not. Is that a problem?"

"It's just a thought. Anyway, we won't take up any more of your time, Mr. Pigeon. Thanks very much. We're concerned about a batch of arsenic trioxide that's come to our attention. Perhaps you might check to make sure it couldn't possibly have come from here?"

"Gladly, gladly, but I can tell you now it isn't ours."

When they got back into the car, Kathy asked, "What do you think?"

Pip said, "Okay, you're a driver and you pick up a consignment of chemicals from some factory somewhere, and you've been told you have to be careful with it. Maybe you don't know it's arsenic, maybe you've just heard that it can knock you out, and you're thinking you could spike a girl's drink with it. So on the way back you stop the van, and open a carton, and take a bit from a container and replace it with something else—flour or caster sugar or something, to make up the weight."

"Wouldn't that be noticed?"

"Maybe not. I mean, if you doctored explosive, the fireworks wouldn't work and you'd be in trouble, but this is to make coloured light. Maybe it just wouldn't be so bright."

"Nice theory." Kathy started the car. "Or maybe he did know it was arsenic. Maybe he didn't just want to knock her out. I think we should talk to Keith Rafferty about how well he really knew Marion. You got time to go there now, or did you want to knock off?"

"No, I'm fine, boss."

"I just wondered." She glanced at Pip's short skirt, high heels. "Thought you might have a date or something."

"Not tonight. I'm all yours."

THEY DREW UP OUTSIDE the block in Bradshaw Street, and were unbuckling their seat belts when Kathy paused. "Hang on," she murmured. The front door of flat number three had just opened, and she saw the figure of Keith Rafferty silhouetted against the light. He turned and yelled something back into the flat. Kathy wound her window down and heard a woman's voice, Sheena's, scream an obscenity.

"And fuck you, bitch," Keith roared. He turned and marched off along the deck. They watched as he sprinted down the stairs at the end and headed towards the street, shrugging the collar of his leather jacket up as a cold gust of wind caught him. He pulled a mobile phone out of his pocket and made a call as he strode off. Kathy started the car again.

They followed him out onto the main street, almost deserted, past shop windows to a pub on the next corner, the Three Bells. He reached the door and yanked it open. A gust of loud music blasted out.

"That's nice, isn't it?" Pip said. "Your wife's just lost her daughter and you piss off down the pub with your mates."

"It'd be interesting to hear what they talk about, wouldn't it?"

"What, fancy a drink do you, boss?"

"Unfortunately Keith knows my face."

"He doesn't know mine." She flicked the sunshield down and examined herself in the mirror, fluffing her hair and pouting her lips. She put on more lipstick.

"You can't go in there on your own."

"Why not? It's only a pub. I'll just keep my ears open, all right? I'll be waiting for a friend."

Kathy hesitated. "You've got my number in your phone? Give me a ring, let me know what's happening. Just be careful."

"Sure."

Pip got out of the car and hitched her skirt a little higher, tossed back her head and made for the pub door. Kathy watched her go with a sense of foreboding.

Ten minutes passed, the car cooling. Kathy gave a shiver and reached for her phone just as it began to buzz. "Hello?"

"Hi! Where are you?"

Kathy could barely hear for the music, a raucous rhythmic thumping.

"You okay?"

"Of course! Well, don't take too long, will you? I'm having fun."

"Do you want me to come in?"

Pip giggled. "You sound like my mother." She rang off.

Another ten minutes went by, then another, and Kathy tapped her hand on the steering wheel, feeling cold and uneasy. She tried Pip's number but didn't get a reply. She waited another five minutes, then jumped out of the car and headed for the door.

The music was too loud, the lights too bright, and the smell of beer rancid. The place was packed, and she had to force her way through the crowd, mostly men, who smelled of sweat and beer and jostled her as she pushed through. She saw a glossy black head of female hair at the bar, but when she got there found it wasn't Pip. She could see no sign of Keith Rafferty either. She saw the door to the ladies' toilets at the back of the room and struggled through to it. Pip wasn't there. Panicking now, Kathy made her way out again, through the throng, ears battered by the noise, and saw another door at the back marked FIRE EXIT. A male voice called, "Oi, darlin'!" She pushed through into a narrow corridor with another door at the far end with the same fire exit sign. Beyond was a small courtyard with boxes, crates and beer barrels. Kathy stumbled over a pile of boxes, through an opening in a brick wall and into a puddled laneway. A white van was parked up ahead, its rear door open, figures huddled. They looked up as she charged towards them. She saw Keith Rafferty's face, eyes ablaze, and then a woman's legs, hanging half out of the back of the van. Another man turned towards her, swearing, hand raised up. She grabbed his fingers and he screamed as she twisted his arm behind his back.

"Police! Stay where you are."

Rafferty was looking around, over her shoulder, as she struggled with the other man. Then he turned and hauled the woman out of the van and dumped her on the ground, slammed the door and turned to go.

"Stay where you are, Keith!" Kathy shouted. She had the phone in her hand now, pressing buttons. "Officer in trouble."

Keith Rafferty turned back towards her, fists up. For a moment they stared at each other, then he deflated, unclenched his hands and held them up. His friend stopped struggling. On the ground at his feet Pip gave a low moan.

"This is all a mistake," Rafferty said. "We were just trying to help the lady. She was legless. We just offered her a lift home. Isn't that right, Brendan?"

ACCIDENT AND EMERGENCY AT Ealing is one of the busiest hospital departments in West London, and it took Brock a little while to find his way to the bed where Pip lay, face ashen, eyes closed.

"How's she doing?" Brock pulled a chair up beside Kathy's. He saw the dark shadows around Kathy's eyes, and when he took her hand he felt a tremor.

"She'll be all right. Rafferty tried to throw away some orange pills when the uniforms arrived. They think they're Klonopin, similar effect to Rohypnol. They've stabilised her."

"Was she assaulted?"

"A few bruises. The way they were handling her . . ." Kathy stopped and took a deep breath. "She hasn't said anything yet. Apparently she may remember nothing."

"Where's Rafferty now?"

"Down the road, at Ealing police station. His mate's called Brendan Crouch, no record."

"Have they been charged?"

"Yes."

"Witnesses?"

"They're taking statements in the pub now."

"Okay, good. We don't have to do anything till morning."

"I think we should speak to them now, while they're still rattled."

Brock looked at her cautiously. "You're sure?"

"Yes."

"Well, I can take care of that."

"I need to be there, Brock. This is about Marion as well as Pip."

"You think Rafferty had something to do with Marion's death?"

"That's why we were there, at the pub." She explained about their visit to the fireworks company and then going to question Rafferty. "I'll bet he's done this before, lacing women's drinks. Maybe the arsenic was an experiment that went wrong, maybe it was more than that."

"Hm. Has the doctor had a look at you?"

"I'm fine, really."

"What have you had to eat tonight?"

She shook her head.

"All right then. First we get you a meal and a good wash, and then we'll go down the road."

At the Ealing police station they were met by the duty inspector, who advised them that the pub interviews weren't promising. "No one saw anything, or at least admits to it. No one even remembers Rafferty and Crouch being there, or DC Gallagher. Sorry."

They decided to interview Brendan Crouch first, in the hope he would give them something. He had a strong Liverpool accent and an air of mystified innocence. "I don't know what this is all about," he said, then looked accusingly at Kathy. "She nearly broke my fuckin' finger."

"How did you meet the woman in the pub?" Brock asked.

"Which woman was that?"

"The one I caught you loading into Rafferty's van," Kathy snapped.

He gave her a cool, considering look. "She approached us. We were having a quiet drink when this tart comes up to us, giving us the big eye. She chats for a while and offers to buy us a drink, but her speech is slurred, and she's obviously had a skinful. We tell her she's had enough, so she asks if we could take her home. Well . . ." Crouch gave a little smile. "Why not? Keith's van was parked in the lane out the back, but she keeled over as soon as the cold air hit her. We were just trying to help her into the van when this lady started screaming at us." He nodded at Kathy.

Through this account, Brock was aware of Kathy at his side, chewing her bottom lip, her nails dug into the palms of her hands, trying to contain herself.

"That's a lie," she said, voice tight.

He gazed at her. "Which bit?"

"All of it."

Brock came in quickly. "That isn't what your friend is saying, Brendan. His version has you making the running. The way he says it, you couldn't keep your hands off her."

Crouch turned his eyes slowly to meet Brock's, then he said, quite softly, "Now there you're wrong, pal. Keith and I spent four years together in the army, and one thing I know about him for sure is that he'd never shop a mate."

It was an elementary mistake, Brock told himself furiously as they led Crouch away, showing your hand before you understand the game. I've been spending too much time in bloody meetings. He glanced at Kathy. She looked subdued, head bowed. "Why don't we leave this till morning?"

She just shook her head.

Rafferty walked in with a swagger in his step. He yanked back the chair as if he was an old hand and sat down and folded his arms. He stared at Brock coldly as he listened to the caution.

"Why don't you tell us what happened in the Three Bells this evening, Mr. Rafferty?"

Rafferty's eyes flicked across at Kathy, then back to Brock. Then he stiffened and looked at Kathy again, frowning. "Hang on, know you, don't I? I didn't recognise you before. You were the one came to our flat, weren't you? The one told Sheena about Marion, right?"

"That's right."

"Well, what the fuck were you doing at the pub? What's going on here?"

"I came back to ask you some questions about Marion, and we saw you going into the pub."

"She was with you, that woman?"

Kathy nodded.

"But she never said she was a copper. She never mentioned Marion. What the fuck's going on?"

Brock cut in. "What's going on here is that you've been arrested for drugging a woman in a pub and trying to abduct her. So answer my question, Mr. Rafferty. What's your version of what happened in the pub this evening?"

But Rafferty just sat back, shaking his head. "Oh no. This ain't right. I'm not saying nothing till I've spoken to a solicitor."

49

"Your refusal to cooperate will go against you."

"Uh-uh. Not a word."

"Very well, we can arrange for a duty—"

"No thanks," Rafferty sneered. "I'll make my own arrangements, thanks."

"We'll speak to you again first thing in the morning, Mr. Rafferty. In the meantime, think very carefully about what you're going to tell us."

When they got outside, Brock said, "Go home, Kathy. Get some rest. You look all in."

"I'm sorry. This shouldn't have happened. I shouldn't have let it happen."

"We'll sort it out. The fact is, they're both up to their ears in it. Let's hope they can lift Rafferty's prints from the bag of pills."

"I'd like to speak to the publican at the Three Bells. I saw him watching me when I went in, trying to find Pip."

"I'll do that, Kathy. You go home. That's an order."

He watched her get into her car, then headed for his own.

THE THREE BELLS SEEMED subdued when he pushed through the doors, with only a few customers huddled at tables. The band on the tiny stage at the back was in the final stages of packing up their gear. They looked fed up.

Brock went to the bar, picking out an older man at the till and nodding to him.

The man noted him with a frown. "What now?"

"DCI Brock. And you're Mr. Cornford?" He'd seen the licensee's name over the door.

"That's right. You lot trying to put me out of business?"

"A young woman was almost raped here tonight, Mr. Cornford."

"So you say."

"Do you know Keith Rafferty?"

"He's a local, comes in a fair bit."

"And Brendan Crouch?"

"Didn't know his name, but he's often with Rafferty."

Brock watched one of the other barmen drawing a pint.

"Fancy one?" Cornford said.

"Saw the look in my eye, did you?"

The publican smiled.

"Yes, it's been a long day." Brock unbuttoned his coat and sat heavily on a stool. "Have one yourself." He put a tenner on the bar, watching the golden, liquid foam into the straight glass. "Has this happened before?"

"Drink spiking? Get it all the time, young lads slipping an extra double vodka into their girl's mixer."

"What about pills?"

"Pills are everywhere you look these days." He hesitated, then went on, "Couple of weeks ago a young woman came in, Saturday lunchtime, said her friend had been drugged and raped the night before, after coming in here. When I talked to her she was a bit confused. They'd been to at least two other pubs, then got separated. When she found her friend later she was in a bit of a mess. I told her to go to the cops if she thought something bad had happened. I don't think she did."

"Two weeks ago?"

"Maybe three now."

"Know their names?"

Cornford shook his head.

"Was Rafferty in that night?"

"Friday night, bound to have been."

Brock thanked him, drained his pint and left. When he got in his car he put a call through to DI Bren Gurney.

SIX

KATHY DROVE A FEW blocks away from the Ealing police station before pulling in to the kerb. She got out her phone and keyed in Nicole Palmer's number.

"Kathy! You've sorted things out?"

"'Fraid not. They're getting worse, actually. You're not in bed, are you?"

"It's only ten. Lloyd just got in." Her partner was also a detective, in North London.

"I need a big favour, Nicole. I'm trying to find out about two guys who were in the army together. There's not much on them on the PNC. I was wondering if you could access their army records, and dig up anything else."

"Sure. I'll get onto it tomorrow."

"I was wondering if you could manage it now. We're interviewing them first thing in the morning. It would really help if I could have something by then."

There was a silence. "You want me to go into the office *now?*"

Kathy sighed. "No . . . I'm sorry. It was a stupid idea. Forget it."

Another long silence. "What are their names?"

"No, really, Nicole. Forget it."

"I've had a couple of drinks. You'll have to pay for the cabs."

IT WAS A SHORT drive to Bradshaw Street. TV screens flickered through curtained windows as Kathy made her way to flat three. It took a long while for Sheena to come to the door. She blinked at Kathy, bleary-eyed, racking her brains.

"Kathy Kolla, Mrs. Rafferty, from the police. I came about Marion, remember?"

"Oh . . . oh aye. I'm . . ." She looked vaguely back over her shoulder. She was wearing a dressing-gown, hair mussed, a cigarette burning in her fingers.

"Can I have a quick word?"

"S'pose so."

There was an empty vodka bottle on the floor in the living room, clothes scattered, TV emitting canned laughter.

"Can we turn that down?"

Sheena blinked, looking around for the remote. Kathy found it and handed it to her. The sound boomed louder, then dipped to a murmur.

"How have you been?"

"Oh, you know. How does a mother feel, eh?"

"Yes. Can we sit down? I'm afraid I've got a bit more bad news. Keith's been arrested."

Blank incomprehension. "Keith what?"

"He's been arrested."

"Keith? Did he hit somebody?"

"We think he spiked a girl's drink, in a pub."

Sheena's eyes came abruptly into focus. "What?"

"Him and Brendan Crouch."

"Jesus Christ. The stupid . . . Where was this?"

"The Three Bells."

"Och no. Pissing on his own bloody doorstep, the stupid . . . Ah'll kill that bastard."

53

"Has he done anything like this before?"

"Is the Pope a fuckin' Catholic? Where'd ah put ma fuckin' drink?"

"With Marion?"

"What?" Sheena's eyes widened, the whites ringed with smeared mascara.

"Did he try stuff with Marion?"

"What . . . what are you tryin' to say?"

"Come on, Sheena. You know, don't you? Marion didn't tell you when she moved three months ago. Why was that? It was to keep Keith from finding her, wasn't it?"

Sheena opened her mouth but nothing came out. She was taking quick shallow breaths. Suddenly she gave a little cry, and looked down at her hand, where the cigarette had burned down to her fingers. She stabbed it in an ashtray and wheeled on Kathy.

"Git out," she said hoarsely.

"I want to help you, Sheena. I want to help you do the right thing for Marion."

"GIT OUT!" she screamed. "GIT OUT! GIT OUT!"

"Calm down." Sheena was looking wildly around, as if for a weapon. "All right, I'm going. Just think about it, Sheena. I'll be here when you want to talk."

BROCK HAD TOLD HER to go home and so, belatedly, she did. The place was cold and she put the heating on and made a cup of hot chocolate, then sat, waiting, trying to think.

Towards two a.m. her phone rang.

"Kathy?" It was Nicole, sounding weary. "Rafferty left the army six years ago. He was in the Second Battalion, Light Infantry, along with Crouch. They served together for four years, in Iraq and Northern Ireland, and on the mainland. There was one incident of interest, in Belfast. A girl accused the two of them of rape. Later she withdrew her complaint and the charges were dropped.

I'll email you the details. You've got the later assault and prostitution charges against Rafferty from the PNC, I take it?"

"Yes. That's fantastic, Nicole. I'm really grateful."

"Make it up to me by coming to Prague, Kathy."

"No chance, I'm afraid. It's already Friday. Next time."

"That's the thing though. There may not be one."

She hung up and ran a bath, then lay down on her bed, unable to sleep.

When the green digits on her alarm clock reached 5:00 she got up and dressed and took the lift down to the ground floor to get her car.

The forecourt to the A&E entrance was alive, ambulances moving steadily through, the steady pulse of trauma beating through the night. Pip was dressed, standing talking to a nurse at the counter. She gave Kathy an anxious smile.

"Hi!" Kathy beamed. "How are you?"

"Fine. Doctor's just told me I can go. They need the bed."

"Great. I'll give you a lift home. No after-effects then?"

Pip shook her head. "It wears off after about eight hours, apparently. Only, I can't remember much."

"Never mind."

"Brock was here."

"Really? When?"

"He left half an hour ago. He took a statement. He was very nice about it all."

They walked together to the front doors. "Oh, it's still dark," Pip said. "I thought it was morning."

"Nearly. What did you tell Brock?"

"About going into the pub. I stood near Rafferty at the bar, trying to get myself a drink, but it was packed. He was talking to another guy, and I heard him mention Marion's name."

"You're sure?"

"Yes. I tried to get closer, and suddenly he turned around and started chatting me up. That's when I phoned you—I told him I was waiting for a friend."

They got into Kathy's car and set off along Uxbridge Road. "Go on."

"They saw I didn't have a drink and insisted on buying me one. I know, it was stupid, but what could I do?"

"He said you spoke to him first."

"Yes, that's what Brock told me, but it wasn't like that. Rafferty pushed himself into my face, very close. He wouldn't let me move. The other one too. It was suffocating in there, and deafening. You couldn't hear yourself think."

"What happened then?"

"I don't know. That's all I can remember."

"Maybe it'll come back to you. Do you remember anyone else nearby, anyone who might have seen what happened?"

She shook her head.

When they reached the house that Pip shared, she said, "I'll just get changed and come back with you."

"Not today, Pip. You have a long weekend. Take it easy."

"I'm not suspended, am I?"

"Nobody's suggested that," Kathy said. *Not yet.*

Brock was already at the Ealing police station when she arrived. He was reading through a file, a mug of coffee and a bacon sandwich at his elbow. "Ah, Kathy. Feel a bit better for a good night's sleep?"

"Great. How are we doing?"

"We start interviewing at eight thirty." He checked his watch.

"I've got something on their military service." She showed him Nicole's email.

"Good." He read. "All part of a pattern, isn't it?"

"Any luck with the prints?"

"Yes, he certainly handled those pills. But that's all we have. We haven't found any witnesses, and Pip can't remember anything useful."

"Then there's me."

"Yes, there's you." He patted the report in front of him. "I've been reading your statement to the duty inspector last night."

"And?"

"And you won't be taking part in the interviews this morning."

"But I think—"

He shook his head. "Bren's coming in. He'll do it with a sergeant from this station."

There was a rap on the door and a uniformed inspector stepped in. She introduced herself and shook hands, then said, "We are honoured this morning."

For a moment Kathy thought she was making a sarcastic remark about them, but the woman added, "Julian Fenwick has arrived."

Julian Fenwick was well known as a high-profile criminal defence lawyer, often seen on TV news bites at the shoulders of notorious crooks, whose guilt and simultaneous release seemed to be guaranteed by his presence.

"He's representing Rafferty?"

"Both of them, apparently. He's with them now."

"How did they manage that, I wonder?"

After briefing Bren, Brock took his place beside Kathy to watch the interviews on closed-circuit TV.

They took Rafferty first, slumped beside his lawyer opposite the two detectives. Bren opened the interview, inviting Rafferty to describe the events of the previous evening. Rafferty replied in a careless monotone. He and his friend had been having a quiet drink together when a young, attractive woman approached them, acting flirtatiously, and wondering if they could get her a drink through the scrum of people at the bar. Soon she had begun to act in a way that suggested she was drunk. When her behaviour became more erratic they agreed to her request to give her a lift home. She collapsed as they got to their van, at which point another woman appeared, claiming she was a police officer, and attacking Rafferty's friend.

Bren and the other detective picked away at the details of this account without making much headway, until Bren suddenly produced the plastic packet of Klonopin pills. Without telling Rafferty that his prints had been found on it, he invited him to agree that he'd been seen trying to dispose of it at the scene in the lane.

Rafferty stared at the packet, then at his lawyer, then at Bren. "Can I have a closer look?" he asked, and Kathy was aware of Brock at her side stirring and murmuring, "Oh dear."

Bren passed over the packet inside its transparent plastic evidence pouch.

"Yes, you're right. I'd forgotten about that."

"Do you know what the pills are?" Bren asked.

Unruffled, Rafferty said, "E? I'm just guessing."

"You think those are ecstasy tablets?"

"That's what I assumed."

"Where did you obtain them?"

"She gave them to me, the girl, in the pub."

"But her fingerprints aren't on the packet. Yours are."

"Well it's true. When she started acting pissed she pressed them into my hand and asked me to look after them for her."

Bren made him repeat this several times.

"So when the other woman said she was a copper, I remembered them and threw them away."

"Oh dear, oh dear," Brock grumbled.

When it came to his turn, Crouch had less to say. He had witnessed the girl approaching Rafferty, and had given his friend a hand, just trying to help, but he hadn't seen any pills. He had been the one who had bought her drink, and he could guarantee it hadn't been tampered with when he put it in her hand.

When Bren finally brought the second interview to an end, Julian Fenwick, who had said almost nothing up to this point, spoke, "Now that we're off the record, Inspector, I wonder if I might have a quiet word with you? Just the two of us." He didn't quite wink up at the camera, but Kathy sensed that he might have.

"What can I do for you?" Bren said as they sat down again at the table.

"There are some disturbing features about this case that I feel I should bring to your attention, DI Gurney, in the interests of avoiding wasting police time and resources."

"Go on."

"The arresting officer was DI Kathy Kolla, yes? She isn't with you today?"

"What of it?"

"Are you aware that she engineered that absurd little cameo in the Three Bells?"

"How do you mean?"

"She sent DC Gallagher in to approach my clients, while she waited outside in her car; she then appeared miraculously in the lane at the critical moment. Obviously she arranged the whole thing. It is the most blatant attempt at entrapment I've ever encountered."

"If you have any criticism . . ."

Fenwick raised his hands. "This is completely off the record, yes? For the moment, at any rate. Do you also know that she met Mr. Rafferty two days ago, at his home, in the course of investigating the tragic death of his stepdaughter, Marion Summers—who was poisoned, so I understand, possibly by someone interfering with her drink?"

"Yes?"

"It is a cliché, is it not, that murders are committed by close relatives of the deceased? Close family are the first suspects, yes? Stepfathers of beautiful young women most of all. Ergo, Mr. Rafferty is guilty as sin. Sadly, though, there is no evidence to support this. Therefore an enthusiastic officer—an *over*enthusiastic officer—might be tempted to create some."

Bren started to say something angrily, but Fenwick waved his hand at him. "No, no, please, I'm making no accusations. At this stage. I've met DI Kolla. She has an interesting record. Impressive, but not really a team player—that was my impression. Bit of a chip on the shoulder? And newly made up to inspector, and no doubt anxious to justify . . ."

Bren was getting to his feet.

"Please don't take offence, Inspector Gurney," Fenwick said smoothly, rising also. "I'm trying to do us both a favour. I suspect the Crown Prosecution Service will be looking very hard at this one." He held out his hand. "Good morning to you."

Bren ignored the hand, opened the door and stood aside.

"What do you think, Kathy?" Brock said.

"I think he has a point," she said heavily.

"Well, I'm afraid he's right about the CPS. Come on." He got stiffly to his feet. "You've got a murder to solve."

SEVEN

KATHY SAT AT HER desk, furious with herself. Across the way, Pip's empty chair was a vivid accusation. *You screwed up*, it said. *You let Pip down.* The worst of it was that Rafferty would now be so much harder to touch. How had he got Julian Fenwick to come out at the crack of dawn? It was just one of many mysteries. What did she really know about Marion Summers, after all?

She stared at the pile of paper on her desk, lacking the stomach to begin. On the top was a printout of calls to and from Marion's mobile. Pip had been working on it, marking it with coloured marker pens and careful notes in girlish handwriting, like a school assignment. Yellow meant the university, it seemed—calls to the departmental office, to the university library, to her supervisor Dr. da Silva. Green meant other work-related, Kathy guessed— the British Library, the Family Records Centre at Finsbury, the National Archives at Kew. Then there was blue for various services—a minicab service, a restaurant, a hair salon in NW3. Why there?

But the most interesting bunch were highlighted in day-glo pink, and seemed to be private numbers. K. Rafferty in Ealing was her mother's home number of course. Then there was S. Warrender in Notting Hill, called regularly up until five weeks before.

T. Flowers and E. Blake were persistent numbers, and also—was this a mistake? Kathy was looking at the last of the six pink numbers, against which the name entered was Marion Summers.

She checked and had it confirmed. Marion had been making regular calls to a second mobile in her own name—that she'd bought and given to someone else perhaps?

The last call Marion made before she died was to T. Flowers. Kathy checked through the record. There had been sixteen calls between them in the previous month, the final one being a call from Marion at 8:16 on the morning of her death. Kathy wished she knew what they'd talked about. Had Marion spoken of someone following her? Had they planned to meet later that day?

E. Blake was interesting too, the pattern of calls odd. Three weeks earlier, E. Blake had sent Marion a stream of text messages, dozens of them. She replied at first, then stopped, but E. Blake went on, bombarding her with calls. It had lasted for four days, then stopped.

Kathy put the phone records aside and considered the papers stacked beneath from the previous day, plus a new heap alongside that had arrived overnight. She made a coffee and got to work, trying to cull out the stuff she could leave till later.

After half an hour she had dealt with the most urgent items, and returned to the phone records. She made a start in checking the names, and established that the E. Blake number was registered to a Mrs. Eleanor Blake, living in Manchester. After being assured that her son wasn't in trouble with the police, Mrs. Blake explained that it was he, Andy, who had the use of the phone, and that she would be very pleased if Kathy could persuade him to cut down on the number of calls he was making, which were costing her a fortune. "He's a student at the university," she explained. "Do you want his address?"

Kathy tried the number of S. Warrender in Notting Hill a couple of times and was diverted directly to a message service. T. Flowers wasn't answering his or her phone either. There was another number that interested her, that of a public phone in Leicester Square. A call had been made from there on the afternoon before Marion was poisoned. There were probably surveillance cameras nearby if she cared to look, but most likely it was just a friend out shopping, Kathy thought. It was all a matter of how far you went, how far you could afford to go, with loose threads everywhere. If you plucked at them all you'd eventually unravel the whole of London, discover what every citizen had been up to on the fatal day.

She looked again at the list in front of her and made up her mind. It was time she found out about Marion's student friends.

THE ADDRESS WAS A narrow brick terrace in a backstreet in Southwark, not very far from the student flats in Stamford Street where Marion had once lived. Her knock was answered by a big beefy young man, unshaven, who yawned and scratched his belly through a threadbare T-shirt as Kathy introduced herself.

"Yeah, that's me," he said, voice croaky but not belligerent. "What's it about?"

"Can I come in?"

"Sure." He shrugged and turned away, leading her down a dark narrow corridor to a small kitchen at the rear. The place smelled of sour damp and burnt cheese and stale beer. There were dirty dishes and empty drink cans and pizza boxes everywhere. He clumsily cleared a seat for Kathy, and leaned back against the sink facing her. "So what have I done?"

Kathy took out her notepad. "Do you know someone called Marion Summers, Andy?"

He blinked, puzzled, then made an exaggerated frown. "Ye-es."

"When did you last see her?"

"Oh, ages ago. Why? What's it about?"

"She died three days ago, on Tuesday. Haven't you seen the papers?"

His mouth dropped open; he appeared thoroughly shocked. "No! That's terrible. How? What happened?"

"We're investigating that now. Where were you last Tuesday?"

He shook his head, running both hands through his hair. "Tuesday . . . Tuesday . . . Well, a maths lecture at ten, followed by a physics prac in the afternoon. I had lunch with two mates at the pub—or maybe that was Wednesday, I'm not sure. No, it was Tuesday."

Kathy took their names. "Are they friends of Marion's too?"

"Nah. Look, I barely knew her. I only met her a couple of times."

"Go on."

"Well, the first time I was having coffee with a friend of mine, Tina Flowers—she's a student, stays in the student flats in Stamford Street, where I used to live. Well, that's where we were, having coffee, when Marion called in to see her. I thought, wow, she was a knockout, really attractive. She and Tina talked about some work they were doing, and then . . ." He shook his head, and his face had gone very pale. "Christ."

Kathy got to her feet. "Sit down, Andy. Put your head between your knees." She filled a glass under the tap and brought it to him.

"Sorry . . . it just hit me. Sorry . . ."

She waited until he finally sat up, sucking in a deep breath. "God, haven't done that since school. How—how did it happen?"

"We think she was poisoned."

"Oh Jesus." He bent forward again, cradling his face in his hands. "That is so unreal."

"Go on with your story. You were at Tina's place."

"Yes. As Marion was leaving, Tina mentioned this party we were going to the next evening, and told Marion she should come, and I joined in and said she must, and she sort of laughed and said maybe. Well, she did. I'd already had a few by the time she showed up. I thought she looked fantastic, really sexy, and I went and chatted to her. She said she was waiting for someone else to arrive, and we flirted, you know. She was really bright and attractive and, well, confident, and I thought she was interested. Only she wasn't really. I think she was just filling in time. The next day I persuaded Tina to let me have her phone number, and tried to call her."

"Twenty-eight times."

"Never! Did I? Bloody hell. You didn't *read* the messages, did you?" His face turned a deep red. "It was a bit of fun, you know? Just mucking about. I mean, I was really keen, but she was having me on, I reckon; just teasing."

"How frustrating. That must have really pissed you off."

"Yeah, it did a bit, but that's how it goes, isn't it? Win some, lose some."

"Who was she meeting at the party?"

"Well, that's the thing, I don't know if there really was anyone. I mean, when I wanted to take her home she said she had to find this other guy and disappeared, but I never actually saw her with anyone, and neither did Tina. But I couldn't be sure; there was a big crowd there. Anyway, after a couple of days trying to talk to her on the phone, I gave up. I don't even know where she lived."

Kathy showed him the mugshot of Keith Rafferty from his police file.

"Blimey." Andy stared at the scowling face. "Who's he?"

"Ever seen him before?"

"Don't think so."

"Okay. So what did Marion talk about, at the party?"

"Oh, you know . . ." He shrugged, then raised his head, an odd expression on his face. "Jesus, I've just remembered. There was something weird she said."

"Go on."

"Well, Tina had told her I was studying science at uni, and she wanted to know if I was doing any chemistry subjects. When I said yes she asked if I knew anything about arsenic compounds. I asked her why, and she said she wanted to poison somebody."

They stared at each other, and Kathy felt a chill creep up her spine. Nigel Ogilvie's remark in the London Library came back to her, about her interest in poisons. "She said that? What words did she use, exactly?"

"Umm . . . *I'm thinking of poisoning somebody,* something like that. I took it for a joke, of course."

"Did you tell her—about arsenic?"

"No, all I know is that arsenic is a heavy metal, but I don't know which compounds are most lethal or anything, or what they taste like."

"She wanted to know that?"

"Yeah. So I told her about Dr. Ringland. He's one of our chemistry lecturers, and arsenic is his research area."

"Did she contact him?"

"I've no idea."

"Where can I find him?"

He told her, and supplied the number of Tina Flowers's flat, and Kathy left him sitting in the kitchen.

THE STUDENT FLATS IN Stamford Street were seething, as if someone had poked a stick in an ants' nest; people were running out the door with hair and scarves flying, late for ten o'clock lectures. Kathy checked in at the office and was told how to find Tina Flowers's room on the fourth floor. It was part of a self-catering apartment of six single rooms sharing a lounge, kitchen and bathroom. One of the other residents of the apartment was in the lounge, ironing clothes. Her name was Jummai, she said, a student from Nigeria. She showed Kathy the door to Tina's room, which she knocked on, waited, then opened. Inside Kathy glimpsed a chaos of crumpled clothes, towels, unmade bed, shoes, CDs and books. The doors of the wardrobe, chairs and table formed improvised drying racks for underwear.

Jummai smiled. "Tina is not tidy," she said. "I think she may have gone to a nine o'clock lecture. She'll probably be back soon."

She seemed very shy, and Kathy chatted to her about her studies, and what life was like in the apartment, trying to put her at ease.

"Do you know a friend of Tina's called Marion Summers? This

is her picture. She lived in this building until three months ago, and I understand she visited Tina here recently."

Jummai examined the photo. "Yes, I do remember her. She is very attractive. She's not in trouble, is she?"

"I know she went to a party with Tina not long ago. Were you there?"

Jummai's face dropped. "Oh, you are looking for drugs."

"No, no, it isn't that. I'm afraid Marion died on Tuesday, Jummai. I'm looking into the circumstances."

The girl looked shocked, and wary. "That is very sad."

"Yes, very. I have to find out as much as I can about her. Can you help me at all? Did you go out with her and Tina?"

"No. I go to church, Tina goes to parties, as you say. She returns late at night and disturbs everyone. She borrows things and doesn't return them. She eats other people's food and doesn't replace it. I don't mean to sound unkind, but that's the way it is."

"I see. How about Marion?"

"I don't know . . . She seemed to be more serious. She dressed well and spoke softly. I think she was helping Tina with her work. I heard them discussing an essay. And money."

"Money?"

"Tina always wants to borrow money."

At that the door to the corridor flew open, there was a muffled curse, and then a dishevelled figure, loaded with several heavy bags, stormed in.

"Ah, Tina!" Jummai said.

"Yeah, what? I can't give you your skirt back yet, Jummai, so piss off."

Jummai rolled her eyes at Kathy. "There is a police officer here to see you, Tina."

"What?" She peered at Kathy. "Hang on, I need a pee." She dropped her bags and disappeared through another door.

She took her time, and when she came back she had a surly set to her face, as if preparing to deny everything. Kathy showed her ID, speculating on what she'd flushed down the toilet. "Let's take a seat, Tina. I'm calling about your friend Marion, Marion Summers. Have you seen the news?"

This wasn't what the girl was expecting, and she cautiously shook her head.

"It's been in the papers. Marion was taken ill on Tuesday, and died in hospital later that day."

The girl did a double take, then looked horrified. She had a pale, elfin face, exaggerated by the dark makeup on her lips and eyes, and cropped black hair. Out of the corner of her eye, Kathy noticed Jummai observing Tina's distress with some satisfaction.

"Any chance of a cup of tea or coffee, Jummai?" she asked.

"Oh . . . yes, all right."

"I can't believe this," Tina whispered. "I spoke to her on Tuesday morning."

"Did she sound all right then?"

"Yes, fine. She said she'd call me later in the week. What happened?"

"It appears that she was poisoned. We don't yet know how it happened."

Tina gave a choking sound and put a hand to her mouth.

"You all right? You want a glass of water?"

The girl shook her head, said hoarsely, "I don't understand. Where was this?"

"At the London Library, where she was working. She had some lunch in the square outside, then came in and collapsed. There was nothing anyone could do. Were you close friends, Tina?"

She hunched forward in the chair, staring at her fingernails, bitten to the quick. "Yes."

"Can you tell me about her?" Kathy spoke gently. "It would help me. Do you mind?"

Tina said nothing at first, then whispered, "She saved me. Last October, when uni came back, I just couldn't deal with things anymore. I was standing in front of the student notice board in the department, trying to decide whether to jump in the river or go home and cut my wrists . . ."

Kathy had already spotted the pink scars on the girl's pale forearm.

"Then this voice behind me said, 'Interested?' It was Marion. She pointed to a notice she'd put up, offering paid research work. I don't know why I said yes. It was the last thing I wanted really, but there was something about her. We went and had a coffee, and she told me what she was doing. She wasn't like me at all— she was very organised and disciplined, whereas I'm the opposite. But it felt like we were . . . sisters. Later on we discovered that our lives had been quite similar. I mean, like broken homes, stuffed-up families. Marion tried harder than me to keep in touch with her mum, but she's useless. Have you spoken to her?"

"Yes."

"Did she ask if she'd get any money out of it?"

"Something like that."

"That'd be right. Anyway . . ." Tina shrugged herself upright and looked around. "What do you care?"

"I went through a bad time when I was about the same age as you, Tina."

"Yeah? What happened?"

"I became a cop."

"Oh." She played with her fingers, twisting them together. "Well, maybe you're like her. She was so strong. She knew exactly what she wanted."

"And that was?"

"To be independent, not to rely on anyone, to be able to live her own life."

"That usually takes money."

"That's why she was working so hard."

"With her studies?"

"And her paid job."

"What was that?"

"She was some kind of research assistant to someone. So what with that and her university work, she had more than she could cope with. That's why she was looking for someone to help her."

"It must have paid pretty well, this other job, if she could afford to employ help."

"Yeah, she said they were pretty well heeled. And impatient."

"Someone at the university?"

"I don't know, she never said."

"So did you see each other socially? Meet her other friends?"

Tina shook her head. "I don't think she had many friends. At least, she didn't talk about them."

"What about a boyfriend?"

"Do you know who it was?"

"I was hoping you could tell me."

Tina shook her head. "She never let on."

Kathy bit her lip with frustration. "You say you and Marion were good friends, but you don't know who she worked for or who her boyfriend was?"

Tina just shrugged.

"But you knew there was someone?"

"She had a new ring one time. It looked expensive, and when I asked her she said an admirer had given it to her for her birthday. She was teasing me."

"Where did Marion move to, Tina?"

"I don't know that either." She saw the expression on Kathy's face and protested, "No, it's true. There were a lot of things she kept private."

A look of hurt came over her face, and Kathy saw a tear form in her eye. She wondered if Tina had been in love with Marion. "Didn't you mind that, Tina?" she said carefully.

Tina sniffed and shook off the question. "I thought it was really mysterious and interesting how she kept things dark. But now I wonder if she was afraid."

"How do you mean?"

"Well, afraid that bad things might happen if she let the different parts of her life come together."

"Did she ever mention being afraid of someone in particular?"

"No, not in so many words. But when something like this happens you look back at everything and wonder, don't you? I remember one time we were walking across the river, and she suddenly jumped, as if she'd seen someone, and as soon as we got to the other side she dashed off with hardly a word."

"I see."

Kathy showed her the picture of Rafferty. The girl hesitated. "I'm not sure."

"What sort of research work was Marion doing?"

"It was all to do with William Morris and the Pre-Raphaelite Brotherhood—that's what she was doing her doctorate on as well. Pretty boring really, but it was good for me—my Eng. Lit. lecturer is mad keen on them and there's bound to be exam questions. He's her supervisor too."

"That's Dr. da Silva, isn't it?"

"That's right."

"What's he like?"

"Fancies himself. You know, shows off to the girls in class. Tells us about these papers he's given at conferences around the world with lots of other important wankers like himself."

Kathy smiled. "How did Marion put up with that?"

"She could handle it. He's supposed to be a world authority on the Pre-Raphaelites, so I suppose she didn't have much choice."

"And Marion was particularly keen on that period."

"Oh yes. The way she talked about Dante Gabriel Rossetti, it sounded like he was the only man she'd ever really loved."

"But he's dead?"

Tina nodded. "Yeah, over a hundred years ago. Sad, really—for Marion I mean."

"What did you do for Marion, exactly?"

"Library searches, mostly." Tina's expression softened as she explained, as if this was a part of her life that had gone well. "I wasn't looking at the main Pre-Raphaelite literature—that's what she was working on. But she wanted me to poke around the edges: old newspapers, memoirs, court records, books, diaries—anything really—by people who might have seen them from another angle, like doctors, lawyers, relatives, other writers and painters. She gave me lists of key words to work from. Marion said the most important thing was the choice of key words."

"Can I see them?"

The girl looked doubtful. "I don't think they'll mean much, but okay." She got to her feet and went to her room, returning with a folded sheet of paper. "This was the original list. From time to time she'd add new words. This is a copy; you can keep it."

"Thanks." Kathy scanned the words, mostly names that meant little to her:

Dante Gabriel Rossetti
Elizabeth (Lizzie) Siddal
Jane (Janey) Burden/Morris
Fanny Cornforth
Annie Miller
Lena Wardle
George Wardle
Madeleine Smith
James Smith
H. Haverlock
Poison
Arsenic
Laudanum
Suicide/suicide pact
Ophelia
The Awakening Conscience
Guenevere

Kathy pointed to the words *Poison* and *Arsenic* and asked Tina, "Why these?"

"Oh, it comes up all the time, you'd be surprised. The Victorians used arsenic for all kinds of stuff." She caught the puzzled look on Kathy's face, and said, "You think she was deliberately poisoned by someone, don't you?"

"It seems probable. Can you think of anyone who would have hated her that much?"

Tina shook her head. "I just can't believe this," she whispered, and tears began to dribble down her cheeks.

Kathy dug a packet of tissues from her pocket. "Here . . . I'll leave you my phone number. You might remember something that will help us get to the bottom of this. We may also need to speak to you later to get a formal statement."

She looked up as Jummai approached with a tray and three mugs. "Sorry, Jummai, I have to go. Thanks for your help. Will you stay with Tina for a bit?"

"Yes, and I will pray for Marion," Jummai said, as Kathy left.

EIGHT

KATHY'S NOSE LED HER to the information counter of the laboratories. It began at the front door to the street, a faint chemical smell reminiscent of the swimming pool, and built up to something more like an attack on the Western Front.

A man in a white coat answered her ping on the counter bell. "Can I help you?"

"I'm after . . ." Kathy had to stop to clear her throat with a cough.

"Yeah, sorry about that. We're having a bit of trouble with the extract fans."

"I'm after Dr. Ringland. Is he in?"

"Sure. Hang on."

Actually, Kathy rather liked the smell. The laboratories that she'd visited at the forensic science facilities were mostly odourless and not at all like the school labs she had fond memories of. What was the point of studying chemistry if there were no stinks and bangs?

A rather handsome middle-aged man emerged after a moment, a worried frown on his face. "Yes? I'm Colin Ringland."

Kathy showed her ID. "Can I have five minutes of your time, Dr. Ringland? Somewhere quiet?"

He showed her down the corridor to a small tutorial room, with a white board scrawled with diagrams of molecule structures. They sat at one end of a Formica table.

"I'm wondering if you ever met a PhD student at this university called Marion Summers."

"Ah, yes, that poor girl. I read the newspaper report, and her supervisor told me."

"Dr. da Silva?"

"That's right. He said you'd contacted him."

"You know him well then?"

"Yes, we live near each other and play squash regularly. In fact I originally assumed it was he who referred her to me, but it turned out she'd heard about my work from one of my students."

"So when did you meet her?"

"I could check if you like, but it must have been about a month ago. She phoned and asked if she could see me about her research, then came over here and we talked for an hour or so. About a week later she followed up with some queries over the phone."

"Would you mind telling me what you talked about?"

"Poisons—arsenic specifically." He raised his hands. "Yes, I know. When I saw in the paper that Marion was believed to have been poisoned I wondered if I should contact you. I discussed it with Tony—Dr. da Silva—who hadn't heard about the poisoning part. He thought it was probably a bizarre coincidence and so I did nothing."

"What's your involvement with arsenic?"

"It's my main research area, part of a joint research project with Jadavpur University in Calcutta and our engineering faculty here. Do you want me to go into details?"

"Maybe an outline."

"It's to do with trying to find an effective solution to the contamination of drinking water with arsenic in West Bengal and Bangladesh. Have you heard about that?"

Kathy recalled what Sundeep had said. "Something, I think."

"Well, the Bengal basin is very densely populated, of course, and there has been a long-standing health problem because of a lack of access to clean water. People were relying on polluted river and pond water, and so in the 1970s UNICEF and the World Bank decided to fund a huge aid program to sink tube wells that would provide clean water from deep below the surface."

"Sounds like a good idea."

"Yes, enlightened western aid to give the poor clean drinking water. What could be wrong with that? The trouble was that the whole region is sitting on thick layers of alluvial mud, and as the rainwaters soak through the mud they leach out naturally occurring arsenic and concentrate it deep down, right where the new wells were to draw their water."

"Wasn't the water tested?"

"Apparently not for arsenic. The geology was unusual and no one expected this. People began to get sick, but slowly. Arsenic is a heavy metal, like lead, and the body has trouble getting rid of it once it's taken in. It gradually accumulates, and people began to show symptoms like blisters, cancers, gangrene and damage to liver and kidneys. But they were also undernourished and sick with other things, and it took a long time to figure out what was wrong, and meanwhile they kept sinking new wells—over 900,000 in fact.

"The result is that millions of people are now at risk; some estimates say as many as thirty million people across the whole region are slowly dying. It's the biggest case of mass poisoning ever. The long-term solution has got to be more effective management of water on the surface—clean reservoirs, proper drains and so on. But in the meantime they need a cheap and simple way of filtering out the arsenic from the wells. That's what we're working on."

"And to do that they need an expert on the chemistry of arsenic," Kathy said.

"Yes, that's me."

"But I don't suppose it was the Bangladesh problem that Marion wanted to talk to you about."

"Actually she was pretty interested; I showed her around the lab and we talked about the work. But no, you're right, it was the basic chemistry of arsenic compounds and how they worked as poisons that interested her, in relation to the Pre-Raphaelites."

"That's what I don't really understand. Did she explain how it was relevant to her studies?"

Ringland smiled. "You sound like Tony—he felt she was making far too much of this. He wanted her to concentrate on other things. Arsenic was used for all kinds of purposes in the nineteenth century, and certainly was a huge health problem. That's what Marion was mainly concerned with. She said she was writing a paper."

"So she was knowledgeable about its use? I mean, properties, doses and so on?"

"That's what she wanted to speak to me about: the different compounds and their effects. Frankly, she didn't have the basic grounding in chemistry. Typical arts student, having trouble with formulae, numbers. She did her best, trying to write it all down, but when I started getting into detail, your arsenates and arsenites and arsenides, your trioxide and your pentoxide, your arsphenamine . . ." He saw the look on Kathy's face and laughed. "Used for syphilis. Pretty brutal. Thank your lucky stars for antibiotics."

"I don't have syphilis at the moment," Kathy said, and watched his face turn scarlet.

"Oh God, no, I didn't mean . . ."

"And neither did Marion as far as I know, but I'll check. Is that what she was interested in?"

"Oh, anything to do with how the Victorians used the stuff—Fowler's solution for warts, Gay's solution for asthma, Frère Come's arsenical paste for cancer . . ."

"And where would you find arsenic these days?"

"Well, somewhere like here, I suppose. We carry quite a bit of it. All under very secure conditions, of course. The university's health and safety procedures are rigorous, believe me. But in any case, that wouldn't be what killed Marion."

"Why do you say that?"

"Well, nobody dies of arsenic poisoning in the UK these days. You're not suggesting that, surely?"

"We're still doing tests."

"You'll probably find it was some food toxin. It's pretty scary what gets into our food."

"Yes, I suppose so. All the same, I'd like to be certain that the poison couldn't have originated from here."

Dr. Ringland looked at her as if she was being obtuse. "But why? I mean, you surely don't think she was poisoned by someone working here in the lab, do you?"

"No, I wasn't thinking that. I just wanted to be sure she couldn't have got hold of something herself while she was visiting."

"Oh no, no chance of that."

"What about Dr. da Silva, has he been in here?"

Colin Ringland raised his eyebrows at her. "Sure, I have shown him around, and he's called in for me a couple of times when I was working."

"Could he have got a sample of the chemicals for her?"

He choked back a laugh. "Utterly impossible. Come on, I'll show you."

He took Kathy into the working areas, showing her the locked storage rooms and cabinets and explaining the security arrangements of keys, alarms, cameras and inventory checks. By the end of it she had to admit it seemed highly unlikely that Marion or anyone else from outside could have helped themselves to the laboratory stocks of arsenic.

AFTER TRYING DR. DA Silva's phone numbers without success, Kathy went back to the office of the Department of European Literature and spoke to the secretary, Karen.

"Dr. da Silva? I saw him earlier." She went over to the window and said, "Yes, his car's there."

Kathy looked down into the street and saw a red BMW sports on a meter. "That's nice. I didn't think lecturing paid that well."

"Family money," Karen sniffed. Her tone was sharp with disapproval, and she turned away to consult her computer. "He's giving a lecture at the moment, another twenty minutes to go. LT108. You could catch him when he comes out."

"Thanks, Karen."

Kathy found lecture theatre LT108, its red LECTURE IN PROGRESS light illuminated, and opened the door. She found herself at the top of a steeply raked auditorium, packed with students, and took a seat halfway down towards the lecturer's dais. A tall, dark-complexioned man was speaking. He was in his mid-forties, Kathy guessed, and spoke with a cultured drawl. His manner was confident and lively, and he emphasised his points with forceful gestures of his hands. From time to time, as he turned to his notes, he would sweep his long black hair back from his brow. His audience was attentive, especially the women, Kathy thought, and she wasn't surprised, for his voice, appearance and manner were all quite compelling. She could see what Tina had meant.

When the lecture finished, Kathy worked her way down to the front against a stream of departing students. A couple of girls had cornered the lecturer, talking animatedly, and he was smiling as he replied, collecting up his papers and moving towards the door. He spotted Kathy, and put a hand up to hold the door open for her. His face was a little fleshier and older than it had seemed from a distance.

"Dr. da Silva, I'm Detective Inspector Kathy Kolla," she said, showing him her ID, and watching his expression freeze. But she was used to that. She held out her hand and he shook it cautiously.

"You want to talk about Marion?" he said quietly.

"Yes."

"Terrible. We're all shocked. We just can't believe it."

"Of course. Is there somewhere we can go?"

He led her to his room, a comfortable corner office with a large window. Books covered every inch of the walls. On the shelf facing her when she sat down were multiple copies of a thick volume, its title—*Dante Gabriel Rossetti*—printed in sumptuous Gothic script, as was the author's name, *Anthony da Silva*.

"Apparently it was on the radio that someone probably put something in her lunch, is that right?" he asked.

"That's what we suspect."

He pursed his lips with distaste. "I can't understand how anyone could do that. There are some very sick people around. I suppose you have to deal with them every day." He gave her a sympathetic smile.

"We have to consider the possibility that her attacker knew her in some capacity, so we're speaking to her friends and work colleagues. How long have you known her?"

"Um, it must be about three years. I first came across her in her honours year, and she'd be almost two years into her doctorate now."

"So you must have got to know her quite well?"

"Well, academically, yes. I met with her on average, what—every couple of weeks during term time?"

"How about socially?"

"Oh not really. We bumped into each other from time to time—departmental drinks, open lectures, that sort of thing. And she came to our house once. Jenny, my wife, put on a little party for my doctoral students. She likes to do that occasionally, check them out." He gave a faint smile.

"And you phoned each other frequently?"

He stared at Kathy for a moment, and she wondered if he was going to deny it. Then he said, "Well, yes, if she had a query about something in her work, or I had to change a meeting, that kind of thing."

His reply was guarded, and Kathy sensed he wasn't being completely open. "Have you been to her home?"

"No. I don't know where she lived, to be honest. I suppose the office will have the address."

"You don't know if she shared with someone?"

"Sorry, no idea."

"What about her friends, other people she went around with?"

"No, I couldn't say."

"I've just been speaking to Dr. Ringland." Kathy saw the surprise register briefly. "He told me about Marion's interest in arsenic poisoning. Can you enlarge on that for me?"

"Oh . . . yes, of course. That is rather strange, isn't it, in the light of what's happened?" He paused, as if debating how to go on. "She was studying the Pre-Raphaelites for her PhD. How much do you know about them?"

"They were a group of nineteenth-century English painters, weren't they?"

"And poets, yes. The 1840s and '50s, the first avant-garde movement in art, something of a sensation at the time—young men breaking the mould, that kind of thing. Their program was to reform art by going back to the fifteenth century, before it was corrupted, hence their name." He was interrupted by his phone ringing. "Excuse me." He picked it up. "Hello? Colin, hi, we were just talking about you. I'm sitting here with Inspector Kolla now . . . Yes, sure . . . You still on for tonight? . . . Great. I'll call you back later. Bye."

He smiled at Kathy. "Sorry about that. Where were we?"

"The Pre-Raphaelites."

"Oh yes. Well, they and their circle—wives, lovers, models—were a fairly sickly lot. I don't know if they were more so than the average Londoners of that period, but it's a striking feature of their story. Dante Gabriel Rossetti's wife, Lizzie Siddal, was a chronic invalid; she died of an overdose of the laudanum she was medicating herself with. His lover Janey, William Morris's wife, was also sickly, and Rossetti himself eventually went barking mad, sharing his house in Chelsea with a menagerie of kangaroos, wombats and armadillos."

He was more relaxed now, slipping into the familiar account he might have entertained students or dinner guests with many times before.

"Now, it's conceivable that arsenic had something to do with all that. One of the revolutionary things about the Pre-Raphaelite painters—Rossetti, Millais, Holman Hunt and the others—was their use of the new vivid pigments that the chemical industry had recently developed, especially a brilliant green called Emerald Green, or Paris Green, made from arsenic. People were shocked by the blazing colour of their paintings, made possible by these new pigments—later the Impressionists used the same colours to achieve their dazzling effects—but they were quite dangerous. The painters absorbed the pigment through their skin, they breathed its fumes and held paintbrushes loaded with it in their mouths. It's said that arsenic poisoning from Emerald Green was the cause of Monet's blindness and Van Gogh's madness. It was Cézanne's favourite colour, and he developed severe diabetes, a symptom of chronic arsenic poisoning."

It was developing into a lecture, and Kathy interrupted. "How does Marion fit in?"

"Ah, well, yes. Marion found all this rather fascinating. Too fascinating, really."

"How do you mean?"

"It seems a little churlish to criticise her scholarship at a time like this."

"I'd appreciate a frank opinion; I believe you're the world expert on this subject."

Da Silva chuckled, letting her know that he recognised outrageous flattery when he heard it, and didn't mind in the least.

"Marion was one of the brightest doctoral students I've ever had. She was extremely serious about her work, applied herself very diligently. She was quite passionate about her ideas. Rather too much so. It is a classic trap for a scholar to become too attached to a pet theory before all the evidence is in. Marion could be quite headstrong, and ambitious too, desperate to break new ground, achieve new insights. It sometimes made her rather extravagant in her formulations. I had to keep trying to rein her in."

"Can you tell me what her particular ideas about arsenic were?"

"Oh . . ." He flapped a hand, his sigh almost a groan. "She tried to extend what was probably just their ignorance about the dangers of paint pigments into a whole philosophy. She speculated that the Pre-Raphaelites cultivated a fascination with death, especially tragic, premature death, and that this was mixed up with their notions of romantic love and sexual freedom. Well, they certainly did have tangled sex lives, but Marion blew it out of all proportion. She was obsessed."

"It does sound ambitious."

"Quite impossible. Absurdly broad for a doctoral thesis." He leaned forward, punching the point home with his index finger, and Kathy saw another side to him, pugnacious and domineering. "She was wandering off into areas in which she had no expertise—forensic medicine, psychology, chemistry, you name it." He gave a snort. "The provisional title of her thesis was *Sex and Death: A Pre-Raphaelite Discourse*. You see what I mean?" He spread his hands. "Somewhat melodramatic."

"But they were pretty melodramatic, the Pre-Raphaelites, weren't they?"

He smiled at Kathy indulgently. "Well, yes, but Marion was writing an academic treatise, not a novel. That was our compromise title. Her first efforts were even more lurid—'lust' figured prominently, if I remember rightly."

"Was there much lust in Marion's life, would you say?"

He held Kathy's eye for a moment, then said, very deliberately, "I have absolutely no idea. She never talked about her private life."

"Did she have a job, apart from her studies? Some source of income?"

Again, he couldn't say, and his mood changed, becoming impatient and bored. He checked his watch.

"What were your movements last Tuesday, Dr. da Silva?"

He frowned. "I was working at home. I'm preparing a paper for a conference in the States, and the deadline is coming up. There are too many interruptions here, so I stayed at home to get it finished."

"Was anyone with you?"

"I'm afraid not."

NINE

THE PHONE WENT OFF as Kathy slid behind the wheel. Her heart sank as she recognised Nicole's voice. "Oh, hi."

"You didn't ring me back. How did it go this morning?"

"Not too well, I'm afraid. It didn't work out as I'd hoped."

"You sound harassed."

"Sorry, I've been flat out with this murder case, that woman who was poisoned in St. James's Square."

"Oh, is that what you're on?"

"It's my first murder since I made inspector, Nicole. I've got to get it right."

"And you will, but you're not giving up on this weekend."

"It's impossible. I'm really sorry. I was looking forward to it."

"Sounds like you need a break, Kathy. Anyway, maybe you'll have cracked it by tonight."

Kathy sighed. "No way. Cases either crack in the first day or they go on for weeks. We've passed the golden hour; it's all hard slog now."

She rang off, and immediately the phone rang again, this time with the librarian Gael Rayner on the line.

"Oh, Inspector, we're under siege here!" She sounded excited.

"What's going on?"

"There's a contingent of foreign press outside, trying to get pictures and interviews about Marion's death. We've had to bar them from coming in. I try to tell them this is the London Library, for goodness' sake, not *CSI Miami*."

"Do you want me to talk to the local coppers?"

"Oh no, it's all right. They're rather dishy, actually. I probably will let them in to shoot a bit of film, but I just don't want them to turn us into the London Dungeon or something. No, it was another thing I thought I should mention to you." Her voice dropped to a whisper. "I'm really not sure if it's relevant. It concerns one of our readers. It may be nothing at all, and I'd hate to make trouble unnecessarily."

"Gael, this is a murder inquiry. You can trust me to handle any information tactfully, but you really can't keep anything relevant to yourself."

She sighed. "Oh well, yes."

"Should I come over there?"

"Maybe that would be best. But not in a police car with sirens, please. It might be best if you were to come to our service entrance at the back, off Mason's Yard. I'll meet you there."

Kathy followed Gael's instructions and made her way to the library's back entrance, past wire fencing surrounding the compound of the builders that Gael had spoken of. The librarian was waiting there, and took Kathy to a small staffroom. Coffee cups stood on a draining board, a few magazines lay on a table at which they sat.

"Can I get you anything? Tea, coffee?"

"I'm fine. What did you want to tell me?"

"Well, it was when the foreign film crew arrived. It caused a bit of excitement in the library, and people went to the windows to see what was going on. And I happened to notice Nigel Ogilvie there. I was struck because he was holding his mobile phone up, although he didn't appear to be calling anyone."

"He was taking pictures?"

"Exactly. And then I remembered . . . I haven't been able to get it out of my mind, that dreadful scene up in the Reading Room, when Marion collapsed. I've gone over it so many times, and now it occurred to me that there was something . . . odd. You remember that it was Nigel Ogilvie who rang for the ambulance?"

"Yes."

"I was paying most attention to Marion, of course, trying to do what I could—nobody else had much idea, and I've done the first-aid course. But at some point I looked up and saw Nigel. I thought it was strange, because he was still sitting in his chair, while everybody else was on their feet. And he was holding up his mobile phone. I assumed he was calling for help, but when I asked him he appeared rather surprised, as if that wasn't what he was thinking at all, but then he said yes, and made the call. This all happened in a twinkling, you understand, and I was much more concerned with Marion. It's only now that I remember the odd expression on his face when I asked if he was phoning for help. I mean, what else would he have been thinking of?"

"Go on."

"I feel like a bit of a rat, telling you this. I've known Nigel for years, and he's a very nice, quiet man, always with a friendly word."

"But . . . ?"

Gael gave a big sigh. "When I thought about it, I recalled seeing him with his phone out in the library before. Then I remembered another time. I was standing at the window on the top floor one day, about a month ago. It was lunchtime, and the trees in the square were bare. I noticed Marion on one of the benches in the central gardens, eating a sandwich and reading a book. And then I saw another person standing on the other side of the gardens. It was Nigel, and I thought he was behaving rather strangely, standing behind a tree, almost as if he was playing hide-and-seek, not wanting Marion to spot him. But then I realised he was holding his phone out, and I thought he must be just checking his messages or something. Now I'm not sure . . ."

"You think he was taking pictures of her?"

"Oh God, I don't know. It sounds so creepy when you say it out loud. I've probably let my imagination run away with me. I mean, he's in *publishing*, for goodness' sake."

"That's probably not an absolute guarantee of virtue, Gael."

The librarian gave a rueful grin. "I'm sure I'm wasting your time."

"Don't worry. And you said he's here at the moment?"

"Yes, in the Reading Room. He seemed rather excited by all the fuss outside. I'll show you the way, only . . ."

"Don't worry, I'll be very tactful."

"Thank you."

But when they reached the Reading Room Nigel Ogilvie wasn't there. Then Gael spotted his papers at one of the tables. "He's probably in the stacks. I think I know where he's likely to be. How are your heels?" She looked down at Kathy's shoes. "No, you'll be all right."

She led the way back into the narrow book stacks, and Kathy understood what she'd meant, for the floors were made of steel grilles.

"This was one of the first steel-framed buildings in London," Gael murmured. "Very innovative for its time. Here . . ."

They turned a corner and Kathy saw Ogilvie between the shelves up ahead, his back to them. She nodded to Gael to leave and advanced on him.

"Mr. Ogilvie, hello."

He turned, holding a book, a vague smile on his face. "Oh, hello! Inspector . . ."

"Kolla. Sorry to interrupt, but I needed to check something with you."

"Oh yes?"

"Your phone, do you have it with you?"

"Er, yes." His free hand strayed to his jacket pocket.

"May I have a quick look?"

He hesitated. "Why?"

"Just details. I'll have to put it in my report. The type."

"Really?"

Kathy put out her hand with a smile and for a moment thought he wouldn't do it. Then, apparently unable to think of a good reason for refusing, he reluctantly eased out the phone. She took it quickly and said, "Oh yes."

She opened it. The controls were different from her own, and she made a few mistakes as she rapidly thumbed the buttons.

"What are you doing? Here—!"

"Would it have retained a record of your call, do you think?" she improvised.

The question threw him for a moment. "What? I don't know. Look, give it to me and I'll try to—"

"Ah, what's this?" There was an image of a camera crew in the square, seen from the Reading Room window. Before that an ambulance standing outside the library. She flicked back, stared at the screen for a moment, then looked up at Ogilvie, whose face had become very flushed. She showed him the image. "That's Marion on the floor, isn't it?"

"What . . . I really don't know . . ." he gabbled. "Maybe, when I made the call, I may have pressed the wrong button. If you'll just give it to me . . ."

"This is important evidence, Mr. Ogilvie. We'll need this. What else have you got?" There was a long silence as Kathy clicked back through the images. "Well, well." She pocketed the phone. "I think we need to talk about this."

"It's nothing, it's just . . ."

"Not here. I want you to come with me to a police station to tell me all about it. And I want to caution you that you don't need to say anything, but . . ."

He stood in dismayed silence as she delivered the caution, then meekly followed her to the Reading Room to collect his belongings. As he gathered them up and fumbled them into his case, Kathy glanced across at Gael, who was sitting at her desk, surreptitiously taking it all in. Kathy gestured her over.

"Ms. Rayner, Mr. Ogilvie and I would like to leave without drawing attention to ourselves. Could you let us out the back way?"

"Certainly." She glanced at Nigel Ogilvie, whose head was bowed. "Is everything all right?"

"Fine," Kathy said. "Just fine."

It was a short drive across Piccadilly to Savile Row and into West End Central police station, where Kathy arranged for Ogilvie to be shown to an interview room to sit alone for a while.

She wondered about phoning Brock, but thought better of it; he'd probably be tied up, and anyway, this was her case. She arranged for hard copies to be made of the images in Ogilvie's phone, and sat down to study them. The earliest was of Marion sitting in the square, viewed from the Reading Room window, before she returned to the library and collapsed. Kathy thought about this, then went in to interview Ogilvie, accompanied by a young woman constable from the station. He sat up with a jerk as they came in.

"Look," he began, "you've got—"

Kathy interrupted, face grim. "We're not quite ready to begin, Mr. Ogilvie. Just some housekeeping first. Your full name, address and home telephone number, please."

He complied, giving an address in Hayes.

"Do you own or rent any other properties?"

"No."

"What about your work address?"

"Surely . . . surely you don't need to involve them?"

"Just routine."

She left again, to make arrangements for a search warrant for Ogilvie's home and office, then returned to the interview room and switched on the equipment, formally opening the interview. She spread the pictures out on the table. "I'm showing Mr. Ogilvie eight prints of photographs found in his camera, all of which show Marion Summers before and at the time of her collapse in the London Library on Tuesday last, the third of April, shortly before her death. Do you agree that you took these pictures, Mr. Ogilvie?"

He bit his lip, a pained expression on his face, pudgy fingers fiddling with the corner of one of the pictures. "This is extremely embarrassing, but it's not what you think. I had no . . . bad intentions."

He gazed at her anxiously, searching for some glimmer of empathy, and saw none.

"They gave me this phone at work, you see—insisted on it, so that they could keep in touch. My publishing director loves phoning me at odd times with his latest brainwaves—during dinner, on the train, at weekends. I hate the damn thing, but I did find the camera quite intriguing, once I'd worked out how to use it. I thought at first that I could take pictures of pages from the books I was studying—I've seen other people doing that—but I found the quality not very good, and decided to stick to photocopies. But I did find it amusing to record incidents of daily life."

"Of Marion Summers's daily life, you mean. Not your wife and kids."

"I don't have a wife and kids. Marion is, *was*, a very striking young woman. I find most of the people at the library rather, well, predictable, but she was an intriguing mystery. She was very beautiful, like the Pre-Raphaelite women she was studying. I liked to speculate about her life, but in the most innocent way."

"How do you mean?"

"Well, I asked myself, did she have a husband? A lover?"

"And did she?"

"I don't know. I never found out."

"Did you follow her home?"

He looked startled. "No."

"Do you know where she lived?"

"No, no."

"How do you know she was studying Pre-Raphaelite women?"

"Ah . . . I noticed the books she was reading and, er, I looked up her borrowing record on Gael Rayner's computer when she was away from her desk."

"You were stalking her."

Ogilvie winced. "No, please, it wasn't like that. There was nothing predatory about it. I was just intrigued. She was so refreshing, a free spirit. And then, when she collapsed like that, it was so terrible, like fate . . ."

"Fate?"

"Yes." He reached for one of the last pictures, and drew it out with the tips of his fingers as if afraid it might burn him. It showed Marion on the floor, her red hair fanning out, surrounded by a sprinkling of wild blooms. "Don't you see? Ophelia . . . You must know it, in the Tate, the Millais painting."

Ophelia, Kathy remembered that the name had been on Tina's word list. Ogilvie looked at her blank face, then his expression crumpled. "Oh my God, this is a nightmare."

Kathy, her voice softening a little, as if in sympathy at his predicament, said, "Please understand, Nigel, that we will discover everything. It is important that you are completely frank with me from the start, or else things will go very badly for you. Now, what part did you play in Marion's death?"

He shook his head so hard his whole body vibrated. "No, no, nothing!"

"Was it a prank, to get her attention?"

"I swear, no."

"You put something in her lunch during the morning, didn't you? Perhaps you just intended to make her a little unwell, so that you could be a good Samaritan and take her home. Was that it?"

Ogilvie moaned, gasping his denials.

"You know how she died, don't you?"

"I've read the newspapers. People in the library have been talking about it."

"What's your understanding of what happened?"

"Well, I believe she went out to have her lunch in the square, as I told you . . ."

He stammered his account, and all the time Kathy was willing him to say the word that hadn't been in the papers: *arsenic*. That would clinch it. But he came to the end without a hint of it, and no matter how she probed, he repeated only, "Poison, that's what I read."

She showed him the picture of Rafferty, and watched a twitch of alarm cross his face. "Do you know this man?"

"Is he . . . Is he . . . ?"

"You recognise him, don't you?"

"I think I may have seen him—in the square. I thought he was watching Marion."

"You know him, Nigel. Did he give you the poison to put in Marion's lunch?"

"Oh dear Lord, no, no, a thousand times no!"

Kathy gave a deep sigh. "You took other pictures of Marion, didn't you?"

"Um . . ." He frowned at the photos, as if trying to recall.

"Before last Tuesday," Kathy prompted.

"No, no. I don't believe so. Really, I wasn't in the habit . . ."

"We have a witness, someone who saw you in the square one day, taking pictures of Marion with your camera."

His eyes widened in alarm.

"I warned you, didn't I, Nigel, about lying to me? It means I can't believe anything you tell me."

"I swear—"

"Do you own a computer?"

His face was now as white as the sheet of paper in Kathy's pad.

"Yes."

"Where is it?"

"At . . . at home."

"In Hayes?"

He nodded, jaw locked.

"And at work, you have the use of a computer?"

"Yes, but—"

"On your desk?"

"Yes."

"Do you live alone?"

"No. I live with my mother. She's elderly, infirm. My father passed away, it was their home. I moved back when my mother became frail."

"I would like your permission to search your house."

"No!"

"You refuse?"

A blush appeared on his cheek and he seemed to puff up a little in defiance. "Yes, I refuse. It's out of the question. It would be far too distressing for my mother."

"Very well. I'm suspending this interview now. I'll arrange for you to get a cup of tea."

When they were outside, Kathy said to the PC, "I'm going to wait for the search warrant, but in the meantime I'd like you to go on ahead to his house. See if there's going to be a problem with his mother's state of health. Be gentle and reassuring. Say Nigel has given us some very helpful evidence and he'll be along shortly. Get her talking. Has he had girlfriends? Does he experiment with chemicals? Does he have a lock-up somewhere? But don't be too obvious."

While she waited Kathy logged on to the Tate Britain website and looked up "Ophelia." The image of the Pre-Raphaelite masterpiece came up on the screen, the demented young woman from *Hamlet* floating in the dark stream, russet hair spreading in the current, wild flowers in the water around her. He was right, Kathy thought. It was her. Apparently the model, Lizzie Siddal, later Dante Gabriel Rossetti's wife and laudanum victim, nearly died of pneumonia posing for the painting in a bath. *Sex and death,* Kathy thought, imagining what Marion would have made of Lizzie's story, suffering for her lover's art.

WHEN KATHY ARRIVED AT the house in Hayes, it was the constable who answered her knock. She shook her head, looking over Kathy's shoulder at Ogilvie sitting ashen in the patrol car, the white van with the search team parked behind, and said in a murmur,

"Alzheimer's, I'm afraid. She's cheerful enough, just can't remember things. I had to remind her who Nigel was. She seemed to think he was still at school."

The search of Mrs. Ogilvie's home made Kathy feel grubby. It was a small, anonymous detached house in a leafy suburban street, which gradually came to life at the intrusion of the police vehicles. The garden was meticulously groomed, the interior fastidiously tidy. If this is worthy of police time, it seemed to protest, then we're all in trouble. And indeed the only guilty secret they found was a small and rather embarrassing collection of pornography in Nigel's bedroom—he was something of a rubber fetishist, it seemed. Apart from that he seemed to lead a pretty boring life, Kathy thought; small wonder he'd found Marion Summers entrancing. They found no trace of chemicals, but there was the computer of course, to be taken away and examined. Nigel watched them from his bedroom window, as it was carried out to the van, then abruptly turned to Kathy.

"You may find some more pictures on the computer, now I come to think of it," he said stiffly. "It had slipped my mind. One afternoon I happened to see Marion get on a bus in Piccadilly. On impulse I hailed a taxi and told the man to follow the bus. I said my daughter was on board, and I wanted to make sure she got to her destination safely, without her being aware of me fussing. He probably didn't believe me. We followed her to Hampstead, a pleasant little mews cottage. I didn't stop. I took a picture and told the driver to drop me at a tube station."

"Do you know the address?"

"Um, I believe I do recall. It's 43 Rosslyn Court."

"Did you go there at other times?"

"Certainly not."

"We shall find out if you're lying again, Nigel."

They left to the twitch of curtains in the neighbouring houses, a heavy dull red sun sinking in the cold western sky, and made their way back into town, to the offices of the publishing house where Ogilvie worked. There they searched his desk and confiscated his computer. His work colleagues seemed rather excited to discover that dull Mr. Ogilvie was a man of mystery, of interest to the police. Kathy waited with the team until it was finished, impatient to move on, to discover if they really had found Marion's refuge at last.

TEN

WHILE THE PATROL CAR and van sped off back to West End Central, Kathy headed up to Hampstead. The mews was a secluded street not far from the heath, number forty-three a small detached two-storey, red-brick house with Victorian sash windows and ornamented chimneys.

The bell tinkled faintly through the stained-glass panel in the front door. There were no lights on in the house. Kathy was fairly well hidden from neighbours by trees in the street and a trellis arch at the front gate, and the streetlights were dim and far apart; a discreet entrance. When there was no reply she used the bunch of keys they had found in Marion's bag to open the door.

The house had a mildly stale, musty smell, as if no one had opened a window for a while. Kathy trod softly down the carpeted hall, checking a room fitted out like an office on the right, then a sitting room and kitchen at the rear, overlooking the tiny paved courtyard. Then she went back to the stairs in the hall and quickly made sure that there was no one in the two bedrooms and bathroom above. Everywhere she had an impression of brand-new, stylish fittings and furniture, and an almost obsessive tidiness.

She returned to the ground floor, to the kitchen. It was small, but immaculately fitted out with the latest Miele appliances. She found a light switch, suddenly bathing the granite worktop in light. Everything was in its place apart from some things left out on the bench beside the sink—a six-pack of juice bottles, two removed, one of which stood open beside a half-filled glass of orange liquid, a saucer containing a small amount of white powder sitting on a set of kitchen scales, and a teaspoon. They were the only things in the whole house that weren't neatly stowed away.

She pulled latex gloves from her pocket and crouched to take a closer look. The powder was crystalline, more like fine sugar than flour. Would Marion have added sugar to the juice because of her diabetes? But there was something about it that didn't look quite like sugar either. She straightened and backed away, then got on the phone for a scene of crime team. "I'll wait outside in the car," she said, and made her way back down the hall, taking with her the half-dozen envelopes she found in the wire mail basket hanging at the back of the front door. They were all advertising material, only one, from a local hair salon, addressed to *Ms. M. Summers*, the remainder to *The Occupant*.

The forensic team had been on stand-by, and arrived quickly. Kathy briefed the Crime Scene Manager at the front steps. "This is the home of Marion Summers, the woman who was poisoned in St. James's Square on Tuesday. I'm interested to know if anyone else has been living here or visited her recently. Also, there's some white powder and bottles of juice in the kitchen. I'd particularly like a chemical analysis. It's possible there may be poisons here."

She put on disposable overalls along with the others, and showed them the powder in the kitchen.

"Not sure what it is," the manager said, squinting at it.

"No. I might phone our pathologist. He's been looking into this."

"Good idea. We'll keep out of here until he's seen it."

Sundeep was very interested. "I'll come straight over, Kathy. And you must be careful about fumes. Best you stay away until I get there."

She rang Brock, then began a closer look of the house, starting with the ground-floor room at the front, which Marion had clearly been using as her office or study. The walls were white, the furniture and fittings modern pale timber and chrome, functional, elegant and very new. In front of the tall sash windows overlooking the front garden and street there was a large table, on which were several neat stacks of books and papers. One of the other walls was lined with shelves of books, volumes of poetry, art and history, among which she noticed Tony da Silva's *Dante Gabriel Rossetti*. A third wall was dominated by a large pinboard covered with postcards, photographs and stick-on notes, circled and connected by threads and felt-pen lines of various colours. The notes bore names, with brief comments and dates, mostly from the nineteenth century, and Kathy assumed that they were people connected with Marion's thesis; several of the names were familiar from Tina's list. A portrait drawing of Dante Gabriel Rossetti, looking poetically windswept, was pinned in the centre, with the dates *1828–82*, and connected by red lines to several women's faces, as well as to *William Morris, 1834–96*. A number of the small photographs were postcards of Pre-Raphaelite paintings, including, she noticed with a small buzz, the Millais *Ophelia*. Alongside it Marion had written neatly, *Lizzie Siddal 1852*.

She began searching drawers and shelves for a personal address book, but without success, then moved on to the rear sitting room, a cosy little room with Victorian-patterned wallpaper and curtains and a marble and black cast-iron fireplace. There was a small dining table there, with only two chairs facing one another across the polished mahogany.

Upstairs there was a similar contrast between the styles of the front and rear rooms, the front bedroom plain and modern with white walls and blinds, the other plush and period, right down to the ornate gilt frame around the huge mirror on the ceiling over the bed. Kathy stared at it, wondering. It reminded her of another such mirror on the ceiling of the bedroom in a flat a boyfriend of hers had once borrowed. It wasn't how she'd imagined Marion at all.

The scene of crime officer working in that room gave a chuckle and said, "Yeah, bit of a challenge if you're not young and beautiful. Looks like there were two completely different people living in this house—Plain Jane at the front, and Naughty Nancy back 'ere. Take a look at this stuff." She showed Kathy a drawer of lingerie.

Another female voice came from the en suite bathroom, a very plush affair with marble tiles and an elaborate double spa unit. "I'd have said this one might have been an expensive hooker, except there ain't no condoms. There's always boxes of condoms." She sounded as if she knew what she was talking about.

"Maybe she only had one client," Kathy offered.

"Yeah, that's a possibility, I suppose."

"So you think there were two women living here?"

"Well no, that's the thing. According to Gerry the fingerprints in both rooms are the same. He's only found one person's prints in the entire house so far. There's a hairbrush in each bedroom and the hair looks identical in each—long, deep red."

There were no men's clothes or toiletries. The whole place, they noted, was immaculately clean and tidy. "In fact," one of the SOCOs said, eyeing the other, "we think it's a bit suss."

"In what way?"

"Like someone's gone over it all, every square inch."

"A cleaner?"

The woman shook her head. "A searcher. A pro, so careful we can't really be sure."

"How do you mean?"

The woman took her to a chest of drawers against the wall and kneeled, pointing to compression marks on the carpet, not quite aligning with the corner of the furniture. "Looks as if it's been moved recently and the carpet lifted. And in the dust on top of the wardrobe, finger marks of someone feeling, but no prints— they were wearing gloves."

After she was dead? Kathy thought about it. Yet they hadn't touched the stuff on the kitchen benches. "She only moved in a few months ago. She would have shifted stuff around."

"Hm, maybe."

Kathy went to the window of the back bedroom, and looked down on the small courtyard and the gate to a secluded car park to the rear. Another discreet entry.

Sundeep arrived and was shown through to the kitchen. Kathy stood in the doorway with him and pointed at the saucer of white powder, feeling uncertain.

"It's probably bicarbonate of soda or something, but I thought we'd better be careful."

"Quite right."

"Though it wouldn't make any sense . . ."

Sundeep put on a mask, then opened his bag and very carefully began taking samples from the saucer, glass and opened bottle. "Anything else?" he asked.

"That's all really. They haven't been through this room yet."

Together, she and Sundeep opened drawers and cupboards. In a corner of one they came across a screw-top jar, unlabelled, containing traces of what looked like more of the white powder. Sundeep took a sample then said, "I've got enough. They can move in here now."

"How long will it take?"

He gave her a grim smile. "Hardly any time. The lab's too slow, so I set up my own apparatus. Care to take a look?"

She wanted to spend a lot more time in the house, but later, when the forensic team was finished. She left, telling them to phone her if they came up with anything interesting.

SUNDEEP HAD SET UP a small laboratory in what had once been a darkroom along the corridor from his pathology suite in the basement. Despite a powerful fan that he switched on as soon as they went inside, the smell of chemicals had permeated the benches, on one of which was rigged an assembly of glass tubes and vessels held in clamps.

"All right." Sundeep rubbed his hands in anticipation and handed Kathy goggles, mask and gloves. He put on the same and began to open jars from a shelf above the bench. From one he took a piece of metallic zinc, and dropped it into a fat test tube, then added a few drops of blue fluid from another flask with a pipette.

"Copper sulphate," he muttered. Again, with a little tug of nostalgia, Kathy was taken back to her schooldays. The chemistry mistress had been stern and grey-haired, she remembered, formidable in her attempts to stop the boys from blowing themselves up or gassing themselves. What had become of her?

Sundeep was adding a small amount of his first sample, of the white powder they'd found in the saucer.

"Now, hydrochloric acid . . ." He took the glass stopper out of a bottle and poured the acid into the test tube, the mixture foaming up as he sealed it. After a few more adjustments, he held a cigarette lighter to the end of a thin glass tube connected to the test tube, and a flame leapt out. "Hydrogen gas," he said, voice muffled by his mask. "And, if there's any arsenic present, arsine gas too."

"How can you tell?"

"Watch." He took a pair of pincers and lifted a glazed porcelain dish to the flame. As they watched, a silvery black mirror was formed on its surface. Sundeep's eyes lit up. "Yes! There it is. That's arsenic, Kathy."

"You're sure?"

"This is my version of the Marsh test. It's very sensitive. It's what eventually put a stop to arsenic poisoning in Victorian England. Before this you could never really tell. There's your culprit: arsenic trioxide."

Kathy stared at the dark mirror, seeing a blurred image of herself in its depths.

Sundeep repeated the experiment with each of his samples. They all contained arsenic.

Kathy rang the Crime Scene Manager at Rosslyn Court to let him know.

"Yes, we took precautions. Funny thing though."

"What's that?"

"We've lifted clear prints from the dish, the spoon, the juice bottle, the scales and the screw-top jar, and they match the ones we've found all over the house. I had them email Marion Summers' prints from the path lab to my laptop here. They match. They're all Marion's."

"NO SIGN OF A forced entry?" Brock was standing in Marion's work room, taking it in.

"No." Kathy had just arrived back from Sundeep's laboratory. "Everything looks completely undisturbed." But the word jarred a little. Was that really the impression it gave? More that it was frozen, the house holding its breath as if waiting to see whether they would discover its secrets. She told Brock about the SOCOs' notion about a careful searcher.

He shrugged. "They get bored, the repetition. Sometimes their imaginations run wild."

The Crime Scene Manager put his head around the door. "We're on our way out. I'll try to get them to hurry up with the DNA results."

"Thanks, I'd really appreciate that." But Kathy was already resigned to what they'd find. "You're quite sure about the fingerprints on the stuff in the kitchen though, are you?"

"Yeah, they're all hers. No sign of anyone else's." He saw her disappointment and added, "Sorry, luv."

"It just wasn't what I expected."

"How could you?" Brock said at her side, studying the notes on the pinboard. There was a china ornament on the mantelpiece below that looked oddly out of place, a figurine of an old woman selling balloons, and he picked it up and turned it over, examining the name, running his finger around the hollow interior. "A young, attractive, intelligent woman, apparently doing well, carefully measures out a heavy dose of arsenic trioxide into a bottle of juice and goes off to the library. After working through the morning she goes out into the square where she eats her sandwich and washes it down with the poisoned drink in full public view. Then collapses and dies an excruciating death. It's hard to fathom." But Kathy could recall other public suicides she'd encountered, histrionic and manipulative, extravagant acts of self-destruction that had filled her with a mixture of despair and disgust.

Kathy unfolded the list of key words that Tina had given her and showed it to Brock, pointing out *Suicide/suicide pact*. "I spoke to a science student at the university who'd met Marion at a party. When she discovered that he was doing chemistry, she told him that she was interested in arsenic, and when he asked why, she said she wanted to poison someone. He thought she was joking. So did I."

"Yes."

"I had developed this picture of her in my mind. I felt I was coming to understand her."

"Tell me."

"Her early home life was a mess, no father and a promiscuous drunk for a mother, things looking bad until her aunt took her in. She settled down, won a scholarship, escaped to London, worked hard, did well. Very organised, independent."

Brock turned and looked pointedly at Kathy. "Sounds like someone else I know."

She coloured slightly. "Oh . . . no. Not at all. No, I was just so sure she was the innocent victim of some creep like Keith Rafferty or Nigel Ogilvie. It seemed so tragic, so unfair—but now this. The SOCOs thought she might be on the game, or at least was being kept by a rich lover. Well, you saw the mirror on the bedroom ceiling, and then there's this house. The rent must be pretty steep. It just wasn't how I imagined her."

"Where could she have got the arsenic from?"

"She'd been getting information from a chemistry lecturer at her university, who is also a friend of her PhD supervisor. She told him it was for her research into Victorian painters. She wanted details of different compounds and doses. And there's arsenic in the laboratories there. I got him to show me around, and he insisted no one could steal any from there. It did seem quite secure."

"From the way you describe her, she was a pretty determined and resourceful character. I dare say she would have found a way if she really wanted to."

"You agree it's suicide, then?" She still half hoped he'd suggest some other way of looking at it.

"I'd have preferred a note, but maybe she sent that to the boyfriend, who's keeping his head down. It's hard to see any other explanation, if the fingerprint and DNA results are confirmed. Alex Nicholson has a taste for poisoners, I remember—she might be interested in this one. I could give her a ring."

The forensic psychologist, Kathy knew, had recently returned to work in London after a spell at the University of Liverpool. Brock got out his phone and dialled. When he rang off he said, "She's free at the moment. Says she'll come over. Anyway, it may not be the result you expected, but it looks like you've cracked it, Kathy, on your own. I'm sorry I've given you so little support on this one, though it seems you didn't need it. You'll be able to take the weekend off after all."

"Oh." She gave a pained smile. "I was supposed to be going to Prague, but with all that was going on, I cancelled."

"Of course you must go. Especially after last night. Best thing."

"What's happening to Rafferty and Crouch?"

"CPS won't touch it. The charges have been dropped."

They were silent for a moment, then Brock said, "Prague in the spring . . . I'm told it's looking good these days. I'm jealous." He smiled at her, a twinkle in his eye.

"With Nicole Palmer, in Criminal Records."

"Hm." He turned back to the pinboard, the little smile still on his face.

TWENTY MINUTES LATER KATHY saw Alex Nicholson step out of a cab at the front gate. She opened the door and went to meet her.

Alex shook her hand and looked up at the building. "This is cute. A gingerbread house. Just the sort of place you'd expect a student of William Morris to live in. I'm envious. Pricey neighbourhood."

Kathy had worked with Alex on several cases, and had found her rather intimidating at first. Slight in build, with a mop of black hair and unconventional, though stylish, taste in clothes, she exuded self-confidence. Some of the others in the team thought that Brock indulged her, but Kathy had to admit she'd been pretty accurate in the past.

Kathy led Alex through the house, letting her take her time in each room, and filling her in on what they knew. They finished in the study, where they sat with Brock at Marion's work table.

"This house . . ." Alex shook her head, looking around. "What do we know about it?"

"Nothing yet. She moved in about three months ago. Forensics think she lived here alone."

"Maybe two people shared it before, and she just inherited it like this?"

"It's possible."

"Because otherwise . . . well, you pointed it out yourself, Kathy — the front rooms and the back, so different." She shrugged and opened a notebook and began jotting. "I'm doing a study of poisoners. They have a whole set of profiles to themselves, different from all the rest. This is my first arsenic suicide, in fact my first arsenic poisoner, so I'm really interested. You thought it was murder at first, yes?"

"Yes. It's taken us three days to find where she lived. She'd kept it pretty much secret."

"So did she intend for you to think she was murdered? But then, why leave that stuff in the kitchen where it would eventually be found? Why not clear it away and leave the mystery open?

Did she then want you to have to search for the truth? Make a public spectacle of her death? I mean, if she wanted to take poison, why not just do it quietly at home? Why choose St. James's Square of all places?"

"Yes."

"And then there's the poison. My God, arsenic! Horrible stuff, a painful, lingering death. You mentioned that she was interested in it?"

"Maybe obsessed by it," Kathy said. "Her PhD supervisor told me she was making it the focus of her interpretation of the Pre-Raphaelite circle, against his advice. And she had been talking recently to a colleague of his in the science faculty about its basic chemistry."

"Her period, the nineteenth century, was the heyday of the arsenic poisoners, wasn't it? She would have identified, is that what you're saying?"

"Something like that. But there's another possibility. Dr. Ringland, the scientist she spoke to, said she was like other arts students—not very good with formulae and numbers. I'm wondering if she was experimenting on herself, trying to experience the symptoms at first hand, without actually wanting to kill herself. But maybe she got the dose wrong."

"Mixed up her micrograms and her milligrams, you mean?" Alex nodded. "Possible. Not so interesting, but possible."

"If she was experimenting on herself, this may not have been the first time," Brock said. "Sundeep might be able to find signs of that in her body."

Alex was staring at the pinboard on the wall. "This is interesting. Have you had it photographed?"

"Yes, the SOCO photographer did that."

"You see the symmetry. The man in the middle, Rossetti, has a woman on each side of him. Do we know who they are?"

"His wife, Lizzie Siddal, on the left in the pose of Ophelia, and his mistress, Jane Morris, on the right. Yes, I noticed that."

Alex nodded. "The victim wife and the mistress. Plain Jane and Naughty Nancy? Is that what you were thinking?"

"What are you getting at, Alex?" Brock said.

"Suicide usually happens after a period of intense internal debate, a struggle between opposing instincts. I'm just wondering if this might be a case of Plain Jane being murdered by Naughty Nancy, or the other way around."

"Come off it," Brock protested. "That's psychology babble."

Alex gave him a tolerant smile. "It's not impossible. Did you notice that Jane's bedroom door has a lock on it, on the inside, whereas the other doesn't? Almost as if Jane were afraid of Nancy, and wanted to keep her out. Marion may have been suffering from DID, dissociative identity disorder, what we used to call multiple personality disorder."

"Isn't that a form of schizophrenia?" Kathy asked.

"No, that's a brain disorder, quite different. DID isn't brought on by substance abuse, either. It's still a controversial diagnosis, but I have encountered several very dramatic examples that convinced me, where two or more quite distinct personalities coexisted within the one individual, taking turns to control their behaviour. There have also been cases of what you might call mutual self harm—one personality trying to hurt another. I don't recall a case of resulting suicide, but I can look into it. There's generally accompanying memory loss, dissociative amnesia. Has anyone mentioned instances of Marion blanking out, losing time?"

Kathy shook her head. "She does seem to have been very secretive though, hiding all sorts of things from people who were supposed to be close to her."

"It's possible that was a defence mechanism, if she recognised that inexplicable things were happening in her life."

Alex pointed at the photograph of a third face on the board, a young Victorian woman directly over Rossetti's image. She stared straight at the camera, her face framed by thick dark hair finished in a braid across the crown of her head. There was no name.

"She looks determined, doesn't she?" Alex said. "And familiar. Know who she is?"

Kathy shook her head.

Brock's phone trilled in his pocket. He spoke into it briefly, checked his watch, then rang off. "I'm going to have to get back. Stay as long as you like, Alex. I thought you might find this one intriguing. Perhaps you have got something with your Jane and Nancy theory. Maybe she hated herself for what she'd had to become in order to survive. We might get you to write something for our report to the coroner."

Alex said she'd get a lift back with him to the West End. As they made to leave she said, "If I had more time, I'd love to deconstruct that pinboard and try to work out exactly how she related her own life to it."

"Couldn't it just be her work for her PhD?" Kathy said, thinking that this was all getting rather fanciful.

"That too. But you're free to pick your own PhD subject, aren't you? Your choice reflects your own preoccupations. You're exploring yourself as well as your topic, and it can become pretty obsessive. Believe me, I know. Just make sure you've got it all recorded, Kathy. Did her computer not tell you anything?"

"It seems she used the machines in her department. We're in the process of accessing her email account."

"What, there wasn't a computer of her own here, or at the library where she collapsed?"

"No."

"What about disks, memory sticks?"

"We haven't found anything."

"Oh, come on! All that gorgeous kitchen equipment and no laptop? This girl was a serious scholar! She'd have at least one computer of her own, and masses of backup."

"Yes," Brock said. "There are a few loose ends still to tie up."

Kathy thanked Alex at the front door and returned to Marion's study. She sat there for a long while, looking at the pinboard, the book titles, going through the drawers once again. She came across a framed portrait photo of Marion, and set it up on the table in front of her, as if she could interrogate the face that gazed calmly back at her through the glass. It was a black-and-white image, like the Victorian photographs on the wall, as if reflected in an arsenic mirror. She took in the enigmatic smile on the lips; the clear, intelligent gaze of the eyes; the humour creases at their corners; and she asked it softly, *How on earth could you do a thing like that?*

She lifted a piece of blank paper and placed it in front of the picture, covering one half of Marion's portrait. The person she saw was open, warm, outgoing. Then she moved the sheet of paper to cover the other side, and now she was confronted by an eye half-closed, reserved, and a half-mouth tight with suspicion. She took the paper away and the two halves merged into a single image, ambiguous now and more difficult to read. It was a simple trick, which worked for anyone's face. You didn't need to have DID to contain two personalities—everyone did. Two contradictory propositions—which was the real one? The answer, of course, was *both*.

Kathy sighed and dropped the photo in her bag and pulled out her phone. She rang Nicole's number and explained the situation.

"I knew it," Nicole said. "I told you so, didn't I?"

"I suppose you cancelled my flight?"

"Of course not. Meet me after work tonight and we'll get ourselves organised."

THEY MET IN A bar in Victoria near both their offices, a place so crowded that they had to stand jammed together at the front window, shouting questions and answers at each other over the roar of conversation. At one point a young man in a dark suit bumped Nicole's arm, sending her sheaf of Prague and easyJet brochures flying across the floor, and they had to scrabble to gather them up. "I told you we needed to get out of London," Nicole yelled. "Did I mention the very attractive Czech that Rusty's got lined up for you?"

ELEVEN

PERHAPS IT WAS A mistake to take the M25, Kathy thought, as they crept towards the third clogged junction in a row on the orbital motorway the next morning. She checked her watch again, calculating their narrowing margin of time. Nicole caught the gesture and said calmly, "Don't worry, we'll make it."

By the time they finally arrived at Gatwick, dropped the car in the long-term car park and sprinted to departures, Nicole had lost her cool.

"Oh damn!" They saw the huge queues at the easyJet counters.

A young man standing at the back of the queue turned to them. "Where're you off to?"

"Prague," Nicole panted.

"Me too. Come on." He took hold of Nicole's arm and led them to the front of the queue, pushing in as a couple moved away from the check-in desk. He had a brisk conversation with the man, who nodded, asked for identification, and bundled them through.

"Brilliant!" Nicole shook his hand as they cleared security and headed to the gate.

He gave her a warm smile. "Practice." He turned to Kathy. "Maybe I'll see you in Prague." He waved and walked away.

"He's gorgeous, and he likes you." Nicole said. "Did you see the way he looked at you?"

Kathy laughed. "I thought you'd fixed me up with a Czech." But her eyes strayed after the young man.

A couple of hours later, Kathy found herself, with a slight sense of unreality, walking briskly along the bank of the Vltava River, sparkling sunlight reflecting off freshly painted and restored buildings, Nicole chatting at her side. They paused at the Jirásek Bridge to take in Frank Gehry's extraordinary Ginger and Fred building, its forms dancing around the corner to point the way into the New Town area of Prague, the Nové Mĕsto. They headed that way, in towards Charles Square, following the directions to the café where Rusty was to meet them.

He was already there, sitting alone at a table. They exchanged hugs and sat down, Nicole chattering to her brother about arrangements for the weekend. Despite the novelty and interest of the city, and the crispness of the spring morning, Kathy was finding it hard to get Marion Summers out of her head. What else should she have done? What signs had she misinterpreted? Then Nicole gave a cry of delight and pointed across the street at a figure with a camera, and Kathy realised it was the man who'd rescued them at Gatwick.

Nicole said, "Go on, ask him over. He fancies you."

"No, I'm not interested."

"Well it's time you were. I'll ask him then." Nicole jumped to her feet and ran across the street. Kathy watched the look of incomprehension change to a smile as he realised who she was, then he gave a shrug and followed her.

"Hello again." He grinned at Kathy. "I guess tourists all go to the same places." He spoke with the same slightly amused, calm voice she remembered from the airport.

"Sit down!" Nicole commanded. "We're going to buy you a drink for saving us."

Despite her embarrassment at Nicole's overemphatic welcome,

Kathy thought he did seem quite pleasant. He had a certain poise. Rusty pulled a chair over from another table and they made introductions. His name was Guy Hamilton, and he was alone, driven by a sudden impulse to get out of London for the weekend.

"Well, you must come and see Rusty's show tonight," Nicole insisted, giving Kathy a nudge under the table.

IN LONDON, BROCK SAT at his desk, nursing a cup of strong coffee. His office window was cracked half open, allowing a breath of cool spring air into the room, and with it the muffled thump and bray of a military band, out on The Mall, perhaps, or Horse Guards Parade. He had intended to concentrate on the office paperwork that had backed up during the week, approving timesheets, the Action Manager's estimate of resources needed, costs, but instead he had the Summers file open in front of him, reading through Kathy's reports. Despite his revulsion at the girl's public suicide, he found himself drawn back to her, wanting to understand.

The phone at his elbow rang; the duty officer. "Got a woman on the line, sir, says she's got information about Marion Summers. Very insistent on speaking to the senior officer on the case. Says her name is Sophie Warrender. Sounds posh." He sounded sceptical, understandably, after so many hoax calls and nutters. "Shall I put her through to the hotline?"

"No," Brock said. *Warrender.* The name had been in the file somewhere. "I'll take it, thanks." A click, then he went on, "Good morning, this is Detective Chief Inspector Brock. Can I help you?"

"Yes, I hope so. My name is Sophie Warrender. I know Marion Summers, the victim in that terrible poisoning case. I'm sure it must be the same person—twenty-six, a PhD student at London University?"

"That's her. How are you connected, Mrs. Warrender?"

"She's been doing work for me, research for my next book. I'm an author, you see." That rang a bell. "We've been out of the country, just flew back last night, and I hadn't heard. I thought I should speak to you."

"Where do you live?"

"Notting Hill, Lansdowne Gardens."

"Ah yes." Brock was scanning the list of Marion's telephone contact numbers. "Can I have your phone number, please?"

She gave him a couple of numbers, which matched with those on the list.

"And you have some information for us?"

"Well, I'm not altogether sure, but yes, I think I should speak to you. Do you want me to come to see you?"

"Did Marion visit your house in Notting Hill?"

"Yes, this is where I have my office. She was here quite often."

"Then I think I'd like to come to you."

He rang off and called for a car. As he prepared to leave, his mobile rang, Suzanne on the other end. He felt a familiar warmth as he heard her voice.

"Are we still on for tonight?"

He patted his wallet with the tickets for the National Theatre. "Of course. Is Ginny lined up to look after the kids?"

"Yes, she'll stay at my place for the weekend."

"Good. Where do you want to meet?"

"At the Long Bar? Can we eat afterwards?"

"Certainly. Tell me, I've just had someone on the phone. Her name sounded familiar, but I wasn't sure. An author. I wondered if you'd heard of her—Sophie Warrender?"

"I certainly have heard of her. I gave you her last book at Christmas. Don't you remember?"

"Ah, yes, of course. The one with the odd title."

"*How Pleasant to Know Mr. Lear.* I thought you told me you read it?"

"Er, most of it. I ran out of time in the end, but it was interesting. She writes biographies, then?"

"That's right, great Victorians usually. She's highly regarded. Are you going to speak to her again?"

"Yes, I'm on my way to her house now."

"In Notting Hill?"

"How the hell did you know that?"

She laughed. "Maybe you should appoint me as a consultant, David. I wish I were going with you. I want you to tell me all about it tonight, especially about the house."

HE TURNED INTO LANSDOWNE Gardens: old-fashioned lantern streetlights, Jaguars and BMWs in the parking bays, mature trees budding into life. The houses, two and three storeys, were late Georgian or early Victorian, Brock judged, with classical porches at the front doors, pale cream stuccoed ground-floor walls and yellow London brick above, with cornices and pediments over the windows. They stood shoulder to shoulder addressing the streets, while behind, he could see in passing glimpses, the backs opened onto shared gardens like long thin private parks lying between the rows of houses.

The Warrenders' house was at a corner with a cross street, and the picturesque tendency that had been apparent in its neighbours, but hidden beneath their classical symmetry, was here given freer rein. Arched attic windows peered over the parapets between the tall chimneys, and a conservatory-like room with a flamboyant double-curved ogee lead roof was attached to the side, surmounted by a small Italianate tower.

A truck and skip stood outside, laden with builders' debris, and Brock had to wait at the balustered front wall while men in white overalls came out of the house carrying drop sheets and pots of paint. When they'd passed, he went to the portico and pressed a brass bell-push.

A middle-aged woman came to the door. Brock's first impression was of bright, intelligent eyes scrutinising him over the top of slender glasses, and auburn hair pulled back. She had a full, attractive mouth with which she formed a careful smile when he said who he was.

"And I'm Sophie Warrender. Do please come in." She led him through the hallway, the smell of fresh paint very strong, and down a short corridor towards the conservatory room that Brock had noticed from the street. It had tall windows on three sides to the garden, the walls in between lined with bookshelves. In one corner a woman was typing at a computer on a large, book-covered desk; in another, a few seats were arranged around a coffee table as for a meeting; in the third stood another writing station, and in the fourth a spiral stair led up into the tower.

Sophie Warrender introduced her secretary working at the desk. "Do you want to finish up now, Rhonda? I think we've broken the back of it. Thank you so much for coming in today."

Rhonda nodded and asked if they wanted coffee, but Brock said not and Sophie took him over to sit at the low table. The door closed behind her secretary, and she began, in a low, confidential voice.

"Marion began working for me almost a year ago, Chief Inspector, helping me with the research for my current book. I write biographies, of nineteenth-century figures."

"Of course," Brock said, "*How Pleasant to Know Mr. Lear*. I enjoyed it very much. If I'd known I was going to meet you I'd have brought it to have you sign it."

She was pleased, looked shrewdly at him, reassessing him. "That's kind of you. Of course, I'd be delighted to sign it. Perhaps we'll have another opportunity. And I take it as a real compliment that you enjoyed the book. In a way we do similar things, don't you think? Trying to tease out the hidden motives and misdirections of the people we study. But I think my task is simpler, working on dead subjects. The living are much more elusive. But since you've read the book you'll understand when I tell you that we've been in Corsica for the past four weeks."

"Ah." Brock remembered part of the Lear biography dealing with his painting expedition to the Mediterranean island.

"When I was doing the research for that book I retraced his steps on Corsica, and it was during those visits that Douglas, my husband, and I found the house that we bought and now have as a holiday retreat. We went over there to get out of the way of the decorators, and didn't keep up with the English news. That's why I had no idea about this tragedy until this morning. I was appalled when Rhonda told me—she just assumed that I knew."

"So Marion was working for you as well as studying for her doctorate?"

"Yes. The job with me was part-time, casual. She could fit it in around her other commitments."

"Her tutor, Dr. da Silva, didn't mention that."

"No, well, he probably didn't know. Marion was on a scholarship of some kind, and there were restrictions on how much paid work she could do, so she just didn't tell them at the university. In fact the research for me did help her own studies, because we were both examining the same group of people, the Pre-Raphaelites—that's why I picked her in the first place."

She hesitated, and Brock waited, letting her tell her story at her own pace. She was frowning, pursing her lips, and he sensed some inner debate going on.

"I suppose other people have described Marion to you?"

"To some extent, but we'd like to understand her better. We haven't found anyone that she really confided in."

"No, I'm not altogether surprised. That was my impression of her, a lone . . . well, not wolf, perhaps. A lone tigress, maybe. She was a very spirited girl, very fervent and single-minded about her work and ideas. Sometimes, when she was talking about the people she was studying, the dead painters and poets and their spouses and lovers, I used to feel that they were her real friends, the ones she felt closest to, who interested her so much more than the living people she had to put up with.

"I can't say I blame her, really—they were fascinating characters, and their lives were all tangled up in such passionate and complicated ways. I'm working on a biography of Jane Burden, the wife of William Morris, the socialist poet and creator of all those wonderful fabrics and wallpapers and pieces of furniture you can see in the V and A. But she was also the very striking model for Dante Gabriel Rossetti, who was infatuated with her and was her lover for years, while his friend William looked helplessly on."

"And Dante's wife was Lizzie Siddal, the model for the drowned Ophelia, who looked remarkably like Marion," Brock said.

"Yes. You have been doing your homework. I'm impressed. I had no idea the Metropolitan Police were so well read." She gave a little frown and said, "Sorry, that sounds patronising, doesn't it? I didn't mean it."

"Well, Victorian biographies probably don't figure high on the reading lists of the Met, though when I think of some of the stuff we have to read I'd say it's a great pity." Brock was trying to recall Kathy's report. "We got the impression that Dr. da Silva felt Marion's interest in these people had a morbid element to it."

"He may be right. That's really what I wanted to speak to you about. Can I ask . . . Rhonda showed me a report in the *Guardian* this morning, that there's a rumour she died of arsenic poisoning. Is that true?"

Brock said, "We haven't officially released that information, but yes, it does seem to be the case. Is that significant?"

"Well, it's an extraordinary coincidence. You see, in recent months Marion became increasingly interested—I would say almost obsessed—with arsenic poisoning. I found myself trying to deflect her with other topics that I wanted researched, but she was quite stubborn. Once she got her teeth into an idea, she just wouldn't let it go."

"How was this relevant to Jane Burden and the Pre-Raphaelites?" Brock asked.

"Arsenic certainly had a big influence on the life of Jane's husband, William Morris. His father established what was then the biggest arsenic mining company in the world, near Tavistock in Devon, which created the fortune that Morris inherited and which allowed him to finance his other projects. Arsenic also cropped up in several coincidental ways in their story—it was used in dyes and paints, in medicines and makeup. They treated syphilis with it and used it in all sorts of patent medicines. All this was well known. It was just a fact of life in Victorian England. But Marion seemed to want to make more of it."

"How do you mean?"

"She had very firm ideas about the way the Pre-Raphaelite women were used by their men. She thought they were exploited and oppressed."

"You didn't agree?"

"Oh, there was a lot in what she said, but I felt the relationships were more nuanced than that—the triangle between William Morris, Jane Burden and Dante Gabriel Rossetti was a very interesting case in point. But where she really lost me was in claiming that arsenic was an integral part of this oppression, deliberately used to keep women sickly and docile."

"Really?"

Sophie Warrender shook her head sadly. "I gathered that Dr. da Silva thought this was nonsense. She was quite scathing about him. But when I cast doubts on the line she was taking she stopped talking about it and became more secretive. And now this. If it weren't so tragic one would say it was a triumphant vindication of her theories."

"Are you suggesting that Dr. da Silva might have given her arsenic?"

"Oh, no." She looked acutely embarrassed. "That would be a shocking thing to suggest. No, it was just such a strange coincidence . . ."

"Too strange?" Brock asked.

She shifted uncomfortably in her seat, then again offered him a coffee. This time he accepted, and followed her out to the kitchen, obviously freshly re-equipped and decorated, with the maker's sticker still on the oven door.

Sophie opened a large stainless-steel-fronted fridge-freezer and groaned. "Oh dear, no coffee. We may have to make do with tea, I'm afraid."

Just then a man came in carrying a large cardboard box filled with groceries. He was powerfully built, late fifties, face red with exertion. He swore and dumped the heavy box on the table, then noticed Brock. "Hello, who are you?"

"Dougie, this is Chief Inspector David Brock, from the police."

"Oh?" He drew himself upright. "How d'you do."

Brock offered his hand. "Mr. Warrender?"

"That's right. What's the problem?"

"It's about Marion Summers, darling," Sophie said.

"You called the police?"

"I thought I should."

He frowned and said dubiously, "Yes, quite right."

"Did you know Marion, Mr. Warrender?" Brock asked.

"Hardly at all. Shocking thing, of course. I suppose you come across it every day." He looked around distractedly. "Where's Rhonda? Can't she sort out this mess?"

"She's my secretary, darling, not our housekeeper."

"She managed to look after the builders for the past month, didn't she? Can't she lend a hand?"

"She's gone home. You know she doesn't usually work on a Saturday. Did you get coffee?"

Her husband grunted. "Bugger coffee. I'm opening a bottle of the Nielluccio." He bent over a case in the corner and pulled out a bottle of red wine. "You'll join us, Chief Inspector? Corsican, fresh from the vineyard."

"Thank you. Perhaps I will. This is a wonderful house. How long have you been here?"

"Over forty years, would you believe." He began opening cupboards, all empty. "Where are the fucking glasses?"

"I think they're all in the dining room, darling." Douglas Warrender stomped out to fetch them and Sophie went on, to Brock, "It is a wonderful house, isn't it? Built at about the same time that William Morris and Company started up in business. That was one reason I was drawn to write about Janey Morris. When I walk through the house I can imagine her here, advising the first owners on wallpapers and fabrics. Dougie's parents bought it when they came back from India in the sixties."

They heard an exchange of voices, then Douglas returned with a tray of glasses, followed by an elderly woman and a teenage girl, both dressed in thick coats and scarves. "Sophie, Joan and Emily want to go out. Tell them it's lunchtime, for God's sake."

"I can't stand another minute in the house," the older woman said imperiously. "The smell of paint is making me quite ill. Emily and I are going out for some fresh air. If we feel hungry we'll get something ourselves."

"Joan, can I introduce you to Detective Chief Inspector Brock," Sophie said. "From Scotland Yard. This is Dougie's mother, Lady Joan Warrender, and our daughter, Emily."

"A policeman! What have you done now, Dougie?" the old woman cried. "Stealing from your shareholders? Plundering the vicar's collection box?"

Warrender gave a pained smile. "It's about that research assistant of Sophie's, Mother. You heard, didn't you?"

"Oh yes!" Lady Warrender was instantly contrite. "I'm so sorry. How awful. And you're leading the investigation into her death?"

"An inspector of mine is the senior investigating officer on the case. She's away at the moment, and I answered Mrs. Warrender's call. Did you know Marion?"

"Only to say hello to. Emily knew her better, didn't you, dear? She helped you with your school assignment."

The girl nodded. She was a plainer, awkward version of her mother. "I liked Marion a lot," she said softly.

Douglas poured the wine into three glasses, as Joan and Emily left, then announced that he would take a sandwich up to his study and go through his mail. Sophie and Brock returned to her office in the conservatory room.

They sat, Brock admired the wine, then said, "You mentioned William Morris's arsenic mine in Tavistock. Could Marion have gone to visit it?"

"Not that I know of. It closed down many years ago. I shouldn't think there's much to see there now. Why?"

"We're puzzled by where the arsenic that killed Marion might have come from."

"But surely that will follow when you discover who gave it to her. Do you have a suspect?"

"The forensic evidence seems to point to Marion having deliberately mixed and taken a poisoned drink herself. We found arsenic in her kitchen."

"What?" Sophie looked bewildered.

"You find that hard to believe?"

"Yes, I do. I would never have imagined that Marion was suicidal. Did anything drastic happen to her while we were away?"

"We're trying to find out. Were you aware of a man in her life?"

"No, she never spoke of one. In fact she never said much about her private life." She frowned, thinking. "I have absolutely no idea where she could have got the arsenic from."

"Did she ever talk about the place where she was living?"

"It was a student flat in Southwark, I believe."

"She moved from there about three months ago. She never mentioned a house in Hampstead?"

"No. It seems I didn't really know her at all."

"Earlier you seemed guarded when you were talking about her tutor, Dr. da Silva."

She sighed. "Yes, I suppose I was. He's a highly respected scholar of international standing, and the author of the definitive book on Dante Gabriel Rossetti. But I felt from what Marion said that the relationship between them wasn't as it should have been."

"Really? In what way?"

"I was only getting one side of the story of course, but from Marion's odd remarks, she seemed to feel that he was an oppressive figure."

"Might they have been in a sexual relationship, do you think?"

"She never hinted at it, but I suppose it's possible."

"When she left her student flat in Southwark she seems to have told no one where she went, as if she was trying to escape from someone. Could that have been Dr. da Silva?"

Sophie Warrender spread her hands in a hopeless gesture. "I really don't know."

"What about this man? He's her stepfather, name of Keith Rafferty." Brock showed her his picture. "Mean anything to you?"

"Oh . . ."

Brock saw the start of recognition in her face. "You know him?"

"Once, as Marion was leaving, we were at the front door together and I noticed a white van parked on the other side of the street. The driver's window was open and he was staring across at us, and I thought what a mean-looking character he was. It was this man, I'm sure of it. I remember Marion suddenly drawing back into the house, looking very pale. She said she didn't feel well, and I made her sit down and got her a glass of water. Later I called a taxi to take her home. The van had gone by then."

"When was this?"

"I'm not sure exactly. This year, I think. January or February."

Brock drained his glass. "Well, thanks for your help. I'd better go now. Please let me know if anything else occurs to you."

When they reached the front door, Sophie Warrender said, "I hope this doesn't sound out of place, Chief Inspector, but I gave Marion a number of my books and research notes to work on while I was away. I really will need to get them back before too long. Will that be a problem?"

"I shouldn't think so. Tell you what, I'll get my inspector, DI Kathy Kolla, to contact you and she can work something out."

"I'd be so grateful." She shot Brock a dazzling smile, then closed the front door.

THAT EVENING, IN THE Long Bar of the National Theatre and afterwards over supper, Brock told Suzanne Chambers about Marion and her connection to Sophie Warrender. Suzanne was as shocked and intrigued by the circumstances of Marion's death as everyone else, but it seemed there was another reason for her interest. She had read all of Sophie Warrender's biographies and greatly admired them, but eventually, after a couple of drinks, she admitted that what had originally drawn her to them was the discovery that Sophie was married to Suzanne's first great love.

"What, Dougie Warrender?" Brock looked surprised, then laughed.

"What's funny?" Suzanne stiffened.

"Nothing, nothing," he said rapidly.

"Did you see him today?"

"I did, actually. A powerful man, bit flustered from the trip back from Corsica. They have a house there."

"In St. Florent, yes."

"You know all about them, don't you? You haven't been stalking him, have you?"

She coloured a little. "Of course not. I saw her on TV once, authors talking about where they do their writing, and she mentioned the house in Corsica, and the one in Notting Hill. But I knew it already. When I was thirteen my best friend at school, Angela Crick, lived next door to the Warrenders on Lansdowne Gardens. I spent a magical summer staying with Angela while my parents were overseas, and fell madly in love with Dougie. He was older, about seventeen, very dark and brooding, my Mr. Darcy. They'd just come back to England from India, where Dougie's father had been a diplomat of some kind. It was my first big passion. His cousin was staying with him at the time, I remember, and he fell for Angela. I wonder what happened to Angela? I remember being devastated when I heard that the Warrenders were moving to New York, but they held on to the house in Notting Hill, apparently. And now you've been there, and have actually met them all."

She looked wistfully into her glass. For a moment, as she had been talking about the Warrenders and the house in Lansdowne Gardens, the memories of those days had come back so vividly, the intensity of the feelings of her youth allowing her to briefly pull away the dulling blanket of years. She thought of Brock's amused reaction to her confession about Dougie Warrender, and wondered if she would be terribly disappointed if she bumped into him again. Probably she would; they probably wouldn't even recognise each other.

TWELVE

THERE WAS A MOOD of new beginnings on Monday morning at Queen Anne's Gate. Detectives who had been seconded to Counter Terrorism Command had returned and were ready for new assignments. Bren and the others looked refreshed, hyped up by their spell away. They gathered in the incident room for Brock's morning briefing, several of them clustering around Pip, whom Kathy noticed as she walked in.

The young DC came over to her and said meekly, "Am I forgiven?"

Kathy smiled, pleased to see the girl back on her feet. "It was my fault, Pip. I should never have let you go in there alone. Let's just put it down to experience."

"I heard they've dropped charges against those guys. I can't believe it. What about Marion? You'll let me go on working with you on that, won't you?"

"Looks like there's nothing to work on." Kathy told her what they'd discovered at the house in Rosslyn Court. Pip was shocked and started to protest, then fell silent with the others as Brock walked in, carrying a tall stack of files.

"I hope you all had a good weekend," he began, "because there's a heap of stuff to clear up now."

She *had* had a good weekend, Kathy thought, though it seemed suddenly remote. Guy Hamilton had joined up with them, at Nicole's insistence, and he'd been good company. He was a structural engineer, he'd told them, waiting to be posted back to a project in the Gulf states.

Brock gave Kathy three files, all liaison jobs with overseas forces through Interpol, tracing fugitives believed to be in London. She wondered if this was him having a little dig at her weekend trip. Without explanation he switched Pip to work with another pair of detectives, and she shot Kathy a penitent look.

When the meeting was over Brock drew Kathy aside and handed her a note summarising his meeting with Sophie Warrender. "You should meet her. In fact I said you might take her to Rosslyn Court to collect books and papers that she'd lent Marion."

There was something about the way he said this that alerted Kathy. "So you want me to go on with that?"

"Loose ends," he said vaguely. "If you've got time."

"I'll get onto it. So you've taken away my little helper."

He smiled. "I thought you might like a break."

Kathy returned to her desk and put a call through to Sundeep Mehta. His advice was precise. "The heavy metals persist in the body. If she had a history of taking arsenic, it'll be recorded in her hair, fingernails and bones. I'll check. But Kathy, this was a massive, lethal dose. Was she an impulsive woman?"

"That's not my impression, Sundeep."

"Well, I'll get back to you."

She settled down to read through the new files, and made a start in following up the most promising leads. All the same, her mind kept returning to the house in Rosslyn Court. Alex Nicholson's comments about the absence of a computer stuck in her mind, irking her for not noticing it sooner. Eventually she rang the secretary at the university and asked her if she could think of anywhere else Marion might have kept personal possessions. Karen explained that postgraduate students were provided with individual lockers. She apologised for not thinking to mention it before. Kathy said she'd come straight over.

When she arrived Karen took her to the postgraduate students' office, a large room with a rank of computer stations to one side and a table and whiteboard at the other. A sink and coffeemaking facilities stood in the far corner, next to a bank of grey metal lockers. Karen took her master key and opened one which had Marion's name written neatly on a label. It was completely empty.

Kathy stared at the void in disappointment, then turned to Karen. "Is there anywhere else Marion could have kept things?"

"Not as far as I know."

"Do you know if she had a computer of her own?"

"Sorry, no idea. We could ask." They went around the room, questioning the half-dozen students working at the keyboards. No one knew.

"How about Dr. da Silva, is he here?"

"Monday . . . he doesn't have any lectures today." She looked out the window. "Car's here. Maybe in the library, or his office. Shall I check?" She dialled a number on the phone on the central table and spoke a few words. "Yes, he's in his office. He says to go on up. Know where it is?"

"Yes—thanks, Karen."

Da Silva answered her knock, swelling up a little as he showed her in, as if wanting to become larger. "Welcome," he murmured. "Please sit down. Any developments?"

"Possibly. It's a bit early to say. We found where Marion was living, in Hampstead." She watched his reaction closely.

"Really? Hampstead? Whereabouts, exactly?"

"Rosslyn Court. Know it?"

"Yes, I believe I do. I'm . . . amazed, frankly."

"Why is that?"

"Well, it's an expensive address. Not exactly student digs."

"Where do you live, Dr. da Silva?"

"Me?" Kathy thought there was a flush of colour in his face.

"Not far from there, actually. I live in Hampstead Garden Suburb, just up the road."

"That is a coincidence."

He gave her a little frown. "Was it any help, finding where she lived?"

"Possibly. But I wanted to ask you again about Marion's access to computers. Surely she would have had one of her own? A laptop, maybe?"

"Well, I told you this before—I really don't know. I can't remember her ever bringing one to our sessions."

"Do you have anything of hers?"

"Eh?" He looked startled, drawing himself upright in his chair. "What do you mean?"

"I just wondered if she might have left anything with you for safekeeping—computer disks, say, or electronic copies of her documents, that sort of thing."

"Oh, I see. No, nothing like that. She gave me printouts of her work mostly. I've kept those. Once or twice she emailed drafts to me."

"I've looked in her locker downstairs."

"Locker?"

"The postgraduate students are given lockers."

"Are they? I didn't know."

"Anyway, it was empty. Can you think of anywhere else she might have left anything?"

"Sorry." He raised his hands helplessly.

"We're wondering if it's possible she might have taken her own life, Dr. da Silva?"

"What, with arsenic?" He looked genuinely astonished. "You've got to be joking, surely?"

"Why do you say arsenic? I didn't mention that."

"You certainly did to Dr. Ringland. He tells me you wanted to know if she could have taken arsenic from his lab." He gave her a teasing smile. "Or indeed if *I* could."

"We have to consider every eventuality. So you don't think it's likely?"

He pondered, stroking his chin. "Well, it's a pretty astounding notion. I wouldn't have thought of her as the suicidal type. That would be a gruesome way to do it, surely? I mean, she wasn't stupid. She was rather fascinated by early, tragic death, I suppose. As I mentioned to you, I felt her enthusiasms were a little . . . overripe, one might say—hysterical even."

Kathy felt her dislike of Tony da Silva's smugness growing, and had to warn herself not to let it cloud her judgement. "Do you recall anything specific in recent weeks? Anything that in retrospect might be taken as a warning, a cry for help?"

"Not really. She did go on at length about poor old Lizzie Siddal and her death. She took an overdose of laudanum, you know. That's opium, morphine. I suppose you've checked that wasn't how Marion died?"

"It seems it was definitely arsenic. Well, if there's nothing else . . ." Kathy got to her feet, noticing again the row of his Rossetti biographies. "I must get a copy of your book, Dr. da Silva."

"Oh, please . . ." He leapt to his feet and snatched one from the shelf. "Be my guest."

"Well, I must pay for it."

"Don't be silly. Your first name is Kathy, yes? With a K?"

"Yes."

He opened the cover, took a felt pen from his desk and wrote with a great flourish, then snapped it shut and handed it to her. "It's my pleasure. Oh, and, er, I loaned Marion some of my own books and papers. I suppose they'll be at Rosslyn Court. Could I make arrangements to pop over there and pick them up?"

Kathy sensed anxiety beneath the casual question and said, "Not in person, Dr. da Silva. At least not for some time. Perhaps if you gave me a list of the things that are yours I could take a look."

He flushed and muttered that he'd do that.

When she got outside into the corridor, she opened the book and read his inscription: *To Kathy, with enormous admiration for your work, Tony da Silva.*

She wrinkled her nose, wondering what he'd written in Marion's copy.

It occurred to her that Tina Flowers might know if Marion had a computer, so she tried to phone her, but she wasn't at Stamford Street, nor was she answering her mobile number, and Kathy returned to Queen Anne's Gate and her paperwork. An hour later Tina rang.

"I got your message," she said. "Is there news?"

"I just wanted to ask about Marion's computer, Tina. What did she use?"

"Oh, I don't know. I never saw it."

"What about you, do you have one?"

"Yeah, a laptop."

"How did you give her the work you did for her?"

"Mostly it was photocopies and handwritten notes, but I did email her stuff sometimes."

"She didn't give you any computer disks to keep for her, did she?"

"No. Has anything happened? Have you found anything?"

Kathy hesitated, then said, "Did Marion say anything at all, well, odd when you spoke to her that last time, on Tuesday morning?"

"Odd? No, I've gone over in my head everything she said, and she seemed normal."

"Not depressed, then?"

"No, quite the opposite. She was happy. Everything was going well for her."

"Did you ever hear her talk about suicide?"

"Well, yes, about the characters she was researching. I was supposed to look out for suicide references. It was on my list of key words, remember?"

"Yes, but I mean at a more personal level. Did she ever talk about wanting to kill herself?"

"No, of course not. She wasn't like that. Why do you ask?"

"We've found where she was living, Tina—a house in Hampstead. She never mentioned that?"

"No."

"Inside we found evidence that she mixed her own drink that day, lacing it with arsenic."

"No!" Tina's voice choked off abruptly, and Kathy heard the sound of a gasp or sob. Then she came back on. "No, I don't believe it. She'd never do that. You've made a mistake."

"I don't think so."

"Why are you doing this?" The girl's voice was suddenly hot with angry protest. "That's the easy way out, isn't it?"

"What do you mean?"

"Blame Marion, she can't answer for herself. Nobody else gets upset."

Kathy waited a couple of beats, then said, "That's not how we work, Tina."

"She would *never* have killed herself."

"How do you know?"

"She was too smart. She had her life together. Despite . . ."

"Despite what? Who?"

Tina didn't answer at first, her breathing harsh down the line. Then, "If you won't find out what happened, I will," and she hung up.

Kathy turned back to her files, trying to concentrate, and was immediately interrupted by another phone call, a man's voice, a Scot.

"It's Donald Fotheringham, Inspector. We spoke on the telephone last Wednesday, if you remember, when you called Bessie Wardlaw, Marion Summers's auntie."

The minister, Kathy recalled. "Ah yes, Mr. Fotheringham. How is Mrs. Wardlaw?"

"Awfy frail, I'm afraid, and quite distraught over Marion's death. It's been in the *Sunday Post*, you know, and the *Glasgow Herald*. That's why I'm here."

"Here?"

"Aye, here in London. I came down on the sleeper. Bessie asked me to try to find out what really happened. She wanted me to speak to you in person. I hope that will be possible."

"Yes, yes of course. Whereabouts are you, exactly?"

"I've got myself a wee room in a hotel near Euston. I can hop on a bus and be with you any time you say. Maybe I could buy you lunch. Would it be too dreadful to suggest a sandwich in St. James's Square?"

Beneath the sombre tones, Kathy thought she detected a little quiver of eagerness in the minister's voice, as if he was finding his mission rather exciting.

"That'll be just fine. One o'clock?"

SHE SPOTTED HIM STRAIGHT away, a tall, rather gaunt figure standing alone beside the equestrian statue. He wasn't wearing a dog collar, but she had the sense of a stranger in a strange land, taking it all in.

She introduced herself and he transferred a plastic bag to his left hand and they shook.

"Good of you to see me," he said. "So this is the place . . ."

Kathy pointed to a bench. "That's where she had lunch, and over there is the library where she collapsed afterwards." She pointed to the frontage of the London Library, shouldered into the corner of the square by its grander neighbours.

"Ironic." He nodded at the figure on the prancing horse. "She told me once she hated King Billie. She hated the Orange lodges. I believe her father was a member of the number one lodge down in Kilwinning."

They walked over to the bench and sat down. It was in full sun and felt warm, as if someone had just been sitting there. Kathy was surprised at how much more foliage there was on the trees after less than a week.

"He left Marion and her mother when she was young, didn't he?" Kathy asked.

"Aye, so Bessie told me. Marion was two. It shaped her life, I suppose, growing up with no father, and a mother whose parenting skills were . . . somewhat lacking, shall we say?"

"Yes, I've met Sheena."

"How is she? Bessie wanted me to ask."

"Well enough. Works in a supermarket in Ealing. She still seems devoted to Keith Rafferty. Do you know him?" She showed Fotheringham his picture.

"No, I don't believe he ever came up to Scotland. Tell me, that looks like one of those official police photos. Does he have a record?"

"He does."

"Ah. Bessie suspected as much. Sheena was a bit evasive about her husband's background." He seemed about to say more, then changed his mind and reached into his carrier bag. "I got one smoked salmon sandwich and a vegetarian one. And two different cans of pop. Please take your pick. I'm happy with either."

"I was glad you were there when I phoned Bessie. I'm afraid I gave her a shock."

"Och, she's coping, but she's had heart problems and has to be careful. Very upset about Marion, of course, but she doesn't show much on the surface. Quite the opposite of her younger sister."

"Bessie was very attached to Marion."

"Oh aye. Mind you, it wasnae all plain sailing. She took Marion out of shame at how Sheena had neglected her, and there were some stormy times when the girl moved in, I can tell you. Marion was out of control, and it took all of Bessie's willpower to bring some discipline into her life."

Out of control. It was a phrase that seemed at odds with the picture Kathy had of Marion. "Had she been abused?"

Fotheringham hesitated. "I wouldnae put it quite like that. But she couldnae stay at that school, not after what happened."

Kathy raised an eyebrow and the minister sighed. "I don't like to rake up these old stories, now that Marion has so tragically passed away. She was a different person then—wilful, headstrong. She formed a passionate attachment to one of the men teachers. We were never sure exactly how it was reciprocated, if at all, but one night she painted their two names in huge letters across the front of the main school building, with an obscene word between. You can imagine the mothers dropping their bairns off the next morning and seeing it. It was all around the town in minutes. Marion was fourteen years old. The teacher was suspended, his wife left him, and two weeks later he hanged himself."

"Really?" Kathy tried to square this with the picture she'd formed of Marion.

"I don't want to make her sound like a monster. The truth of what happened at the school was never established, and she could be a delightful person, and intelligent, very intelligent. But sometimes, if she was thwarted, a darker side took over. There were times I feared for Bessie after she moved in with her. The neighbours used to tell me about the terrible rows they had. Then finally she seemed to settle down. She made friends with some sensible girls at her new school, and applied herself to her studies. We were very proud of her when she got the scholarship to London. It was the reward for all Bessie's efforts. And now this. To be the victim of such a thing." He shook his head sadly.

"Mr. Fotheringham, I should tell you that new information has come to light which suggests that Marion may not have been murdered."

"What?"

"After some difficulty we found the house where she was living. And inside we discovered evidence that she herself prepared the poisoned juice that she drank here, on this bench."

The man's mouth dropped open. "You're not suggesting suicide?"

"That's the way it looks."

"Oh dear. That's terrible. Such a death. And so public. Would it have been painful?"

"Yes."

"There was a spell, in her late teens . . . Bessie discovered that she was cutting herself. But we thought she'd got over that."

They sat in silence for a while as Mr. Fotheringham digested this. Then he said, "You had difficulty finding her house, you say? Surely Sheena could have helped you there?"

"No, it seems Marion moved from the student flats where she was living three months ago, and didn't tell her mother."

"That's strange, is it not? Why would she do that?"

"We don't know. We wondered if she was hiding from someone."

"Who?"

Kathy shrugged. "We considered her stepfather, Keith, but didn't find any real evidence."

Fotheringham's eyes narrowed at her equivocal phrase. "I should pay Sheena a visit while I'm here. She was never one of my flock, but Bessie would expect it of me."

"Well, if you bump into Keith, just be careful. He's got a short fuse."

"I'll bear that in mind. And what about her student friends—is there someone I might speak to? I'd like to be able to tell Bessie something of her life down here."

"There's one, Tina Flowers, you could try. She's taken Marion's death hard, and refuses to believe she might have killed herself. It might help her to talk to you too. I'll contact her if you like, and give her your number."

Kathy rose to her feet. "Thanks for the lunch, Donald. Keep in touch while you're in London. Let me know how you get on, and I'll update you if we get any more information."

She left him pondering on the bench in the shadow of King Billie. When she got back to her office she found a note with the answer to one of the lines she'd been following up: the present owner of 43 Rosslyn Court was registered as Marion Summers, as from the twelfth of January. Kathy read the paragraph several times, her pulse quickening. How was this possible? How had a penniless student come to own an expensive house in Hampstead?

Her request for access to Marion's known email account had not been as successful. It was an MSN Hotmail account, and the data would have to be released by Microsoft in the USA, subject to approval by the FBI, and with all the recent terrorist investigations, delays were expected.

THIRTEEN

SUZANNE CAUGHT THE TUBE to Notting Hill Gate, then walked briskly down the busy thoroughfare of Holland Park Avenue heading west. It was a fine morning for a walk, a breeze sending the clouds scudding overhead, the pavements damp from an early shower. After a while she turned right into the quieter streets of Notting Hill and began to zigzag to the north and west until she came to the curve of Lansdowne Gardens. It was years since she'd been there, and she was amazed at how it had changed, so much so that she almost stopped and turned back, afraid that the memories she treasured would be ruined by this actuality. It wasn't that the buildings had been redeveloped, nothing like that—she recognised several of the more distinctive ones as she passed. Rather they had all been buffed and scrubbed and painted, extensions tastefully tucked around, gardens immaculately groomed, security discreetly visible. She remembered how it had been that summer she'd stayed with Angela, forty years before, a scruffy run-down district of old houses in decay, subdivided into bedsits and improvised flats, the warm evenings echoing with the sound of the West Indians' reggae and the hippies' Stones. And now look at it. The gloss of evident wealth made her feel vaguely disconcerted, as if the appearance of an old friend had been turned plastic by a particularly exacting face-lift.

As she approached the corner with Lansdowne Rise, she hesitated, catching sight of the Italianate tower and the attic windows. *Oh Dougie,* she thought, *fancy you still being here after all this time.* Talking to Brock about those days had stirred so many memories that she'd decided to steal a little time to visit the place again before returning home to Battle. But now she felt like an intruder, a thirteen-year-old once again.

Someone was in the garden, a woman with a headscarf stooping to pick jonquils. As Suzanne stared at her, she raised her head and focused, giving a vague smile.

"Good morning."

It was Dougie's mother! What was her name again? Jean? Jan? Suzanne opened her mouth to say good morning in reply, and before she could stop herself said, "It's Lady Warrender, isn't it?"

"Yes, that's right." The elderly woman frowned, straightening stiffly and looking at Suzanne more closely. "Have we met?"

"Well, yes, we have, actually. A very long time ago, in the sixties. I was a friend of Angela Crick, who used to live next door."

"Angela? Why yes, of course, I remember Angela. And you are . . . ?"

"Suzanne. Suzanne Chambers."

The frown deepened on Joan Warrender's face and then suddenly cleared into a delighted smile, a twinkle in her eye. "Of course! Little Suzanne! Such a pretty girl, and—I'm not wrong, am I?—rather taken by my Dougie?"

Suzanne felt herself blush. "No," she smiled, "not mistaken."

"I'm afraid he's not here at the moment, but I'm about ready for a cup of tea. Won't you come in and join me, if you have the time?"

"Well . . . I'd love to."

Suzanne stepped through the wrought-iron gate and followed Joan Warrender around the garden to the back of the house. At the kitchen door the older woman kicked off her Wellingtons and stepped into a pair of slippers, carrying the flowers to the sink.

"I was just thinking how much the neighbourhood has changed since I was here with Angela," Suzanne said, and Joan laughed.

"Oh my goodness, when we arrived from India, we thought we'd landed in a slum. Roger bought the house from a highly misleading photograph and information sent by a local agent desperate for a sale. We weren't here long as it happened, before Roger took the job in New York, but we hung on to the house, and look at it now."

"You had an elephant's foot for an umbrella stand in the hall, didn't you?"

"You're right! Shockingly incorrect now, I dare say. I'm afraid it didn't survive our various travels. Poor Hathi. He was practically a family pet in India—the elephant, I mean. Dougie was heartbroken when he died. How clever of you to remember his foot."

Suzanne could barely picture Dougie's tall, rather severe-looking father. "Is Sir Roger here too?"

"No, he passed away fifteen years ago. I have my own little apartment now. Come and see."

Suzanne picked up the tray of tea cups and biscuits and followed the other woman out along a passage to a small sitting room with a view over a mass of daffodils leading down to the shared private garden at the back of the house.

"I have my bedroom through that door there, and my own bathroom, so I'm quite independent." She talked about the other members of her family. Dougie was something big in finance, his only daughter, Emily, waiting to take her place at Oxford that autumn. "And you may have heard of Dougie's wife, Sophie. She's a well-known author."

"Yes, I'm a great admirer of her books. As a matter of fact she's the reason I happened to come by this morning. She contacted a friend of mine a couple of days ago, and he came here and when he told me about his visit it brought back memories and I was curious to see the house again after all this time."

"I see. But who was this friend of yours?"

"He's a policeman, with Scotland Yard. He came to speak with Sophie about the girl who worked for her, who was poisoned."

"Oh, that was shocking." But Joan Warrender looked more intrigued than dismayed. "Did he tell you the inside story? What do they think really happened to her?"

"I'm afraid he didn't say."

"Oh, but you must find out and tell me. I'm quite fascinated." She gestured at the TV sitting in the far corner of the room. "I watch all the crime and forensic shows."

"Well," Suzanne said, wanting to give her something, "he's obviously intrigued by the case. There seem to be some strange features, apart from the poisoning itself."

"Oh yes? Like what?" The elderly woman was leaning forward avidly.

Suzanne would never normally have shared Brock's comments with anyone else, but Joan's relish was hard to resist. "Why arsenic, and where did it come from? And it seems that she had money that is hard to account for."

"Yes! I remember noticing a ring one day. I asked her about it and she wouldn't say. As for the arsenic, well, I suppose they have that sort of thing in universities, don't they?" She raised an eyebrow suggestively, her eyes bright and alert.

Suzanne looked at her, trying to read the innuendo. "Lady Warrender," she said slowly, "what are you saying?"

"Joan, dear. Call me Joan, please. I'm only stating the obvious. The fact that I saw her once in the company of a certain rather debonair older man who happened to be at the university is purely coincidental."

"Well, she was a student—perhaps he was her tutor."

"He was."

"How do you know?"

"I asked her afterwards. She seemed rather secretive."

"There's nothing wrong in a student meeting with her tutor, surely?"

"Getting into a taxi in Covent Garden, holding hands?"

"Well . . . You should speak to David—Chief Inspector Brock, my friend."

"Oh, no." The intensity of Joan's manner suddenly evaporated and she burst out laughing. "I'm no Miss Marple. It was probably perfectly innocent. I couldn't even be sure that they were holding hands. I think I convinced myself of that to make things more interesting. Sophie would be appalled at me spreading tittle-tattle."

They finished their tea, and Suzanne said she would have to go. As she showed her to the door Joan said they should meet up again for lunch the next time she was in town, as long as she promised to tell her more juicy details of the Marion Summers case. As she walked away down Lansdowne Gardens, Suzanne thought how strange it had felt to be in that house again, and to meet Dougie's mother after so many years. She felt rather surprised at herself for coming here, and a little foolish. It was a relief that Dougie hadn't been at home, and she felt embarrassed at the thought of him catching her there, and also rather guilty regarding David. Should she tell him about her visit? Probably not—but then, he might be interested in Joan Warrender's "tittle-tattle."

She passed Angela's old house. They had lost touch years before, and she wondered where her school friend was now. She decided to detour by way of Portobello Road, where the two of them had spent hours together in the street market. On her way she passed a smart bookshop with a poster in the window with Sophie Warrender's photograph, looking very sophisticated and assured. *Hear Notting Hill author Sophie Warrender talk about her biographies*, it said. *Wednesday 11 April, 7:30pm. Admission by ticket only.* Suzanne hesitated, then went inside.

FOURTEEN

THERE WERE DOZENS OF responses to her Interpol inquiries for
Kathy to deal with the next morning, and it was almost lunchtime
before she got to an envelope with Dr. Mehta's name in the sender
box. It contained several pages of a faxed report, tagged with one
of Sundeep's compliments slips with a handwritten scrawl: *Kathy,
Forensics sent me this draft for my comment. What do you think?
Sundeep.*

He had underlined several sentences and put question marks in
the margin, just in case she needed guidance. The marked pas-
sages were: *The screw-top jar found in the kitchen cupboard had
previously contained sugar, traces of which were found beneath the
As_2O_3 . . . Both the teaspoon and saucer bore coffee residue . . . The
glass of contaminated orange juice also contained traces of sodium
bicarbonate.*

A vivid mental picture came into Kathy's mind, of the café in
Charles Square on Saturday morning. Guy had ordered a glass of
orange juice and at some point they'd all simultaneously noticed an
orange moustache formed on his upper lip. Rusty had laughed and
pointed it out, Guy sheepishly wiped it away, and then they were
all laughing, the ice broken, suddenly all best mates. Kathy smiled

to herself a little regretfully. They'd had so little time together, and now she wished she was back there with them. With Guy.

When they had emerged in the small hours of Sunday morning from the hot smoky cellar in which Rusty's group had been playing, a huge silver moon hung over the city and a freezing wind caught them by surprise. Guy had put his arm around Kathy and she pressed close against him, seeking warmth. They'd become separated from the others on the way back to Nicole and Kathy's hotel, walking in companionable silence. When they reached the doorway he asked if he might call her when they got back to London, and they swapped phone numbers, writing them on the palms of their hands. Then they kissed goodnight. He was catching a different flight back and she hadn't heard from him again. They'd had plenty to drink in the cellar, and she supposed he'd lost her number. She felt a twinge of regret.

She shook herself. What was Sundeep getting at? She picked up the phone.

"Ah," he said. "You got my notes. So?"

"The things weren't clean when she used them to mix the drink."

"Yes. So?"

"I don't follow, Sundeep. So what?"

"Come on, Kathy." Impatient now. "If she was conducting some kind of experiment on herself, wouldn't she have used fresh dishes? Wouldn't she have stored her precious arsenic in a clean jar? Incidentally, there's no evidence of previous arsenic ingestion in her hair or nails."

She saw where he was going now and felt a quickening of her heart, but pressed him. "Suicide then, rather than an experiment gone wrong?"

"Murder, Kathy, murder! Her breakfast things were taken out of the dishwasher by someone knowing her prints and DNA would be all over them. The whole thing was staged."

"You're sure?"

"No, how can I be? It's just a conjecture. But it makes sense to me."

"Wouldn't Marion have noticed that the plastic cap seal on the juice had been broken when she opened it in the park?"

"Not necessarily, if it was screwed back on tight. Would you?"

"Mm. There was no sign of a forced entry."

"Because he had a key."

Kathy heard the restrained excitement in his voice. "He?"

"Yes, *he*." Sundeep's voice had sunk to a hoarse whisper. "Marion's body has told me something else."

"How do you mean?"

"I did some more tests on her blood serum."

Kathy waited, then realised that he was determined to make her coax it out of him. "And what did you find, Sundeep?"

"I found Beta-human chorionic gonadotrophic hormone."

"What's that?"

"Beta-hCG is present in the blood serum of pregnant women."

"But you said she wasn't—"

"She wasn't—but she had been. It persists in the serum for five or six weeks after the end of the pregnancy. I'd say she had a miscarriage about two weeks before she died."

"A miscarriage or an abortion?"

"Well, it could be that too, yes."

"Can you tell how long she would have been pregnant?"

"I think not long, since there were no other visible signs. I'd guess no more than two months."

They were silent for a moment, then he said, "You'll look into it?"

"Yes, Sundeep, I'll look into it."

She hung up, pushing the Interpol files to one side. The house, she thought, she had to find out about the house. Then she remembered Brock asking her to take Sophie Warrender there. There had been something loaded in the way Brock had made the suggestion, as if he felt the author could help Kathy in some way. So she dialled the Notting Hill number and arranged to meet Sophie Warrender at Rosslyn Court in half an hour. Then another thought occurred to her. Marion had gone to great lengths to keep the compartments of her life separate. Maybe it was time they were brought together. She rang Tina's mobile.

"Yes?" The girl sounded breathless as if she was walking fast.

"It's Kathy Kolla, Tina."

"Oh. What do you want?"

"I'm about to go to the house where Marion was living. I'm meeting the woman she had that other job with. I wondered if you'd like to come along? I can collect you if you're not too busy."

The line was silent for moment, the heavy breathing stilled. "Okay."

"You won't miss a lecture or something?"

"Doesn't matter."

"Where are you?"

"On Waterloo Bridge."

"Walk over to the Strand and I'll pick you up there in ten minutes."

Kathy hung up, wondering if she was doing the right thing.

TINA WAS STANDING AT the kerb, clad in a T-shirt and short skirt, stamping her feet and shivering in the cool breeze, despite the sun. She slid in beside Kathy and immediately wanted to know about the house and the Warrenders, then reverted to silence. Kathy didn't push her.

Sophie Warrender was waiting by the front gate of number forty-three, a younger woman by her side, both wearing winter coats. Kathy parked behind their Mercedes and introduced herself and Tina.

"I hope you don't mind me bringing my daughter, Emily," Sophie said. "I may need a hand carrying the books."

"Did you know Marion, Emily?" Kathy asked.

"Yes, I liked her a lot." The girl lowered her eyes, sounding shy or withdrawn.

"They were good friends," Sophie said. "Marion helped Emily with her A-level schoolwork a couple of times, and you helped her too, didn't you, darling? Indexing or something, on her computer. Emily's waiting to go up to Oxford in the autumn," she explained. "I've had her helping me with my researches too."

"What sort of computer did Marion have, Emily?" Kathy asked.

"A laptop, but I don't know if it was hers. She wasn't very used to it."

"And did you and Tina never meet?"

Both shook their heads, eyeing each other with interest.

Sophie was looking up at the front of the house. "This is quite charming, isn't it? But expensive to rent in this part of town, surely. Was she sharing with a group?"

"Apparently not."

"Really? How could she afford it? I paid her very little really."

"Good question. You got any ideas, Tina?"

Tina shot Kathy a dark look, muttered, "No."

Kathy led the way to the front door, and took them through the downstairs rooms. The other women all seemed astonished by the newness and quality of the fittings.

"It's very tidy, isn't it?" Sophie said.

"Wasn't Marion usually tidy?" Kathy asked.

Sophie said, "Oh yes, I think so. Always very organised."

Tina nodded. "You should have seen her room at Stamford Street. She couldn't believe the mess the rest of us lived in."

Sophie gazed around Marion's orderly workroom, then went over to the table. "It's all here—my notes, the books, the photocopies we spoke about, and the work she's been doing this past month." She flicked through pages of typescript. "Everything I asked. It's almost as if . . ." Sophie hesitated, and glanced at Tina.

"Go on," Kathy said.

"Well, I'm probably imagining it, but it's almost as if she'd tidied everything up, knowing . . ." Her voice faded.

"Knowing she was leaving for good?" Kathy prompted.

Sophie nodded.

"Knowing that people like us would be standing here looking at it." Kathy went on. "So perhaps you can tell me if you find anything else here that strikes you as odd. I'll let you sort out your things while I have a word with Tina. Maybe you could make out a list of what you're taking."

"Of course."

Kathy took Tina's arm and led her out to the sitting room at the back of the house and sat her in one of the two armchairs in front of the fireplace. She took the other, and said, "I think it's time we helped each other, Tina. You said I was wrong in thinking Marion poisoned herself. Well, I'm prepared to keep an open mind on that, but I need help. There's some reason you're so sure I was wrong, isn't there?"

Tina met her eyes for a moment, then looked away. "Nothing special."

"The pathologist has discovered that she was pregnant, and lost the baby just a couple of weeks before she died. Did you know that?"

Tina looked shocked, and shook her head. "No!"

"She didn't give you a hint? Think about it, Tina. You said she was the same as usual in the weeks leading up to her death, but surely there must have been something?"

"I had no idea about a baby," she whispered. "But there was something, something new, that she said was very exciting . . ." She frowned, trying to remember exactly what Marion had said, but the memory seemed elusive. "Exciting and scary, that's what she said. But I thought she was talking about her work. I was sure she was. That's why I didn't think it had anything to do with what happened. Could she really have been talking about a baby?"

"Try to remember exactly what she said."

Tina's mouth twisted with effort, but she shook her head.

"Maybe it'll come back to you. But what I really need to know is, who was the father?"

Tina shook her head hopelessly, and after awhile Kathy gave up pressing her. "Did you get in touch with Donald Fotheringham?"

"Yes, I phoned him. We're meeting later this afternoon. I'd like to hear about Marion's early life."

"Good. He wanted to speak to someone close to Marion. Maybe talking to him will make you remember something that might help me."

Tina looked around the room. "But now I feel as if I didn't know her at all."

Sophie Warrender's voice called from the hall. "Hello? We're just about finished here."

Kathy got to her feet and went out to them. Emily stood behind her mother, both women carrying bags full of papers and books. Sophie handed Kathy a list. "This is everything we've taken. Thank you so much."

"That's fine. Tell me, did Marion mention a boyfriend to you?"

"DCI Brock asked me the same question. No, she didn't."

"How about you, Emily? Did she say anything to you?"

"No."

"Why?" Sophie asked. "Was there some mystery man in the background?"

"Apparently. She lost a baby two weeks before she died."

Sophie looked surprised, Emily more so, her mouth dropping open. "Oh God, that's terrible!"

"Yes. We would have expected him to come forward, but he hasn't."

"Perhaps he's married," Sophie said, and a small frown crossed her face. "My husband's mother, who lives with us and met Marion a couple of times, saw her once getting into a taxi with an older man. When she asked Marion about it, she seemed embarrassed. She said it was her tutor. Do you remember, Emily?"

"Yes." The young woman bobbed her head awkwardly. "In Covent Garden."

"Did Marion say anything else about Dr. da Silva to you?"

"Only that she got quite frustrated by his directions to her," Sophie said. "I told your chief inspector. They seemed to have quite a few disagreements. But I never got the impression from her that there was anything romantic going on. How about you, darling?"

Emily bit her lip, looking very pale. "I'm not sure. She told me once that I should be careful when I got to Oxford and watch out for men who tried to pretend that they were interested in my brains, when all they were really interested in was something else."

"You think she was referring to her tutor?"

Emily nodded. "Yes."

There was a small sound at Kathy's back, and she turned to see Tina standing behind her, listening to their conversation.

"Well . . ." Sophie Warrender checked her watch. "We must go. Thanks again." She shook Kathy's hand. "Please let me know if I can help in any way. I must say I find this all very disturbing. I shall miss Marion a great deal. I would really appreciate it if you would let me know how things progress. Maybe I could write a letter of condolence to her parents. Do you have their details?"

Kathy gave her Sheena Rafferty's address, then Tina said quickly, "Can I get a lift back with you? Anywhere near a tube station would be fine."

Sophie shot a questioning glance at Kathy, then said, "Of course."

Kathy closed the door behind them, returned to Marion's work-room and sat down at the table. Through the front windows she watched the three women getting into the car and felt a surge of frustration. She was sure Tina knew more, but the girl had long ago developed a tight-lipped resistance to authority. She wondered if she might open up more to Emily, or Donald Fotheringham.

She looked around her as Marion would have done, the last time she sat there, just over a week before: the orderly stacks of papers on the table, the neat line of pens, the bookshelves on one side, the pinboard on the other. She stopped and looked again. Something was different, and it took her a moment to realise that the display of pictures and connecting threads was changed in some way. Something was missing, she felt, though she couldn't place what it was, and she experienced an uncanny sensation, as if Marion herself had come back in the interval and rearranged her board.

Kathy picked up the list of items that Sophie had taken. There was no mention of the pinboard, but perhaps she hadn't thought that important enough. She took out her phone and dialled Sophie's mobile. No, the other woman said, they hadn't touched anything on that wall. Kathy's sense of unease faded as she realised that forensics had probably returned to collect further samples, then surged back when she remembered that she had the only house key. They couldn't have got in without her knowledge. She looked around the room again, searching for some other sign, and her eye stopped at a gap in the bookshelves. It hadn't been there before, she was almost certain, because she thought she remembered what had been—Anthony da Silva's biography of Dante Gabriel Rossetti. That didn't appear on Sophie's list either.

Before she left she checked the windows and doors once more, finding no signs of forced entry, then took photos of Marion's room with her mobile phone.

KATHY FOUND THE ESTATE agent at her second attempt. Bryan Dawkins showed Kathy into a small glass-partitioned room in one corner of his office. He was a plump, cheerful, enthusiastic man— as who wouldn't be, Kathy supposed, given the price of houses in the neighbourhood.

"Yes, we handled the sale of 43 Rosslyn Court," he said. "I read about that dreadful poisoning in the London Library, of course, but I just didn't make the connection with our Ms. Summers. Please take a seat."

"Tell me about the sale of the house."

"She spotted it herself. Apparently she'd been looking in this area, and saw our sign outside the house. She came in and asked for particulars, and I showed her around. She fell for it immediately, it was exactly what she was looking for, so she went ahead, all pretty straightforward."

"What was the selling price?"

"Seven twenty-five. She didn't haggle."

"Seven hundred and twenty-five thousand pounds?"

"Yes. It was a good buy. It'd only just come on the market. The seller had done it all up—new kitchen, bathrooms, wiring, everything—then his company posted him abroad and he had to sell up."

"Did she discuss how she was raising the money?"

"Her solicitor dealt with all that. After we shook hands that day I didn't see her again. There was one condition that caused a bit of discussion. They wanted to settle in three equal payments spread over six months. The seller wouldn't have it, and in the end Ms. Summers agreed—must have fixed up bridging finance, I suppose."

"So she didn't give any indication where the money was coming from?"

"'Fraid not. Is there a problem?"

"Not really. Just trying to get a picture of the lady," Kathy said. "We haven't been able to speak to her immediate neighbours yet. Know anything about them?"

"Yes, I do actually. We handled both properties within the past five years or so. One is a Middle Eastern gentleman, rarely stays there I gather, and the other is a doctor and his family, at present doing a stint at a hospital in Alberta, Canada. So it's not surprising you haven't been able to catch them at home."

"What about the furnishings in the house, Mr. Dawkins? Did the previous owner leave any of them?"

"Oh no, it was completely bare. Everything in there now will have been put there by Ms. Summers. I believe she did have someone in to redecorate the place when she first moved in. I recommended someone."

Kathy thanked him and got the name of the solicitor who had acted for Marion; his office was further along the high street. On the way there she phoned her contact at Forensic Services, who confirmed that they had not returned to the house since Kathy had been there on the previous Friday.

"I think someone's been in there since we left," she said. "Could you do another check for fingerprints? Especially the downstairs front room, the study."

The man groaned. "Come off it, Kathy. We're up to our ears. I thought this one was well and truly tied up. Suicide, yes?"

"Maybe not. I'll put in a formal request."

"Well, it probably won't be this week, unless you can persuade my boss."

"Also, could you send me a complete set of all the photographs you took in the house, please? Thanks."

THE SOLICITOR HAD RECOGNISED Marion's name in the newspaper reports, but hadn't thought to contact the police. Or rather, Kathy suspected, he had decided not to get involved. He seemed to know very little about his client and had done no other business for her apart from the house purchase.

"Confident, intelligent young woman. Seemed very pleasant. Tragic business."

"Did she talk about her personal circumstances?"

"Said she was a student. A relative in Scotland had left her an inheritance that she wanted to invest in property as her security for the future. I agreed that the house she had in mind would serve admirably."

"Did she say anything about this relative? A name?"

"No, I don't believe so. The only thing was that she wasn't sure when probate would be granted, and she didn't want to lose the house. We tried to delay completion, but the seller wanted things wrapped up."

"What happened?"

"The money came through. She paid."

"How?"

He frowned. "A bank draft, as I recall. Is that important?"

"Possibly."

"Do you suspect fraud?"

"I'm trying to establish if Ms. Summers had any substantial debts at the time of her death, and hence what her assets might amount to."

"Hm, well, it wasn't a building society mortgage."

He got to his feet and went to the door, saying a few words to a secretary, then returned to his seat. "Won't be a moment."

"Do you know if she had another solicitor?"

"She didn't mention it. You're thinking of a will, perhaps? Have you traced her next of kin?"

"Her mother's living in London, other relatives in Scotland, but none of them seems to have been aware of a substantial legacy."

"I see."

The secretary brought in a file which the solicitor consulted. "Yes, here we are. A draft from the Banque Foche SA in Geneva made out to ourselves in the sum of 1.1 million euros. After completing the purchase there was a balance of almost twenty thousand pounds that we returned to Ms. Summers."

"Why a Swiss bank, did she say?"

"Apparently the relative had business interests in Switzerland."

"Do you know this bank?"

"No, I can't say I've come across them before, but there are many banks in Switzerland."

"All very discreet, no doubt."

The solicitor allowed himself a small smile. "No doubt."

FIFTEEN

"THIS IS DETECTIVE CHIEF Inspector David Brock," Kathy said curtly, coming into the room quickly and pulling up a chair at the table.

Nigel Ogilvie blinked at him uncertainly. "Er, how do you do?"

Brock grunted noncommittally and sat heavily in the other chair, tossing his newspaper onto the table. He folded his arms resignedly as if he had far better things to do, and his eyes strayed back to the paper, folded to the sports page.

"The last time we met," Kathy said, "you suddenly chose to reveal that you did know where Marion Summers lived, a fact you had denied up until that point. Now that you've had a few days to think about things, I wonder if you have any other information you'd like to share with us?"

"Um, well, no, I don't believe so."

Kathy stared at him for a long moment, so hard that he was obliged to look away. "You should bear in mind that we've now downloaded all the contents of your computer, including material that you probably thought you'd trashed."

Ogilvie bit his lip and remained silent.

"You're very interested in poisons, aren't you?" she went on, scanning the sheets of paper on her clipboard. "Aconitine, strychnine, digitalin, hyoscine hydrobromide, hemlock, arsenic . . . Obsessively interested, one might say."

"It's my work," Ogilvie blurted. "I had to research poisons. That's what the project is all about. I told you."

"Your boss disagrees. The title of the book was *Deadly Gardens*, yes? He wanted you to find gardens where people had died in sinister circumstances—hanged, drowned, guillotined, burned at the stake. He tried to discourage you from focusing so much on poison, but you seemed to take no notice."

Nigel's face burned. *That little shit Stephen. How he must be enjoying this!*

"So much so that he's had to give the project to somebody else."

"What?"

"Didn't you know? He did say that he'd had a lot of trouble getting hold of you recently. Apparently you never answer your phone. Too busy taking pictures with it, probably."

"Look, I—"

"And poisoners! Hamlet's stepfather, Dr. de la Pommerais, George Lamson, Dr. Crippen. Did they have interesting gardens? Well, did they?"

"Not them, especially . . ."

"Then why, Nigel?" Kathy leaned forward across the table. "Why this obsession with poison? You can imagine what the prosecution barrister will make of that, can't you?"

Ogilvie paled. Out of the corner of his eye he saw Brock reach suddenly forward. He stiffened, but the chief inspector was only turning his newspaper over to the crossword.

"It wasn't like that at all," he gasped. "I had a plan."

"Oh, I'm sure of that."

"No, no. For the book," he gabbled. "I was going to work through different means of death, and it seemed logical to start with poisons, because poisonous plants can grow in gardens. And also . . ." He hesitated.

"Go on."

"Well, to be frank, Marion did have something to do with it.

When I started my research in the library, I went to *P,* and there she was."

"What?"

"The layout of the London Library is different. They don't use Dewey Decimal, the subjects are arranged alphabetically. It's one of the charms of the place." He chuckled nervously. "You can get quite unlikely subjects sitting next to one another. People say it's very serendipitous." He saw the stony expression on Kathy's face and added quickly. "That means—"

"I know what it means. What's that got to do with anything?"

"Marion was studying Pre-Raphaelites, and so when I was looking for Poisons I met her, further along the shelves. We were both in the *Ps.*"

"So it gave you an excuse to get close to her."

"Well, not like *that.* I mean, she was also interested in poisons, because of her work—laudanum and arsenic, especially. So we exchanged information."

"Tell me."

"Oh, let me see . . ."

Nigel Ogilvie launched into a rambling account of various sources of information on nineteenth-century poisonings that he'd shared with Marion.

Kathy pressed on, probing Ogilvie with bits of information they'd gleaned from his computer. "Who's Colin Ringland?"

"What?"

"His name's on your hard drive."

"Is it? Ringland . . . Ringland . . . Oh yes, Marion gave me his contact details. Someone at her university who was interested in arsenic. I spoke to him on the phone once. Something about Bangladesh; I didn't think I could use it."

When she'd exhausted this line Kathy moved on to the photographs downloaded from his phone, pressing him about Marion's house, and about a large shoulder bag she was carrying in several of the pictures.

After an hour she paused and looked at Brock. He glanced up, as if dragging himself away from some other train of thought entirely.

"Mm, yes," he said. "Her computer. What is it about that, I wonder?"

Ogilvie looked at him in surprise. "Pardon?"

"You were very uncomfortable each time DI Kolla brought it up. You crossed and uncrossed your legs, fiddled with your watch, scratched your nose. What was all that about, I wonder?" Brock asked this with an almost kindly interest, as if this was something two reasonable people could surely resolve.

"No, no. As I said, I don't know if it was hers, and I really can't remember the make. Truly, I've racked my brains."

"So why the anxiety each time it was mentioned?"

"I haven't got it!" Ogilvie yelped, holding himself rigid as if trying to stop his body from betraying him. "I don't know where it is, I swear to God!"

Brock studied him for a moment. "I'm almost inclined to believe you, Nigel. But there's something there, isn't there? Something you're not telling us."

"BUT THERE'S NOT A trace of his DNA at Rosslyn Court," Brock objected. "And no sign of arsenic at his home."

Kathy nodded. It was true; they'd tested his clothing, the keyboard of his computer, his fingernails and every inch of his bedroom and garden shed and found no indication that Ogilvie had ever been in contact with arsenic, let alone acquired enough to poison someone. "But we did establish a connection to Dr. Ringland, who has buckets of the stuff."

"Mm." Brock didn't sound convinced. "We'd better organise an audit of that laboratory." He checked his watch. "Another meeting. I'll leave you to it."

Auditing a university laboratory wasn't something Kathy had been faced with before and she wondered how to set about it. She decided to phone Sundeep Mehta for advice, and he immediately offered to help. They discussed how it should be done, and afterwards, while Sundeep organised an inspection team with Forensic Services, Kathy worked her way through the university administration until she got to speak to the senior academic responsible for the laboratory. The man was guarded and clearly worried when Kathy explained the reason for her call.

"You're not suggesting that we were the source of the poison, are you?"

"We know that Marion Summers visited the laboratory, and so far that is her only connection to a source of arsenic that we've been able to discover. So I'm sure the university will be as anxious as we are to eliminate this possibility as soon as we can."

"Yes, yes, of course. But she could hardly have just walked in and helped herself." The academic left the conclusion unspoken.

"We have no reason to suspect Dr. Ringland or his team of any lapse, but it would clearly be best if they didn't carry out the audit themselves."

They discussed the issues at some length, and Kathy began to realise the time and effort that would be involved. There wasn't only the physical security of the laboratory and its materials to consider, but also the paperwork trail of purchase orders, stock records and disposal arrangements. They agreed to meet the following day to draw up detailed plans for inspection and forensic analysis, supervised by a joint committee. In the meantime, the academic agreed to close down the laboratory and seal its premises and records.

BROCK WAS PLAYING DEVIL'S advocate, Kathy thought to herself that evening, as she sat on the sofa in her flat with a glass of wine and the remains of an Indian takeaway. He hadn't been entirely convinced by Sundeep's claim that the scene in Marion's kitchen was staged, and was becoming impatient with the lack of progress. He wasn't the only one: the case had dropped below the press radar now, and Forensic Services were clearly reluctant to spend more time on it. It had reached that messy stage, she thought, of inconclusive leads and dubious theories. A young woman, secretive and possibly hysterical, disturbed by a recent miscarriage, stages an attention-seeking cry for help, miscalculates and kills herself. End of story, move on.

Except that somehow Marion had got her hands not only on a few grams of arsenic, but also on three quarters of a million pounds, and they had no idea from where. And then there were the predators—Keith Rafferty, Nigel Ogilvie, perhaps Anthony da Silva and the unknown father—standing in the background.

She turned again to the photographs on her laptop of Marion's study, those taken by the SOCOs on Friday and on her phone that afternoon. She'd been mistaken about the pinboard, it seemed — there was only one small change, the removal of that unidentified photograph of a woman brooding over Dante Gabriel Rossetti in the middle. Everything else was the same. And da Silva's biography of Rossetti was gone too, as she'd thought. The obvious culprit had to be da Silva himself. Perhaps there had been a compromising inscription in the book, and he'd had a key and come back to check on things once she'd told him that they knew about the house. But why wait till then? And what was the significance of the missing photograph? It was equally possible that Tina or Emily had helped themselves to these trophies from Marion's room. Were they aware of the significance to Marion of the unnamed woman?

She'd had large prints made of some of the crime scene photographs, and with these she formed a collage on her wall reproducing the display on Marion's pinboard. Was this something she should follow up? Until the woman's picture disappeared she would have said it was, literally, academic. It occurred to her that she could construct her own version of this, with the images of the people involved in Marion's death. She sorted through her papers and began to stick their photographs—Keith Rafferty's stark police file photo, a brooding image of Anthony da Silva from the back of his Rossetti book, a snap of Nigel Ogilvie from his own phone camera, looking owlishly startled, and, at the centre, the black-and-white photograph of Marion herself. Was there some sort of parallel here?

She gathered up her file and noticed her bag in the far corner of the room, still only half unpacked from the weekend. It seemed a long time ago now. She thought again of Guy Hamilton, in Dubai or Qatar or wherever it was, and at precisely that moment, as if by induction, her phone rang and with a jolt she heard his voice.

"Kathy, hi. It's Guy. Guy Hamilton, from Prague? Is this a bad time?"

"No . . . no, not at all, Guy. How are you? Are you in the Gulf?"

"No, they delayed the trip for a few days. I'm just waiting, twiddling my thumbs. I wondered if you felt like going out for a drink or something."

"Sure. When?"

"Well, now, if you're free."

"Okay . . . yes! That would be good."

"Great. You live in Finchley, right? I'll come and pick you up. What's the address?"

She told him and hung up, feeling her cheeks burning. Then she jumped to her feet and started to get ready.

When he pressed the buzzer she took the lift down to the ground-floor lobby, and saw him waiting on the other side of the glass doors, stroking the ginger cat that was curling round his ankles. He was wearing the soft suede jacket she remembered from Prague. He looked up as she opened the door, and they grinned at each other and exchanged a quick kiss on the cheek.

"I think she likes me," he said, and it took Kathy a second to realise he meant the cat.

"She belongs to Jock, the manager. Basically she vets everyone who calls."

He led her to a little Porsche parked near the gate, and when he said he didn't know the area she directed him to a wine bar she thought would be all right, not too far away. As he drove they tentatively re-established contact, feeling different now on home ground. He was quiet, grateful that she had been free at such short notice when he'd been at a loose end, waiting to go away.

He corrected himself when they settled themselves in the bar. He hadn't meant that he'd called her because he was at a loose end. The fact was that he'd intended to do that anyway, but assumed he wouldn't be able to until after this trip.

"Same here," Kathy said, feeling unexpected pleasure at the confession. "I was going to call you."

"Oh, great! Well . . . cheers."

They talked about the weekend, casting it in a retrospective glow that reflected on their evening now, warming them with shared intimacy as Kathy remembered the characters they'd met at Rusty's show, and Guy recalled the one with the dark glasses, falling over the dustbins outside.

"I've been so flat out since I got back," she said, laughing. "I'd forgotten that."

"Busy time, eh?"

"Always."

"The same case? The girl who was poisoned?"

"That's right. I should have moved on, but I can't seem to shake it off."

"But it was suicide, didn't Nicole say?"

Kathy hadn't realised that Nicole had been talking about it. "That's what it looked like, but . . ."

"You're not so sure?"

Kathy shrugged.

"I know the feeling," he said. "Reason tells you that you've got the answer, but it doesn't feel right, eh? I get that all the time."

"But surely, as a structural engineer, you have the maths to tell you if you're right or not."

"I wish. No, you have the maths to tell you if it'll work, but is it the best answer? Is there another way of looking at it you haven't thought of?"

"That's exactly right. And I think Marion was struggling with the same problem." She told him about Marion's pinboard, its network of relationships, and how she felt she needed to do a similar thing.

"But you'll have computer programs for that sort of thing, in the police, don't you? I've seen it on TV, the murder wall, glowing in gothic darkness."

She laughed. "Yes, we have one of those, but I need something at home, that I can think about over a glass of red."

"We have programs we can put on our laptops, for analysing complex relationships of things—people, cash, construction events. I use that sort of thing all the time."

"Maybe I need someone like you to give me a few lessons," she said.

"I think you do." He grinned.

They talked some more about his job with a big international firm of engineers, based near the BT tower. He also began to open up about himself, his family in Esher, mentioning a three-year relationship that had recently ended.

"How about you?"

Kathy hesitated. "It tends to be difficult, with the job. The last two men in my life"—no *three*, she thought, *God*—"were police officers, and that made it easier in a way . . ."

"But also like living over the shop?" he offered. "Yeah, I had a girlfriend in the office once and it was a bit claustrophobic. Bloody difficult actually, when things went pear-shaped."

"Yes," she agreed, remembering.

"Maybe you need to branch out a bit. Sample some other profession."

He was right, she thought. Time for a change. The others hadn't done her much good.

After midnight she began to stifle yawns, and he drove her home. "Listen," he said as they got out of the car and walked to the glass door, "I could show you some of the software we use for creating networks. We could download it onto your laptop and you could work out your own pattern, like Marion's. If you're busy I could just drop a disk into your letterbox . . ." He stopped and stared at the bank of letterboxes that was built in next to the door. She followed his gaze and saw what looked like a cat's tail protruding from one of the slots.

"That's my box," she said.

"It looks . . ." They went closer. "Isn't that your manager's cat? How did she manage to get in there?" There was no way the cat could have squeezed through the opening.

"It's a joke," Kathy said. "Jock's always fooling around."

But she felt uneasy as she opened the door and they went into the hallway, from which the residents had access to the backs of their boxes. She pulled her keys from her bag, but already she'd seen the trickle of dark liquid oozing from the lip of hers. She slipped the key in the lock, swung the small door open, and then jumped back as a cascade of bloody offal spilled out onto the floor.

"Aww!" Guy gagged at her side as the sickly smell hit them. "What the?"

The bloody mess was all over the floor and the back of the other boxes—and her shoes, Kathy noticed.

"Is it Halloween or something?" Guy said. "Is it kids? Tell me that's not the cat."

As if in answer, something slowly slid forward out of the box and tumbled to the floor. It was the rear end of a cat, its hips and two legs, dragging behind it the ginger tail.

They stared at in horrified silence for a moment, then Kathy pulled out her phone and rang a number. "Jock? It's Kathy Kolla from 1203. I'm in the front lobby. I think you should come."

It took several minutes for Jock, muttering and swaying, to appear from his small flat at the back of the block. He swore when he saw the mess, then turned pale as he made out the tail. "Is it Trudy?" he wailed. "Is it my baby?"

They worked together to gather up the remains and mop away the blood. Jock went off to call the police, muttering that it would do no good.

"Oh, Guy, your jacket." Kathy looked at the stain on his sleeve "We should sponge it off. You'd better come up to the flat."

"Well," he said, as the lift rose to the twelfth floor, "that was nasty." His face clouded. "It couldn't have been meant specifically for you, could it, Kathy? I mean, one of your old customers, or something? Someone who knows where you live?"

"No," she said. "No chance of that." But Kathy was mentally checking through the people she might have annoyed enough recently to do something like this—the Roach clan, the Fab Five . . .

While she sponged his jacket he roamed around the room, becoming interested in the pictures on the wall. "I see what you mean," he said. "Yes, I'm sure I could find something to help you with this."

She tried to sound interested, but she couldn't get the business downstairs out of her head. It was Keith Rafferty's style, she decided, picturing the ugly leer on his face. Did he try something like this on Marion? After a while she sensed that Guy wanted to stay, but she wasn't ready for that. Eventually he thanked her and shrugged on his jacket, and she showed him out to the lift. They kissed goodbye, promising to meet again when he came back from his assignment, and she returned to her flat, feeling exhausted. She opened the door to her small bedroom and switched on the light, and saw Trudy's little head staring up at her from her pillow.

SIXTEEN

BROCK STOOD AT THE window on the sixth floor of the headquarters building and stared impatiently out across the roofs to
his own office, two hundred yards away. The door opened behind
him and his boss, Commander Sharpe, strode in.

"Sorry to keep you, Brock. Lot to catch up on. So where were
we?"

"Personnel." Brock resumed his seat. "I think we've just about
finished."

"One other matter." Sharpe drew a document from his file and
handed it over. The letterhead was *Metropolitan Police Service: Di-
rectorate of Professional Standards*, and the subject title, "Complaint against Detective Inspector Katherine Kolla, Homicide and
Serious Crime Command." The complainant was Keith Rafferty,
represented by Julian Fenwick.

Brock skimmed the document, then handed it back.

"That's your copy, Brock. You're familiar with the circumstances?"

"Oh yes. The man's a thug, both him and his friend Crouch.
They were in the army together. Apart from the matters on his
police record, it's highly likely that they raped a woman in Belfast

DI Kolla had grounds for suspecting Rafferty's involvement in the death of his stepdaughter, Marion Summers."

"Yes, but Fenwick makes a strong case that she mishandled the investigation. You see there, where he charges her with provocation, intimidation, entrapment and fabricating evidence."

Brock was tired of this. He'd spent the past three weeks covering Sharpe's back. "Look, Dominic"—Sharpe looked startled, as if unaware that Brock even knew his first name—"Kolla is a first-rate officer and we've been working under extremely difficult circumstances while you were away, with an acute shortage of manpower. She used her initiative under intense pressure. This"—he waved the document—"is crap."

"Nevertheless, *David* . . ."—Sharpe gritted his teeth—"Fenwick has a habit of making such cases stick, as we know to our cost. He says he will seek an injunction if we don't immediately prevent Kolla from making further contact with Rafferty or Crouch, pending a full investigation of their complaint. I believe we should comply."

"That would be tantamount to an admission of fault."

"I don't agree. I think it would be a prudent precaution, and I want you to see to it."

Brock sighed. "Very well."

"There's no question of her being suspended from duty at this stage," Sharpe went on. "Just a transfer to other inquiries."

"A CAT'S HEAD IN your bed?" Bren raised his eyebrows. "Who's this, the kitty Godfather?"

"It's Keith Rafferty, that's who it is." Kathy glanced at Pip, who was listening with a look of disgust on her face. "His style, wouldn't you say, Pip?"

"Yeah, absolutely. What a creep. But how did he get into your flat?"

"Yes, how did he manage that?" Bren looked concerned.

"That's what I'd like to know. I've changed all the locks, and tried again to get our manager to install CCTV, but he says he's too heartbroken to deal with things like that at the moment. You should be careful, Pip. He might have a go at you too."

"Are you sure it's Rafferty?" Bren said.

Kathy shrugged. "Maybe it was just the tooth fairy having a bad day." She sighed and ran a hand over her face. "Look, I've been through it in my mind and I just don't see who else would want to have a shot at me like this."

"Maybe I should pay him a visit," Bren offered.

"No thanks, Bren," Kathy said. "That's probably exactly what he wants. Anyway, I'd better go. I've got a university laboratory to audit."

All the same, as she walked away the image of the tiny bloody head on her pillow came back to her, and she suppressed a shudder.

The laboratory staff were gathered in the front lobby of the building, whispering together in small clusters, watching the officers in protective clothing going in. Through the glass panels of the doors Kathy caught a glimpse of Sundeep Mehta with a clipboard, issuing instructions.

"So just how long is this going to take?" Colin Ringland's voice had become indignant. "It's extremely disruptive, and potentially dangerous and costly. We have experiments set up, work in progress."

"Have you spoken to Dr. Mehta, Dr. Ringland?"

"The Indian chap? He just breezed in and kicked everybody out. I tried to explain that we'd already sealed off the critical area, but he wouldn't listen."

Kathy got out her phone and rang Sundeep. Through the glass she saw him reach into his pocket. "Sundeep, it's Kathy. I'm outside with Dr. Ringland, the lab director. Can you spare a moment for a quick word?"

"Very well, Kathy. Give me a minute."

When Sundeep came out they went together to a small meeting room where Kathy recorded Ringland's litany of concerns and complaints, coaxing Sundeep to respond patiently. When they were finished, she remained with Ringland.

"Thanks," he said, mollified. "I suppose you've got a job to do. But I can't imagine how the Summers woman could have got her hands on any arsenic from our lab, I really can't."

Funny thing about language, Kathy thought, how it gives people away—*the Summers woman*. You'd never say, *the Ringland man*.

"I asked you before if someone else could have got it for her."

"Tony da Silva, that's what you mean, isn't it? Have you thought that she might have wanted you to think that?"

"How do you mean?"

"Tony told me that you were thinking she took the stuff deliberately. Maybe she wanted to implicate Tony while she was at it."

"Why would she want to do that?"

"Hah!" He gave a bitter laugh. "Because she was a manipulative bitch who was prepared to do anything to get her own way."

"Even kill herself?"

"Maybe she got the dose wrong. I told you before that she wasn't very good with figures."

"Yes you did, didn't you? But why implicate her supervisor?"

Ringland shrugged—rather evasively, Kathy thought. "I don't know. Out of spite, I suppose. They didn't always see eye to eye."

"I don't always see eye to eye with my boss, but I don't try to implicate him in my suicide."

"That's what I mean—she was unstable."

"You said manipulative, wanting to get her own way. So how was Dr. da Silva stopping her?"

He shook his head dismissively. "I'm just saying she gave him a [ ] of grief. She was a difficult student, okay? She demanded a lot [ ] attention. We all get them from time to time. She was a par- [ ]larly bad case."

"Did he sleep with her, Colin?"

"Christ!" Ringland rocked back in his seat. "Who told you [ ]t?"

Kathy smiled. "That's not really an answer, is it?"

"Look . . ." He was flustered now. "You'd have to ask Tony. I certainly don't believe so, and you'd be advised to take student gossip with a grain of salt."

"Or a grain of arsenic." Kathy got to her feet. "Thanks for your help, and for your patience with our audit. We'll get out of your hair as soon as we can."

She was stepping out the front door when her phone rang, and once again she heard the excited, slightly breathless voice of the librarian, Gael Rayner.

"Kathy! Sorry, but we've had another incident."

"Another one?"

"Yes, an assault, right here in the library stacks."

"What kind of assault? Not another poisoning?"

"No, much more physical. Someone just attacked Nigel Ogilvie. One of the other readers heard the commotion and found him, unconscious. I rang triple nine for an ambulance, and now you. I thought you'd want to know."

"Yes, of course. I'm on my way."

The ambulance was parked outside the library's front door on St. James's Square when Kathy arrived, the stretcher being loaded into the back.

She showed her ID. "How is he?"

"Heavy bruising, cuts, probable concussion and fractured ribs and radius. He was conscious when we arrived, said he'd fallen down the stairs, but that's not how it looks."

"Okay." Kathy checked the motionless figure in the neck brace, eyes closed. "Where are you taking him?"

"UCLH."

Gael Rayner opened the front door of the library and waved Kathy in. "We locked all the doors after I phoned you, just in case the assailant was still here. I wasn't sure if that was the right thing to do." Her eyes were bright with excitement.

"That's fine. Tell me what happened."

Gael led her in through a crowd of chattering readers in the entrance hall. "One of our members, a Mr. Vujkovic, was in the stacks and heard an argument on the floor below. Then there was a cry and a crash. He went down to investigate, although he's not a very agile man, so it took him a little time. He found Nigel lying among a pile of books that had fallen out of the shelves."

They hurried back through the library to the book stacks, to where several elderly men were standing in a cluster at the foot of a flight of stairs, beside a tumbled heap of books scattered across the floor. One of the men was introduced as Mr. Vujkovic, and he shuffled forward and repeated the story in broken English.

"The ambulance officer told me that Nigel said he'd fallen down the stairs," Kathy said.

"No, no," Mr. Vujkovic said. "There was much struggle, much argument. Maybe push down stair, yes, okay, but not fall."

"Was he arguing with a man, or a woman?"

"I think man. I couldn't see. Nigel scream like pig in slaughter-house."

Two uniformed officers had arrived, and Kathy sent them off to search the building, guided by one of the librarians. She looked around at the scene. There was blood on the steel grille floor, and also traces of sand on the bottom step of the staircase.

"Do the builders come up here, Gael?"

"No, they shouldn't."

"But if we go down a level we'd come to the door out to the area where they're working, is that right? Show me."

They went down the next flight and emerged into a corridor. Along the floor Kathy found other traces of sand and cement dust. They came to the door that Gael had let Kathy in by the previous week when she'd come to interview Nigel Ogilvie. It was un-locked. Kathy pushed it open and walked out into the passageway beside the building site, following it to the open entrance gates. The site hut was nearby, and fixed to its parapet was a security camera covering the site entry and street outside. She knocked on the door, and explained to the site manager what had happened.

"This was about forty minutes ago," she said.

"No problem."

He fiddled with the machine in the corner of his office, and then replayed it backwards.

"There!" They watched as a white van materialised across the courtyard, and a man ran backwards out of it and into the library's compound. Running the recording further back they established that the white van had arrived fifteen minutes earlier. The image of the driver, wearing overalls and a peaked cap, was indistinct, but Kathy was able to make out the van's number. It took one phone call to establish that it belonged to Brentford Pyrotechnics.

THE TYRES SQUEALED AS Kathy turned into the car park of the fireworks factory, the blue light pulsing. She pulled up at the office entrance and marched into the reception area. A girl at the front desk jumped as she demanded to see Mr. Pigeon, and hurried to the door of the adjoining office. The manager appeared, greeting her with a cautious smile, and led her into his room.

"Another query, Inspector?"

She handed him the number of the van taken from the CCTV. "Is this your van, Mr. Pigeon?"

He studied the slip of paper. "I think that may be one of ours. Why?"

"I'd like to know who the driver is and where it is now."

"Is this a traffic matter? Has it been in an accident?"

"If you could just answer my questions, please."

Pigeon frowned, then seeing the look on Kathy's face lifted the phone and dialled an internal number. After a short conversation he said, "The driver is Keith Rafferty. He left about an hour and a half ago to take a consignment out to a job in Epping, due back after lunch, around two. Now, may I ask what this is all about?"

"Your van was recorded just over an hour ago at an address in Central London at the time of a serious assault. The driver was filmed going into the building where the assault took place."

"My goodness. You suspect Keith?"

"You know he has a criminal record, do you?"

Pigeon's eyebrows rose. "I can't say I was aware of that, no. One moment."

He went over to a filing cabinet and withdrew a file. There were a couple of pages inside. "No, there's no mention of a record. Was it serious, what he did?"

"Assault, living off immoral earnings. He did gaol time. There was also a rape case that was dropped for lack of evidence."

"Oh dear. I had no idea. He had a very glowing reference from a security consultant . . ." he scanned one of the pages, "by the name of Crouch."

"Yes, they were in the army together. Crouch was also implicated in the alleged rape."

"Oh. Well, that is most disturbing. So you want to interview Keith?"

"I certainly do, but I'm also interested in another matter, possibly connected. You remember when I was here before that we talked about the security of your chemicals?"

"Of course, and I showed you our clearance documents and our latest security vetting."

"We didn't discuss the possibility of one of your own employees removing material."

"Yes, but I told you, deliveries are weighed and recorded as they arrive and the use of all chemicals carefully tracked and accounted for."

"What about a delivery driver, maybe helping himself to small quantities from shipments *before* they're checked in? Would that be possible?"

Pigeon's mouth opened to protest, then a little cloud of doubt passed over his eyes. "Well, I'd say no, but I suppose I could check. You think Keith Rafferty . . . ?"

"I'd appreciate it if you would keep this to yourself for the moment, Mr. Pigeon. He may have had a friend in the laboratory who would cover up for him. I think it would be a good idea if you carried out your own checks and got back to me, preferably within the next twenty-four hours."

"I see. Well, yes, I'll see what I can do."

As she got back into her car, Kathy had a call from Brock.

"Kathy? Where are you?"

She explained about the assault at the London Library and her trip out to the fireworks factory. "I'm going to arrest Rafferty as soon as he gets back."

There was an ominous pause, then Brock said, "No. I want you back here, Kathy. Quick as you can."

"But—"

"Quick as you can, Kathy." The line went dead.

SEVENTEEN

"BREN TOLD ME ABOUT the cat," Brock said.

"Yes, well, you can understand how I feel then." Kathy sat rigid in the seat facing him across his desk, knowing he could see her anger blazing like a beacon, a part of her regretting this unfamiliar feeling of rebellion against him, another part relishing it.

"All the more reason for you to drop it," Brock said. "He's trying to goad you, make you step over the line. Don't worry, he's not going to get away with it. I'm going to put Bren onto the Ogilvie assault."

"No!" Startled at the vehemence of her own reaction, Kathy felt the blood rush to her head. She bit her lip, then continued, more measured, "He doesn't have the background."

"Then you'll have to give it to him." Brock sat back in his chair, studying her. "How do you see it, then, Kathy? Do you think Rafferty killed Marion?"

She hesitated. "I don't know. Oh, he's capable of it, and we know he likes tampering with girls' drinks. It's also possible that he raped her and made her pregnant, but there's the business of the unknown benefactor who stumped up three quarters of a million for her house."

"You have a suspect?"

"Her supervisor, Dr. Anthony da Silva, a flirt with his students, married to a wealthy lawyer, living conveniently close to Marion's new house. It's even possible he had Rafferty working for him, doing his dirty work."

"That'd be a risky business relationship," Brock mused. "Why the attack on Ogilvie?"

"I think he knows more than he told us—maybe something he picked up from snooping around Marion. Maybe da Silva got Rafferty to persuade Ogilvie to keep quiet."

"That's possible, I suppose." The atmosphere in the room had relaxed a little. "Brief Bren, Kathy. Get him to follow it up. As for Marion, if we really have got a murder on our hands, rather than a suicide, I'd like to get Alex Nicholson to take another look. Why don't you draw up a profiler briefing for her. Keep it simple— victimology, scene, forensics—you know the form."

Kathy nodded.

"Then concentrate on Interpol. Maybe you should go over to see them at Lyons. Have you ever been?"

She shook her head, feeling sorry that he felt he had to offer her a little treat in compensation. "I'll speak to Bren."

He was a solid, dependable detective, who'd got her out of trouble on more than one occasion, and she knew she could rely on him. He listened patiently to her briefing, asked a few pertinent clarifiers, and gave a brisk nod. "I'll take him apart, Kathy, don't worry."

"Well, watch your back, Bren. Remember there's two of them, him and Crouch."

"They won't even know it's happening until it's too late."

"How are you going to do that?"

"Don't know yet." He gave her a benign smile; one he'd picked up from Brock, she thought.

She returned to her desk and drew up a summary of the Marion Summers case, which she emailed to Alex Nicholson, then forced herself to concentrate on the Interpol requests. It wasn't as if they weren't interesting—a fugitive Australian con man thought to have slipped into Britain on a tourist bus from Holland, a Bulgarian people-trafficker believed to be hiding from vengeful colleagues he had cheated, a Russian couple who had probably abducted a missing child. She picked up the phone and got back to following the lines of inquiry she'd already begun, putting Keith Rafferty and Nigel Ogilvie out of her mind.

That evening, as people began to stretch and yawn and reach for their coats, Bren came and sat on the edge of her desk.

"Ogilvie is sitting up in his hospital bed, enjoying the attention of the nurses. He insists that he lost his footing on the stairs while he was carrying a pile of books and that there was no one else involved. The witness, Mr. Vujkovic, and the doctor say otherwise. The doc showed me pictures he took while he was dressing the wounds—you can actually see the print of someone's boot on his thigh and shoulder. But Ogilvie won't change his story. I showed him Rafferty's picture and he feigned ignorance, but you could tell he was scared shitless. I don't think he's going to change his tune, unless we can get to the bottom of what's been going on from some other angle."

"What about Rafferty? Did you speak to him?"

"Yes. He didn't deny that he'd gone to the rear of the London Library. He said someone who wouldn't give his name phoned him and asked to meet him there, concerning Marion's death. But when he got there no one showed up, and after ten minutes he left without seeing anyone. His knuckles were grazed and slightly swollen—from carting boxes, he said." Bren smiled grimly. "Leave it with me."

A bit later Pip came by Kathy's desk.

"Sorry, boss," she said, head down, contrite. "This is all my fault."

"Swings and roundabouts, Pip. All in a day's work. How are you going?"

"Oh, good. I'm working with the boys on a series of bank robberies involving fatal shootings."

"Well, you take care."

"It's all right. I'm not usually so stupid." She hesitated, fiddling with a file in her hand. "I did finish off one little job you gave me. Do you want it, or should I give it to DI Gurney?"

"What is it?"

"The posy of white flowers Marion had." She opened the file. "*Cistaceae*, of the rock rose family." She offered Kathy a sheet with photographs and information on the plant taken, Kathy noted, from the Internet.

"Oh . . . well done."

Pip handed her another sheet. "In the Victorian language of flowers, the gum cistus of the *Cistaceae* plant family symbolised imminent death. Literally it meant, *I shall die tomorrow.*"

"And that's exactly what she did. You think it was some kind of message from someone?"

"Could be."

"Any idea where they could have come from?"

"Not really. You see the five petals around the yellow stamens in the centre?" She handed Kathy an enlargement of the photo Gael had sent over.

"Yes?"

"We should get an expert to look at them, but from what I've been able to find out, they're *Cistus monspeliensis*, Montpellier cistus. It's a wild flower."

"Montpellier?" Kathy said. "The south of France?"

"That's right, that's where they're most common. But where would you find them in London?"

But Kathy was thinking that Corsica was off the south coast of France. The place had cropped up in Brock's notes of his meeting with Sophie Warrender, and again when Kathy had checked where Tom Reeves had disappeared to. Calvi, it turned out, was also in Corsica. It seemed like a sign of some kind, or more likely one of those coincidences that just happen.

Pip said, "Shall I give this to Bren?"

"No, leave it with me. We don't want to confuse things. Thanks." She gave Pip a little smile and she grinned back.

"Sure, boss."

As Kathy was getting ready to leave for the night, she decided to ring Donald Fotheringham to see how he was getting on with Tina.

"Like a house on fire, Inspector."

"Really?" Kathy tried to imagine it. They seemed the most unlikely of companions. "That's good."

"Aye. She's an interesting lassie, and a good friend to Marion. I was afraid at first that we wouldnae hit it off. I spoke to her flatmate, a girl called Jummai, who seemed to feel that we wouldn't, but all went well after I explained to Tina that I just wanted to get to the bottom of what happened to Marion. After that she agreed to let me help her."

"Doing what?"

"Well, she believes that Marion's death has something to do with the work she was doing for her thesis."

"Did she explain how? It doesn't seem very likely, surely?"

"Aye, that was my feeling too, and she didn't really explain, but I went along with it, because I wanted to learn more about Marion's life down here. And to tell you the truth, I've been finding it all very interesting."

"What have you been doing?"

"We've been at the British Library, following the trail of Marion's book requests. Tina has Marion's reader's card, and seems to be able to access her records."

Kathy wondered where she'd got that from.

"When we get the books we work together, reading, looking for references that might mean something. She has a list of key words."

He sounded so enthusiastic that she wondered if he'd been looking for an excuse not to go back home. Well, Kathy thought, at least it'll keep them both out of trouble. She couldn't imagine Keith Rafferty having much problem with what they were doing. "And did you find anything?"

"We only started today, and to be perfectly honest I can't see where it will lead, but at least it gives me a chance to chat to her about Marion." He paused, and his voice took on a more loaded tone. Kathy thought the Scottish word would have been *canny*. "She mentioned that you had shown her Marion's new home, Inspector. Very nice, she said, in a pricey part of town. I wondered how she could have afforded it."

"We've been wondering the same thing, Donald. Apparently the estate agent believed she had come into an inheritance, from a Scottish relative with business interests in Switzerland."

"Switzerland!" Fotheringham exploded. "The only Swiss interests in the family that I'm aware of is Bessie's cuckoo clock. I'll check with Bessie when I call her tonight, but I hadn't heard of a death in the family lately, and if there had been I'd be very surprised if there was any money involved."

KATHY CAUGHT THE TUBE back to Finchley Central and walked through darkened suburban streets towards her home. There had been rain, and water dripped from branches overhanging the pavement and hissed beneath the tyres of passing cars. She hesitated as her block came into view, scanning the shadows for the shape of a human figure When she reached the light of the front door to the lobby, she checked back over her shoulder before turning her key in the lock. There was a single envelope waiting in her scrubbed-out mailbox, with Jock's handwritten scrawl of her name on the front. Inside were sets of keys, a note from the locksmith explaining what they'd done, and a bill.

She caught herself holding her breath as she stood in the lift waiting for the doors to close, as if half expecting someone to leap in at the last moment. The same when the doors slid open at her floor. There were two new locks on her door, and she fiddled with the keys, feeling like a gaoler. She went into the silent flat, checking it quickly, then took off her clothes and had a shower.

Afterwards, feeling a little easier, she boiled some pasta and added a jar of sauce from the fridge.

Brock was protecting her, she told herself, not from Rafferty but from herself. He was still convinced that she was identifying with Marion in a way that was disturbing her judgement. But their stories weren't the same. Unlike Marion, whose early life had been disrupted, poverty-stricken and possibly abused, she had grown up in a perfectly happy, protected middle-class family in the London suburbs. It was only at the age of twelve that things had veered dramatically off-course. On a hot summer's afternoon her father, that proud, rather distant and intimidating figure, had driven his car into the support structure of a bridge on the M1. The ensuing investigation revealed that he had not only corruptly abused his civil service position to aid property developers, but had also invested everything the family owned in a failed business deal. Abruptly Kathy's childhood, seen now as a golden haze of lost innocence, was over. Her mother, affectionate but weak, was unable to cope. Together they moved up to Sheffield to live with Aunt Mary and Uncle Tom by the steelworks in Attercliffe.

It was the failing mother/rescuing aunt part that had struck Brock, Kathy supposed, that and her escaping back to London at the first opportunity. But otherwise their stories were quite different. Her own mother had barely survived the move and died soon after, and her own school career in Sheffield had been less than glorious, her escape route the police force rather than university.

All the same . . . She stared at Marion's picture on the wall. And perhaps the differences between them made it impossible for Kathy to get inside that other mind. The academic stuff, for instance, the historical research that Tina seemed to think so important, what chance did Kathy have of finding her way through that? Tina must have da Silva in mind, she thought. Could da Silva, the pompous, opinionated tutor with whom Marion had apparently quarrelled, have been her lover?

Kathy had added a few more trophies to her wall alongside the images from the previous night. A picture of the unknown Victorian woman was there now, taken from the SOCO pictures, and another of Montpellier cistus, though what these images meant, and how they were related, wasn't clear to her.

But Donald Fotheringham had mentioned Tina's list of key words, and it occurred to her that it might help her too to navigate Marion's mind. She searched through a pile of papers on her table and found it again, a list of seventeen items, the first ten of which were people's names. Some of the names were up there on the enlarged photograph of Marion's pinboard, and with the help of Tony da Silva's biography of Rossetti, Kathy was able to work up a few notes on their stories and relationships to the central figure of Rossetti.

Lizzie Siddal was his sickly wife, the model for Millais's *Ophelia*; Rossetti married her in 1860 after a protracted relationship when it appeared that she was on the point of death. She had survived another couple of years before taking the fatal dose of laudanum.

Janey Morris, née Burden, the wife of William Morris, was the great love of Rossetti's life, with whom he was infatuated for about twenty years until they broke off their affair in 1877. She was also a model for the Pre-Raphaelites, painted over a hundred times by Rossetti.

Fanny Cornforth was another of Rossetti's models and his mistress, and he was reputed to have also had a "flirtation" with Annie Miller, who posed for Holman Hunt's painting *The Awakening Conscience*. This painting, reproduced in da Silva's book, showed Annie as a Victorian woman caught rising from the lap of a gentleman visitor in a living room furnished in plush Victorian style, rather, Kathy thought, like Marion's own back room. Most striking was a large mirror on the wall behind the guilty couple, reflecting their awkward pose from behind. It had a gilt frame, very similar to the one in Marion's bedroom, almost as if she'd composed her own interior to reflect Holman Hunt's scene of adulterous temptation.

All of these names could be found on Marion's pinboard, connected by a web of scarlet threads, as well as many others: Edward

Burne-Jones linked with Georgiana Burne-Jones as well as Maria Zambaco; William Holman Hunt with Annie Miller and also Fanny Waugh and Edith Waugh. Kathy began to see the board as a mapping of the complicated amorous entanglements of the group—some legitimate, others secret and adulterous.

But the other names on Tina's checklist, the Wardles, Smiths and Haverlock, were not on Marion's pinboard, although small images of all three of the paintings on the list were there.

Kathy referred again to the extensive index at the back of da Silva's book and found *Wardle, George*. She turned to the reference and read:

George Wardle was associated with William Morris between 1865 and 1889, becoming manager of Morris and Company and acting as a steadying influence on Morris's business ventures. He and his wife Lena Wardle became part of the wider Pre-Raphaelite circle following their marriage in 1861, the year in which Morris, Marshall, Faulkner and Company was founded. Lena was notorious as the Scottish poisoner Madeleine Smith, who came to London after her acquittal in Glasgow for the murder of Pierre Emile L'Angelier in 1858. Her history was well known within the Pre-Raphaelite circle; at the time of her trial, Rossetti, upon seeing her portrait in a newspaper, declared that she would never be hanged as she was a *stunner*, their favourite term of approbation for an attractive young woman, potentially a model. Later, when she had moved to London and married Wardle, Rossetti wrote a satirical short play for the private amusement of Jane Morris, in which Lena Wardle poisons William Morris in order for her husband George to acquire the company.

Kathy stared at the words *the Scottish poisoner*, and had a feeling that she had discovered the identity of the unnamed woman on Marion's board. A few minutes on the Internet confirmed it. There were dozens of references to Madeleine Smith on the web, providing various photographs and drawings that had been made of her and recounting her story.

Madeleine Smith first met Emile L'Angelier in 1855 through a mutual friend in Glasgow. Madeleine was an attractive twenty-year-old, the granddaughter of one of Glasgow's best-known architects. Emile was twelve years older, a French Channel Islander who had been travelling in Scotland on the lookout for an advantageous marriage to a well-connected young woman. He had already spent some time cultivating a lady in Fife, without success. He now focused on Madeleine, who was swept off her feet, entering into a secret affair with him which lasted for eighteen months. Eventually Madeleine began to cool. Realising that her family would never agree to a match with Emile, and being now pursued by a much more eligible man, she told Emile that she wanted to end the relationship, and asked for the return of the hundreds of love letters she had given him. He refused and said that he would never allow her to marry another man. Under Scottish law at that time, a woman who had sexual intercourse with a man, and who stated her intention to marry him, both of which Madeleine had confirmed in her letters, was technically regarded as already his wife. Madeleine begged him to be reasonable, and during the course of March 1857 they continued to have nocturnal meetings at the window of her house, during which she gave him cups of coffee and cocoa. He complained several times to his landlady of feeling ill after these meetings, and following their final meeting on the twenty-third of March he collapsed and died. The cause of death was established as arsenic poisoning, Madeleine was found to have bought several batches of the poison, and she was arrested and brought to trial.

The trial of Madeleine Smith was one of the great murder trials of Victorian Britain, Kathy learned, and continued to provoke debate. Some saw her as a rich, promiscuous psychopath, others as the victim of a ruthless predator. Her sympathisers speculated that Emile, when he finally realised that he was going to lose Madeleine as he had the lady in Fife, committed suicide by himself taking arsenic, leaving a trail of diary notes and conversations with his landlady to implicate his lover. Others suggested that he had indeed poisoned himself, but never intended death, hoping instead to move Madeleine to change her mind. They pointed to the fact that Madeleine was quite open about buying the poison, which was not uncommon in those days, and that Emile's first diary entry alleging poisoning predated her earliest purchase.

Madeleine was defended by a brilliant and eloquent advocate, who nevertheless privately believed her guilty. The jury decided otherwise, bringing down the peculiar Scottish verdict of *Not Proven*, which one wit described as meaning "Not guilty, but don't do it again."

Well, it had happened again, or something rather similar. Kathy sat back, looking over the notes she'd made. The tale resonated so strikingly with Marion's own that it was impossible to ignore, but what did it mean? That Marion had become obsessed by the Victorian woman and killed herself in some kind of macabre parody of Madeleine's story? Or that someone else had killed Marion, in such a way that she would understand exactly what was happening to her? The thought was chilling: a coded murder that only Marion would have been able to interpret.

The buzzer of Kathy's entryphone sounded, the sudden noise making her jump.

"Hello?"

"Hi, Kathy?" She thought she recognised the voice through the electric crackle, and her heart gave a little thump. "It's me—Guy. Hi. I've got something for you. Is this a bad time?"

"No, hello, Guy. You want to come up?"

"If that's okay. Twelfth floor?"

"That's it." She pressed the button to unlock the front door, cleared the remains of her dinner and went out to the lobby to meet him.

The lift sighed to a stop and he stepped through the doors with a big grin, clutching a bunch of daffodils. His cheek felt cool, his coat damp from a light drizzle.

"Come in."

"Are you okay? I've been worrying about you, after that cat. Any developments?"

She didn't tell him about the head on her pillow, and changed the subject. "Lovely flowers!"

"I noticed you didn't have any in your flat. Maybe you don't like them?"

"I love them. I'm just too lazy to buy any. Let me put them in water. Take off your coat and help yourself to a glass of wine. Have you eaten?"

"I grabbed a sandwich at work. My time's all mixed up at the moment, waiting for the word to go."

She noticed that he was edgy, unable to keep still. "Still nothing?"

"No, they keep delaying. How about you? We could go out to eat if you like."

"I had something too. I've just been doing some homework."

"I see that." He was twisting his head, looking down at the printouts about Madeleine Smith. "Um, 1857? Aren't you a bit late to solve this one? Ah . . ." He looked at the wall. "I see you've got some more pictures for your network. That's what I came to give you."

He pulled a disk from his pocket and offered it to her. "We can load it onto your laptop and set up a generic network for you to play with. You can scan in your images and make different kinds of linkages, groups, whatever you like. You want me to set something up?"

She didn't really think she'd use it—she preferred being able to look up at the things on the wall whenever she was passing—but she liked that he wanted to do this for her. She stood behind him, watching, as he sat at the table and played with the machine, and then, when he'd got something working to his satisfaction, she pulled a seat up beside him and followed his instructions. As she got used to the system, she did have to admit that it was neat, however she didn't have a scanner in the flat, and most of the images weren't on her computer, so they came to a dead end.

"I'll get you a scanner," he said.

She laughed. "You can't do that."

"They're dirt cheap. Call it a birthday present."

"Bring me one back from the Gulf," she said, "and I'll pay you back."

He went over to the images on the wall. "But you have some flowers. What are they?"

"Wild flowers from France, apparently, but what they mean, I don't know."

"But you'll find out, eh? Hot on the trail." He laughed, a nice warm laugh. It was a long time since she'd heard anyone laughing here, she thought.

He must have seen the frown on her face, for she suddenly realised he was staring at her. "You're very self-possessed, aren't you?" he said.

"Am I? You too, yes?"

"Me? Oh, I don't know . . ." He came over and sat beside her on the sofa. "I sometimes feel I don't know what I am anymore."

"How do you mean?"

"Well, if you're serious about your job—as you are, as I am—you have to let it shape you, don't you think? I mean, you may start out with certain qualities and that's why they pick you, but then the job develops them, exaggerates them, so you can perform. Like, I have to go onto a big project site, where thousands of guys are slaving away, twenty-four hours a day, to meet their deadlines, and I maybe have to go up to this bloody great concrete thing they've just finished and say, 'No, that's not good enough, you have to tear it down and do it again.' I know they're going to argue and try to twist my arm, and I know I can't step back, I can't feel sorry for them, because that's my job. They think I'm this hard bastard, but I'm not really. It's just the person I have to be in that situation. Well, hell, it must be the same for you, right?"

She nodded.

"That wouldn't be so bad," he went on, "if it was just like a suit of armour that you could step out of at the end of the day, and be yourself again. But it isn't like that, is it? It's become part of you, this other character, you've changed to make room for it . . . Sorry, I'm going on a bit."

"No, it's true, what you say. I'm just the same. Right now my boss is telling me to forget about Marion Summers. He thinks I'm getting too involved. I tell myself he's wrong, but here I am, sitting in my flat trying to get inside her head. What kind of life is that?"

"Exactly. I think what I'm trying to say is that I sometimes wish I could just have my old self back, because then it would be easier to tell you how good it feels, just sitting here, talking to you."

She reached out her hand to his, then leaned forward and kissed him gently on the mouth. Later she led him into her bedroom. The sheets and pillows had been replaced, but she still had a mental image of the cat's head. She needed him to wipe it away.

EIGHTEEN

THAT SAME EVENING, SUZANNE returned to the bookshop in Notting Hill. She almost hadn't come—there weren't convenient trains and the thought of driving up to London for a brief and probably unrewarding talk was unwelcome. But she was intrigued by the thought of seeing Dougie's wife in the flesh, and in the end she had decided to make the trip. She felt slightly guilty about being in town without telling David, but he might have wanted to come too, and she'd felt obscurely embarrassed by the idea. This was part of her sentimental journey down memory lane, she told herself, probably the end of it, and she avoided asking herself if she hoped Dougie might be there, though surely there was little chance of that.

But he was there, she saw, as soon as she opened the door and stepped inside. At first she was slightly dazzled by the light, then there he was, standing in a group beside a pyramid of his wife's books, glass of wine in hand. She recognised him instantly, although when she came to register the details—thinning dark hair slicked back, fleshy jowls, pouchy eyes, heavy build—they were nothing like the teenage Dougie of memory. But those middle-aged features couldn't hide the dark magnetic eyes, the curling smile of the lips, the interrogating tilt of the head she remembered so vividly. The impact was so immediate and so breathtaking that she actually had to turn away and lean against the end of a bookcase until she had calmed down a little. She didn't approach him, but handed over her ticket and took a glass of wine, then concentrated on examining the bookshelves furthest from the group until the bookshop manager called for people to take their seats. She sat near the back at the end of an empty row, and focused on a novel she'd picked out, and so didn't recognise the elderly lady with a stick who came in late, helped by a younger woman. Suzanne looked up and gave an automatic smile which faltered when she saw that it was Joan Warrender, Dougie's mother, taking the place beside her. Lady Warrender smiled back, then gave a little frown, as if trying to remember why the face was familiar. Then her eyes became sharp. "Why, hello again."

"Hello, Lady Warrender," Suzanne murmured, feeling her face colouring, as if she'd been caught stealing apples from the old lady's tree, or something equally absurd.

"Ladies and gentlemen, readers, lovers of fine books . . ." The woman by the pyramid of biographies called for their attention and began a glowing introduction to the author. Dougie had sat down somewhere at the front, and Suzanne couldn't see him. There was applause, then Sophie Warrender got to her feet.

"How pleasant to know Mr. Lear," she began.

"He reads, but he does not speak, Spanish,
  He cannot abide ginger beer;
  Ere the days of his pilgrimage vanish,
  How pleasant to know Mr. Lear!"

Sophie smiled at the gathering. "Edward Lear's autobiographical poem said it all for me. Getting to know him through researching and writing his life was indeed a very pleasant experience."

The talk was followed by questions. How did she pick her subjects? How long did it take her to do the research? Who were her own favourite authors? Then it was announced that she would sign copies of her books, and the audience began to get to their feet.

"You must come and meet Dougie," Joan Warrender said, with a glint of what might have been mischief in her eye.

"Oh no, I don't want to intrude."

"Nonsense. Of course you must, after all these years." Joan Warrender turned to the young woman at her side. "This is my granddaughter, Emily. Emily, meet an old friend of your father's, um . . ."

"Suzanne Chambers. How do you do, Emily." They shook hands, and Suzanne reluctantly followed them as they slowly made their way through the throng to the front of the room.

Douglas Warrender was standing near the table at which his wife was seated, signing her books. He was talking to the book-shop manager who, Suzanne suspected from her animated gestures and smiles, rather fancied him. She wasn't really surprised, for despite the years he still had the powerful physical presence she had found so overwhelming that summer long ago. Her heart beat a little faster as she allowed herself to be led forward.

"Dougie!" Joan interrupted peremptorily. "I've got someone you must meet. A childhood sweetheart."

"What?" He turned to look at them with an amused expression on his face, and then his eyes snagged on Suzanne's and they gazed at each other. "Good Lord," he said softly. "Is it . . . ?"

"Suzanne," she said brightly, a little too loud, before he could make a mistake. "Suzanne Chambers. I was Angela Crick's friend."

He stared at her for a moment, then said, "I want to hold your hand." They all stared at him in astonishment. Suzanne, startled, was dimly aware of his wife pausing in her signing and looking up at them.

"Remember?" he said.

Then she gave a laugh, remembering vividly, and said, "Anyone who had a heart."

"Can't buy me love," he replied, with a big, wicked smile.

"Don't throw your love away. Oh, Dougie. I do remember."

The others still weren't sure, too young, or in Joan's case too old, to remember the hits of 1964.

"So how do you know my father?" Emily broke in.

"I stayed in the house next door to yours for a couple of months, with a school friend who lived there."

"But there was something else, wasn't there?" Joan said, again with that edge in her voice. "Oh, that's right, you're the wife of the detective who called about Marion. Do you remember, Dougie, last Saturday, that man?"

The smile on Dougie's face froze.

"We're friends," Suzanne said quickly. "Not married."

"Oh, sorry," Joan went on relentlessly. "But that was how you came to call at the house on Monday, wasn't it?"

"Monday?" Douglas said. Sophie's pen had stopped, suspended over a book, while she listened.

"I was in Notting Hill, and after hearing my friend mention that he'd met your wife, whose work I admire so much, and realising it was the same house I used to know, I couldn't resist seeing it again. Lady Warrender was in the garden, and very kindly invited me in."

"I see," Douglas said carefully. "And now you're here."

"Yes. As I said, I'm a great fan of Sophie's." She glanced at Sophie, who was now distracted by an enthusiastic reader haranguing her about a very interesting great-grandfather, ripe for biography.

"Well, you must meet her." Douglas's poise had returned. "Have a glass of wine with us while she finishes off that queue. So what are you up to these days?"

Emily was whispering in her grandmother's ear and pointing to the gardening section, and the two of them moved away, leaving Suzanne alone with Douglas. She accepted the glass he offered and told him a little about her shop in Battle, and he seemed genuinely interested.

"So how come you know this copper?"

"Oh, I've known David for ages."

"Just good friends, eh?"

"Yes." She gave a casual laugh, and silently asked Brock to forgive her.

"What was the girl next door called again?"

"Angela Crick."

"I can't picture her."

"Long straight blond hair, quite pretty. Your cousin Jack was madly in love with her, do you remember?" She didn't add that she had also been madly in love that summer. She wondered how much he did remember.

"Oh, Jack, of course!" He grinned. "I remember now. And have you kept up with Angela?"

"No, haven't heard of her for ages. How about Jack? What's he doing now?"

"Ah, he died, I'm afraid. Massive heart attack, ten years ago."

"Oh, I'm so sorry."

"God, I need a drink." Sophie had appeared at Douglas's shoulder, and was regarding Suzanne keenly.

"Of course, darling. I want you to meet someone I used to know, a very long time ago."

He made introductions, then Suzanne had to explain her presence once again while he found Sophie a glass.

"So you were an old girlfriend of Dougie's? And you came into the house on Monday, did you?" She had a faint smile, but made it sound dubious. "I'm afraid it was probably a mess. We're still trying to get the place straight after a major renovation."

"No, it looked lovely," Suzanne said lamely. "I had such fond memories of it, the high ceilings, the elephant's foot in the hall . . ."

"The what?"

She explained, feeling more and more uncomfortable talking about Sophie's own house from a time before she knew it, as if Suzanne were claiming some prior knowledge.

"How disgusting."

Suzanne assumed she was referring to the elephant's foot, and was relieved when Douglas reappeared with Sophie's wine. He seemed offhand now. "Get that down, old thing," he said abruptly, looking at his watch, "and then we really must go. God, these things are a bore." Then he caught his wife's eye. "Not you, darling. You were brilliant, as always."

"Yes," Suzanne said. "Absolutely gripping."

"Nice to meet you again," Douglas said, offering his hand. "Good luck with the antiques business." Then he took his wife's arm. "Let's round up the others."

NINETEEN

"YOU SOUND HAPPY."

Kathy looked up at Bren's voice. She realised she'd been humming to herself. "Oh." She grinned. "I'm all right. How about you?"

"Spring flu," he said, looking exhausted. "Not me, so far. Working its way through the family."

"Oh dear. The girls?"

He nodded wearily.

"How's it going with Rafferty?"

He shook his head. "Nothing much, except that he does seem to spend a hell of a lot on the horses. How's Interpol?"

"Interesting." She knew he was running two other cases, and didn't press.

"You should wangle a trip to Lyons," he said, moving off, then gave a violent sneeze.

She did feel happy. It was amazing, really, how a little thing could change the whole way you felt. Well, it hadn't been that little . . .

But she still felt impatient about Marion's case. She had worked out that, of the ten people on Tina's list of key words, five had been connected with "the Scottish poisoner"—there was Lena Wardle and Madeleine Smith herself, then her husband George

Wardle, and James Smith, who had attended and been a witness at her wedding, and finally H. Haverlock, whom she had discovered to be the other witness. At some point she was going to have to talk to da Silva, but she wanted to go armed and prepared, knowing the right questions to ask, the right weaknesses to probe.

She remembered the letter Marion had received from the American university, and wondered if they might have some information. It was too early to phone them, and she made a note to try that afternoon. For an hour she worked on her Interpol files, then put her pen down. It occurred to her that Sophie Warrender should be able to throw some light on the Madeleine Smith angle, and picked up the phone. The author seemed less friendly than when they'd met at Marion's house, but she agreed to meet Kathy at her home in Notting Hill in an hour. On impulse Kathy looked her up on Google, where her eye was also caught by an entry for Douglas Warrender. It referred to a speech he'd given at a banking conference, and gave a reference to his company, Mallory Capital, with an address in St. James's Square.

KATHY WAS IMPRESSED BY the house when she caught sight of it along Lansdowne Gardens, its new paintwork gleaming beneath a blue spring sky. When she rang the doorbell it was answered by a woman who introduced herself as Rhonda Bailey, Sophie's secretary, and led her across a hall and down a passage lined with green wallpaper printed with a pattern she thought similar to the William Morris designs illustrated in da Silva's book.

Sophie was on the phone, arguing with someone about a publicity campaign, and Rhonda showed Kathy to a seat and offered her a cup from a pot on the coffee table, then returned to her keyboard.

After a while Sophie slammed the phone down and turned to Rhonda. "Bloody idiot. How does he expect to expand sales if they won't invest a little in publicity?" She took off her glasses and stood up, coming over to Kathy. She seemed agitated and didn't offer her hand. "So, what can I do for you, Inspector?"

"There were a couple of little things I thought you might be able to clear up. Sorry, I can see you're very busy. Would you like me to come back later?"

Sophie waved a dismissive hand. "No, no. Now's as good a time as any."

"Well, first of all, I know I asked this before, but are you absolutely sure you didn't inadvertently take a copy of Anthony da Silva's Rossetti biography from Marion's house?"

She watched Sophie's hackles rise again. "Absolutely not! I already have that book—it's over there—and neither I nor Emily removed it. What's so bloody important about it anyway?"

"Sorry, I just have to account for everything. It really doesn't matter. Can I ask you if you recognise this woman?" She handed over the photograph of Madeleine Smith.

Sophie glanced briefly at it. "No. Why?"

"Her name was Madeleine Smith, and she married William Morris's manager, George Wardle."

"Oh, the murderess. Yes, I know who you mean. What are you after?"

"It seems Marion was very interested in her, and since she had been accused of poisoning her lover with arsenic . . ."

"Oh, the morbid fascination with arsenic angle, yes, I see. Look, I went over all this with your boss, what's his name? Brock. It was the reason I contacted him in the first place. I told him about Marion's theories about the role of arsenic in Victorian society. I really do rather resent having to repeat myself."

"He told me about your conversation, Mrs. Warrender, but it was Madeleine Smith in particular I wanted to ask about. Did Marion discuss her with you?"

Sophie frowned. "We did talk about her, now you mention it. Marion sympathised with her predicament—you know, having that lover who would rather ruin her than let her go. But there was something else . . . She'd had some disagreement with Dr. da Silva about Madeleine Smith, I think. I seem to remember she got quite agitated about it. Do you recall, Rhonda? Were you here that day?"

"Actually, she told you that Madeleine Smith was the key to the whole business."

"Did she?" Sophie raised her eyebrows. "I don't remember that."

"What business?" Kathy asked.

"Well, the disagreement she was having with Dr. da Silva, whatever that was."

"It wasn't really of any interest to my work," Sophie said. "She did tend to go off at a tangent. I had to remind her several times who was paying for her time." She checked her watch pointedly. "Was there anything else?"

"Not really. I'm sorry to have interrupted you when you must be so busy after your time away."

"Yes, it has been rather hectic. Bloody phone, after four weeks of blissful peace."

"I've never been to Corsica, but I'd like to. An ex-boyfriend of mine is in Calvi. Is that near where you are?"

"Not far. Our house is in the north of the island too, at St. Florent, between Calvi and Bastia, the main city in the north. He didn't join the Foreign Legion, did he? That's where they're based."

"Really? No, I'm sure he didn't." But thinking about it she wasn't so sure. "He said Corsica is beautiful at this time of year," she lied, "with the wild spring flowers over the hills. Is it like that where you are?"

"Oh, absolutely, the maquis is an ocean of blooms."

"You're lucky to have a job that you can take away with you to a place like that. It must be more difficult for your husband. He's in banking, isn't he?"

"What is this, *Parkinson?*"

Kathy smiled. "Sorry. My inquisitive nature."

"Well, yes, it is more difficult for him, but he's reached a level where he can more or less make the rules. Modern communications are wonderful, of course, and if they need him for a meeting he can always fly back."

"But wouldn't he have to change planes at Paris or Nice? It must take all day."

"You have been doing your homework, haven't you? Are you thinking of going out to see this Beau Geste of yours? Once the tourist season starts next month you can get direct flights from London to Bastia, but Dougie doesn't have to bother. They send over a private jet to pick him up. It lands back at City Airport, and a car has him at his desk in no time."

"Ah. Did he come back around the time Marion died, by any chance?"

Sophie stiffened, and Kathy was aware of Rhonda looking up.

"Why on earth do you ask that?" Sophie demanded angrily. "Or is it just your inquisitive nature?"

Kathy shrugged, trying to make light of it. "You could say that. I'm interested in Marion's movements around that time, and any sightings of her by people who would have recognised her would be useful. Your husband's office is in St. James's Square, isn't it?"

"Well, let me assure you, Inspector, my husband did not leave Corsica at that time, and I must say I'm beginning to resent the intrusive attentions of your boss's little coterie. Rhonda will show you out." Face flushed, she swung away, shoving her glasses aggressively back on her nose, and began noisily shuffling her papers.

Kathy left, wondering what *little coterie* she was talking about.

BROCK WAS TALKING IN his room with a couple of other detectives when Dot tapped on his door. "Sorry, but I've got a Mrs. Warrender on the line. She says you know her, and she's very steamed up about something."

"All right, we've just about finished here." He went round to his desk chair as the other two left. "Hello? David Brock speaking."

"Yes, I've got a bone to pick with you, Chief Inspector."

The woman sounded furious. "What's that, Mrs. Warrender?"

"You know bloody well what's that. I came to you in good faith with what I knew about Marion, as any honest person might, and the next thing I and my family are being subjected to underhand surveillance and questioned as if we were suspects."

Brock scratched his beard, wondering what she was going on about. "I really think there must have been some mistake."

"Mistake? I've just had your inspector here, accusing me of theft and lying about our movements, and practically implying that my husband was mixed up in Marion's death."

"DI Gurney?"

"What? No, the blond woman, Kolla. She insisted on seeing me under the pretext of being interested in some irrelevant nineteenth-century character, and the next thing she's asking leading questions about my husband's movements. But that's only the latest intrusion. No doubt your other informant has briefed you about her spying activities?"

"I'm sorry, I have no idea—"

"Your so-called lady *friend*. Is she an undercover officer too?"

"Mrs. Warrender, please. I have no idea what you're talking about."

"Suzanne Chambers, she said she was. Just two days after I speak to you she turns up at my house and invites herself in and interrogates my elderly mother-in-law, mainly about my husband. Then two days later—yesterday evening—she turns up again at a reading I was giving in our local bookshop. Again she insinuates herself into my mother-in-law's company, using her to interview my husband, who was also there. She claimed they'd once been teenage friends, though my husband says he can't remember her. Are you claiming you don't know about this woman?"

"I do know a Suzanne Chambers," Brock said slowly. "But I'm sure she wasn't in London yesterday."

"Look," Sophie snapped, "this has got to stop, do you hear me? Do you seriously suspect my husband of wrongdoing? Because if you do, I'm getting straight on to our lawyers."

"No, no, I'm sure we don't. I really think there's been some misunderstanding here. Suzanne Chambers certainly doesn't work for the Metropolitan Police or any other security agency, and has not discussed with me any contact she may have had with you, which I'm sure was not in any way sinister. I'll certainly speak to her about it. As for DI Kolla, the Marion Summers case is still ongoing, and she was trying to tidy up loose ends. I'm sorry if her approach seemed offensive. I'm sure it wasn't intended to be, and I'll speak to her too." He stopped himself, wondering why he was bending over backwards like this. It was the revelation about Suzanne, of course. He remembered her slightly dreamy comments after the National Theatre, about Douglas Warrender being her first great love. What on earth was she playing at?

"I'd appreciate that," Sophie Warrender said, sounding somewhat calmer. "And anyway, I thought the Marion business was cleared up. Didn't you decide she'd committed suicide?"

"The forensic evidence leaves some room for doubt. We need to explore all the options for the coroner."

"You still think it possible that someone murdered her?"

"There are unexplained gaps in our information. The identity of the father of the child she lost two weeks before her death, for example."

"Yes, Inspector Kolla mentioned that when we met at Marion's house. I had no idea."

"You said you weren't aware of a boyfriend, didn't you?"

"Yes. To be honest I imagined her as completely celibate. Stupid of me."

"Well, she guarded her privacy rather closely, it seems. I'm sorry we seem to have been at cross-purposes, Mrs. Warrender. Leave it with me."

He rang off and dialled Kathy's number. "Kathy? Brock. What are you doing at the moment?"

What she was actually doing was trying to check on private flights between London City and Bastia at the beginning of the month. What she told Brock was, "I'm working on the Interpol cases."

"I've just had Mrs. Warrender on the line, complaining about your visit."

"She did seem a bit stressed today. What was the problem?"

"She said you implied that her husband was involved in Marion's death."

"No, I didn't do that. Interesting that she chose to see it that way though."

"I thought we'd agreed that you were going to concentrate on Interpol?"

"Yes. It was just a loose end. A book went missing from Marion's house after I took Sophie Warrender over there. I just needed to check she didn't have it."

Brock frowned. "Kathy . . ." He sighed. "Just leave her alone, will you?"

Then he added, "You haven't spoken to Suzanne recently by any chance, have you?"

"No, not for ages. Why, is she all right?"

"Yes. I just thought . . . Never mind."

Brock rang off and dialled Suzanne's mobile.

"Yes? Oh, David! I'm serving a customer. Can I ring you back?"

"Quick as you can." He put the phone down, thinking that her voice had sounded odd, almost guilty.

She rang back after a moment. "Hello. Are you all right?"

"I'm fine, but Sophie Warrender isn't." He told her about the phone call.

"Oh dear. But honestly, she's making a mountain out of a molehill. I decided to detour to Notting Hill on Monday on the way home because of our conversation. It's changed so much, so smart and rich, when it used to be practically a slum. Anyway, her mother-in-law, Lady Warrender, was in the garden, and we got chatting and she invited me in. I hadn't planned it. Then I saw a notice for Sophie Warrender's talk in a local bookshop. I wanted to hear her speak, but I didn't think I'd make it, otherwise I'd have mentioned it to you. But at the last minute I decided to dash up, hear the talk and dash back. I had no idea that Lady Warrender would be there, or Dougie, who she insisted on introducing me to. Honestly, David, it wasn't important."

She'd lain awake the previous night rehearsing this, and she thought it sounded all right, except that she'd said "honestly" twice, which she knew he regarded as a sure indicator that someone was lying through their teeth. And his response sounded heavy and sad, as if he was very disappointed, and of course the whole thing had been clumsy and stupid.

"Suzanne, this is an ongoing murder investigation. Like it or not, you are associated with me. You can't just go calling on witnesses at a time like this."

He sounded exasperated, as if he'd never imagined he'd have to explain such a thing to her. Which of course he didn't, except that she had a life too, and she hadn't exactly engineered this. She wanted to promise to have nothing more to do with the Warrenders, but she couldn't quite do that. When she'd got home last night she'd looked up her old friend Angela Crick on friends reunited.co.uk, and found her details listed with other old pupils of St. Mary's Grammar School for Girls. And that morning, during a lull at the shop, she'd emailed her and they'd arranged to meet. They could hardly do that without talking about Dougie Warrender.

KATHY TOO WAS RELUCTANT to let this go. She felt annoyed. Brock wasn't usually like this, checking her every move. And she wondered why Sophie Warrender had been so defensive. It was all very well Brock telling her to get on with something else, but her mind had ideas of its own. She turned over the note about the American university and was checking the international code when Brock rang her again.

"Tina Flowers," he said. "That's Marion's friend, yes?"

"Yes."

"Forget what I said. Drop what you're doing. There's a car outside for us."

TWENTY

LILY CRIBB WAS A mature-aged Open University student, and was feeling quite numb. Perhaps you should expect this sort of thing to happen when you come up to town, she'd told herself, but still, she hadn't felt as shaken since her dad had dropped dead outside the pub.

She had been sitting at one of the desks in the Humanities Reading Room. The desk was rather splendid, made of oak with an inlaid green leather top and lit by a specially designed reading lamp, and it was still hardly marked by use. Despite its craftsmanship, Lily hadn't quite come to terms with the newness of the building and its fittings; she harboured a secret prejudice that really great libraries like this should be old and venerable, like the circular domed reading room of the old British Museum library which this building had replaced. She would admit, though, that the new structure was quite magnificent. She thought the main entrance hall with its wave-like ceiling very grand, rising up to the glass cube in which the King's Library was housed, and she did admire the care that had been taken over every detail, like the little light on the built-in console in front of her, which had begun flashing to tell her that the book she had requested was now available at the desk. She remembered the thrill of anticipation that flashing light provoked; the book was a memoir of life in East Anglia in the closing years of the nineteenth century, which she had managed to track down with some difficulty, and which she hoped would give her some crucial insights into the social impacts of the Great Eastern Railway, which was the subject of her thesis. The thought of what she might discover was so exciting, in fact, that she'd thought she'd better visit the loo first.

There she encountered more thoughtful design, with a nice balance of functionality and restrained elegance which she noted approvingly. Her eye travelled around the room, checking the basins and taps, the lighting, the tiles, wondering if she could learn something for her own bathroom makeover, which was germinating in her imagination. Her eye stopped at the door of one of the toilet cubicles, beneath which a shoeless woman's foot was jammed.

A heart attack? A drug addict, even here? She tapped on the door. "Hello? Are you all right?" Silly question. She thought she heard a faint moan, but the door was locked, so she hurried out to get help.

"After that it all happened so fast," she told Brock, who was sitting opposite her, listening patiently. She felt he was a sympathetic interrogator, a still centre in the middle of the panic her discovery had provoked. "As soon as they opened the door I realised who it was."

"You knew her?"

"Tina? Oh yes, I've met her here before. The first time she was lost—it was her first visit and she didn't know her way around. She looked so young and bewildered I felt sorry for her. She was looking for the India Office Records, I remember, and though I hadn't the faintest idea where they were, I did know how to set about finding them. After that we bumped into each other a few times. She was doing a research project for her university course— cultural studies, whatever that means."

"Did you ever see her talking to anyone else?"

"Let me think . . . Yes, I did see her one day in the café in the forecourt—what they call the 'piazza'—at the front of the library.

She was with several other people. I took them to be university students too, but I'm afraid I can't remember anything about them."

"You've been very helpful, Mrs. Cribb. I'll give you my card in case you think of anything else, no matter how trivial."

His benign smile was like a blessing, she felt, but his eyes were very sharp.

KATHY WAS OUTSIDE THE main entrance of the library, in the forecourt Lily Cribb had described, by the café ominously called The Last Word. "One of the waitresses remembers Tina being here about an hour ago, at that table over there, and thinks she saw someone standing talking to her. A man, she thinks, but she's not sure. No one else seems to remember anything, and there are no cameras covering the area where she was sitting."

Brock looked around. The day was overcast, a sharp, cold wind whipping the people hurrying across the piazza. They were wearing scarves and hats, collars turned up against the chill. If Tina was poisoned here her attacker would have been captured on a camera somewhere nearby, but it might be impossible to get an image of their face. "Where have they taken Tina?"

"UCLH," Kathy said, remembering that it was the same hospital they'd taken Nigel Ogilvie to. "At least we were able to tell them to look for arsenic poisoning."

Behind them uniformed officers were trying to take statements and answer questions as people milled around in confusion, their routines disturbed by the dramatic arrival of ambulance and police cars. Brock drew Kathy aside.

"Look, this changes things, Kathy. We now have a pattern—two women students in the same university department, until recently living in the same building. Maybe we've been sidetracked by the mysteries of Marion's life. Maybe it's more straightforward—another student, perhaps? Or someone who works at the student flats?"

Kathy thought about Andy Blake, the science student who had known them both. Had she accepted his story too readily? Or the disapproving Jummai? She said, "I had my money on their tutor, Dr. da Silva."

"Hm. I think this is beginning to look like what Sundeep first feared, a serial psychopath, who likes watching women die painful deaths in public view. Surely da Silva wouldn't be so stupid as to pick his own students. Do we have his picture?"

"I can get one sent over. So, I'm back on the case?" Kathy said.

"I don't think you were ever off it," he replied dryly.

AS KATHY MOVED AWAY she saw Donald Fotheringham, waving to her from a knot of people standing with the uniformed police. She went over.

"Donald. You're here too? Were you with Tina?"

"Aye." He was pale, quivering with agitation. "Emily and I were with her over there, having lunch with her at the café. We left her on her own. I walked up the road to Euston station to find out about getting a train back to Glasgow. As I was coming back I saw the ambulance leaving the library. I never imagined it might be for her. What happened for pity's sake? Nobody seems to be able to tell me."

"She collapsed, Donald. It looks very much like what happened to Marion."

"Oh, dear Lord."

"Show me where you were sitting."

They went over to the café, surrounded now by police tape. A scene of crime team was unpacking their gear, a detective talking to a couple of waitresses.

Donald pointed out the place where they'd sat, the same table the waitress had said, and tried to recall the people at nearby tables without much success.

"I'll show you some pictures later, Donald. Can you tell me what Tina had to eat and drink?"

"Well, the sandwich I bought her—turkey breast salad, it was. And a black coffee. She already had a bottle of water she was drinking from."

"Okay." Kathy called over to one of the SOCOs and passed this on. "Now, what about Emily? Do you know where she is?"

"She said she was going back home. We'd spent the morning helping Tina with her researches, and I said I'd buy them both lunch before she left."

"You weren't aware of anyone watching you this morning?"

"Good heavens, no. Is that what you think, that he was watching us all the time?"

"I just don't know, Donald. Do you have a mobile number for Emily?"

"Yes . . . here."

Kathy tried it, but got through to a recorded voice inviting her to leave a message. She asked Emily to get back to her as soon as possible.

"Do you feel all right, Donald?" she asked. "No nausea, stomach pains?"

"No, nothing."

"We'll get a medic to have a look at you. And Emily seemed okay when she left?"

"Perfectly."

"How long ago was that?"

Donald looked at his watch. "About an hour and half ago. I should go to the hospital to be with Tina. She has no family in London."

"We'll go together. I've just got a couple of things to do. Why don't you take a seat over there and see if you can remember anything else?"

She went back and had another word with Brock, then rang Sundeep Mehta's number at the mortuary, knowing he wouldn't answer his mobile if he was working on an autopsy. After a moment he came to the phone. She told him what had happened and heard his sharp intake of breath.

"Where is she, Kathy?"

"UCLH."

"I'll get over there straight away."

Kathy dug in her pocket for her notebook and found Sophie Warrender's number. The phone was answered by her secretary Rhonda, who sounded almost as if she were expecting Kathy's call. She put her through, and the now familiar voice said stiffly, "Sophie Warrender here. What do you want?"

"I'm trying to contact your daughter, Emily, Mrs. Warrender. Do you know . . . ?"

"Yes, she said you'd tried to ring her. I told her not to respond. I've spoken to your superior, and neither I nor any of my family have anything to say to you."

"She's safely at home, then, is she?"

"Safely? What are you talking about?"

"There's been an incident, this time at the British Library, around the time Emily was there today. I wanted to make sure she was all right."

"Incident?"

"Another poisoning. Are you sure that Emily isn't showing any signs of nausea or stomachache?"

"My God! I'll get her to a doctor straight away."

"Good idea. Then I'll need to come over to speak to her. It is very important."

Kathy returned to Donald Fotheringham, sitting beneath the statue of Isaac Newton in the centre of the forecourt, like a spindly caricature of the massive bronze that loomed above him, both crouching forward on their seats, brooding on their problems. A paramedic was packing a bag at his feet and nodded to Kathy as she came over, saying that Donald was in the clear.

She led him to the car waiting outside on Euston Road, and they drove the short distance to the new blocks of University College Hospital. At the accident and emergency department they were told that Tina was in a coma, and they took a seat in a quiet corner to wait.

"You said you were going to speak to Bessie about a wealthy relative leaving Marion some money," Kathy said.

"Oh aye, I asked her. As I thought, she'd never heard of such a thing. That really doesn't ring true, Kathy—is it all right if I call you that?"

"Sure."

"Well, Bessie's theory, and mine too if I'm honest, is that Marion had found a sugar daddy. She was a bonny lass, no doubt about it."

"Yes, you're probably right. A sugar daddy who wants to remain anonymous."

"Aye, well, Tina had her own ideas about that."

"Go on."

Donald Fotheringham hesitated, seeming torn between an innate love of gossip and a deadly sense of rectitude. "She seemed to have the idea that Marion's tutor, Dr. da Silva, was the fly in the ointment."

"Really. Did she have any evidence of that?"

"I couldn't say."

"So what was this work you were doing? You said you were following up Marion's borrowing list."

"Aye, that's right. Tina was convinced there was something hidden there that would lead her to Marion's killer."

"But how? Did she give you any idea?"

"No, she said I had to keep an open mind. I must say it all seemed a bit far-fetched to me. How could Marion's studies of the Pre-Raphaelite Brotherhood cause any problems today?"

He took a notepad from his jacket pocket. "This was our most recent topic." He showed her a heading in capitals, underlined, followed by a string of references and notes: *India Office Records*— GENERAL SIR HENRY HAVELOCK ARCHIVE.

Kathy stared at the title. "Who's he?"

"The hero of Lucknow, do you no' remember your history?"

"I'm afraid not."

"He was a great man, took part in the First Afghan War, then commanded a division in the Anglo-Persian War and returned to

India in time for the Mutiny, where he relieved the siege of Lucknow and promptly died. There's a statue of him in Trafalgar Square, which that wee leftie Ken Livingstone wanted rid of. Do you no' remember?"

"What did he die of?"

Donald consulted his notes. "Dysentery, on the twenty-ninth of November 1857."

The year Madeleine Smith was tried for murder, Kathy thought, but what was the connection? Something tugged at her memory.

"What does this have to do with the Pre-Raphaelites, Donald, do you know?"

"That's what we were trying to find out. Marion had studied this archive, apparently, but Tina didn't know why. She wanted us to go through every item. It was a collection of documents donated by the Havelock family to the library, apparently."

Then Kathy remembered one of the names on Marion's list of key words: *H. Haverlock*. Of course, that's why the name was familiar; the witness at Madeleine Smith's wedding to George Wardle, although his name was spelled slightly differently from that of the soldier. Was that the connection?

Kathy looked up to see Sundeep pushing through the door from the ward. He came over as she rose to her feet.

"It's arsenic all right," he said. "Just what I feared, a serial poisoner. Is it the libraries? Is that the connection? Dear God, you'll have to close every library in the city. There'll be panic."

"Maybe not, Sundeep. Tina was a friend of Marion's, a fellow student. That's more likely the connection. How is she doing?"

He shook his head. "I don't think she's going to make it. The next hour will be critical, but even if she survives, they'll keep her in a coma for a further twelve hours at least, so there's nothing we can do here. They'll let us know if there's any change." He wiped a hand across his face. "I was going to phone you, about the audit at the university laboratory. We're still checking some of the details, but it looks pretty clear that their security is tight. The only lapse we've found concerns Dr. Ringland. Every time one of the experimenters withdraws a dangerous chemical from the store they have to get their order countersigned by Dr. Ringland or his deputy. But the heaviest user of arsenic is Dr. Ringland himself, for his experimental work, and he doesn't always get a countersignature from one of the others. It's an understandable lapse—I'm sure I'd have done the same myself. As the person ultimately responsible for laboratory security he would have regarded himself as above suspicion."

"What does he have to say?"

"He can account for every requisition. The trouble is, we only have his word for it." Sundeep checked his watch. "I have to get back. Let me know how things develop, won't you?"

Kathy returned to the seat beside Donald. He looked at her anxiously and she shook her head and told him what Sundeep had said. Then she added, "What about Emily? Do you think Tina talked to her about what she was searching for?"

He sighed. "It's possible, I suppose. The two of them were more on the same wavelength than me. I just followed Tina's instructions, but Emily had suggestions of her own. Do you think she's in danger too?"

"Not if I can help it. I'm going to speak to her now, Donald. Do you want a lift anywhere?"

"No, I'll stay here."

"Okay. Give me a ring if there's any change."

SOPHIE WAS WAITING FOR her when she arrived, tense and anxious. They stood in the hallway, talking in low voices.

"They say Emily is all right, thank goodness. What on earth is going on, Inspector?"

"Tina collapsed after lunch, and has been taken to University College Hospital. She's in a coma, and her condition is critical. It does seem like a repeat of what happened to Marion. Emily was with her just before it happened, so I need to speak to her."

"Very well, but I insist on being with my daughter when you speak with her."

"Certainly, if Emily's happy with that."

Sophie led the way into a lounge with a large TV screen at one end. Emily was sitting staring at the blank screen. She jumped to her feet as they came in. "What's happened? What's going on?"

Kathy repeated what she'd told her mother, and shock filled Emily's face. "But . . . how?"

"We're waiting for tests to be completed, but it does appear as if she was poisoned in much the same way as Marion."

Emily clapped a hand to her mouth and gave a choking sound.

"We think it may have happened at the café where you had lunch together. So you haven't felt any symptoms yourself?"

The girl shook her head. Her face was pale and she looked as if she might pass out. Her mother went to her side on the sofa and put an arm around her.

Emily looked up at Kathy, tears filling her eyes. "Is she dead too?"

"The doctors are fighting to save her. They had a better idea what to do this time, but I'm afraid things don't look good."

"I should go to her."

"She's in a coma. There's nothing we can do at the moment. What's important is to make sure you're all right, and for you to tell me anything that might help us."

Emily stared anxiously at Kathy. "Didn't Tina say anything?"

"I'm afraid not."

Emily rocked forward on the edge of her seat, arms clutched around herself, shaking her head. "I can't remember anything special. We were with Donald. He wanted to buy us lunch before I left to come home."

"Who is Donald?" Sophie demanded.

"Oh, this man who knows Marion's aunt. He wanted to help us."

Sophie looked at Kathy in alarm. "How do we know he knows her aunt, for goodness' sake? Are you questioning him?"

"Yes, I've already spoken to him. That's how we knew Emily

was there. Can you remember any of the people that were sitting nearby, or passed you in the café?"

She shook her head. "It's just a blur."

Kathy talked her back through the events of the morning, working forward again to their going to the café. "You're sure you can't remember anyone looking at you, following you? Perhaps someone that Tina may have known?"

Something seemed to register with Emily. She gave a little frown, then said slowly, "I did notice someone. I'd seen him there before, at the British Library, a day or two ago. He didn't approach us, but I did have the feeling Tina recognised him."

"What did he look like?"

"Oh, quite respectable. Dark hair swept back. Um . . . in a suit, I think."

"I'll get some photographs for you to look at, but meanwhile, it might save a little time . . . You remember that biography of Rossetti we spoke about this morning, Mrs. Warrender?"

"The da Silva book?"

"Yes. I wonder if I could have a look at your copy?"

"What?"

"Please. I'll explain when you bring it."

Sophie hesitated, then rose to her feet. "All right, but don't say a word until I get back, Emily."

When she had gone, Emily gave Kathy a weak smile. "Would you like anything, a cup of tea?"

"No thanks. What about you? A glass of water?"

"I'm all right."

Sophie returned, handing Kathy the book.

"Thank you." Kathy turned to the inside flap of the back cover, and showed Emily the author's photograph.

The girl gave a start. "Oh! Yes, I think . . . It does look like the man I saw. Who is it?"

"Dr. da Silva is a teacher on Tina's course," Kathy said carefully. "Did Tina mention him to you?"

"Yes, and Marion too. I just didn't know what he looked like."

"What did Tina say?"

"Oh, that she didn't trust him, that Marion had had a problem with him. That sort of thing."

"Yes, well, it's natural that he would be in the library, and he's one of the people we'd want to establish as a possible witness."

"I see."

Neither of them looked convinced by Kathy's explanation, and she went on, "I'd like you both to treat this conversation in confidence for now. We'll be talking to him, among many others. Can you remember exactly when you saw him before?"

"Not really. Probably Tuesday. Yes, I think Tuesday afternoon."

"All right. So, how did you come to be helping Tina?"

"Well, it was when we gave her a lift after we met with you at Marion's house. You remember, Mum?"

"Yes, you said you'd helped Marion from time to time, and Tina asked about what you were going to read at Oxford, and when you said you had spare time at the moment she invited you to help her doing her library searches."

"That's right. I was quite keen, as least to try it for a few days, just to get an idea about her work. Only, well, I think the main reason she asked me was to pump me about what I'd been doing with Marion."

"How do you mean?"

"I didn't realise at first, but what she was researching wasn't her own university studies. She was trying to retrace what Marion had been doing in the weeks before she died. She seemed to feel that would explain what happened to her."

"But how could it do that, darling?" Sophie said. "Did she say?"

"She thought that Marion had discovered something really important. Something that would have a huge impact."

"About what?"

"I think—it's only what I guessed from listening to her—I think it had something to do with him." She pointed at the cover image on da Silva's book. "Dante Gabriel Rossetti."

Sophie sat up sharply. "Oh . . . my God."

Kathy said, "What is it, Mrs. Warrender?"

"Well, it seems rather obvious, doesn't it? Anthony da Silva is the leading world authority on Rossetti, and Marion was his student, with whom he often quarrelled about her theories and interpretations. Suppose she discovered something catastrophic about his research? It wouldn't be the first time that the reputation of a leading researcher has been utterly destroyed, the academic world turned on its head, by a discovery—of plagiarism, say."

The same thought had already occurred to Kathy, and she said, "Do you think Tina might have discovered something like that, Emily?"

"It's possible, I suppose. She didn't tell me if she had."

"And how did she seem today?"

Emily frowned. "She wasn't herself. Something was worrying her. The books she wanted weren't available and she was very agitated. Donald and I tried to cheer her up, but she got angry." She wiped her eyes.

"So," Sophie said, turning to Kathy. "What are you going to do now?"

"I'd like to take Emily back to my office to look at photographs of some other people."

"And then what? I mean, she may be in danger too, don't you think? In fact she could also have been an intended victim this lunchtime."

"I'll make sure she gets back safely, and then it might be as well if she stays at home for a few days."

Sophie reluctantly agreed to let her daughter go, and Kathy drove her back to Queen Anne's Gate and sat her down with a cup of tea while she prepared a set of identification photos. Apart from Tony da Silva, which she confidently picked out, she hesitated over one other, Keith Rafferty, frowning, then shaking her head.

"Maybe not," she said.

"But a possible?" Kathy prompted, trying to sound neutral. "Could you have seen him with Dr. da Silva, for instance?"

Emily thought about that, then shook her head. "Sorry, no, I don't know. Maybe it's just that he looks like every thug you've ever seen on the news."

While she was there, Kathy drew up a statement summarising what Emily had said for her to sign, then arranged for a patrol car to take her back to Notting Hill. As it drew away Kathy saw Alex Nicholson step out of a cab and hurry towards her.

"Brock phoned me with the news, Kathy," she said. "I came as soon as I could."

TWENTY-ONE

THEY GATHERED IN ONE of the smaller offices, with a window overlooking a small courtyard at the back of the building. "It's quieter in here," Brock said. "We need to be able to think. There's a mood of panic setting in. I have to decide whether we should close every library in the city."

He described to Alex what they knew of the circumstances of Tina's collapse and what they were now doing, gathering witness statements and camera material at the British Library and beginning interviews with all Tina's friends and student acquaintances that they could trace. As Kathy was adding what Donald Fotheringham and Emily Warrender had told her, Dot put her head round the door and handed Brock a note in her neat script, which he read out. "Officer on duty at UCLH reports Tina Flowers pronounced dead this afternoon at 1606. Autopsy first thing tomorrow."

There was a moment's heavy silence in the room. Outside the window, a light drizzle glistened on the mossy brick wall. Finally Alex spoke, her voice low.

"You don't have to close every library, Brock. Poisoners are the most organised of offenders, and there's nothing random or erratic about this. The two women were specifically targeted in the most calculated way. Their killers went to great lengths and took great risks to kill them in just this way."

"Killers?" Brock queried. "You don't think they're the same one?"

"I think it's possible that there's more than one, operating together."

Brock and Kathy looked at her in surprise. "Why?"

"Both scenes were difficult to arrange. Think of the first—the setup of apparent suicide arrangements in Marion's kitchen could only be done after the killer was sure that Marion had swallowed the poisoned drink and it had taken effect, otherwise she might return and find it. So we have the killer in St. James's Square witnessing her collapse, then travelling six miles to Hampstead to improvise the kitchen scene, with very little time to spare. They couldn't know if Marion might have her address in her wallet, allowing the police to go straight to Rosslyn Court. It would be much easier if there were two people, one in St. James's Square and one in Hampstead.

"In Tina's case the problem is different. It's one thing to spike a girl's drink in a crowded bar, and another to pour a lethal dose of arsenic into someone's cup of coffee in front of the victim and surrounded by witnesses. Easier if there's two involved, one to cause a distraction."

Kathy said, "Rafferty and Crouch, they're a double act. We've seen that at first hand." She told Alex about their experience with Pip.

Alex wasn't so sure. "The classic profile for this kind of highly organised killer would be: intelligent, socially competent, an eldest child, in skilled work. But what's the motive? My best advice is, follow the money trail that bought the house." She hesitated, then added, "If there is a killer."

Again the other two stared at her.

"Everything I just said," Alex went on, "assumes an outside agency. But the easiest way to explain the logistical difficulties of the crime scenes is if the girls did it themselves, a double suicide.

Sundeep's objection to Marion using dirty utensils may not be significant. She had recently lost a child, she was about to commit suicide, she was in turmoil, very disturbed."

"Not according to—" Kathy began, then stopped.

"Who?"

"Tina."

"Exactly. They were close, weren't they?"

Kathy nodded. "Tina told me that Marion had saved her life when she'd wanted to end it all."

"It sounds a cruel thing to say, but there's an element of exhibitionism in both deaths, if you care to look at it that way—agonising deaths in full public view. About the most difficult thing to arrange, for anyone except the victim."

They fell silent again, the rain steadier now. Then Alex added, "Doesn't mean they didn't get help, though. The arsenic had to come from somewhere."

AFTER THE MEETING BROKE up, Brock had to go over to the Scotland Yard building to brief senior officers about the public safety aspects of the case. As he gathered up his papers they agreed that Bren would concentrate on Rafferty and Crouch, and Kathy on the university connections. When she returned to her desk Kathy thought about Alex's comments, then made a couple of calls regarding the Banque Foche in Geneva. Next she dialled the number on the Cornell University letterhead from Marion's student mailbox, and got straight through to Dr. Grace Pontius, who was perturbed when Kathy introduced herself.

"Metropolitan Police?" she said. "How can I help you?"

"It concerns a letter that you sent to Marion Summers, dated the twenty-seventh of March. Do you recall it?"

"Sure. I was expecting to hear from Marion. Is something wrong?"

"I'm afraid so. Marion died suddenly nine days ago, on the third of April. Her tutor, Dr. da Silva, didn't contact you?"

"No. Oh my God. And the police are involved?"

"The circumstances of her death are still not clear. She died of arsenic poisoning."

"What? But that's shocking. How could something like that happen?"

"That's what we're trying to find out. You wrote about a conference she was coming to at your university?"

"In August, yes. Tony must be devastated."

"He's going too, is he?"

"Yes, they were both presenting papers on their research. The topic of the conference is gender and culture in Victorian England, so it's right up their street. Tony is presenting a paper on Dante Gabriel Rossetti, of course. He's the world expert."

"Yes, I know. What about Marion's paper?"

"Well, she gave me a fairly sensational title: *Murder, literal and phenomenal, in the work of Dante Gabriel Rossetti*. But she was a bit slow giving me a synopsis. She did say that it would cause a stir."

"I see. But I suppose Dr. da Silva would know all about it."

"I assume so. I met Marion with him when I was in London last year, and I was very impressed by her. I'm sure it would have been a very good paper. It's really devastating that this has happened. Maybe if Tony has a copy we might get him to present it as a tribute to Marion. So how can I help you, Inspector?"

"I'm talking to anyone who may have had contact with Marion around the time she died. Did she say anything to you when you spoke that struck you as odd in any way?"

"No, not at all. She'd got a grant from her university to help her to attend our conference, and she was very excited about coming. I got the impression that everything was going really well."

As Kathy rang off, Bren came over to her desk. He'd been in touch with Keith Rafferty's boss at Brentford Pyrotechnics, Mr. Pigeon, who'd promised Kathy he'd check their arsenic supplies.

"He can't find any discrepancies, Kathy, but I got the impression he's not completely confident. Your last visit seems to have rattled him. He's given Rafferty the boot."

"Sacked him?"

"Yeah, he reckoned Rafferty lied on his original job application."

"What did Rafferty have to say?"

"Told him he could keep his job. Didn't seem much bothered."

Kathy thought. "You said he was spending money on the horses."

"Yes, a fair bit, from what I could gather. Just gossip, mind you, down the pub."

"Maybe it would be worth checking at the local betting shops."

"Yeah."

Kathy worked on the phone for a while, coordinating teams at the library and university student flats. Later, when Brock returned from his briefing, he called Kathy up to his office.

"They've decided not to close the libraries," he said. "Public warnings instead. Won't do much for the café business. What have you got?"

"Several witnesses who saw her in the library today, but no one at The Last Word except for the waitress. Forensics haven't been able to find any traces of arsenic in the café. It's likely her coffee cup was put through the washing machine before we got there. They're working through the contents of all the rubbish bins. So far nothing from Tina's student roommates." Then she told him about her call to America.

"You're wondering if Marion was going to embarrass Dr. da Silva at the conference?"

"Something like that. Sophie Warrender suggested that she may have discovered some problem with his scholarship—plagiarism, maybe. And according to Donald Fotheringham, Tina had da Silva in her sights. And . . . I think someone's been in Marion's house since we locked it up." Kathy hadn't put this into any of her reports, still uncertain if she was right.

"You haven't spoken to da Silva?"

"Not since Monday, to ask him about Marion's computer. I told him then about the house in Hampstead. What do you think? We have nothing concrete. Should we wait until we do?"

Brock thought, then shook his head. "I'd like to meet him." He checked his watch. "Six. Let's see if we can catch him on home ground. Do we know anything about his family?"

"Wife's a rich lawyer, apparently."

"See what you can find out while I order a car."

By the time it arrived, Kathy had put together an outline of the da Silva household. "Wife is Jenny da Silva, a commercial lawyer with Braye Sneddon Wilkes. Her father is Sir George Thorpe."

"The furniture chain?"

"Yes. That's where the money comes from, presumably. First marriage for both of them. She's forty-two, he forty-six."

"The difficult age," Brock murmured.

"Is there an easy one? They have two children: Mortimer, nine, and Leslie, seven."

"A perfect family."

"Yes. I had Googled him previously, and there's no doubt about his reputation. Terrific reviews for his Rossetti book from the *TLS* and *New York Review of Books*, and a profile in the *Observer* magazine."

"Lot to lose, then."

They came to the broad, tree-lined streets of Hampstead Garden Suburb, the model development laid out a hundred years before, and found the da Silvas' house, a substantial rendered semi-detached villa. The red BMW Z4 M Roadster was sitting in the driveway.

"He's at home," Kathy said.

They walked up to the door in the fading light and Kathy rang the bell. After a while the door was opened by Jenny da Silva.

Kathy liked her straight away. She had a warm, open smile and looked as if she might be just about to tell you a good joke she'd heard. There was a streak of flour on her brow where she'd pushed her hair back, and Kathy noticed a half-full glass of white wine on the hall table behind her. She seemed very practical and competent, and just looking at her Kathy felt she could tell that her wealthy father hadn't spoiled her, but had made her serve her time in the packing department or accounts during the school holidays. She had managed the production of children into a compact timeslot before resuming her career, and was now a success in her own field and married to a star in another. An admirable life, and Kathy knew that they were about to trample all over it.

And Jenny da Silva knew it too, Kathy saw. As she showed her ID and introduced herself and Brock, she saw the smile drain from the other woman's face, as if she'd always known that something like this was going to happen.

"We'd like to speak to your husband, please, Mrs. da Silva."

"Oh dear, what's happened? Nothing serious, I hope?"

"If we could just speak to him."

"Well . . . you'd better come in." She stood back and they stepped into a generous hall, where they waited while she went into one of the rooms that led off it. The sound of a TV newscast was cut off abruptly, and they heard Tony da Silva's voice. "Who? What?" He came out, wiping a hand across his face as if he might have been caught having a nap. Recognising Kathy he said, "Ah, Inspector," and thrust a hand forward awkwardly.

"This is my colleague, Detective Chief Inspector Brock, Dr. da Silva. We'd like to have a word with you."

"Do you want to use the living room, darling?" Jenny spoke from the doorway, a sleepy child in her arms. "I'll take Leslie up to bed."

"Right, yes." He led them into the rear room and offered them seats, sitting stiffly on the edge of his. "What can I do for you?"

"You have a student, Tina Flowers."

"Oh yes?" He stared fixedly at Kathy.

"You know who I mean?"

"Um, I think so. Third year? Yes. Why?"

"Did you see her today, by any chance?"

His eyes moved from one to the other, and he seemed unable to speak at first. Then he said tightly, "Today? No, I don't believe so."

"You're sure?"

"Can't recall seeing her, no."

"Would you mind telling us your movements today, Dr. da Silva?"

"Umm, normal sort of day. Ten o'clock lecture, afternoon tutorials. Why?"

"The lecture finished at eleven? What did you do then?"

"Bit of library work, then a sandwich in my room."

"Which library did you use?"

"The university . . ." He hesitated, staring at Kathy's face, then corrected himself. "No, I went up to the British Library today, for an hour or so."

"So what times were you there?"

"I'm not sure exactly. Look, what is all this?"

"Please try to estimate when you were there. It is important."

"I can't see how. Well, I suppose I got there some time after eleven thirty, and was there for perhaps an hour, that's all."

"And did you see Tina Flowers while you were there?"

"I told you, no. Why are you asking me this?"

"Tina collapsed at the British Library early this afternoon. I'm sorry to have to tell you that she died later."

Tony da Silva said nothing, jaw locked, staring at Kathy.

"Tony?"

His wife's voice from the doorway roused him, and he slowly turned to face her.

"Are you all right?" she said. "What is going on? What's the matter?"

"I'm afraid that another of Dr. da Silva's students died in suspicious circumstances this afternoon."

"Another . . . like Marion Summers, do you mean?"

"Yes."

"But that's appalling. Where did this happen? At the university?"

"At the British Library. Dr. da Silva was also there at about the same time. We were hoping he might be able to help us find out what happened."

"You were there?" Her husband didn't respond, apparently locked in some inner struggle. "Tony!"

He drew a deep breath and looked away, through the French windows to the back garden, now almost lost in the gathering dark. "Yes," he said heavily. "I was there."

In Tina's wallet they had found a photograph of her and Marion together, both laughing at the camera. From this they had made a copy of Tina's face alone, and Kathy now showed this to Jenny da Silva. Her expression froze.

"You know her?"

Jenny glanced over at her husband, but he didn't respond. She looked at Kathy. "She was here, last night."

There was a moment's silence as this sank in. Then Brock said, "I'd like you both to come with us to make a properly recorded statement."

"I can't leave the children," Jenny said, a note of panic in her voice. "And I won't say another word, not until I've discussed this with my husband."

"It's all right, Jenny." Tony da Silva roused himself. "You don't need my wife. Tina did come here yesterday evening. I'm happy to make a statement."

"Tony?"

"It's fine, darling. There's absolutely nothing to worry about." He turned to Brock, a glimmer of his old confidence returning to his voice. "I'm sorry, you caught me unprepared. I was dozing when you arrived, and when you told me about Tina, I just went into shock. I really can't believe this."

He fetched his jacket, kissed his wife on the cheek and left with the two police. When they got into the car he began to say something, but Brock stopped him and cautioned him. He cautioned him again when they were seated in an interview room at the local police station, not far away on Finchley Road.

"Let's begin with Tina Flowers's visit to your house last night, Dr. da Silva. Tell us about that."

"Ah . . ." Da Silva cleared his throat and took a sip of water from the plastic cup they'd provided. "I should explain that I didn't know Tina well. She's in a course I teach, and she's attended my tutorials, along with many others, but I had no real personal contact with her. I didn't realise, for example, that she was a friend of Marion Summers, until she told me last night. That was the purpose of her visit. Apparently she had got it into her head that the reason Marion had died was because of something she'd discovered in the course of her research work. Tina was very agitated when she came to see me. When I told her that her notion seemed totally implausible to me, she exploded, and said that she'd discovered some notes of Marion's, written in a library book, which proved I'd plagiarised her work. This was utter nonsense. I've never done any such thing and I told her so. She blustered and said she had the evidence, and I told her in that case to go to the university authorities or the police, and I kicked her out. I must admit I was shaken by the whole episode, just coming out of the blue like that. She was close to violence, trembling and spitting with rage, and I got pretty angry too. You see? I'm telling you all this although I know it doesn't show me in a good light, given what's happened. But I haven't seen her since, I swear. You asked if I'd seen her at the British Library today, and I said no. That's true. If we were there at the same time I certainly didn't see her."

"An extraordinary coincidence, though," Brock said.

"Yes, well, no, not really. I went there because of her visit, to see if I could find this book she'd been talking about. She wouldn't have been able to borrow it—the BL isn't a lending library—so it would have to be there still. I checked a couple of Rossetti titles, then I ran out of time and had to go. I was intending to have another look tomorrow."

"So you were concerned about Tina's accusation," Kathy said.

"Not about the ridiculous accusation of plagiarism, but I was concerned that Marion might have written something disparaging or contentious about me in a book that was circulating out there in the public domain."

"Would she have done that?"

Da Silva shook his head wearily. "I don't know. We had been at cross-purposes in the last month or two. I told you how headstrong she was, didn't I?"

"Do you have a copy of her paper for the Cornell conference?"

He looked at Kathy in surprise. "You know about that? No, no I don't. She was rather secretive about it, actually. I've no idea why."

"It was about your subject, Rossetti, wasn't it?"

"I don't know. Her title was rather general as far as I recall, and she refused to discuss it with me."

"That's a little odd, isn't it? A student refusing to discuss the paper she was going to give at a conference with her supervisor, who's the world expert on the subject?"

"Look, I don't see the relevance of this."

"Well, let's speculate," Kathy persisted, leaning forward. "Suppose Marion had discovered something that would reflect badly on your reputation, and had decided to reveal it at the Cornell conference. You'd give a great deal to stop her, wouldn't you?"

"No, there was nothing like that." He reached for the cup of water, then changed his mind when it became apparent that his hand was shaking.

"Did you ever give or lend Marion money, Dr. da Silva?" Brock came in.

"Certainly not!"

"We can check, you know. Do you have an account with a bank in Switzerland?"

His eyes widened. "No."

"The Banque Foche in Geneva. Have you or your wife had any dealings with them? A bank loan, perhaps? A money transfer?"

"I swear, I've never heard of them."

"Did you ever have sex with Marion Summers?"

"No, no!"

"Tina thought you did."

"Did she?" He was gasping now, red-faced. "She had no cause."

"Did you know that Marion lost a baby two weeks before she died?"

Da Silva stared at him, wide-eyed.

"Were you the father?"

"Oh dear God. No, no."

TWENTY-TWO

KATHY DIDN'T ENJOY THIS, the patient grinding away at a story until only the true bones remained. If Brock shared her impatience and weariness with the process he didn't show it, taking da Silva back again and again over old ground, looking for discrepancies. He was implacable and endlessly attentive, as if willing to go on all night.

During a short break Kathy found a message on her phone from Guy, asking if they could meet that evening. She rang him and said that wouldn't be possible.

"Still working?" he asked.

"Yeah, we've got a suspect strapped to the table."

"What a fun job you have. How about tomorrow, the weekend? We could go to Prague."

"I wish. Maybe. Depends. How about you? Still waiting on your marching orders?"

"Won't be till next week now."

"I'll ring you tomorrow," she said.

"I'm counting on it."

She swallowed her coffee and reluctantly got back to her feet to restart the interview. As they headed for the door, she said to Brock, "I don't think we're going to get anywhere."

"Any ideas?"

"I'd like to search his office at the university."

"We'll get a warrant in the morning."

"I'd rather tonight, before he has a chance to remove anything. He's forewarned now."

"Okay. You go and see to it. I'll keep going with him."

It was almost eleven that night before Kathy delivered Tony da Silva back to his front door. Before he could get his key in the lock it was opened by his wife, who said not a word as he trudged in. From the look on her face Kathy guessed that his evening of interrogation had only just begun.

She continued on into the centre of the city, to the Strand campus of the university, where she located the night security staff and presented her warrant. After making a couple of phone calls, one of the guards escorted her to the Department of European Literature, and the office of Dr. da Silva.

"Don't need me, do you?" he said, switching on the lights. "I've got rounds to make, be back in an hour."

"Fine." She put on latex gloves and looked around.

She saw it straight away. Among the rank of copies of da Silva's biography of Rossetti, there was one more worn and battered than the rest. She laid it on the desk and opened it to the title page. There, in the rather florid script she knew from her own copy, she saw a dedication:

To M.
He sees the beauty
Sun hath not looked upon,
And tastes the fountain
Unutterably deep . . .
Tony da Silva

The rest of the book was annotated with comments in another hand—Marion's. Kathy closed the book and slid it into one of the plastic bags she'd brought.

It took her longer to find the rest, but when she did come

across it, tucked into a hanger of one of his filing cabinets, she discovered he'd made things easy for her by keeping everything together in a single buff envelope. When she opened it and tipped out its contents, the first thing that slid into view was the picture of Madeleine Smith. The buzz of recognition was followed by a rising excitement as Kathy began to scan the documents that followed out of the envelope. There were photocopies of entries from a diary, written in a flowing copperplate style and dated from the late 1850s through to 1869. There was also a sheaf of colour scans of portrait paintings of Pre-Raphaelite women and various other reference notes and photocopies. Kathy spread these out and came to the last item, some pages clipped together, which seemed to be the draft of part of an essay or academic paper. The top page was numbered four, the earlier pages apparently missing, but her heart gave a leap when she read the italic header at the top of each sheet. It said, *Murder, literal and phenomenal, in the work of Dante Gabriel Rossetti—Marion Summers.*

already well aware of Madeleine Smith, having followed her trial for murder at the time that he was working with Morris and Jones on the Oxford Union project, where he was overheard stating that she would never be hanged because she was a "stunner"[13], and they met for the first time not long after she arrived in London with her brother Jack in 1858[14]. It is the author's contention that he painted her portrait no less than nine times during the following two years. The models for these pictures have been variously identified as Jane Burden,[15] Annie Miller,[16] and "Unknown,"[17] as well as, confusingly, Ellen Smith,[18] a "laundress of uncertain virtue"[19] who sat for a number of other paintings by Rossetti. However an overwhelming case can be made for Madeleine Smith as the subject of all these nine portraits, and is set out in a separate paper by the author.[20] Guinevere (1859), fig. 3, in particular bears a striking resemblance to a contemporary photograph of Madeleine Smith, fig. 4.

It is also now clear that Dante Gabriel Rossetti and Madeleine Smith became lovers during this period. The crucial evidence for this and other events to be discussed in this paper is provided in the diary of Henry Haverlock, an artist on the periphery of the Pre-Raphaelite circle, and friend of Jack Smith. This diary was discovered recently by the author, hidden in a London archive.[21]

(note: expand on predatory nature of R's relationships with his models—also lover of Jane Burden at this time)

According to Haverlock,[22] the affair came to an end when Elizabeth Siddal, Rossetti's former mistress, whose whereabouts are unknown during this period, reappeared, apparently on the point of death, and "manipulated"[23] him into fulfilling his earlier promise to marry her. Soon after this was accomplished, Madeleine Smith married George Wardle, becoming Lena Wardle.

The circumstances of the married life of Dante and Lizzie Rossetti are well known: the late-term miscarriage of a child in 1861, Lizzie's depression and increasing use of laudanum, and finally her death in February 1862. There has always been speculation about the coroner's verdict of accidental death as a result of an overdose of laudanum.[24] The couple had gone out to dinner with the poet Swinburne, who said that she had been in good spirits. When they got home Lizzie went to bed, but Rossetti left again, ostensibly to work, though it was rumoured that he went to visit a lover. When he returned at half past eleven he claimed that she was in a deep sleep, with a suicide note pinned to her nightgown, and that he was unable to wake her. He then removed the note, alerted his landlady and a neighbour, and sent for a doctor who lived nearby. The doctor pumped out Lizzie's stomach, but was unable to revive her. Other doctors were called, and Rossetti then walked to the home of his friend Ford Maddox Brown in Kentish Town and showed him the note, which they burnt. They both returned to Blackfriars in time to witness Lizzie's death. At the inquest the housekeeper, who was devoted to Rossetti, made a point of saying that she had no suspicions about the circumstances.[25]

However, the Haverlock diary now contradicts this version of events. It confirms that Rossetti had resumed his affair with Lena Wardle in the latter stages of Lizzie's earlier pregnancy in 1861, and was increasingly impatient with his wife's erratic moods and embarrassing behaviour in public. According to Haverlock,[26] it was Lena that Rossetti visited after his wife went to bed that fatal night, to beg her to help him to put an end to the torment of his intolerable marriage. Haverlock records that she gave him a preparation of one-fifth of an ounce of arsenic, enough to kill forty men, the same amount as she had given the unfortunate Emile L'Angelier in Glasgow. Rossetti returned to his wife, whom he woke and gave the preparation, disguised in laudanum. Her known addiction to laudanum, the presence of the empty laudanum bottle by her bedside, and the strong smell of laudanum from her stomach contents, all persuaded her doctors to look no further for the cause of her death. The suicide note was apparently a fabrication of Rossetti's, in case doubts were raised.

Haverlock tells us something else about the events of that fatal night. It seems that Rossetti waited some time for the arsenic to take effect before calling for help, and during this time Lizzie became alarmed by her condition. She already suspected that he had been to see his mistress, and it is likely that the taste and gritty texture of Lena Wardle's preparation had registered with her. When she began to experience intense stomach pains, she was able to write a short note to the housekeeper, Sarah Birrill, which she hid under her pillow. Sarah found this the following day, but kept the contents to herself. Torn by conflicting loyalties, and unwilling either to destroy or reveal the note, she later contrived to have it buried with Lizzie in her coffin.

Rossetti's extreme distress and remorse following the death

of Lizzie is well attested, affecting all of his immediate circle, including his brother William, Swinburne, and the painter and poet W. B. Scott, as they became embroiled in his attempts to contact the spirit world through séances.

(note: phenomenal murder as a trope in the poetry and paintings of DGR following 1862)

The story revealed by Haverlock reaches its bizarre climax in 1869. In his diary for that year he tells us that,[27] seven years after Lizzie's murder, Sarah Birrill finally told Rossetti about Lizzie's note. It was apparently this that provoked his extraordinary efforts to reopen Lizzie's grave, in order, as he claimed, to recover poems that he had buried with her body.[28]

The revelations contained in Haverlock's account overturn much of the existing scholarship on Dante Gabriel Rossetti's life and work. In particular it raises fundamental questions about: the identification of models in a number of his paintings and as subjects of his poetry; the interpretation of his work and actions for the critical period 1858 to 1869 and beyond; the psychology of the man; the interpretation of images and metaphors of death in his work after 1862. Clearly the complete corpus on Rossetti is now superseded, and will have to be rewritten.

"All right there, love?"

Kathy looked up, startled by the security guard's voice. "Yes, thanks. Fine."

"Ready to go, or are you staying all night?"

"No, I'm finished. I'll just leave a note of what I'm taking." She gathered up the contents of the buff envelope and put them into a second plastic bag, then wrote out an official docket, ripped off the top copy and left it in the centre of da Silva's desk.

"Don't suppose he'll be best pleased when he gets that in the morning," the man said.

"No," she agreed. "I don't suppose he will."

TWENTY-THREE

WHEN KATHY ARRIVED AT the office the next morning DC Pip Gallagher brought her a cup of coffee.

"You look as if you need this," she said. "Late night?"

"Yes. Good one, though."

"Aha." Pip gave her a wink. "I'd heard rumours."

"What?"

Pip just smirked.

"Pip! What are you talking about?"

"Nothing. Just when the Summers case is hotting up too. I wish I was back with you again. What I'm doing now is dead boring."

"Well, you could help me with something if you've got a bit of time to spend with Google."

"Sure, what is it?"

Kathy gave her a copy of the dedication written in the front of the da Silva book. "See if you can trace the quotation, assuming it is one."

"Any clues?"

"It could be from a Pre-Raphaelite poem, Dante Gabriel Rossetti maybe."

"Okay, I'll have a go."

She wandered off and Kathy got down to work. There were test reports to wait for, and in the meantime CCTV footage from the British Library to check. Some of the witnesses who had been there the previous day would have to be reinterviewed to see if they could identify da Silva.

Towards noon she got a call from Brock. "He wants to see us with his lawyer."

"Julian Fenwick?"

Brock laughed. "He didn't say. Two o'clock, all right?"

"Fine."

When she went out to a nearby café for a sandwich and drink, Kathy was aware of herself gingerly tasting each before she ploughed into them. She suspected that all across London people were doing the same.

TONY DA SILVA'S LAWYER wasn't Fenwick. Instead he'd come with a female solicitor Kathy had met a couple of times before, and she wondered if it was a deliberate choice for someone on the point of being accused of murdering two women.

"Yes, Dr. da Silva?" Brock began. "You want to add something to our interview last night?"

Da Silva didn't look as if he'd slept, his face pale and puffy, his voice limp. "When I went to my office at the university this morning," he said, "I found this." He unfolded Kathy's docket in front of them, as if hoping it might still turn out to be a mistake.

"Yes?"

Da Silva glanced at his lawyer with a look of desperation, and she frowned and said, "My client is anxious to have his property returned. The material listed on this paper is of academic interest only and of no relevance to your inquiries."

"Of very considerable academic interest, I would have said. And highly relevant to our inquiries. But perhaps Dr. da Silva could enlighten us as to how they came to be in his possession. The book, for instance?" Brock lifted it from his bag and thumped it down on the table between them.

Da Silva's eyes opened wider, staring at it in its clear plastic bag. "I am the author of that book," he said, and his voice was unsteady and slightly hoarse, as if his throat was dry. "It is one of my copies."

"Really? Your handwritten dedication at the front is addressed 'To M.' Who's that?"

Da Silva swallowed and shook his head.

"Sorry?"

"Can't recall," he whispered, almost inaudible.

"Well, let me help you," Brock said. "You see the tear at the top of the cover on the spine? And the crease lower down, across the R in Rossetti?" He reached again to his bag and brought out two packets of photographs. From the first he selected a picture of Marion's bookshelves. "Scene of crime photograph taken at Marion Summers's home at 43 Rosslyn Court, Hampstead, on Friday the sixth of April. See the date at the bottom?"

The solicitor was leaning forward, adjusting her glasses to see the photo. Da Silva didn't move.

"And on the shelf here"—Brock pointed—"a copy of that very same book, with identical tear and crease on the spine cover." He gave the lawyer time to examine it. She glanced back at da Silva, who didn't meet her eyes.

"And here is another photograph of the same bookshelves, taken on Tuesday the tenth, four days later. The book has disappeared, from a locked house." Brock reached out and spread his hand on the plastic pouch. "And now here it is, in the possession of Dr. da Silva, its pages covered from back to front with the handwritten notes and fingerprints of the dead woman, Marion— 'M.'"

The silence stretched painfully, and the solicitor finally snapped it with a crisp, "I'd like a break to discuss matters with my client."

"No." Da Silva shook his head, hunched between his shoulders. "I want to explain." He took a deep breath, eyes fixed on the table in front of his fingers. "Nine months ago Marion came to me with some ideas about Dante Gabriel Rossetti and Madeleine Smith. She had noticed a resemblance between Madeleine and some portraits painted by Rossetti. No one had ever made such a connection before, and the dates of the portraits were significant, because they were painted before either Rossetti or Smith were married. Rossetti was famous by this stage and a notorious womaniser, and Marion speculated that the chemistry would have been irresistible to each of them, for their own reasons. Madeleine, you remember, was an infamous figure, more or less in exile from her home and loved ones, and desperate to make a new start in London.

"What appealed to Marion about this, of course, was the sensational nature of Madeleine's past, the arsenic murderess. Which I suppose was exactly what did not appeal to me. It was all flimsy speculation, based on a supposed resemblance of portraits. My book was in the final page-proof stages, every word and image finalised, and it was out of the question for me to hold things up to include Marion's far-fetched ideas. I told her to forget it and concentrate on her topic. She didn't, of course. Quite the opposite. She became more and more obsessed with the implications of a murderess acting as a kind of hidden agent within the Pre-Raphaelite circle, previously unrecognised. As with any historical story, even one as thoroughly researched as the Pre-Raphaelites', there were plenty of gaps and contradictions if you cared to look, and she wanted to explore them all.

"Then she came up with her theory about Rossetti murdering his wife. I was horrified. I told her I would have to reconsider being her supervisor if she wouldn't be guided by me. Her response was to hide what she was doing. She became secretive, postponed our meetings. Then I got a call from Grace Pontius in Cornell. She said she'd confirmed an invitation to Marion to present a paper in the summer, and asked me what I knew about this amazing new body of research that she was going to reveal at the conference. I was shocked. I knew absolutely nothing about it.

"So I tried to contact Marion, and I discovered that she'd

moved, and nobody knew where she was living. She wouldn't answer my phone calls or emails, and when I saw her once in the library she hurried away before I had a chance to talk to her. I began to think that some really big scandal was brewing—that Marion, out of stubbornness and spite at my refusal to consider her theories, was planning to challenge my reputation as a scholar in the most public and damaging way imaginable. I couldn't stop thinking about it, picturing myself turning up at Cornell and sitting through a paper by my own student about which I knew nothing, destroying the basis of my book, my work, my career."

"No," Brock murmured. "Well, you couldn't let that happen."

"What could I do? I tried appealing to Grace. I said that Marion's research really wasn't ready for public exposure, and it would be a kindness to her to make her wait. But Grace smelled a rat. She said that Wallcott at Princeton had heard something about Marion's work from one of his colleagues who met her by chance in the university here, and Grace was afraid Princeton might publish her first if she cancelled. I was beside myself."

"So?"

"Then I remembered that I'd met Marion's mother. She turned up uninvited to a faculty tea party for students and their relatives, a year or more ago. Appalling woman. When she learned I was Marion's supervisor she cornered me. I think she was half drunk, horribly flirtatious, and I had to listen to the story of her life before Marion realised what was happening and dragged her away. But I did remember her name, Sheena Rafferty, and the fact she lived in Ealing somewhere. She was in the phone book, and I went to see her. I assumed she'd know where Marion had moved to, only she didn't. Her husband, Keith, was there, and when I left he came after me and said he might be able to find out where Marion lived, if I made it worth his while. He asked for fifty quid in advance. I suppose he was testing me, to see how badly I wanted to know. Maybe he sensed that I was desperate. So I paid him and he said he'd get in touch."

"When was this?"

"About a month ago, the middle of March."

"What happened?"

"Nothing. He didn't get back to me. I was going to contact him, but then I heard the terrible news about Marion and did nothing until Inspector Kolla told me last Monday that Marion had been living in Hampstead. I tried to find the address from the phone book but couldn't, so I phoned Sheena Rafferty again. She wasn't in, but her husband was. I told him that Marion had some papers of mine that I wanted back, and asked if her mother had access to the house."

"Couldn't you have asked us that?" Brock objected.

Da Silva bit his lip. "I did ask DI Kolla, but she wasn't cooperative, and she pretty much gave me the impression that I was under suspicion, so I didn't press the point. I didn't really know what I was looking for, you see, and wanted time to search."

"Go on."

"Rafferty said he probably could now find out where the house was, and also get me a key, if I was prepared to pay."

"How much?"

"A thousand pounds."

"Really? And you agreed?"

"I tried to haggle, but he wouldn't have it. I think he believed there was something going on between Marion and me that I wanted to cover up, an affair or something. In the end I agreed, and within a couple of hours he came back to me. We met at a pub; I paid him the money and he gave me an address and a key. That evening I went to the house and removed the things you found in my office."

"Will Rafferty confirm this?"

Da Silva looked squeamish. "Unlikely, I should think."

Brock sat back in his chair, linking his fingers over his chest, and turned to Kathy. "What do you make of that, DI Kolla?"

"Bullshit, sir," Kathy replied evenly. She reached forward and took the book out of its plastic bag, opened it to the title page and read:

He sees the beauty
Sun hath not looked upon,
And tastes the fountain
Unutterably deep . . .

"That's your handwritten dedication to her, isn't it, Tony? You saw the beauty, did you? You tasted at the fountain, unutterably deep?"

He reddened. "It's from one of Rossetti's poems."

"Called 'Dream-Love,' yes."

"It was one of her favourites," he blustered. "We'd discussed it in a tutorial some time ago. I was being . . . ironic."

A muffled snort came from Brock.

"Doesn't sound like irony to me," Kathy went on remorselessly. "It sounds like a frank expression of love. You were lovers, weren't you?"

He bowed his head. "No. There was a time when I felt we might have been. She seemed to encourage me, when she needed my support to get her scholarship. Then, when it was confirmed, she changed her tune. My dedication in her book was . . . unwise. I could see that it might be misinterpreted. That's why I took it from her room, before anyone could draw the wrong conclusions."

A frown crossed his face and he seemed to rouse himself as if a bubble of his old self-esteem had risen to the surface. He looked Kathy in the eye and said, "Haven't you ever fallen foolishly for the wrong person, Inspector?"

"Yes," Kathy replied. "But I didn't have to kill them."

After they had gone, Brock said to Kathy, "You didn't mention the stuff left in the kitchen."

"No, forensics removed it on the day we found her house. I hoped he might let that slip. Only the killer knows about that."

"But there is a problem, isn't there? If he murdered Marion and planted that arsenic in her kitchen on the third of April, why did he wait until nearly a week later—after you'd told him that Marion lived at Rosslyn Court—to remove the things from her study?"

The same thing had been bothering Kathy. "It would all depend on the timing," she said. "It was like Alex said, he couldn't stage the scene in the kitchen until he was sure she had taken the poison and that it had worked. Then he couldn't be sure how much time he would have. He had to move fast, setting up the evidence and leaving straight away. It was only later, when he realised that he was being treated as a potential suspect, that he decided to remove any embarrassing material he could find in her house."

"Hm." Brock scratched his chin thoughtfully. "So we have a number of fixes on the murderer's movements: he visited Rosslyn Court prior to the murder, maybe on the Monday, to lace Marion's juice with arsenic; he was in St. James's Square at lunchtime on the Tuesday to witness her having her lunch and being taken away in an ambulance; and he was in Rosslyn Court again immediately afterwards to stage the scene in the kitchen. If da Silva's your man, there must surely be a record of him and his little red sports car on a camera somewhere. Find that and we're in business."

But by the end of the day they had found nothing.

ANOTHER TAKEAWAY SUPPER, ANOTHER glass of wine, Kathy sitting brooding on her sofa, facing her own private murder wall. She was conscious of how different the two halves were. The left half, the photos of Marion's pinboard, which initially had seemed rather chaotic and confusing, now appeared as a well-balanced composition, a tightly knit pattern built around the central figure of Dante Gabriel Rossetti, balanced on each side by the two women, Lizzie Siddal and Jane Morris and brooded over by Lena Wardle, while the other players in their drama orbited around. By contrast Kathy's own diagram, on the right, seemed disorganised and unresolved, images floating around an empty centre, without clear connections. She had two victims, Marion and Tina, and she put her pasta aside and rearranged them on the wall so that, like Lizzie and Lena, they were balanced to left and right of the centre. But there was no centre. Instead she had three suspects, Keith Rafferty, Nigel Ogilvie and Tony da Silva, rotating around a void.

She returned to the sofa and ate some more, considering this. The three men were very different from one another, yet were tied together in various ways. They knew each other, and were connected by self-interest, circumstance and assault. Could they all have been involved in the murders of the two women? Or were they merely satellites of some other missing figure in the centre? The photo of Marion's white flowers was pinned over to one side, and Kathy recalled Pip's comment about their meaning, *I shall die tomorrow*, and their name, Montpellier cistus, from the south of France. And maybe Corsica. She remembered how defensive Sophie Warrender had been when she'd asked if her husband had returned to London during their stay on the island.

She felt edgy now, unable to settle, going over her conversation with Sophie Warrender. She had mentioned London City Airport, and how easy it was for her husband to get into his office from there.

Kathy picked up her phone and got through to the duty officer's desk at headquarters. In a little while she had a contact name and phone number for security at the Docklands airport, and placed the call. The man sounded bored, happy to have something to do, and she hung on while he got to work on his computer, checking private flights for the period around the weekend before Marion died.

"No," he said at last. "There were only two private flights between here and Bastia around that time—Friday the thirtieth of March and Sunday the first of April. But no Douglas Warrender on the passenger list."

Kathy sagged. "Oh well. Maybe he used another name?"

"Doubt it. There was only one passenger each time. But it was a woman. Flew out Friday returned Sunday. Name of Marion Summers."

Kathy blinked. "Gotcha," she whispered, and took down the

details of the charter company and flights. A feeling of excitement grew inside her. Poor old Sophie, she thought.

She got to her feet and plucked the picture of the white flowers from its place on the edge of the diagram and moved it to the vacant spot in the middle. As she stepped back to consider, the sound of her buzzer jarred into her thoughts.

"Kathy?" Guy's voice sounded tinny over the intercom. "Are you okay? I was passing and saw your light . . . Sorry, I should have phoned first. Just wanted to check everything's all right."

"Come on up."

She met him at the lift and they kissed cheeks.

"Sure I'm not butting in?"

"'Course not." Seeing him again, she felt a surge of pleasure. "I'm really glad you came."

He grinned. "Any developments?"

"Not really." She took his hand and led him into the flat. "Take off your coat. Wine?"

He saw the half-eaten plate of curry on the sofa and said, "Oh, you're in the middle of eating."

"Want some? There's plenty more."

"Um, well . . . smells good. I'm starving actually. I was going to suggest . . ."

She poured him a glass of wine and went to the microwave.

"Bastia?"

She turned and saw him looking at her notes beside the phone.

"You planning another trip? Sorry." He looked sheepish. "None of my business. But you sound happy."

"Not a trip, no," she said, bringing over his plate. "Bastia's where the flowers came from." She nodded towards the wall and he turned, puzzled, to look.

"Ah, they're in the centre now. You think that's the key? You have a new suspect?"

"I think so. I don't have his picture, but I know who he is. He's been hard to find. I don't know it all yet, but I think I may be getting somewhere at last."

"Didn't you need my program to work it out?"

She laughed. "Sorry. I like having it up there on the wall where I can soak it in at odd moments, when I'm thinking of something else, so inspiration can catch me unawares."

"And it's caught you now? That's why you're happy?"

"It makes you feel good, when something slots into place, doesn't it? And then you kick yourself because it was staring you in the face all along and it seems so obvious."

"So this guy doesn't know you're on to him?"

"Not yet. I've got some more homework to do first, then he'll find out."

Guy raised his glass. "Well done. I'm really glad for you, Kathy." But he looked subdued.

"You all right?"

"I go tomorrow. They just told me this evening. That's why I came round. I didn't expect you to be here, but I came anyway."

"Ah. Did they say how long you'll be away?"

"A year, maybe two. I'll have regular trips back home, of course." He sounded sad.

"Well, we'd better make the most of it while you're here, hadn't we?"

TWENTY-FOUR

THE OFFICE WAS QUIET the next day, Saturday. Kathy imagined Bren looking after his sick little girls, Brock visiting Suzanne down in Sussex, Pip recovering from a night out. She made herself a coffee, feeling simultaneously elated and bereft. She'd said goodbye to Guy at seven that morning, wanting to spend the day with him, but they both had things to do, and he'd said he didn't want her to see him off at the airport.

She called a contact at Interpol and asked for information on Marion Summers on Corsica on the weekend before she died, then began searching the police databases for information on Douglas Warrender. There was a concise biography in the current *Who's Who*, with his present post listed as managing director of Mallory Capital, education at Oxford (BA Hons PPE 1969) and Harvard (MBA 1972), and current address at Mallory Capital, St. James's Square, London SW1.

Towards midday she got word from Interpol that Marion had been registered for two nights in a small hotel, Les Voyagers, in the centre of Bastia.

Kathy was suddenly ravenous, hungrier than she'd felt for ages, and was thinking about lunch when her mobile phone rang. Hoping that it was Guy, she answered eagerly. "Hello?"

The person at the other end paused, then spoke in a soft voice that she didn't recognise. "Detective Inspector Kolla?"

"Yes?"

"My name is Douglas Warrender. I believe we should meet."

Kathy stiffened in her chair. "Concerning what?"

The man gave a little grunt of amusement, then said, "My wife tells me that you were asking about my relationship with Marion Summers. She—my wife—gave me your number."

"I can set up an appointment for you to come in and make a statement, Mr. Warrender."

"No, not that. I'd rather meet you off the record, an informal chat, to explain a few things." The words were mildly stressed, but Kathy picked up the tone of command in the voice. "I think it might save you a lot of time and effort," he added.

"Where did you have in mind?"

"I'm presently sitting on a bench in St. James's Park, just a short walk from your office. It's a pleasant morning, quite warm. You might like to join me. Say in ten minutes?"

Kathy rang off, wondering how he knew she was at work that morning, or how he expected them to recognise each other. But he did, rising to his feet at the same moment that she recognised the face she'd found on the Internet. It didn't really do him justice, she realised, as she walked across the grass towards the bench beneath a spreading plane tree; the image on the web had been rather bland, but in life he seemed forceful and intelligent, regarding her with a shrewd, calculating eye. Kathy wondered if Marion had seen some echo of Rossetti in him.

He held out his hand, and they sat.

"You have a recorder?" he asked.

"Yes."

"It's up to you, but I shall speak more freely if this conversation is not recorded." He seemed quite open, rather relaxed.

Kathy held his eyes for a moment, then nodded and took the machine out of her pocket and laid it on the seat between them. He reached forward and switched it off.

"Thank you. You're interested to know if Marion had a lover, I understand. She did. It was me." He paused. "You're not surprised, I see."

Kathy said nothing, and he went on.

"We first became interested in each other last October. It was a stormy day, I remember, a Saturday, the wind lashing the trees. She had come to our house for a work session with my wife, and Sophie was late getting home from whatever she was doing. Marion and I had a coffee, and began to talk, and very quickly we both realised that we found something compelling in each other. I rang her the next day and asked if she'd have lunch with me, and that was how it began."

Kathy watched him, trying to imagine herself as Marion, becoming *interested*. She noticed the fleshy cheeks, the wings of grey hair behind the ears, groomed to look casually unself-conscious. Maybe it was unfair, comparing him to Guy, but he wasn't her idea of *compelling*. But he must have represented something that Marion wanted—or had it only been about money?

"We became lovers. But it was grubby, inconvenient. Brief meetings in hotel rooms soon lose their charm, and her student friends interrogated her when she went back to her flat. Also there was a problem with her tutor and her stepfather, both pestering her. So I bought her somewhere more agreeable, a refuge, where we could be ourselves, together. You've been there, I understand, with Sophie."

The raised eyebrow was almost teasing, Kathy thought, with the implication, *You took my wife to see my mistress's love-nest.*

"It cost you three-quarters of a million," Kathy said.

"Mm? Yes. So?"

"That's a lot of money."

He looked amused. "Well, I was very attached to her. But . . . do they give you a Christmas bonus, Inspector? No? Well, that represented less than half of mine last year. A small price to pay for a true passion, a meeting of souls."

"Aren't you bothered that her mother and stepfather will get it now, your Christmas bonus?"

He looked more serious suddenly. "Marion signed a document, making it over to me in the event of her death. It was her idea. She didn't like the thought of the Raffertys getting their hands on it any more than I did. Of course we didn't imagine it would ever have to be invoked. The money was nothing. She meant much more to me than that, Kathy. Let's be frank."

Kathy flinched at his use of her first name, and she saw him register this. "Go on."

"That's it, really. She moved into Rosslyn Court in January, and I visited her there whenever I could. It was a wonderful haven for me, away from the pressures of work and the strains at home."

"What about Sophie?"

"Ah . . ." He spread his hands, his face taking on a look of philosophical detachment. "Sophie is a marvellous woman, terrific author, very focused on her work and at the same time a great mother—but she doesn't really need me, not anymore. Nor I her."

"Did she know about Marion?"

"I believe she did wonder if there might be someone else. But she never brought it up, and I felt that she had simply decided to close her mind to that possibility. I'm certain she didn't think it was Marion. I suspected that the month in Corsica was a kind of test. She was insistent on it, and I felt I was under observation, to see how I'd react."

"And how did you react?"

"By the book. On the surface we were a perfect couple, making friends with other holidaying couples at the local restaurants, entertaining neighbours around the pool. But I was in touch with London, and missed Marion dreadfully. When she told me she'd lost her baby, I was devastated. She was distraught. I felt so helpless . . ."

He frowned, as if this was an unfamiliar and disturbing sensation.

"I did fly back to London to see her for just one day—there was a board meeting I told Sophie I had to attend. Marion was very low, and I arranged for her to see a doctor friend. Then later I flew her out to Bastia. It was the weekend before she died. She seemed in better spirits. I spent as much time with her as I could. We drove into the hills and she picked the wild flowers. It was the last time I saw her."

For a moment Kathy caught a vivid glimpse of Marion, in despair, giving herself up to the arrangements this strong man was making for her.

"What about the baby?" Kathy asked. "Were you planning to leave Sophie and start a new family?"

"Yes." He said it decisively, but there had been a small initial hesitation.

"And now?"

"Well, that may rather depend on you, Inspector. My first reaction, when I heard the terrible news, was to tell everyone the truth about us. I was in shock—I suppose I still am. I wanted to declare to the world that this was the woman I loved. But as time has passed I have come to appreciate how much other people would be hurt by that truth. And Marion is dead, so what would be the point? I was intimately involved with Marion Summers, but I had absolutely nothing to do with her death. I want to convince you of that. I have been completely frank with you, told you things that my wife does not know. I am in your power. You can tell Sophie, or not. Please think carefully before you decide."

"Hm." Kathy looked down at a squirrel loping across the grass, its tail tracing graceful loops through the air. She kicked her shoe against the ground, nagged by the feeling that she had missed something—maybe some words or intonations that had seemed out of place—but she had been concentrating so hard on catching every nuance that she'd barely had time to register them before she'd had to move on. She wished now that she had insisted on recording him. She shrugged off the thought and said, "Tell me about Keith Rafferty."

BROCK WAS NOT SPENDING his Saturday morning with Suzanne in Battle, though he was thinking about her. It was his first day without a call from the office in weeks, and he was feeling restless and at a loose end. He had gone to the Bishop's Mitre in the High Street near his home for a pint and a pie lunch while he read the paper, but the news was depressing and he was troubled by the way he'd left things unresolved with Suzanne. He should have been more, well, *balanced* about her sudden determination to dig into her own past. The fact was, if he cared to admit it, he had been jealous of Dougie Warrender, and Suzanne's barely disguised eagerness to meet up again with her first big crush. He had even gone so far as to get a profile of the man from an expert in corporate affairs in the Fraud Squad. A formidable operator, was the word, and very wealthy. "He had some disagreement with his father when he was at Oxford," he'd been told, "and the old man cut off his allowance for a while, so he paid his way by playing poker with the rich kids. Disarmingly straightforward, when you meet him, but don't let that fool you. Many have, to their regret."

He turned away from the chatter of conversation at the bar and took out his phone. Suzanne's answering machine came on, and he left a message.

"A SCOUNDREL, WELL, YOU must know that." He seemed amused by her question.

"How do you know him?"

"Marion told me about him. She hated the way he looked at her, and tried to get her alone."

He stopped, as if he might leave it there, but Kathy said, "And?"

Another little smile, as if to say, *smart girl*. "He would hang around the place where she lived, in Stamford Street, and follow her, spying on her. One time he trailed her to a pub where we were meeting. That must have made his day. Later he contacted me. We met, and he demanded money to keep quiet about our relationship. I persuaded him that I could make life a great deal more uncomfortable for him than he could for me. He backed off. He was one of the reasons for moving Marion out of Stamford Street."

Another pause, before Kathy said again, "And?"

He looked puzzled. "That's about it, I think."

"What about Nigel Ogilvie?"

"Ogilvie? Oh, the little creep in the library. Yes, well, that was Rafferty's doing, not mine. Ogilvie was there when Marion collapsed—I suppose you know that. Apparently in the confusion he palmed a computer memory stick that fell out of her bag. It contained copies of letters that Marion and I had exchanged. He contacted me, with a view to selling it to me—for a highly inflated sum, naturally."

"Nigel Ogilvie, a blackmailer?" Kathy found this hard to visualise.

"Mm. He needed cash. He has a taste for expensive West End call girls, apparently. Did you know that?"

Kathy shook her head, readjusting her mental image of Ogilvie.

"In his case I decided to pay—not as much as he first demanded, but we finally agreed on a more than fair price. I didn't want to meet the man personally, but I did need to impress upon him that there must be no copies made, so I employed Keith Rafferty to make the exchange and emphasise the point. That was a mistake. I get the impression that he may have been overemphatic."

"He put Ogilvie in hospital."

"Well I certainly didn't ask him to do that. Does he say I did?"

Kathy didn't reply.

"It's a lie if he does. In fact I wouldn't be surprised if he did it so that he could keep a good part of the money for himself. He also has a financial weakness, in his case for the horses. Is there anything else I haven't covered?"

"I would like to see that memory stick."

Warrender gave another of his easy smiles. "Oh would you? And why would I agree to that? It contains some very private correspondence."

"You want me to find out who killed Marion, don't you?"

He gave her a bleak look. "Yes, I do." He reached a hand into the pocket of his jacket. "I could tell you I wiped it . . ." He brought out the small device. "This is for your eyes only, and then I want it back. I don't want this circulating around the Met for laughs."

"I shall have to show my boss, and report our conversation today."

"DCI Brock." He nodded. "No one else? You promise?"

"That'll be up to him."

He hesitated, then shrugged and handed it to her. "Please get him to agree."

"Tell me," Kathy said, "what's your theory about what happened to Marion?"

He frowned and turned away. The squirrel was now prancing in front of a group of laughing Japanese, showing off. "I was rather hoping you could tell me that. You now know much more about it all than I do. What I very much do not want is for my involvement to distract you from the real culprit." He turned back to her and his eyes dropped to the memory stick in her hand. He seemed about to add something, then changed his mind. "Surely you have some idea? Won't you tell me?"

She said nothing, and he shrugged and got to his feet.

"I won't say it's been an unalloyed pleasure, Inspector. Too uncomfortable for that. But I feel easier for having told you all this."

Kathy stared at him but he just smiled. "Let me know if you get tired of policing. There're plenty of opportunities for talents like yours, in jobs that give Christmas bonuses."

He walked off across the park towards the Mall, and as she watched him go, one of the missing thoughts came back into Kathy's mind with a jolt: he had said, *She picked the wild flowers.*

Not just wild flowers, but *the* wild flowers, as if he knew about how she'd been puzzling over that posy. And the timing of his confession was odd too, days after her conversation with his wife, which in itself had hardly been challenging enough to cause him to spill the beans about his relationship with Marion. It was almost as if he had known that she already knew about it. A sick feeling was growing in her stomach. He had known far too much.

IT WAS MID-AFTERNOON BEFORE Suzanne answered his call. He was at home, trying to concentrate on finishing Sophie Warrender's biography of Edward Lear.

"Sorry, David," she said. "We've been so busy in the shop. The fine weather has brought everyone out. How are you?"

"Fine, fine. I thought I might pop down this afternoon. I booked a table at the Old Pheasant for us for tonight."

"Oh. That would have been lovely."

"You've got something on?"

"Well, an old friend of mine, in Hampshire, has invited me to go over there this evening. I said I'd stay the night."

"Ah. That's nice for you."

"We haven't seen each other for years. I'm sorry, I should have mentioned it, but it only just came up. This is your first free weekend for ages, isn't it? Are you at a loose end?"

Her words were hurried, he thought, her voice unnaturally bright. "No, no. Plenty to catch up on."

"Maybe next weekend, eh?"

"Yes."

They had a brief conversation, rather rushed at her end and desultory at his, before they hung up. Brock threw Edward Lear aside, thinking of the time he'd almost lost her once before.

TWENTY-FIVE

KATHY EVENTUALLY FOUND HIM in Weatherspoon's Bar in Terminal Four at Heathrow. It had taken a phone call to Scotland Yard to get her through security to the passenger-only departure concourse on the first floor. The place was crowded with travellers, anxious, excited or bored. His head was buried in a paperback, and he didn't look up when she sat at his table. After a moment he reached out a hand to feel for his glass of beer, but she got there first and slid it away. He looked up, puzzled to see that it had moved, then blinked and focused on Kathy. His mouth opened.

"Kathy!"

"Guy."

She watched his expression go through several shifts as he took in the sombre look on her face. Then he sighed, and said, "Oh God. You know."

Her first thought, seeing him sitting there, had been to whack him one and pour the beer over his head, but now she felt only very sad.

"I want to know why."

He sighed again. "Oh, a friend of mine got into a bit of trouble over a big loan he took out to buy a flat."

"A friend of yours."

"Yeah, his name's Helmut. We work in the same office. Anyway, one day he got a phone call from this bloke who said he could sort out the problem, if he was willing to do a little job for him in return. He wanted Helmut to go to Prague for the weekend, all expenses paid, and make friends with an attractive woman. It sounded like a breeze. Only Helmut couldn't go. He's married, and his wife's really sick. That's what made it so important. I said I'd do it for him."

Kathy took a deep breath. Spare me, she thought. But how the hell had he known about Prague? "When was this?"

"Just the evening before we went. It all happened so quickly I didn't have time to think of the consequences. I'm really sorry, Kathy. It just seemed, you know, something to do for a friend, and a bit of a laugh. I didn't count on . . . on really liking you. I hoped you'd never know. How did you find out?"

"I'm a cop," she said bitterly. "Sometimes we get to know more than we'd like."

"Yeah, he didn't tell me that, or I'd have been more cautious. But by the time you told me what you did, we'd got to know each other and were having a good time, and I didn't want to stop. When I got back from Prague I asked Helmut what it was all about. He said he'd been told you were working on the murder of a close friend of this other guy, and he wanted to keep an eye on how things developed. He said he wanted to know the truth of what had happened, because he didn't trust the police and the lawyers not to stuff it up. Helmut got the impression he might be prepared to take matters into his own hands if that happened. The way he told it, I felt some sympathy for him."

"So when was the last time you saw Warrender?"

"Is that his name? I only met him the once, first thing this morning, after I left you. When I finally got the word to go to the Gulf he wanted to meet me in person, to get a personal briefing. I didn't want to go, but Helmut was insistent." He shrugged hopelessly.

"And you told him about the flowers on my wall."

He nodded. "Yes. He was very interested in that."

His eyes went up to a monitor and he said quietly, "My flight's boarding, Kathy. Are you going to arrest me?"

She gave a snort. "What for, screwing a police officer under false pretences? I don't think that's in the book."

"I'm sorry. I really am. I feel like a total shit. But it wasn't all false pretences. I meant what I said about—"

"Don't." She got to her feet and walked away, pushing through the crowds without seeing them.

WHEN SUZANNE LOOKED UP Angela's address in Winchester she found that it was near the centre of the city, and she imagined the two of them, old friends, soaking up the historic atmosphere of the ancient college and cathedral precincts, visiting Jane Austen's tomb and perhaps her house at Chawton nearby, places she hadn't been to since she was a child. But Angela had other ideas.

She had been divorced for four months, and was still working through some of the *issues*. From what Suzanne could gather, the separation had been relatively straightforward—Angela had got the house in Winchester and her husband the flat in London, and neither money nor the adult children had been a problem. But the matter of his thirty-year-old girlfriend, which she'd begun by dismissing as grotesque and pathetic, had affected her in ways she still hardly knew how to acknowledge. For a start, the relationship hadn't collapsed within a few months as she'd predicted, but was looking increasingly solid. But it was the inescapable contrasts, between the other woman's youth and her own age, between beauty in its full flush on the one hand and laboured facsimile on the other, that had gradually got to her in deep and harrowing ways. She had started out shrugging these things off as spurious, but they had come to mean everything. Her life was her own, but it was over. What did she have?

Well, booze for a start, and from the moment Suzanne walked through the front door and the first glass of bubbly was thrust into her hand, she found herself caught up in a race towards oblivion, quite liberating and amusing at first, then increasingly rather alarming. It was clear that Angela had already had a few, but she carried them pretty well, greeting Suzanne with tremendous warmth.

"Oh God, when you contacted me I just couldn't believe it! Seeing you again—you haven't changed a bit!—takes me back to those wonderful days, when everything seemed possible and just so, so wonderful!"

But she didn't really want to talk about those wonderful days, about which she had only the haziest memories. What she really wanted to talk about was being deserted for a very much younger woman.

"No, look, I have to say she really is a *very* charming person. The kids tell me she is, and they would know, having seen so much more of her than I have. And very pretty. Well, good luck to them both. I feel . . . like I have a whole new life in front of me. It's a fabulous feeling. God, I've even started smoking again, after thirty years! That's how old she is, incidentally. Did I mention that? Come on, drink up. A toast—to real friends."

There was no sign of food in the kitchen, and when Suzanne said she'd like to take Angela out for dinner, there was talk about a really marvellous little restaurant not far away, but when Suzanne suggested she phone up to book, it being a Saturday night, Angela got distracted in the middle of searching for their number when she found a photo of herself and her family in happier days, which provoked a sudden tearful collapse.

They eventually crawled into their beds without dinner and without having talked about Dougie Warrender and Notting Hill.

The next morning, very hungover, Suzanne made her way downstairs towards the smell of coffee. Angela seemed to be in slightly better shape than her, and apologised profusely for being such a bad host.

"God, we didn't have a thing to eat, did we? But I'm going to make it up to you, with breakfast for a start. Bacon, sausages, eggs, mushrooms . . ."

Suzanne shook her head vigorously, the motion making her feel even more nauseous. "No, really, Angela. A bit of toast and coffee will be just fine for me."

But Angela had made up her mind, and Suzanne sat at the kitchen table, trying not to retch, as her friend attacked the sizzling frying pan.

"So you met Dougie Warrender again! What's he like? As charming as ever?"

"Yes, just the same." She was about to say "much older, of course," but wisely decided to avoid that tack. "Very rich. He's a merchant banker or something. And the houses, yours and theirs, are immaculate. Have you been back there recently?"

"No, not since we moved, ages ago. And you say that dragon of a mother of his is still there too? You had a real thing for Dougie, didn't you? Did you have sex?"

"No, of course not! I was only thirteen."

"I did, with his cousin Jack. But maybe that was the next year. Didn't I tell you?"

"No, I don't think so. You were sent off to boarding school."

"Yes. In fact that's *why* I was sent off to boarding school." She giggled. "He was ever so gentle, and afterwards he told me all the family secrets. I wonder what he's doing now. I might get in touch."

"I'm afraid he's dead, Angela. Dougie told me. Heart attack, ten years ago."

"Oh God."

Suzanne saw Angela's shoulders slump, and rapidly tried to head off a change of mood. "What family secrets?"

"Oh, I don't know. I can't remember. We should have champagne and orange juice for our celebratory breakfast."

"Oh no, I couldn't, Angela."

"You'll feel much better if you do. Hair of the dog."

"No, really."

"Oh well. Here we go."

She placed a plate of heaped fried stuff under Suzanne's nose, then sat down with her own and began to tuck in.

"In India," she said suddenly. "What Dougie got up to in India, that's what Jack's secrets were all about."

"Really? What did he get up to? He didn't tell me much, as far as I can remember. In fact I can hardly remember him saying anything at all. He just stood around or hit a ball in the gardens, looking sultry and gorgeous. Any time he actually spoke to me I was reduced to a jelly."

"It was about a girl . . . What do they call them in India, is it amah or ayah? A nanny or housekeeper?"

"Dougie had a love affair with his nanny?"

"No." Angela giggled. "With his ayah's daughter, I think. I can't remember much, except that it ended tragically somehow. Come on, eat up."

"How tragically?"

"Oh, I don't know, doomed teenage romance, I suppose, class and race, that sort of thing. Are you sure about the champagne? I think I will."

Suzanne managed to escape before lunch, when the first gin and tonic appeared, pleading a crisis at the shop.

"You have a shop!" Angela beamed. "How marvellous! I've often thought of starting up a little business, you know—a little hobby, really. Perhaps we could go into partnership together. Maybe something organic, beauty products or something. What does your shop sell?"

"Antiques."

"Oh." Angela's face dropped, and Suzanne made for the car.

BROCK TOO HAD WOKEN with a hangover that morning—mild, but enough to make him feel grumpy as he shuffled about the kitchen, making coffee and toast. It wasn't just the hangover; he had woken with the clear conviction that Suzanne had been lying to him. It was such an ugly and improbable thought that he'd tried to dismiss it, but it wouldn't go away. Yesterday he had been merely exasperated by her contacting the Warrenders during his murder investigation, but now her secretiveness and evasive explanations seemed to cast that intrusion in a murkier light. Why hadn't she told him she was coming up to London last Wednesday? And who was the nameless, genderless friend from the past that she'd had to spend the night with?

He stewed on this for a while, then swore and tried to immerse himself in the paperwork he'd brought home. After a couple of hours of that he put on an overcoat and set off down the lane that ran along the railway embankment to the house of a neighbour, whose dog he sometimes took for a walk. As they reached the park, he recalled that the last time he'd done this was with Suzanne's grandchildren, Stewart and Miranda. It occurred to him how much he would miss them all, if things fell apart with Suzanne again.

THE SHOP WAS BUSY when Suzanne returned to Battle later, the spring weather bringing people out for a drive down to the coast. Her assistant Ginny was barely coping with the press of customers in the crowded rooms, and Suzanne immediately hung up her coat and got to work. It remained like that all day, so that she had no time for a lunch break, and she was feeling weary on her feet when the Dutch couple, who had been in earlier, returned for another look at the Georgian silver. She was showing them a tray of spoons when she became aware of a figure standing behind them and to one side. She glanced at him, then blinked. "Oh! Hello."

"Hello," Brock said. "I wonder if you could tell me if this is Pre-Raphaelite?" He pointed to a silver locket in the cabinet beside them.

Suzanne smiled, feeling rattled by his sudden presence, but answered deadpan. "Oh no, a bit later. Art Nouveau, probably around 1900."

She took it out of the cabinet and placed it on the counter, and the Dutch couple turned to peer at it.

"I like it," said the Dutch woman. "Are you going to buy it?"

"I think I may. For a colleague at work. She's getting engaged." Brock turned back to Suzanne. "I've caught you at a busy time."

"Yes." She looked at the grandfather clocks ticking against the far wall. "I'll be closing in half an hour."

"Why don't I go across to the King's Head and wait for you there?"

The Dutch couple exchanged a glance, eyebrows raised.

"Good idea. I'll wrap your locket and bring it over."

In the event it was an hour before she appeared.

"Sorry. Couldn't get away." She thought how serious he looked, stooped over his pint, and felt anxious suddenly, aware of a cold space between them. "Are you all right?"

"Fine. Your G and T may be a bit warm. Want me to get another?"

"No, this will do very well. Cheers." She took a gulp then began to blurt out how glad she was he'd come, but he spoke at the same time, head still bowed.

"So how was your friend?"

"Rather sad. She got divorced recently and she's not coping very well. She's taken to the bottle in a big way. I wished I hadn't gone. It doesn't work sometimes, renewing old friendships. We're not the same people."

He looked up at her, as if trying to work something out, and she added, "I would much rather have gone to the Old Pheasant with you. You were upset, weren't you?"

He hesitated a moment, then reached out his hand and stroked hers. "Just feeling a bit fraught. It's been a heavy few weeks."

"I know." She squeezed his fingers. "Who's getting engaged?" She nodded at the gift-wrapped locket she'd brought.

"No one yet, but there's a rumour going around that Kathy's got herself a new man."

"That is good news. Let's hope he's better than the last one. How's she getting on with her murder case?"

"The poisoning?" She heard the reserve in Brock's voice. "I think we're getting there."

"I'm sorry I blundered in like that, David. I had no idea the situation was so sensitive. There's no suggestion that Douglas Warrender was involved, is there?"

He waited a couple of beats, then said, "Warrender? I don't think so. Why?"

"I'd just hate to think . . . after me getting tangled with them again . . . you know."

"But you're not, are you?"

"What?"

"Tangled with them—are you?"

"No! Of course not. I just feel embarrassed about the whole business."

"Well, don't be. I'm sure your old flame is in the clear."

"Oh good."

"Let's forget all about it."

"I will. That's a promise. Shall I ring the Old Pheasant?"

"Already done," he said.

THE NEXT MORNING, LONG after Brock had driven off back to London for his Monday-morning briefing, Suzanne got a call from Angela Crick.

"You got home all right then, Suzanne? I felt so guilty about making you miss your dinner on Saturday. Why don't we do it again next weekend and I'll make it up to you?"

"Oh, that would be nice, Angela, but it's so busy here in the shop at the moment. I was rushed off my feet when I got back. Maybe we could leave it for a while."

"Oh well. I had something else to tell you about Dougie Warrender."

"Really? What was that?"

"I remembered more about the girl in India, the nurse's daughter. It's funny how things come back to you when you're doing something else. I was putting the bottles out in the recycling bin. They come today, you see . . . Anyway, I noticed this little green bottle, and it just triggered this memory. It all came flooding back. Poor Jack." She sighed.

"What memory, Angela?"

"Don't you want to save it till we get together again? It is rather juicy."

"No, please, tell me now."

Angela giggled. "You *are* interested in him, aren't you? Well, according to Jack . . ." Angela's voice dropped to a whisper, as if telling a children's ghost story, "Dougie got her pregnant and then murdered her, with poison, from a little green bottle."

The line went silent. Finally Suzanne said, "I don't believe it."

Angela laughed again. "No, of course not. I'm sure it was all rubbish, but according to Jack it's what people said at the time. Mind you, Jack was always trying to shock me with outlandish stories."

"But what did he say happened, exactly?"

"He claimed Dougie told him that the Warrenders had to hush it all up and leave India and come back to the UK, like me being packed off to boarding school. Notting Hill must have been a bit of a shock for them, in those days, after India. No wonder Dougie made up whopping tales."

Suzanne felt a tight pain in her chest, and realised she was holding her breath. "What kind of poison was it? Do you remember?"

"What kind? I haven't the faintest. What does it matter? It was just gossip and scandal-mongering, that's all."

Angela went on for some time, but Suzanne didn't take in much of what she said. When she finally hung up she sank into a chair, wondering what on earth she should do. Then the bell on the shop door tinkled and the Dutch couple came in. "All right now," the man said, "we've finally made up our minds."

TWENTY-SIX

My darling,

it's five days since you left and already it seems forever. I console myself with our secret knowledge. Every day I feel it growing inside me, a part of you, feeding on me. But I am lost without you. Yesterday was miserable. Tony spotted me in the university library and threatened to make a fuss about my scholarship unless I agreed to a tutorial. Loathsome man. I had to go to his room where he demanded to know what I was working on. I fudged and he hectored, oh how he hectored, a dreary repetitive rant about how I am on the wrong track. Little does he know! He demanded to see my Cornell paper, but I said it wasn't written yet, though I don't think he believed me. He made the foulest cup of coffee I've ever tasted, and afterwards I was very sick. I had to go home and lie down. It wasn't like the usual morning sickness, much worse. I'm sorry to sound miserable.

I just miss you so.
Your M.

"Two days later she miscarried," Kathy said, as Brock looked up from the printout. "There are lots more like that, as well as copies of her work documents."

"Can we be sure it's genuine?"

"That's the thing, isn't it? He handed the memory stick over to me, knowing we'd read this. I've sent it to the lab, to see if they can establish when the text was written or amended."

"But you felt Warrender was on the level?"

Kathy hesitated. "He sounded very plausible, but there were things he said, as if he knew exactly what I knew, and how far he had to go. It seemed to me that there was only one way he could do that." And finally Kathy told him about Guy Hamilton, and confronting him at the airport. "If Warrender had spoken to me an hour later I wouldn't have been able to see Guy before he left, and I'd never have been sure."

Brock gave an angry growl, his eyes narrowing. "That's very disturbing, Kathy. Is it really possible? How could Warrender have set it up? How could he have possibly known you were planning to go to Prague?"

"That's what I've been trying to work out. I think it must have happened after we arrested Keith Rafferty. My guess is that it was Warrender who arranged for Julian Fenwick to represent Rafferty and Crouch. From them he'd have learned that I was investigating Marion's death, and could have got my mobile number, which I gave to Sheena Rafferty."

"You think they were listening in to your phone calls?"

"It's possible. Or they might have had someone following me when I met Nicole Palmer that Friday evening and overheard me get the information about our trip from her. Guy said Warrender only approached him at the last moment, on that Friday night before we left."

"Either way, it's too damn personal, Kathy. I don't like this at all."

"Yes."

"How did Bren get on with Rafferty? Did he make any headway?"

"Not really." Bren had phoned in that morning, struck down by the flu. Kathy had spoken to him and he'd been apologetic. There had been so many other things demanding his attention. She was sympathetic, but angry all the same. Her anger had been growing over the weekend, as she'd tried to work out the machinations that had allowed Warrender to follow her moves. And now, the memory of Guy at the airport gave her heart another wrench.

Brock saw it, the anger burning inside her. He leaned forward, eyes on her, and said, a note of caution in his voice, "But if that letter is genuine, Kathy, it sounds as if da Silva was making an earlier attempt to poison Marion, doesn't it?"

"Not with arsenic. Sundeep established she hadn't previously taken it. But it could have been something else." What it reminded her of, in fact, was the diary entries of Emile L'Angelier complaining about feeling sick after visiting Madeleine Smith. And of course Marion would have been very familiar with those.

"All right," Brock went on, sounding brisk, wanting to rouse Kathy from her introspection. Clearly she had been fond of this Guy, he thought, and was understandably upset, but they had work to do. "Da Silva is our prime suspect. How do we nail him?"

"He's been careful. We haven't been able to find him on cameras at the critical scenes, except the British Library."

"We're saying he murdered Marion to prevent her from presenting her paper at Cornell that would destroy his life's work, is that right? Is that credible?"

"He certainly sounded pretty desperate about it."

"Then why kill Tina?"

"Because she'd followed the same trail as Marion and found the same source."

"How would he know that?"

"She must have told him when she came to his house the night before she died. Donald Fotheringham told me that he, Tina and Emily had been investigating the archives of the Havelock family in the India Office Records at the library."

"Yes," Brock said, "the woman who found Tina at the library, Lily Cribb, told me that she'd first met Tina trying to find the India Office Records. It seemed odd."

"I think that Haverlock's diary must have been stored there in the Havelock family's archive. I wonder how Marion found it. It must have seemed like a miracle. If we're right, it was her death warrant." Kathy thought. "By last Monday, when da Silva found Marion's notes in her house, he would have realised that the source of Marion's revelations was Haverlock's diary, but he still wouldn't have known how to find it—her paper only refers to a London archive. It was still tucked away in the India Office Records. On the Wednesday evening, when she called at his house, Tina must have told him she'd found it. He would have gone spare, thinking he'd put a lid on it all with Marion's death."

Brock said, "And the following day he would have been tracking her, trying to find out where the diary was."

"Yes. The trail will be there in the record of the books that Tina called up at the British Library. If we can show that she had found the Haverlock diary before she went to see da Silva, that would then put her in the same situation as Marion before she died."

Brock nodded. "Circumstantial, but it might just be conclusive."

Kathy returned to her desk and called over Pip Gallagher, who was working for her again now.

"You okay, boss?" Pip asked. "You seem a bit down."

"No," Kathy said, too abruptly. "I'm fine, Pip. I just wish I knew where the hell da Silva might have got arsenic from, if it wasn't from the laboratory."

"How about Rafferty? Da Silva admitted paying him money. Maybe it wasn't just for the key to Marion's house."

"That is a thought. Look, I want you to drop what you're doing and go over to the British Library and get them to give you a list of all the documents Tina requested in the week before she died. I'm particularly interested in a diary written by someone called Haverlock, which we think is held in this archive in the India Office Records." She handed Pip a note of the references. "Find out if she requested it, okay?"

"Sure. I was never that hot as a reader, but I'll give it a go."

It felt like a penance, Kathy thought, as she worked through the day, poring over the details dredged up by her team, cross-checking the witness statements.

Finally Pip phoned in. "I've got it, boss. Tina was here all right, looking at stuff from the Havelock archive. She requested the Haverlock diary on the evening of Wednesday last."

Kathy sighed, rubbing her hand across her face. "Great."

"What do I do now?"

Kathy thought. "I think we'll need to retrace Tina's steps. Leave it for now. Tomorrow, I want you to go round all the libraries we know Marion and Tina went to, and get a complete record of their borrowings."

The line was silent for a moment, then Pip said, "Really?"

"Yes, really."

Kathy put the phone down. The evening was drawing in, the streetlights flickering on outside the window. She felt a tightness in her chest, her stomach. Maybe Brock had been right, she thought, this had become too personal— Rafferty's threat of legal action against her, Jock's cat, Prague, Guy. *Rafferty*. What was his part in all this, the predatory stepfather? She remembered sensing a false note when Douglas Warrender had described his relationship with Rafferty. If Warrender had arranged Julian Fenwick's services, then it suggested that Warrender and Rafferty were closer than Warrender had implied. And Rafferty knew them all—Warrender, Ogilvie and da Silva—all of them locked together somehow, using and reluctantly protecting each other, a single nut to be cracked. She closed down her computer, shrugged on her coat and caught a District line tube out to Ealing Broadway.

KATHY FOLLOWED THE DECK to the door of the Raffertys' flat and rang the bell. Sheena Rafferty answered, not recognising Kathy straight away. Kathy explained that she had some important information of a personal nature to explain to her, if she could spare a moment.

"I dunno," Sheena looked doubtful. "Keith told me not to speak to you."

"It could be to your advantage, Sheena. It won't take long."

The word *advantage* did the trick, as Kathy knew it would. She didn't enjoy deceiving Sheena, but she was sure that Marion would have thoroughly approved of what she had in mind. She followed Sheena into the sitting room. Two half-drunk glasses stood on the coffee table, a gin and a beer. Sheena reached for the gin and a cigarette.

"Make it quick, will ye? Keith's takin' a shower. He's lost his job and he's not in a good mood." The rumble of plumbing promptly stopped.

"How have you been?"

"Fine, fine. What is it ye want exactly?"

"It concerns your daughter's estate, Sheena."

"Estate?" She looked dubious.

"Her property, her assets, that will come to you, as her next of kin."

"What, like an insurance payout?" she said hopefully.

"I'm not aware of any insurance, but it's possible, I suppose."

"Och, well, what about compensation, victims of crime? I'm a victim too, you know."

"Again, I don't know about that. What I have in mind is potentially much more significant."

There was a roar from the doorway. "What the fuck are you doing here?" Keith Rafferty stood with a towel around his waist, skin pink from the shower, eyes blazing. "I'm calling my lawyer right now."

"No, hang on, darlin'," Sheena said quickly. "The Inspector's come to see me, about Marion's assets."

He hesitated. "What assets?"

"She's just about to tell me, is that no' right, Inspector?"

"Yes."

"Well, go on then," Keith said.

"This is a private matter I have to discuss with Marion's mother,

Mr. Rafferty. I'm well aware of your lawyer's insistence that I should have no further contact with you, and I don't feel comfortable having you present. Maybe I should speak to you another time, Sheena, when you're alone."

"Now wait a minute"—Keith stuck his jaw out—"if you've got anything to say to my wife I want to hear it."

Kathy shook her head and rose to her feet.

"Sheena!" Keith snapped. "Tell her you want it that way."

Sheena winced under his glare and nodded. "Aye. I want Keith to hear."

"Well, if you're quite sure. This is only an advisory visit, you understand, to make you aware of a potential situation that could concern you."

"What?" Sheena looked mystified, Keith aggrieved.

"Get on with it," he snarled.

"Are you aware that Marion owned a house?"

Sheena's eyes widened. "What sort of house?"

"A very attractive detached property, in Hampstead." Kathy turned to meet Keith's eyes. He looked away.

"Hampstead? Owned it, you say?"

"That's right. It's in her name alone, no mortgage."

"But . . . how much would that be worth, then?"

"Quite a lot. Three-quarters of a million, at least."

Sheena gasped. "But how? Marion was a student. She had no money."

"No, but she had an admirer, a wealthy man who bought it for her, as a present."

"Oh my dear Lord! My wee Marion? Who is he, this feller?"

"I'm afraid I can't disclose that."

Kathy felt Keith's eyes on her, burning, trying to work out what she was up to.

"Oh!" Sheena gave a sudden trilling giggle, jumping to her feet. "Did ye hear that, Keithy?! Did ye hear that?"

"Yeah. So what's the catch?"

"Yes," Kathy said, "I'm afraid there is a catch. Marion signed a document giving the house back to this man in the event of her death."

"Oh . . ." Sheena collapsed again onto her chair, horror on her face.

"But," Kathy went on, "and this is the reason for my coming to speak to you, that may depend on the results of our investigation into Marion's death."

"How do you mean?"

"Well, you see, this man is naturally a person of interest to us, having been so much involved in Marion's recent life. And if it should turn out that he was responsible for her death, well, the courts might decide to set aside that document, as amounting to the profits of a crime."

There was silence for a moment. Then Keith said softly, "But is that likely? Do you suspect this man?"

"I'm not at liberty to say, Mr. Rafferty. The case is still wide open at this stage, and we're sifting through a great deal of evidence. I just thought I should alert Mrs. Rafferty to the fact that if we were to lay charges against him at some point in the future, then she should consider seeking legal advice. Three-quarters of a million pounds is a great deal of money."

"Aye," Sheena said dazedly. "It sure as hell is that."

TWENTY-SEVEN

BROCK DROPPED THE REPORT into his out-tray and sat back with a sigh, rubbing both hands across his face. It was all very well giving advice and direction to Kathy and the others, but he had learned to doubt such advice when it came from senior figures who hadn't actually touched the evidence for themselves, hadn't heard the subtle doubt in the witness's voice, had forgotten how contradictory and confusing the options were. Alex Nicholson's suggestion that they might be investigating a double suicide had already occurred to him. Tina's death seemed like a mirror image of Marion's, following Marion's example, perhaps even fulfilling a pact of some kind between them. Kathy had known Tina, and Brock had sensed her sympathy for the student and her scepticism of Alex's idea, just as she had resisted from the start the possibility of Marion's suicide. He suspected that Kathy identified with Marion's struggle, and with Tina's, too closely for that.

But what did he know, stuck behind his bloody desk reading other people's reports? And then there was that disconcerting thing, the sudden appearance of Douglas Warrender on the scene, immediately after Brock had reassured Suzanne that he wasn't involved. Had Suzanne heard something? He wanted to talk it over with her, but that would only complicate things further, and probably put her in a compromising position.

He heaved himself out of his chair and reached for his overcoat. "I'm going up to the British Library to see how they're getting on," he said to Dot as he strode through her office.

"The new HR Deputy Liaison Officer is coming to see you in an hour, don't forget."

"Put him off. Urgent business."

Just getting out of the office lifted his spirits. When he reached the forecourt of the library he paused and took it in once again, peaceful now, the police tapes gone, tourists mingling with students and researchers, people cheerfully drinking coffee in The Last Word café. He went across to the library entrance beneath the lowering roof planes, catching a glimpse of the towers and finials of St. Pancras station next door. At the inquiries counter inside he showed his ID and was directed to an office in the administrative area nearby. There he found Pip Gallagher bent over a pile of books. She jumped up when he greeted her, looking guilty, like a student caught falling asleep over her homework.

"They've given me this table and they're bringing me the books that Tina asked for in the past couple of weeks, Chief. I'm trying to make notes for Kathy." She gestured at a clipboard on which she had laboriously written comments beneath the titles of each volume.

"Big job," Brock said.

"Yeah." Pip sighed. "I'm not sure if I'm doing it right. Kathy wants to establish some kind of logical trail that Tina followed, leading up to the diary that undermines da Silva's work. I've got the borrowing or request records for both Marion and Tina at all the libraries we know they went to—that's the British Library here, the London Library where Marion collapsed, the National Archives at Kew, the Family Records Centre in Finsbury, and the University of London Senate House Library."

She spread the printouts over the table, and Brock immediately understood why she was looking so glum.

"Lot of books," he murmured.

"Yes. I've started with Tina's lists, putting them in date order, and starting at the beginning."

"Makes sense."

"I wondered if she might have left any notes in the books, or written anything in the margins. No luck so far. Basically I'm trying to write a short description of each book, so Kathy can get an idea of what they're about."

"And you started here because . . . ?"

"Well, Tina was attacked here, and also she spent most time here recently. She wasn't a member of the London Library like Marion, so she has no borrowing record there, although they do remember her visiting a couple of times and having a look around. She did leave a record at the other places, but I haven't got to them yet."

Brock realised the size of the task Pip had taken on. It would take her weeks. "Hm." He scratched the side of his beard, looking at the lists. "Most of the titles look like books about Victorian history and art, don't they? Are they all like that?"

"Some are about poisons and criminal cases." She pointed at one, *The Cult of the Poisoner*, and another, *The Arsenic Conspiracy*. "And there are some that you can't really tell." She indicated *After Midnight* and *The Brinjal Pickle Factory*, which were among the later entries on Tina's list. "They could be about anything; you wouldn't know from the titles. There's a few like that. Why *The Brinjal Pickle Factory*? God knows what that's doing here."

Brock was intrigued. "Okay. Well, I might have a look at the lists while you carry on checking the books."

Pip looked apprehensive, clearly wondering what the chief was up to, as he took off his coat and jacket and rolled up his sleeves.

He began by looking for items that cropped up most frequently, books that Marion and Tina had kept returning to. They seemed predictable enough: volumes of poetry, diaries and letters relating to the Pre-Raphaelite Brotherhood. Then he tried to relate borrowings to what they knew of the key events in Marion's life—when she moved out of Stamford Street, when she lost the baby, and immediately before she died. It seemed that Marion had first discovered the Haverlock diary, hidden in the Havelock archive, the previous September, after which she made regular requests to see it. At the same time she'd been checking other volumes from the Havelock archive, including the two memoirs that Pip had mentioned, *After Midnight* and *The Brinjal Pickle Factory*, both written by a Robert Harding. Marion had also searched for items from the archive at other libraries, presumably to see if there could be other copies of the Haverlock diary in existence. Her requests for "Haverlock" were apparently unsuccessful, but it seemed that she had found the Harding books at both the National Archives in Kew and the London Library, and had requested them at both places. Brock wondered why. Tina must have noticed these requests, he thought, because they had been among the latest items she had been investigating. In fact, *The Brinjal Pickle Factory* was the last book that she had requested from the British Library, on the morning of her death.

"Have you had a look at this *Brinjal Pickle Factory* book?" Brock asked Pip.

"Yeah, it's like a cookbook, Chief." She poked around in the pile of volumes in front of her and handed him a slim hardback. Its dark green covers were faded, its pages yellowed, and when he opened it he caught the musty smell of old, unread pages. It wasn't just a cookbook, he discovered, more a memoir by a former colonial administrator of his early years in India before the war. Skimming it, he could find no references to arsenic or the Pre-Raphaelites that might have provided some clue as to why it was on the lists.

"How about *After Midnight* then?"

It turned out to be much the same. Its subtitle was *A Memoir of Bengal, 1947–71*.

Brock scanned the index at the back of *After Midnight*, a catalogue of the great names of the early years of independent India, Pakistan and Bangladesh, from Mountbatten and Jinnah to Sheikh

Mujib. There was no mention of Havelock or Rossetti, but his eye did pick out *Warrender, R. 82.*

He turned to page eighty-two and found the reference:

Among our staff in Calcutta at that time was Roger Warrender, later Sir Roger, newly arrived in early 1948 with his attractive young English bride, Joan. Roger had had a great war, by all accounts, serving with Wingate and the Chindits in Burma with distinction in 1943, and later in the counteroffensive against the Japanese invasion of India in 1944. He had enormous panache and energy, and the turbulent conditions in Bengal at the time of Independence soon called upon all his courage and stamina, not least when Joan fell pregnant with their first-born, Douglas, under trying conditions. They became among our longest serving staff, both playing significant roles in our evolving relations with the ruling groups in East and West Bengal. They departed finally in 1963, to London briefly, before moving on to New York, where Roger took up a senior position with UNICEF.

"Found something, sir?" Pip said.

"Call me Brock, Pip, for goodness' sake." He showed her the page. "Looks like Marion was doing a bit of homework." He took the book and the lists of borrowings over to a nearby photocopier and worked for a while, then returned them to Pip's table.

"I'll let you get on," he said, and strolled off, humming to himself, leaving Pip with a puzzled frown on her face.

KATHY LOOKED FLUSTERED, NEGOTIATING with her Action Manager and someone from head office over a file of time sheets. From the doorway Brock could see that it wasn't going well. He called over, "Kathy, can you spare a moment?" She looked relieved, and left the others to it.

"I just paid a visit to Pip at the British Library," Brock said.

"Oh?" She looked surprised. "Any luck?"

"She's plodding on. But maybe you can tell me something about this . . ." He spread out the photocopies he'd made. "These two books are in the Havelock archive, along with the Haverlock diary, and Marion also requested them at Kew and the London Library." He'd highlighted the entries with a coloured marker. "They're about India. But when I looked in the index of one of them, *After Midnight*, I found a reference to the Warrenders. Here." He handed Kathy the copied page, which she read.

"Reading up about her boyfriend's family history," she suggested.

"Yes, only she discovered this book last September, see? And Douglas Warrender told you he didn't meet Marion until October, didn't he?"

"But she was working for Sophie Warrender, so the name would still have been of interest to her."

"Mm, yes. Why look for the same book in three different libraries, though?"

Kathy said, "I didn't realise that Douglas's father was with UNICEF in New York. I wonder if he was involved with the well-drilling program in Bengal, where he'd been working all those years. Dr. da Silva's friend, Colin Ringland, told me about it. It's his area of research. It's funny, isn't it, how they all seem to be interconnected."

Brock thought. "Perhaps we need to shake them up a bit, open up some of these connections."

"Yes, I agree."

"Any ideas?"

"I'll think about it."

He watched her go back to her desk and thought, *She's up to something.* He knew her well enough after all this time.

KATHY DIDN'T HAVE MUCH longer to wait. As she sat down with a fresh cup of coffee her mobile phone rang, the number she'd given Sheena Rafferty. It was Keith, sounding all the more shifty for trying to appear guileless.

"Yeah, erm, look . . . I was thinking about what you were saying to Sheena the other night, and it made me put two and two together, like."

"And what did you come up with?"

"Eh? Well, some things began to make sense. You were talking about Warrender, right?"

"Was I?"

"Well, I know he was Marion's squeeze. I think I may be able to help you with your inquiries."

"That's very public spirited of you, Mr. Rafferty. You'd better come in and see us."

"No, I don't think so. Mr. Warrender has got friends all over the place. I just want a little chat, somewhere neutral. You know the Swan in Lambeth?"

"Okay, but I'll have a colleague with me."

"No, don't do that. Just you and me, okay? Make it five, tonight."

THE PUB WAS DIMLY lit and almost deserted, the air sour with stale beer. The publican didn't look up as she came in, both he and a customer at the bar engrossed in their newspapers. She spotted Rafferty sitting at a small table in a far dark corner with a pint of bitter in front of him and, to her surprise, Nigel Ogilvie at his side, sipping anxiously at a Bloody Mary. Kathy went over to the pair.

"Wanna drink?" Rafferty said nonchalantly.

"Not from you I don't," Kathy replied. She sat on a stool facing them and took a tape recorder out of her coat pocket.

Rafferty waggled a finger at it, frowning as if at her bad manners. "This is for your ears only, darling. I don't want my words floating around CID and God knows where else."

Kathy placed it on the table but didn't switch it on. "All right.

What's the story?" She looked pointedly at Ogilvie, who flinched and busied himself with a cocktail stirrer in his glass. The left side of his face was still puffy and discoloured from the incident in the library, and he seemed to have lost weight inside his raincoat, which was buckled up as if for a rapid exit.

"After I saw you," Rafferty said, "I got to thinking about one or two things." He leaned forward to interpose himself between Kathy and Ogilvie, who shrank further into his coat. "About arsenic, for instance."

"What about it?"

"A month ago I was in my local and got chatting to this bloke. He bought me a drink and asked me what I did for a living. I told him I was a driver for a fireworks company, and eventually, when we'd had a few, he asked if I could get hold of fireworks cheap for some friends of his. He said they built their own rockets, for a hobby. He mentioned the sort of stuff they'd be interested in—black powder mainly, but other chemicals too. He mentioned arsenic."

"Did you believe him?"

"No, not really. I thought he might be a cop, trying to set me up. They do that you know." Rafferty smirked. "He had that look about him. But you never know." He reached for his pint, gulped, smacked his lips.

"So what did you do?"

"I said I could find out, but I'd need some money up front, my search fee. I asked for a fifty and settled for a pony. He said there was a deadline—some competition they were going in for—and we agreed to meet the next night at the pub. I thought about it and decided not to get involved. The next evening I parked the van outside the pub and took a couple of pictures of him when he arrived. Insurance, in case he got difficult; I thought I could ask around about him."

Rafferty opened his wallet and took out two photographs. The first showed a man illuminated from a streetlight overhead, his features mostly in shadow, the second in profile in the pub doorway, both blurry. Kathy didn't recognise him.

"Anyway, when I told him I couldn't help him, he didn't make a fuss."

"So when was this, exactly?"

"Four weeks ago? About that."

Two weeks before Marion died. By then she and Douglas Warrender knew about the baby.

"Did you find out who he was?"

"Didn't try. Said his name was Benny, that's all I know."

"You met a man in a pub who maybe wanted to buy arsenic? Is that it?"

"Hang on. After you called round the other night, I thought about it again. Who was this bloke? Who were his friends? And I also thought about that other thing I was supposed to have done, beating up old Nigel here. So I went to see him." He clapped an arm around the unhappy Ogilvie. "Go on, Nigel, tell the Inspector."

"Well . . ." Ogilvie briefly met Kathy's eyes, then took a keen interest in his cocktail stirrer again. "What I told you about the attack on me in the London Library, it wasn't the whole truth. I mean, I didn't know who the man was, but I did know why he was there. I didn't tell you because I was afraid. He warned me, you see, in no uncertain terms, to tell no one. He even said that he'd hurt Mother. But I wanted to tell you, and when Keith came to see me, well, it wasn't just my word against a total stranger anymore.

"You see, when Marion collapsed, in the confusion, I picked up a computer memory stick I noticed lying on the floor, meaning to hand it in. Only I forgot about it till later, and then I thought I should open it, just to see whose it was, so that I could return it to them. I soon realised that it had belonged to Marion, and that it contained private correspondence with a lover. I'm afraid—I didn't mean to, you understand—I read enough to get his name, 'Dougie,' or Douglas Warrender, and the fact that he lived in the Notting Hill area and had an office very close to the library."

Kathy listened without comment to this tale, probably larded with half-truths and omissions to make it flow, and imagined how greedily Ogilvie would have pored over every detail of Marion's correspondence.

"So I contacted him direct, in order to return it to him."

"For a price."

"Certainly not!" Ogilvie puffed up in outrage. "Although I did feel that his reaction was one of suspicion rather than simple gratitude. In fact I became quite wary, and insisted that he come to the library to pick it up, where I felt safe. I told him to come to the front counter at midday, where I would meet him. However, at a quarter to, when I was still in the book stacks, I was approached by a man I'd never seen before, who said he'd been sent by Mr. Warrender. But far from offering me thanks, this man was threatening and abusive, and when I objected he became actually violent. He hit me several times and threw me down the stairs, before he left with the memory stick."

"So it wasn't Keith here who hit you?"

"No." Ogilvie raised his chin defiantly. "I told you that before."

"What did this man look like?"

"Him." He pointed a chubby finger at the photographs. "That's him, the same man. In his late forties perhaps, with grizzled hair. A Londoner by his accent. A very tough character. That's what persuaded me to tell you, when Keith showed me these pictures. Now you can do something about it. Only, I'll need protection. If they ever find out I've spoken to you . . ."

"We can't prosecute this man for attacking you without your evidence, Nigel."

"No! I don't want that. Keith said . . ." He looked anxiously at Rafferty. "He said it would help you, if I told you this, with your main case, Marion's murder. That's all I want."

"And you've done that, Nigel. Good lad." Rafferty patted him on the shoulder. "Now piss off."

Ogilvie scrambled to his feet, ducked his head and made off. Kathy looked back at his departing figure and caught a glimpse of the face of the other customer at the bar, before he shifted away behind his paper. Brendan Crouch, Rafferty's partner in crime.

She turned back to Rafferty. "You don't expect me to believe that, do you? We caught you on camera at the library at the time he was attacked."

"Yeah, I was there, but I didn't do it. Fact is, I knew Warrender. I happened to see him with Marion one day, in the West End, having a drink together, all very cosy. I thought, what's she doing with an old bloke like that? It's not right. I was thinking of Sheena, see? How she'd feel about it. So I kept an eye on them, and when she left I spoke to him, asked him what his game was. You've spoken to him, have you? Smooth bugger, yeah? He told me they were just good friends, but to keep it to myself, slipped me a few quid and said he might be able to put a bit of work my way. That's why I was at the library that day. He asked me to meet another guy at the back entrance to lend a hand to pick up some merchandise from someone inside. I was to make sure the negotiations weren't disturbed. Only I got held up in traffic and I was late. By the time I got there it was all over. I heard the fuss and scarpered."

He saw the doubt on Kathy's face and leaned closer, dropping his voice, his breath beery. "Listen, I'm just trying to be helpful, okay?" He tapped the photographs. "I don't know who this guy is. Maybe he's nothing to do with Warrender. Maybe you can't use it. But I could be more helpful."

"Go on."

"Maybe I could arrange for arsenic to be found in Warrender's car, or on his clothes. Would that help?"

Kathy looked thoughtful, reached for Ogilvie's glass and took out the plastic cocktail stick. It had a sharp point, for spearing cherries or slices of lemon. She brought it down on the back of Rafferty's hand, not quite hard enough to puncture the skin. He blanched and his head jerked back, his hand still pinned by the spike.

"Rafferty, if you so much as think of doing anything so stupid, I'll have you locked away forever. I'm not interested in your lies. I want the truth."

She tossed the stick back in the glass.

Rafferty rubbed his hand, his eyes sliding over to his partner at the bar. "Fuck you. The truth is that Warrender had Marion killed. We both know that."

"Do we?"

"Yeah. I don't know why, but he did. Maybe she got too greedy, or wanted him to leave his wife, the usual crap. He tried to make it look like suicide, didn't he? Fucking weird way to do it, if you ask me. But he's a scary guy, underneath that smooth suit. I reckon he wanted her to suffer, and for her to know that. And he's smart and rich. You won't catch him easily."

"What about Tony da Silva? You know him too, don't you?"

"Her tutor? Yeah, he contacted me, trying to find out where Marion had moved to. Said it was urgent academic business. Oh yeah, sure." He pulled a face.

"What do you think it was?"

"Well, he fancied her, didn't he? And she wasn't having any."

"So maybe he killed her."

"Nah. Doesn't have the balls. And he didn't know where she lived. Not until afterwards."

"How do you know that?"

"I told him eventually, after she was dead."

"Yes, he said you gave him a key. Is that right?"

"Not so as I'd admit it. He phoned me at the weekend, wanting me to tell you, confirm it was after she died. I said forget it."

"Of course he could just be using you to disguise the fact that he did know where she lived."

Rafferty thought about that, then shook his head.

Kathy gathered up the photos. "If we can't identify these I'll get you to come in to look at some mugshots. Assuming this isn't just some bloke going for a drink."

She got to her feet and walked out.

WHEN SHE GOT BACK to the office she tried without success to find a match for the man in the photographs. In the end she sent them off to technical support to have them enhanced, and by the next morning she had a reasonably clear large image of his face pinned up on the board, still none the wiser as to his identity. None of the others recognised him, until Bren came in, sniffling and red-nosed, sucking throat lozenges.

"What's Harry been up to then?" he rasped as he passed the picture.

"You know him?" Kathy asked. "I haven't been able to find him in records."

"He's not a crook, he's a cop, or used to be. DS Harry Sykes, retired about four years ago."

"Know what he does now?"

"I can probably find out."

After making a couple of phone calls he came back with the information that Sykes was now working for a West End brokerage by the name of Mallory Capital.

TWENTY-EIGHT

THE PRINCE CLOSED THE file with a sigh. It had a very smart cover, gold embossed, which he liked, but the contents were impenetrable—bear spreads, cliquets, vanilla options—what did he know of such things? He just wanted to spend the bloody money. "Might one smoke, Douglas? One never can tell these days."

"Of course, Ricky. I'll get you an ashtray."

As he passed the window Warrender glanced down into the street and saw a police car double-parked right outside the front door. He gave a little frown, then noticed a solitary man standing in the central gardens of the square. The figure was clad in a long black coat, with a shock of white hair at its head, and was standing motionless, apparently looking straight up at him. Then the man took a hand from his overcoat pocket and lifted it to his ear. Almost immediately, as if by magic, he heard a telephone begin to ring in the outer office. When the buzzer sounded on his desk, Warrender was almost expecting it.

"Hello?"

"I'm so sorry, Mr. Warrender, only it's the police. They say it's urgent. A Detective Chief Inspector Brock. I tried to tell him . . ."

"It's all right, Carol. I'll speak to him. And get Harry to bring the car round to the front, will you?"

"I'm not sure I can. The girls downstairs just told me that he's been arrested."

"What's an iron butterfly again, Douglas?" There was more than a hint of frustration in the prince's voice.

"It's the four-option strategy, Ricky, with three consecutively higher strike prices and a long or short straddle in the middle. Look, I might get Jason to come and talk you through the technical steps again, okay?"

"It's just that Daddy will expect me to know what it's all about," the prince grumbled.

"Of course. Just excuse me one moment."

He went out and spoke to his secretary, then took the call at her desk. "Hello? Warrender here."

"DCI Brock, Mr. Warrender. I need to talk to you, concerning Marion Summers's death."

"Yes, well . . . later this afternoon perhaps."

"This won't wait. I'm outside in the square. We can talk here if you wish, or go up to West End Central."

When Warrender crossed the street into the gardens he saw that Brock had seated himself on the bench near the statue, where, he knew, Marion had taken her lunch, fifteen days before.

"Did she always choose this seat?" Brock asked.

"Unless someone else got here first."

"So that you could see her, from your office?"

"Yes."

"So you might have looked out and watched her sip the poisoned drink."

"Except that I was in Corsica that day, and she knew it."

"Did you arrange to have it done?"

"Certainly not. Is that why you've arrested my driver?"

"He's not under arrest. He's helping us with our inquiries. We have a witness who claims that he tried to obtain arsenic on your behalf."

"What? That's absolute rubbish. What witness?"

"The witness has also suggested that your relationship with Marion had become impossible, her demands too great."

"Well," Warrender replied coolly, "that just shows how ill-informed your so-called witness is."

"All the same, it happened at a time when you were faced with a major disruption in your life, weren't you? Were you really ready for the rupture it would cause, with your wife, your daughter, perhaps your mother? The loss of the house you've shared with them all those years? The gossip in your professional circles? Were you ready for all that? To take on a child again, mewling and puking and keeping you awake half the night?"

"You sound as if you're talking from experience. I have one very considerable advantage over my first efforts to start a family—I can now afford to outsource most of the difficulties. Marion made me feel thirty years younger. I looked forward to it as the start of a new life."

Brock was watching Warrender carefully all through this, measuring his answers, trying to gauge his credibility.

"Weren't you just a little concerned by that—how shall I put it?—that rather obsessive side of Marion's character? Her ruthless need to be recognised, at all costs?"

"You're speculating. You didn't know her. Look, didn't you read the contents of the memory stick I gave your inspector at the weekend? If you're that desperate for a culprit, there are a few clues there, I should have thought."

"Yes, but apparently you didn't give us the original memory stick that belonged to Marion. According to our experts, each of the items has been recorded onto its memory within the last week, and we can't be sure when they were originally written, or by whom. The whole thing could be a fabrication, made for the purpose of feeding us false leads, which, as you say, point away from you."

Warrender sucked in his breath. "The original contained some other things, intimate things, that I wasn't prepared to show you. I thought that even if I deleted them your people might be able to retrieve them. I couldn't risk that, and so I transferred the items I was prepared to share with you to a new stick and destroyed the old one. But the entries are all genuine, believe me. And as far as I can see they point in only one conceivable direction—her tutor, da Silva. Rereading those letters, those notes of hers, I feel very angry now that I didn't see the signs; her instinctive revulsion towards him, the way he attempted to pursue her, and how she fell ill and lost the baby after finally agreeing to see him."

Warrender sat on the edge of the bench, fists clenched, and his voice dropped. "And most of all, the way she was killed. Arsenic, for God's sake! Don't you find that just too damn symbolic and . . . and . . . *anachronistic* for anyone living in the real world? Sounds to me like the ultimate academic put-down."

"You know Dr. da Silva's close friend at the university, Dr. Colin Ringland, don't you?"

Warrender looked up sharply. "How do you know that?"

"You're mentioned on the website of his research unit."

"Oh, the consultative committee. Yes, I do know him, although he has no idea that I was involved with Marion. But you're thinking, 'Dr. Ringland equals arsenic,' yes? Well believe me, I've been nowhere near his laboratory during the time I've known Marion. My connection with Colin Ringland goes back four or five years, and arose out of my father's will."

"I think you'd better explain that."

"My father was with the diplomatic service for many years, mostly in the Indian subcontinent. I was born out there, and we all had a tremendous affection for the place. We returned to the UK in the sixties, and then my father took a post with UNICEF in New York, where he particularly focused on their programs in Bengal and Bangladesh, which he knew well. One of his most ambitious projects was to bring clean drinking water to that area, because illness and death from contaminated water were widespread. He initiated the tubewell programme, to tap clean aquifers deep below the surface.

UNICEF financed the sinking of almost a million such wells, and the immediate health improvements were dramatic. Unfortunately, no one had any idea that the deep water was contaminated with naturally occurring arsenic. It took many years for its insidious effects to become apparent, and when the scale of the problem began to be realised there was some panic, scapegoats were sought. This was long after my father had retired, but a group of activists identified him as the main culprit and attempted to bring a case against him in the American courts. Things got out of hand. He was actually accused of being a murderer at one point. Quite absurd. It was all very tragic and he was devastated. He died before it was resolved, and left a provision in his will to establish a trust fund to sponsor research into solutions to the problems of groundwater contamination. I am now the chairman of that trust, and one of our principal beneficiaries for the past couple of years has been Dr. Ringland and his research team. So naturally I'm acquainted with him, and meet him at several progress reviews each year.

"You know, many of the people in Bangladesh who have suffered from the poisoning of the tubewells regard it as fate, of a particularly cruel kind, as if there had been a curse upon them and the whole enterprise from the start. And it has occurred to me that Marion's death could be seen as a vicious extension of that fate. Without the tubewells there would have been no research program at the university, and without Dr. Ringland's research program, his friend da Silva would have had no access to arsenic with which to murder Marion and Tina."

"DID YOU BELIEVE HIM?" Kathy asked.

Brock scratched his beard. "Both he and Harry Sykes have solid alibis for the time of Tina's poisoning, and both were a lot more convincing than Rafferty. What's his game, anyway? Does he think there's a reward?"

"I think," Kathy said slowly, "that he may be hoping to get his hands on Marion's house."

"Really? How did he work that out? I wouldn't have thought he was smart enough."

"I suggested to his wife, Sheena, that Warrender might lose his claim on the place if he was implicated in Marion's death."

Brock looked sharply at her. "Ah, did you indeed?"

"We wanted to shake them up."

He gave a growl and she braced herself for a bollocking. But after a moment he shook his head and said, a little too calmly, "I think this case has become a bit personal for you, Kathy. I can understand your distaste for both Rafferty and Warrender, but it seems to me, on any objective measure, that Tony da Silva is still our prime suspect. Damn it, he has no alibi for the first murder and was actually at the scene of the second. He had access to arsenic at his friend Ringland's laboratory, and he had a powerful motive Marion was about to destroy his career. I think maybe we're being too clever by half. We'll have him in again, and do it the slow way, bit by bit, again and again, until we find the cracks."

SOPHIE WARRENDER ANSWERED KATHY'S knock, her mood very different from when Kathy had last seen her. She looked drawn and worried, her forehead furrowed by lines that hadn't been apparent before.

"She says she wants to see you," Sophie said, "but she's not at all well, so please be careful. It seemed to hit her on Friday, the day after Tina died. She's hardly eaten a thing since then, or come out of her room. You'll see the change in her. I've had the doctor look at her twice and he's quite concerned. I even thought she might have been poisoned herself that day without realising it and was suffering the after-effects, but the doctor says not."

Emily was sitting in her mother's office, curled up in a corner of a chesterfield sofa, a thick woollen cardigan over her shoulders although the room was very warm. She did look diminished, her eyes large and red-rimmed in her pale elfin face. She had an old leather-bound volume on her knee, gripped in slender white fingers.

"Emily's been digging about in her grandfather's collection up in the belvedere, haven't you, dear?" Sophie's bright, encouraging tone sounded strained. "What have you got?"

Emily raised the book wordlessly for her mother to see.

"Wilkie Collins, yes, well . . . We call it the belvedere"—she pointed to the spiral stair leading up into the Italianate tower visible from the street—"because it was originally open, but Dougie's father had it enclosed and turned it into his private library, his refuge." She seemed momentarily at a loss, then said, "Can I get you tea, Inspector?"

"That would be lovely, thanks."

"Right." She looked doubtfully at her daughter, then said, "Shan't be a moment."

Kathy sat on the sofa, turning to face the girl. "Thanks for agreeing to see me again, Emily. I know it's not easy, especially if you're not feeling well."

"I want to help if I can." Her voice was barely a whisper.

"Have you remembered anything else about that day at the British Library? Maybe noticing anyone at the café?"

Emily shook her head, a loop of auburn hair dropping over an eye. "No, I'm sorry."

"Maybe you could take me through exactly what you did with Tina, that would have been on the Tuesday, when we met at Marion's house, then on Wednesday and Thursday?"

Kathy took notes as Emily haltingly described agreeing to help Tina on the Tuesday, then on the following day going around several libraries with Tina and Donald Fotheringham, trying to establish what Marion had been doing. Several of the librarians recognised Tina as having worked with Marion previously, and were sympathetic, supplying lists of requests, and what with those, and what Tina and Emily could remember of their own work with Marion, they had built up a considerable list.

Kathy nodded. They had found library printouts in Tina's bag at the British Library, as well as in her room at Stamford Street.

"And on the rest of Wednesday and Thursday?"

"Tina gave us topics to investigate. She and Donald were looking into an old archive in the India Office Records, and I was to try to find out more about the inquest into the death of Lizzie Siddal, Rossetti's wife."

"Did Tina say what they were looking for in the India Office Records?"

"Not really. She thought Marion had found something important somewhere, and she knew she'd requested items from there."

"But she was obviously very interested in the events surrounding Lizzie's death."

"Yes. She seemed to think that had been very important to Marion's research. She also . . ."

"Yes?"

"She said we mustn't tell anyone else what we were doing, especially anyone from the university."

Sophie Warrender returned at that point, carrying a tray of tea things, and followed by her mother-in-law, Lady Warrender, who was rather unsteadily bearing a large Dundee cake on a plate. Kathy got to her feet to help, and was introduced to the elderly woman.

"Here we are." Sophie arranged the things on a side table and began to pour while Joan handed round the cake. Emily gave a sharp shake of her head.

"It's freshly baked, dear," Joan said. "I've been enjoying myself in the kitchen. And it's your favourite. You must eat, you know."

Emily put a hand to her mouth, looking as if she might be sick. She got to her feet and ran out of the room.

"Oh, darling . . ." Sophie rose as if to follow her.

"Delayed shock," Joan said briskly. "I've seen it many times before. Time will be the healer. Drugs only delay things." She chomped a slab of cake and smacked her lips.

Sophie sank down again. "Poor girl. She's been very shaken up. Was she able to help?"

"I think so. I'm trying to get a clearer idea of what Tina was doing in the forty-eight hours before she died."

"We almost saw her again, the evening before."

"Oh?"

"Yes, she'd been going to come with Emily to our local bookshop where I was giving a talk about my last book. Apparently she was quite interested, and I told Emily she should come and have a meal with us afterwards. Only she decided at the last moment she couldn't make it." She lifted the book Emily had been reading. "*The Woman in White.* Oh dear."

DONALD FOTHERINGHAM RANG KATHY as she got into her car. He was back in Scotland now, and apologised for leaving without saying goodbye. "I got word that one of my flock had passed away suddenly, and it was important for me to be here. I felt I'd really told you as much as I could."

"I'm glad you called, Donald. I was going to ring you. I believe Tina had been intending to go to a talk given by Emily's mother on the Wednesday evening, but didn't. Do you know what happened?"

"Oh aye. I was invited too, but it wasn't really my cup of tea, and to tell the truth I was feeling pretty exhausted by that stage. But those young women were tireless. Tina especially, she just kept on going. That's why she missed the talk that evening—she wanted to stay at the library till it closed, though we'd been at it since first thing that morning. She said she thought she was getting somewhere, but as I told you, she didn't share it with us."

"I see. And the next day?"

"She seemed tired and frustrated. You know, I've been chatting to Bessie about what we were doing, following Marion's trail all over London without really getting to the heart of the matter, and she said that it had been that way with Marion since she was a lassie. She would play hide-and-seek with her auntie, leaving little messages around the garden that Bessie had to follow. And later, as a teenager, she was awfy secretive. She had a china ornament in her room, an old balloon seller it was, and she hid letters inside it, though Bessie found them, sure enough."

"That ornament was in Marion's house, Donald, but there was nothing hidden inside it."

"No, well, I'm sure her adult ways would have been more subtle. Perhaps we'll never know the whole truth about Marion."

"We'll certainly do our best. Thanks again, anyway."

"But there was something else I wanted to tell you about. I went to see Marion's mother before I left, and gave her my phone number, just in case she needed to get in touch. Well, to my surprise she did, just an hour ago. It seems she's become somewhat disenchanted with her husband Keith, and wanted to get something off her chest. She told me that he and his army friend, Crouch his name is, have a wee racket going, robbing the dead."

"Pardon?"

"They read the death notices in the paper, then visit the deceased's house while everyone is at the funeral. A particularly unsavoury kind of thieving, you might say. Apparently they've been doing it for a long time—since they were in Ireland together with the army. Sheena has known about it for some time too, only now it's become a little personal."

"How do you mean?"

"I rather gathered that Sheena is hoping for a windfall following her daughter's death, and is concerned that Keith will try to get his hands on it. The thing is, when Keith studies the funeral notices, he marks the ones he intends to visit with a cross. Sheena has kept a note of many of their names. She wouldn't want to contact you herself, but was quite happy for me to do it on her behalf, if you were interested."

"Oh yes, Donald," Kathy said. "I'm interested."

KATHY COULDN'T FIND PIP at first in the offices of the British Library, hidden behind a mound of books, and when she finally dug her out, the DC blinked and looked disoriented, as if surfacing from a great depth.

"Blimey, you been here long, boss?"

"No, just arrived. How's it going? Brock said you're doing a great job."

"Did he?" She brightened a little. "Not sure if I am, but still."

"Show me."

Pip took her through the books she'd checked so far, without discovering anything that looked significant.

Kathy said, "I've just learned that Tina spent last Wednesday evening in here, working on something, and I'm wondering what it was."

"Wednesday . . . here we are." Pip showed her the printout. "Just two requests."

Kathy looked at the entries: the Haverlock diary and Sir Robert Harding's second book about Bengal, *After Midnight*. "Have you looked at these?"

"*After Midnight* is here somewhere. Brock asked me about that. I haven't seen the diary yet. Shall I ask them to get it?"

"Yes, do that, and I'll buy you a coffee while we're waiting."

When they returned from the café there was a note waiting on the desk: *Request for Diary, author H. Haverlock, Add. 507861.86 . . . NOT AVAILABLE.*

They found a library assistant who said, "May be lost, or withdrawn for repairs."

"Or on loan to someone else?" Kathy suggested.

The woman shook her head. "It'd say." She tapped at her computer for a moment. "No, it's down as not yet returned by the last person who requested it."

"That would be Tina Flowers."

Another shake of the head, her finger running across the screen. "She returned it last thing on Wednesday. The final request was the following day, the twelfth, at eight minutes past nine, as soon as we opened. By a Dr. Anthony da Silva."

Kathy thought. "Did he request anything else that day?"

Another search, then the woman showed them the entry on the screen: *After Midnight: A Memoir of Bengal, 1947–71, author R. Harding, Add. 507861.103.*

"But we have that here," Kathy said. "Unless there's more than one copy."

"No, that's it. It was returned later that morning."

"So he asked for both books that Tina had been investigating the previous evening, and now one of them is missing."

"How would he know what she'd requested?" Pip asked. "Could he have accessed her records?"

"No." More tapping. "But he was here that evening. See? He requested several books—about arsenic by the looks of it. Maybe he met her, saw what she was reading."

"It makes sense," Kathy said when they returned to Pip's table. "He had finally traced the source of Marion's revelations in her paper to the Cornell conference, and he knew that Tina had found it too."

"So he stole the book and murdered her. Kind of explains everything, doesn't it?" Pip said.

"Looks like it." Kathy reached for the Harding memoir from the book pile, and opened it to a handwritten dedication on the inside cover: *To my very dear friend Toby Havelock, a mischievous memoir, from one old India hand to another. Bob Harding.* She flicked through the book. "And this, about the twentieth century, would have been of no interest to him."

"Brock found a reference to the Warrenders in there," Pip told her, and Kathy nodded.

"Yes, he showed me a copy." She checked the index and read the passage again. "Marion must have found this while she was searching through that family collection, and noticed the reference." Kathy tried to imagine Marion's method, skimming hundreds of books for obscure clues and trails, scanning their chapter headings, their indexes, for her key words. Arsenic, for instance.

She looked it up in the index of Harding's book, and there it was, page 213. She turned to the place, and found no such page. It had been very neatly sliced away, close to the binding. "Look at this," she said, showing Pip.

"You think da Silva vandalised it before he returned it?"

"Who knows? I'd better tell Brock what we've discovered."

When she got through to him and described the sequence they had uncovered, he was grimly pleased.

"Well done," he said. "I thought the answer must lie in those books somewhere. We'd better have him in."

"Yes."

"You sound unsure."

"No, I'm just wondering what was in that missing page of the Harding book. It may be nothing at all to do with da Silva of course, but I'm wondering. Suppose there was something there about using arsenic as a poison, some traditional Indian preparation perhaps that Harding described, which maybe Marion discovered and told her tutor about, and then da Silva used it on his two victims."

"I see, yes. Another link. All right, but there are other copies of that book, aren't there? I seem to remember it appeared on the lists of both the National Archives and the London Library borrowings. I remember wondering why they needed to look at it in three different places."

"I'll check."

Kathy rang off, still uneasy. She hadn't mentioned it to Brock, but what had really unsettled her was her session with the Warrenders. She was haunted by Emily's sickly appearance, the unhealthy glitter in her eye and air of despair, and her mother's comment that she thought she may have been poisoned too. And the terrible thought *Not another one, please God*, had been followed by an even more shocking one: *Three young women, following obsessively in each other's footsteps, like a suicide chain.*

No, Kathy told herself, not that. Brock's right, da Silva's the one.

"Come on," she told Pip. "Let's take a drive. Where was the

next place that Marion found this *After Midnight* book, after she discovered it in the archives here?"

Pip checked. "The National Archives."

"Okay, we'll go there."

TWENTY-NINE

THE NATIONAL ARCHIVES, HOUSING nine hundred years of official records back to the Domesday Book, is housed in a modern
building on a curve of the river near the botanical gardens at Kew.
They found their way to a member of staff who listened to what
they were after, intrigued by the request, and got to work on her
computer.

"Yes, it's here."

"Do you have its borrowing record?"

"I can get that." They waited a moment, then, "Not terribly pop-
ular, only two calls in the past year: T. Flowers a couple of weeks
ago, and before that M. Summers last August."

"No Anthony da Silva?"

"'Fraid not. Do you want to have a look at it?"

"Yes please."

The woman returned after a while with the now familiar small
green volume in her hand, and gave it to Kathy. This time the
dedication in the flysheet read: *To the Public Records Office, in ap-
preciation of your generous assistance in the preparation of this little
book. Robert Harding KCMG.*

Kathy turned to page 213 and found it to be, as at the British
Library, missing.

KATHY SAW THAT THE greenery in the square had thickened and darkened during the past week into more mature, summery foliage, although perversely the weather had turned cold again and grey. They mounted the front steps, went into the library and asked for Gael Rayner.

"Any news?" she said, voice hushed.

"Not really, Gael. We're trying to retrace Tina Flowers's movements in the days before she died, last Thursday."

"Oh yes, we heard all about that, and of course your colleague came to collect the record of Marion's borrowings." She nodded at Pip. "We just couldn't believe it, Marion's friend, taken in the same way. We're all still in shock."

"Did you ever meet Tina?"

"Yes, she came a number of times with Marion, helping her with her work. And after Marion died she came back again. She said she wanted to tidy up some loose ends in Marion's research. She was obviously distressed by what had happened. I should really have charged her for a temporary reference ticket, but I felt sorry for her and let her in on the strength of Marion's membership. But we couldn't let her borrow books."

"Right, so we don't have a record of what she was looking at here. Can you remember if she came in last week at all, in the days before her death?"

"Oh yes, she was certainly here, her and the other girl helping her."

"Emily Warrender?"

"That's right. I'm a great admirer of her mother's work."

"Would you have any idea what they were doing?"

"Well, they had unsupervised access to the stacks, so I wouldn't know really. Let me think . . . Yes, I do remember Tina asking about one book in particular, because she couldn't find it."

"Do you remember what it was?"

"It was in History, or should have been. But I don't think I can remember . . . hold on, I may still have my notes." She took a sheaf of papers from a filing tray and thumbed through them. "Yes, this is the one, I think. Its shelfmark was *H. India*—that's H for history—and *Social etc.* We arrange our books differently here, you see, not by DDC." She deciphered her notes. "Apparently it was shelved under *Harding, R.,* but I don't seem to have a title. I'll have noted it as misplaced. Do you want me to check?"

"I think we know what it was, Gael—a book called *After Midnight*? It was a memoir."

"You're right, I do remember now. They spent quite a lot of time looking for it."

"Do you have the borrowing record for that book?"

"I can check." She called it up on her computer and said, "Only one borrower—Marion herself, last September. Nobody else."

"And she returned it?"

"Yes, on the twenty-sixth of September."

"So what happened to it? Did someone steal it?"

"Unlikely, I think. We assumed it must have been returned to the wrong place in the shelves."

"How could that happen?"

"Well, either by mistake or on purpose."

"Why would anyone do it on purpose?"

"To hide it. What better place to hide a book than in a library?" She smiled. "You look surprised. Obviously you were a very law-abiding student."

"How do you mean?"

"I'm afraid it's a not-uncommon practice in university libraries. If a book is in demand by students and on restricted access, the first one who gets to it places it on another shelf, where its location will be known only to them, although the computer will say it's not on loan. Very frustrating for everyone else."

"But this book wasn't in demand," Kathy said. "Only Marion was interested in it, apparently."

"True. Let's see its publishing history." Another flurry of computer keys and she said, "Well, it was obviously a self-published memoir, a vanity publication, probably just for friends and relatives, with a very small print run. You might find a copy in the British Library, otherwise it's probably vanished into obscurity. Is it important, do you think?"

"I really don't know, Gael. I might ask Emily. Tell me, is Marion's tutor, Dr. Anthony da Silva, a member of the library?"

"Oh yes, I know him. He was here a lot when he was researching his wonderful book on Dante Gabriel Rossetti, but I haven't seen him lately. Not for a while. Shall I check his borrowing record?"

"Please."

"Here we are. No, nothing this year. His last loan was that new biography of Stanley Baldwin, last December."

"Thanks for your help."

Kathy phoned the Warrenders' house from the car. Emily was a little more settled, apparently, after a lie-down. They put her on.

"Hi Emily," Kathy said. "Just a small thing. We're tracing Tina's movements before she died, as I told you, and I understand you both spent some time in the London Library last week, looking for a lost book. Do you remember that?"

"Mmm, yes, that's right."

"Do you remember what it was?"

"I think . . . some sort of memoir? I'm not sure. We never found it."

"Why was it important?"

There was a moment's silence, then Emily replied, "Tina thought Marion had been looking at it. I think Tina thought there might have been something there about how Lizzie Siddal died. That's what she was most interested in, some discovery of Marion's that got her tutor really upset."

"She said that, did she?"

"Yes, she did."

Kathy phoned Brock, and told him what they had learned.

"Good," he said. "We'll have to interview Emily later to get that on record, but that's good enough. Come on in and we'll get to work."

THE ROOM WAS DRAB and dispiriting, as if to tell those who were interviewed in it that anything they might come up with had certainly been heard between these grubby walls before.

"Since we saw you last, Dr. da Silva," Brock began, "we've had a chance to check some of the things you told us." He stopped and stared at the man across the table.

Da Silva tried to meet his eyes, but only succeeded in looking shifty. He was a changed man, Kathy thought, the arrogance gone along with the colour from his face. His clothes looked crumpled and soiled, as if he'd slept in them on someone's sofa, and she wondered if his wife had thrown him out. He took a pair of glasses out of his pocket and put them on with an unsteady hand, as if for protection.

"WE'VE BEEN TRYING TO confirm your account of your movements on Tuesday the third of April, the day that Marion Summers was poisoned, but without success. None of your neighbours saw you that day, you made no calls through your house phone nor received any. There's no evidence of you being at home that day at all."

Da Silva's solicitor began to object, but Brock simply nodded his head patiently and then went on, questioning the tutor again about the details of that day, what he'd had for lunch, what letters he might have written (none), and emails he might have sent from his home computer.

"No, nothing like that. I told you, I was completely engrossed in the paper I was writing for a conference presentation that was overdue." His voice was different, like a nervous public speaker whose throat is stretched tight with tension.

They would require his computer, Brock said, and would carry out a search of his home although from his tone he didn't expect to find much. He moved on to the days following Marion's death, and da Silva's visit to her house.

"I spoke to Keith Rafferty," Kathy said. "He denied that he'd supplied you with a key."

Da Silva made a noise intended as a scoff but that came out as a choke. He took a sip from the plastic cup in front of him and said, "That's no surprise."

They turned to his relationship with Dr. Ringland and access to his laboratory, laboriously working through every detail until eventually the solicitor said, "I think that's really enough. As you can see, Dr. da Silva is suffering greatly from the strain of these terrible events, of which he is entirely innocent. Unless you have something specific to ask him, I'm going to advise him to say no more."

"It's true!" da Silva blurted out, loud enough to make his solicitor glance at him in alarm. "You . . . you're trying to make me out to be some kind of predator, preying on girls like Marion and Tina. But I'm innocent! I was proud of Marion, proud of her as a father might be proud of his daughter, proud of her development, of her intelligence and insight. Proud of her independence too, of her refusal to accept my opinion on trust, difficult as that sometimes was."

There were tears in his eyes now, and the three other people in the room, despite their long experience of such situations, drew back a little in embarrassment.

"When she hid her Cornell paper from me, and I began to suspect the way in which it was intended to undermine me, I felt bitterly betrayed. Her disloyalty was like a knife in my heart. But I never, for one moment, thought of hurting her. That is obscene."

Silence filled the room, then Brock said mildly, "Where were you on the afternoon and evening of Wednesday the eleventh of this month, Dr. da Silva?"

"What?"

"A week ago, between the hours of three and eight. Please think carefully before you answer."

Da Silva frowned, then reached into his jacket pocket and brought out a small diary. "Umm . . . lunch with Dr. Ringland, a two o'clock lecture, then . . ." He looked up. "I believe I went up to the British Library."

"What was the lecture?"

"Victorian literature."

"To?"

"Third-year arts students mainly. Why?"

"Tina Flowers was in that class, wasn't she?"

"Um . . . it's possible, I suppose."

"And then she went to the British Library, where, shortly after four o'clock, she requested two books. Do you know what they were?"

"How could I?"

"Because the following morning you returned to the library as soon as it opened, and requested those same two books, books so obscure that almost nobody else has ever requested them."

"Um . . . I believe I do remember. Marion had told me about them."

Brock shook his head impatiently. "You followed Tina after the lecture up to the British Library, and watched her order the two books, one of which was the source of Marion's revelations in her Cornell paper. You had been unable to find that book because it was stored in one of the special collections, the papers of the Havelock family, a name slightly different from the one you'd been searching for—Haverlock."

Da Silva sat rigid in his chair.

"Where is that book now, Dr. da Silva? You collected it the following day, but never returned it. Where is it?"

He said nothing, jaw locked.

"Did you hide it somewhere in the library?" Kathy pressed.

For a moment it seemed he would keep silent, but then he gave a kind of shudder and whispered, "She just read and read and read, completely engrossed, but she seemed to make no notes, nor photocopies, before the library was closing and she had to hand it back. So the next morning I was there before her and took out the book. It was a scurrilous store of gossip, that's all; a travesty, full of innuendo and rumour. Marion should never have considered it seriously. It was unconscionable that it should cause so much distress. I knew exactly what Rossetti would want me to do with the damn thing, and I did it."

"You did what?" Kathy asked softly.

"I destroyed it," he said defiantly. "I tore it into shreds and flushed it down the loo. There, I destroyed a library book. You can arrest me for that."

"But Tina had read it," Brock said, "just as Marion had before her, so you had to destroy her, too, didn't you?"

GUILTILY, KATHY FELT LIKE da Silva's portrayal of Marion as a disloyal daughter. Brock was energised by the arrest, firing instructions to the team—her team—to fill the gaps in their case against da Silva. She worked with him, of course, following up his ideas, adding her own, yet all the time she held back a little, feeling they'd got something wrong. It worried her that he hadn't been immersed in the case as she had been, but was that just pique at having him take over now? But if there was some flaw, it was up to her, who should have developed a deeper understanding of the dynamics, to put her finger on it.

She puzzled over this later that night, when she finally got home and sat on her sofa with a burger on her lap, staring up at her wall. The diagram, she had to admit, looked pretty convincing with da Silva in the centre, the perfect counterpart to Marion's pattern on the left with Rossetti in that central place, ringed by his women, and Kathy could almost sense that Marion would have approved. So what was wrong?

She went to bed without an answer, overtired and uneasy. She soon fell into a deep sleep, only to wake again after a couple of hours. Her brain immediately began whirring with images of imagined scenes—Marion collapsing in the library, Pip in the pub with Rafferty and Crouch, Ogilvie tumbling down the library stairs, Douglas Warrender meeting Marion in Bastia, then returning across flower-covered hills to suffer a poolside barbecue with his family and friends . . .

No, that was wrong. She opened her eyes in the pitch-dark room, remembering Warrender's remark in St. James's Park: *We were a perfect couple, making friends with other holidaying couples at the local restaurants, entertaining neighbours around the pool . . .*

A perfect couple, not a perfect family. Was Emily with them? Kathy realised they'd never checked.

And suddenly it came to her that what had been wrong from the start was the way in which Marion and Tina had died. It was entirely plausible that da Silva, or Douglas Warrender, or even Keith Rafferty, might have desperately wanted Marion dead. But how would they do it? A hit-and-run, perhaps. An attack in a dark street. A strangling in a car, the body dumped. Something desperate, brutal and anonymous. But not arsenic poisoning.

The way Marion died had felt . . . what? Bizarre, certainly. Eccentric? That wasn't quite it. Rather elaborate and clever, with its references to her studies. Too much so. Like a student prank. It reminded Kathy of those student pranks at school on April Fools' Day, the bucket of water balanced over the door, the boot polish on the door handle, the collapsing chair. Elaborately staged, spectacular in their effects and at their best—or worst—cruelly matched to their intended victim.

She simply couldn't imagine any of those men doing it that way. The diagram on her wall was all wrong, she realised. She had been so influenced by Marion's, with its brooding male at the centre. Perhaps it wasn't like that at all.

A final image came into Kathy's mind, of Emily sitting sobbing on the leather sofa, as pale and racked as the two victims, whose symptoms she almost seemed to mimic. Da Silva wasn't the only one who'd been at the British Library when Tina died. Emily had been there too.

THIRTY

SUZANNE ALSO SPENT A disturbed night. Angela's story about Dougie had unsettled her more than she'd been prepared to admit to herself. He had been her first great love, a dazzling figure against whose memory later boys had been measured and invariably found wanting. Even much later, when she matured and married, the summer in Notting Hill remained a lost Eden in her mind, to be nurtured and occasionally savoured in secret. Angela's story had thrown all that into a new, grotesque perspective, and one that, if it were remotely true, resonated horribly with the case David was working on. She shuddered to think of the ramifications if she told him; but suppose Angela, who obviously hadn't heard of the connection between Marion Summers and the Warrenders, did eventually pick it up, and decide to tell her story to the police? Where would Suzanne be then? One way or another, she didn't see how she could keep it to herself without some kind of reassurance that the story was nonsense. She couldn't approach Dougie, that was unthinkable, but in the end she decided that there was perhaps just one person who might put her mind to rest. And so, that Wednesday evening while Brock and Kathy were charging Tony da Silva with Marion's murder, Suzanne had phoned the house in Notting Hill and asked to speak to Lady Joan Warrender.

Joan remembered her straight away. She was polite, but naturally puzzled at being approached like this, especially after Sophie had told them all about how angry she'd got with DCI Brock.

"But how exactly can I help you?"

"I wondered if I could meet you briefly in the next day or two, perhaps over a cup of tea, Lady Warrender."

"Oh, I really don't think that would be a good idea. Things have been said, you know, people upset. Sophie is very touchy about it. This is a very tense time for us all."

"Of course, I do understand." The old woman sounded so stern, and Suzanne tried in vain to think of some way to mollify her. It had been a bad idea approaching her like this.

"Perhaps if you gave me some idea of what it's about?"

"Well, I happened to meet another old friend recently, Angela Crick, who used to live next door to you, remember?"

"Yes?" Joan sounded bemused.

Suzanne ploughed on. "She told me a story that your nephew Jack had told her, all those years ago, about something that happened in India when you were living there, to do with Dougie."

"In India? About Dougie? Good Lord, what sort of story?"

"Well, it wasn't very nice, and I'm sure it was completely untrue, but I thought it might be a good thing if I could talk it over with you, and get to the bottom of it, so that I could get back to Angela and put her right. I didn't like the idea of her repeating it to anyone else."

Suzanne heard a little gasp from the other end, and imagined the old woman sinking onto the chair in the hall beside the telephone, trying to gather her wits.

"I'm sorry, Lady Warrender. I shouldn't have bothered you. I'm sure I can take care of it myself."

"But . . . no, if it concerns Dougie . . . Have you spoken to him?"

"I thought it best to speak to you first."

"Yes, you're probably right. Oh dear. Very well, let's meet. Not here at the house, and not in a café either—I can't hear anything in places like that anymore. Meet me at the churchyard of St.

John's, just up the hill from us. I often walk up there for a little
exercise. Tomorrow? Shall we say eleven?"

FIRST THING THAT MORNING Kathy checked the passenger lists
of both airline and private flights between London, Nice and Bastia for the months of February, March and April—something, she
told herself, she should have done weeks ago. She established that
Douglas and Sophie Warrender alone had travelled out on the
tenth of March, returning on the sixth of April.

Impatient as she was to follow this up, she couldn't get out of a
scheduled team meeting, and sat through it barely concentrating
on the briefing about a new computer system. When it was finally
over she picked up the phone and dialled the number of the Warrenders' house. Sophie's secretary Rhonda answered.

"I'm afraid Sophie's out this morning, Inspector, working in the
library."

"Ah. Is Emily with her?"

"No, she's at home. Do you want to speak to her?"

"No need to disturb her. Actually it would be better if I spoke
to her in person. I'll come over right away."

Bren tried to intercept her on her way out, but she put him off.
She would have found it hard to explain the sense of urgency she
felt. Rather than wait for a car from the pool, she caught a passing
cab, and made good time to Lansdowne Gardens.

"That was quick." Rhonda opened the front door to let Kathy in,
then hesitated. "After you rang off I wondered if this was wise."

"How do you mean?"

"Emily's really not very well at the moment, in fact she's still in
bed, and Sophie's very protective. She probably wouldn't approve
of you interviewing Emily with neither her nor Lady Joan here in
the house."

"Well, let's ask Emily, shall we? She is eighteen, isn't she?"

"Yes, and I'm sure it would be all right, but . . ."

Kathy sensed something equivocal in Rhonda's voice, as if she didn't want to be accused of wrongdoing, but at the same time wanted to help.

"Were you here at all during the month Sophie was away, Rhonda?"

"Yes, I came in each day and kept an eye on the decorators and reported on progress to Sophie from time to time."

"Was Emily here?"

"Yes, she and Lady Joan didn't want to go to Corsica, so they stayed here, more or less camping in their rooms in the middle of all the mess. Emily was helping Marion with her research most days, and Joan got out in the garden when she could. Look, I'll tell you what. Why don't you wait in the office, and I'll tell Emily you're here?"

"Fair enough."

Kathy walked down the short corridor to the room at the end where Rhonda and Sophie worked. The tall sash windows filled it with light, and the shelves of books gave it the appearance more of an elegant library than an office. She was examining the books on Sophie's desk when Rhonda returned.

"We're considering Alice Kipling for the next book, after Janey Morris is done with," she said. "Rudyard's wife, one of the MacDonald sisters. Her sister Georgiana was married to the Pre-Raphaelite painter Edward Burne-Jones and got very chummy with William Morris, commiserating over the fact that both their spouses were unfaithful."

"All these Victorians seem to be interconnected," Kathy said.

Rhonda laughed. "Too right, you need a bloody good database to sort them all out."

"Lovely room to work in."

"Yes. Have you been up to the belvedere yet?" She nodded to the spiral staircase in the corner.

"No. Is it interesting?"

"I think so." She said it with an emphasis that made Kathy pause. "Why don't you pop up now? Emily's getting dressed."

"Okay."

She mounted the stairs, arriving in the corner of the square tower room which Joan's husband, Roger, had converted into his eyrie. The original owner of the house had an interest in astronomy, and had had it built as an open loggia to house his telescopes, but Roger had enclosed it, leaving narrow windows in each of the corners with views out over Notting Hill, and with timber bookcases and a desk filling the walls between. The room had a lingering smell of cigar smoke, which had thoroughly permeated the wood. The ceiling and floor were both polished timber, so that the room had the feeling of a large cigar box.

Kathy sat in the red leather antique office chair, feeling the snug fit of the room around her, a sanctuary for contemplation. A thick leather-bound tome lay on the desk in front of her, and she read the title in gold letters on the front, *British Pharmaceutical Codex*.

There was a place marker, a piece of folded, stained paper, and when Kathy opened the book and removed the paper she found that it was a piece of old wallpaper, faded green in colour, with a pattern of swirling leaves. It marked a section headed with the title *Arsenic*.

She read for a moment, then heard feet on the stairs behind her. She turned to see Emily's pale face appear.

"What are you doing?" The girl reached the top of the stair and took in the open book on the desk, the unfolded piece of wallpaper. "Oh!" She bit her lip. "I put that away! How . . . ?"

Kathy held her eyes, saying nothing, and suddenly Emily gave a little wail. "You know, don't you? You know!" Tears started from her eyes and she sank to her knees, wrapping her arms around herself, and began to sob.

SUZANNE FOUND JOAN WAITING on a seat in a quiet shady spot at the side of the church. She was wearing an overcoat and hat against the cool breeze, and had a large bag on her knee.

"Ah, there you are," she cried, and Suzanne shook her hand and sat beside her.

"Thank you so much for agreeing to see me. I did feel awkward about approaching you."

"Yes, well, in view of Sophie's sensitivity on the subject, I think it best if we don't mention it to anyone."

"Yes, but you see, it was because of those sensitivities that I thought I should talk to you about this."

Joan frowned. "About what Angela said about Dougie in India? So what did she say?"

"I don't know if you remember, but Angela and Jack were very close in those days, and she said that he'd told her that the reason you all left India and returned to the UK was because of a scandal about Dougie getting a girl pregnant—the daughter of one of your servants, actually."

Suzanne was aware of the elderly woman at her side becoming very still.

"I'm sorry, this is probably distressing for you, and I'm sure utterly mistaken, but I thought if you could tell me the truth of the situation I could put Angela straight, and stop her repeating the story."

"Was there anything else?"

"Well, yes, there was actually. She said that the girl took poison and died, and there was a fuss. You see, I'm afraid that if Angela were to read something like the report in last week's *Observer*, which mentioned that Marion had been working for the writer Sophie Warrender, she might, well, I don't know, start talking to other people about it."

Joan was silent for a moment, then said quietly, "I see. And you didn't tell her about that connection?"

"No, I didn't."

"And have you discussed this story with anyone else?"

"Not a soul."

"Good." Joan took a deep breath and went on, "You did the right thing to speak to me. Because there is not a shred of truth in it. It sounds like some kind of fanciful tale that Dougie must have told Jack to make our days in India seem more interesting and exotic. I remember him telling him another ridiculous story about the elephant's foot, about how he shot the beast, quite absurd. Good Lord, Dougie was only sixteen when we left!"

That didn't seem an altogether conclusive argument to Suzanne, and there was something else about Joan's explanation, a kind of resentful, defensive tone in her voice, that seemed out of key. But she said cheerfully, "Oh good, I thought it must be something like that."

"So you'll tell Angela this?"

"I will."

"If she's not convinced, you can tell her to look up the diplomatic papers for the period at the National Archives in Kew. They're accessible to the public now. Emily looked them up, when she was helping Marion. There's not a whiff of scandal, but plenty of glowing praise for Roger's splendid service. I can give you the references if you like."

"Oh, thank you." Again there had been a defensiveness about Joan's reply, almost as if it were a prepared defence, but then, Suzanne thought, she had probably been deeply offended by the suggestion that their time in India might have been soiled by any kind of scandal. "I am relieved. I'll tell Angela in no uncertain terms, and I'd better tell my friend, Chief Inspector Brock, as well, so he knows, in case it ever comes up."

"What? No! Certainly not. You mustn't do that."

Suzanne was startled by the vehemence of the other woman's words, and felt that she was suddenly seeing a younger, more abrasive version of Lady Warrender, imposing her will on those around her.

"I think it would be sensible to tell him."

"No, do you hear? You'll do no such thing!"

Suzanne flushed and turned away. It had been a long time since anyone had spoken to her like that. "Well," she said slowly, "that's really for me to decide, Lady Warrender."

The old woman gave a strange, guttural growl and hunched away. There was a moment's awkward silence, and then she let out a deep sigh. "Oh dear," she said, her voice now frail again and winsome. "I'm afraid it is one of the tragedies of old age that one can so often see the wise and safest course, but is unable to summon up the ability to persuade others. You really must do whatever you see fit, my dear. Please, we mustn't quarrel about it."

"No," Suzanne said with relief. "I don't want to do that."

"Now look, see what I've brought." She opened the bag on her lap and drew out a gold cardboard box. Opening the top, she showed Suzanne the chocolates inside. "I've been busy this morning. The kitchen is my refuge these days, and one of my great joys is making treats for my family and friends. Do you like liqueur chocolates? Of course you do, everyone does. And what are your favourites? I have made them all—rum raisin, cumquat brandy, crème de menthe. They're all here. Come now, let's be friends. Take your pick."

Suzanne smiled. She didn't really want a chocolate, but she could hardly refuse. She chose a rum raisin. She bit into it and its syrupy heart oozed into her mouth and down her throat.

"Good?"

"Delicious."

"Try another."

"TELL ME," KATHY SAID.

"You know. You've found her, haven't you?"

A jangle of alarm sounded in Kathy's head. *Found who?* "Emily, tell me quickly!"

But the girl suddenly clamped a hand over her mouth and jumped to her feet. She clattered down the spiral staircase in a rush, and Kathy got to her feet to follow her. By the time she reached the foot of the stair Emily was gone. Kathy looked at Rhonda, who was staring at her in consternation. "Where is she?"

Rhonda pointed at the door to the hall, and followed as Kathy ran out, calling Emily's name. They heard a cupboard door bang in the kitchen, and found Emily standing at a bench holding a glass jar of white powder, which she was shovelling into her mouth.

Kathy cried out and lunged at the girl, jerking the jar out of her grip, then grabbed her by the hair and dragged her over to the sink where she used her free hand to turn on the tap and force Emily's head under it, then stuck her hand in the girl's mouth. She choked and struggled, but Kathy forced her fingers into her throat until she was sick. She turned back to Rhonda, who was looking horrified, and said, "Has she seen anyone else this morning?"

"No, no one, only her grandmother."

"Where is she?"

"She went out for her morning walk, as she always does, to St. John's church, up the hill."

"Call an ambulance, Rhonda, and don't let anyone touch that powder."

She half carried, half dragged Emily out to the hall and sat her in the chair beside the phone while Rhonda made the call. She didn't want to leave Rhonda alone with Emily, but the girl looked utterly defeated, and Kathy was gripped by a terrible anxiety. She fired some more instructions at Rhonda, then flew out of the house and raced down the street, at the same time calling on her mobile for help. A man getting out of his car stared at her in surprise as she sprinted past, down to the corner, then up the long rise towards the stone spire of St. John's. As she drew closer, heart hammering in her chest, she made out two people sitting on a bench against the church wall. She thought she recognised the elderly figure in the burgundy hat and coat, and the other looked a little like Suzanne. Astonished, Kathy realised that it *was* Suzanne. She called out.

SUZANNE HEARD THE SHOUT and looked up to see a fair-haired woman running up the hill towards them. She paused, her hand with the second chocolate almost at her mouth, then lowered it again.

"Kathy?"

She turned to Lady Warrender, and was shocked by the curl of utter hatred on the old woman's mouth, as if for the first time seeing the real face behind the genteel mask.

THIRTY-ONE

SUZANNE SAT PROPPED UP against the pillows. It was absurd the fuss they were making. After the second bout of sickness had passed she'd been reasonably comfortable, though her stomach still ached. Dr. Mehta had been in to see her, eagerly discussing symptoms with the A&E registrar. And Kathy, to whom she'd given a statement. But not yet Brock, though she knew he was pacing impatiently outside in the waiting room. Finally she took a deep breath and asked a nurse to let him in.

He came like a storm front through the ward, black coat flying, face dark, trolleys rattling in his wake. "How the hell are you?"

She smiled. "Completely fine."

He subsided onto the chair beside her bed. "You're white as a sheet. What are they giving you?"

"Everything's under control."

"That's what Sundeep said, but I didn't like the look on his face, as if he was already planning the PM."

They lapsed into silence, and then she said, "Has Kathy explained?"

"She gave me some sort of account. I understand you felt you had to check the story you got from your friend, about Warrender poisoning someone, in India."

"I didn't know if it was relevant. I had to be sure before I told you, David. I'm so sorry, after I promised—"

"Hush." He took her hand. "My fault. I should have been a better listener. I've been taking you for granted."

She shook her head. Another silence, while someone was wheeled past, groaning. Then Suzanne nodded at the parcel under Brock's arm. "What's that?"

"Oh, when they told me to go away for an hour, I went for a walk and came across a bookshop." He handed her the package. "A get-well present."

She peeled away the wrapping to reveal a thick volume, a biography of David Hockney. "Aha . . . lovely."

"I thought I'd give the nineteenth century a miss," he said. "And the girl assured me no one gets poisoned."

She had turned to an image of palm trees against a blue sky, and said, "California . . . I believe there's an antiques dealers' convention in Sacramento next month."

She said it with a certain edge, reminding him of the last time she'd planned a big trip and he'd let her down.

"Well then, we should go."

THEY FOUND MORE SCRAPS of the wallpaper in the garden outhouse, and a tub in which, according to Sundeep, the paper had been soaked in vinegar, a weak acid, in order to dissolve the colouring of Paris Green, copper acetoarsenite, used in the William Morris print. The women had then apparently mixed washing soda with the solution, to precipitate the insoluble copper carbonate and leave a clear solution of arsenic trioxide, which could be concentrated and eventually collected as a fine white powder.

"Emily was good at chemistry at school," Kathy said. "She was going to read it at Oxford. She must have discovered what was going on between her father and Marion, and when her parents went off to Corsica, she and her grandmother decided that something had to be done. She found the old books on the chemistry of arsenic in her grandfather's eyrie, where he'd pondered over them, trying to understand what had gone wrong with his tubewell project in Bengal, and she realised that the arsenic-coated wallpaper being stripped from their walls, hidden under layers for over a hundred years, could be the instrument of retribution. It must have seemed like poetic justice somehow."

But this was all conjecture, for neither Emily, in a hospital ward, nor Joan were saying a word. Douglas too, devastated by what had happened, denied all knowledge of the tale that Angela had told Suzanne. It seemed that forensic analysis of her home-made arsenic-laced chocolates would certainly support a charge of attempted murder by Joan against Suzanne, and possibly, though more circumstantially, of murder by Emily against Tina. But if they held their silence, there was frustratingly little evidence to connect them to Marion's death, and Kathy could imagine the sympathetic effect of the two defendants on a jury, and the psychologists' reports that the defence would call up, representing the crimes as desperate acts of temporary insanity by two essentially decent people.

There was still, Kathy felt, a void at the centre of the story, a darkness, like Sundeep's arsenic mirror, hiding some crucial element that no one would admit.

THE LONDON LIBRARY WAS busy when Kathy arrived. A group of Welsh librarians on a trip to London were being given the tour, and Kathy waited for a while in the main hall for Gael Rayner to be free. It seemed such an improbable place for an act of violence, she thought, and yet, at the British Library, Marion had uncovered a little book which might have destroyed a man's reputation and very nearly, perhaps, provided a motive for her murder. Maybe it wasn't the only innocent-looking text she'd found.

"Kathy! Hello. Any developments?"

"I believe there are, Gael. We've charged Emily Warrender and her grandmother Joan with murder and attempted murder." She saw the astonishment register on the librarian's face. "Yes, I know. It seems they didn't like the idea of Marion and Emily's father being lovers."

"Sophie Warrender's husband? Oh my God!" Gael shook her head, taking it in. "And is there something you need here? Evidence of some kind?"

"Maybe, if I can find it. Tell me, do you have any books on balloons?"

"Balloons?" She stared at Kathy, then, seeing she was serious, collected herself and sat down at the computer. "How about *The Aeronauts: A History of Ballooning, 1783–1903*, by Rolt, L.T.C.?"

"Could be."

"You want me to get it for you?"

"I'd like to look at its place in the stacks."

"Its shelfmark is *S* for science, *Ballooning*. Come on, I'll show you."

They went through to the floors of book stacks at the back of the building, coming to the Science and Miscellaneous section, then working alphabetically through to *S. Ballooning*, between *S. Astronomy* and *S. Biology* against the long side wall. Kathy began to remove books, until she found what she was looking for, a small green volume tucked between two others, its shelfmark *H. India*.

"This is in the wrong place," Gael said.

"Yes, it is, isn't it?" Kathy said, and turned to page 213. It was intact.

of unparalleled devotion to the service. There was, however, one incident in 1963 which cast a disastrous pall upon all our efforts, a potential scandal so serious indeed as to threaten a diplomatic rift at the highest level.

One of our senior diplomats, let us call him W, had a son, a cheeky and unruly brat in his childhood, who had developed into a precocious youth, whose sense of seemly conduct left much to be desired. This youth, D, was raised by a devoted ayah, a modest Christian woman of impeccable character, who had a daughter, a year younger than D, who was flattered by his attentions. She became pregnant by him, and, so it was said, overcome with shame and unable to face her mother, she took her own life by eating arsenic, a horrible fate. Then a younger sister revealed the association with D, and rumours began to circulate that he had been with her on the night she took the poison, and that he had forced her to take it. Her family was incensed, their cause was taken up by opportunistic politicians in Dacca, and the affair threatened to take on the dimensions of an international incident.

Fortunately I was able to call upon my extensive contacts in the Pakistani cabinet to bring the scandal under control. A compensation package was agreed between W and the girl's mother, mediated principally by myself and a good friend in the Justice Ministry. W and his family were hastily posted back to London, and official references to the affair deleted from the records. For W it was an ignominious end to a meritorious, if somewhat unconventional, term in Bengal.

On a more positive note, however, shortly after this unfortunate episode was concluded I convened a round table of Western diplomats to reach a consensus on our response to the new constitution for Pakistan promulgated by General Ayub Khan; a meeting, I think one can in all modesty claim, that was a triumph for British diplomacy.

"Harding was a shit," Douglas Warrender said. "He was pompous, smug and dull, everything my father wasn't, and he hated us as a result. The scandal over Vijaya's death was a godsend for him, and he wallowed in it. When my father heard that he was publishing his memoirs in 1973, he demanded to see Harding's manuscript, and threatened to sue if they didn't remove page 213. It was a lie, you see, about my involvement in her death. Vijaya took the poison without telling me or anyone else. The book had been printed, a short run that Harding intended mainly for his friends, to big-note his mediocre career. In the end he agreed to cut out the offending page, but out of spite he kept one uncut copy which he presented to the London Library, where he was a member. Marion found it.

"I told you before, didn't I, about the sense of tragic fate that hung over my father's attempt to help the people of Bengal? Well, it was even worse than I said. You see, although my father defended and supported me, I don't think he was ever quite sure if the accusation that I had murdered Vijaya was true. I believe he threw himself into the tubewell program as a kind of atonement for the wrong that had been done to her. And then, you see, Marion's interest in arsenic in the nineteenth century led her to this stupid book. She was a very smart researcher, Marion. Very thorough, as Dr. da Silva also discovered."

"What did she propose to do with it?" Brock asked.

"Despite her apparent self-confidence and independence, Marion had a deep streak of insecurity. Although I had given her the house, the baby and many promises, she didn't really trust me to go through with it. She actually thought—it sounds so sad and pathetic to say this now—she thought she could guarantee my fidelity by holding that damn book over me. She actually said she would give it to me on our first wedding anniversary. I laughed. I told her that it was history, no one was interested in that stuff any more. But I was wrong, wasn't I? I think Emily overheard us, and told Joan. She couldn't allow it to come out again. My father had gone through so much."

"I HEARD THEM TALKING together in the house one day. They thought no one else was at home. I heard Marion say she'd hidden the book somewhere no one would ever find it. Then she told Dad she didn't want him to go to Corsica. She said that he couldn't have us both, he would have to decide. He said he had to go, but he would tell everyone when they got back."

Emily was sitting in an armchair in her room in the private clinic, Kathy recording their conversation, Brock listening in silence. Her solicitor was seated at Emily's side, silhouetted against the windows and a view of bright sunlight glittering on green foliage. But Emily seemed shrouded in a dark world of her own, her voice faint, eyes rimmed with shadow.

"It was the first I knew about their affair. I couldn't believe it. I didn't know who to talk to. I couldn't tell Mum, I just couldn't. So I spoke to Gran. She said she'd suspected as much. She didn't tell me what was in the book, but she said it was pure poison, and must never be found. She said Dad had got into a scrape like this once a long time ago, and that it was up to us to put a stop to it, as she had then. Marion was a parasite who would destroy all our lives, she said, but if we were strong enough we could put everything right, while Mum and Dad were in Corsica.

"I thought, I really did think, that she meant we would confront Marion and make her leave Dad alone, maybe give her money, but Gran said that wouldn't work with someone like Marion. She said there was only one way to stop her."

Emily buried her face in her jumper and began to cry, soft, choking sobs. They waited, and waited, and she began again.

"I said no, I couldn't do something like that, but Gran said it was simple, she knew a way, but if I didn't want to be involved she would do it on her own. Only she needed a little help with the preparation. I tried to argue with her—I did! But she had made her mind up. Well, you know Gran."

By now Kathy felt Emily wasn't talking to them anymore, but instead to someone inside her head, her better half, perhaps, to whom she'd made this appeal many times before.

"We'd talked about the wallpaper before. Gran knew the stories about old green Morris wallpapers containing arsenic, and we'd spoken about warning the decorators. She wanted me to find out how to extract the poison. When I refused, she said, oh well, she'd have to resort to some other method, take Mum's car and run Marion down in the street, or push her under a train on the tube. She'd have tried too, so in the end I looked up Grandpa's old books in the belvedere and worked it out. I never thought we could make much, and I hoped it might just keep Gran quiet, but then I had to help her—I was afraid she'd poison herself with the fumes, boiling up all that wallpaper, night after night, after the workmen had left. I was amazed when we ended up with as much as we did."

There was a touch of eagerness in this, as if the experiments, the trials and errors, had been rather exciting. Kathy imagined the two of them in the darkened house, witches preparing a deadly brew.

"I spent as much time with Marion as I could, helping her, and I got to know her routine. I followed her home one day and found out where she lived, and Gran found a set of Dad's keys in his study. I also knew about the packed lunch she prepared each day, always the same, a sandwich, a chocolate biscuit and a bottle of juice.

"When it came to that last week before Mum and Dad came back, Gran said we had to act. On the Monday, while Marion was away at the library, we drove over to Rosslyn Court and let ourselves in. We found her bottles of drink in a kitchen cupboard and poisoned each one, then we returned later that evening and waited outside the house. We thought, if she drank one of the bottles that evening we could wait until it was all over, then go in and arrange the things to make it look like she'd done it herself. But she didn't. When she went to bed we phoned her, pretending it was a wrong number, just to be sure. When we returned the next morning we saw her leave for the London Library just as normal, and when we went inside we saw that one of the bottles was missing."

"What about her computer?"

"I borrowed it from her on the Monday, saying I needed to transcribe work I was doing for her, and on the Tuesday morning I took her spare hard disk from her study. Once we knew she was dead we threw both of them away."

"Okay. So after you realised she'd taken one of the bottles with her on the Tuesday, what happened then?"

"I took Gran to St. James's Square, then returned to Hampstead. Soon after one o'clock she phoned me to say that she'd seen Marion having lunch in the square, and drinking from the bottle. Then she phoned again to say that the ambulance had arrived, and I went into the house and set up the things in the kitchen."

"And Tina?"

"Ah . . ." A sad, exhausted sigh. "I begged her to let me help her with what she was doing, because she was so determined to find out what had happened. She just wouldn't leave things alone, trying to find that book. I could tell, that day at the British Library, that she'd found it. She wouldn't say, but she was boiling inside. She said we'd soon have the answer, so I had to do something. I bought us a coffee, and . . . put stuff in hers."

"But Tina knew nothing about your father's story," Kathy said. "The book she was searching for was the Haverlock diary, wasn't it?"

Emily gave Kathy a despairing look. "I wasn't sure. We felt that if she was following the same trail as Marion she was bound to find the book that incriminated Dad. We felt we had no choice, you see. I hated it, the whole thing. It made me sick to think of it, but I had to just shut my mind and do what Gran said, otherwise I knew it would be a disaster."

But Brock wasn't buying that. "You knew Marion was pregnant, didn't you?" The girl gave him a sudden sharp look.

"No," she said softly.

"You picked it up from the conversation you overheard." Kathy saw a moment's consternation on Emily's face and knew that Brock was right. "And you assumed that she was still pregnant when you killed her. How could you know otherwise?" He leaned forward and said, "Your grandmother didn't have to persuade you, Emily. You thought Marion deserved to die, didn't you?"

Emily held his eye, silent for a moment, then whispered, "Yes."

AT THE END OF the following week Brock invited Suzanne and Kathy, along with Alex Nicholson and Sundeep Mehta, to dinner in a newly refurbished restaurant not far from Rossetti's house in Chelsea. Both Joan and Emily Warrender had been charged with the murders of Marion and Tina, while Bren had arrested Keith Rafferty and Brendan Crouch on a string of burglary charges arising from the information passed on by Donald Fotheringham. It was important, Brock felt, to acknowledge the end of the business and move on, and while he might have done this with Suzanne alone, and no doubt would in time, for the moment he sought safety in numbers. Despite their good humour, there was, he felt, an air of mortality about the occasion, only heightened by the stylishness of the surroundings and the size of the eventual bill. Earlier in the day there had been a painful interview with Sophie Warrender, and her distress lingered on, for Brock at least, like a shadow in the background. She had reminded him of her comment when they had first met, that their work was similar, searching for the truth beneath the surface of things, but now she realised the bitter fallacy of the comparison. The difference between probing the past and the present was pain.

But Sundeep was in good form. The son of his friend, who had made the initial misdiagnosis, was off the hook, and during the course of vetting Colin Ringland's laboratory, Sundeep had become friendly with the scientist, to the extent of agreeing to collaborate on the medical ramifications of the research into the poisoned wells. Now he was debating with Alex about the death of Lizzie Siddal, and whether the doctor who examined her could really have mistaken arsenic for laudanum as the cause of death. Alex had been reading up about the case and was intrigued by a number of aspects. What was the nature of the insanity that grew in Rossetti after Lizzie's death? And why did he insist that he must on no account be buried in the same cemetery as her? But Marion's theory about the involvement of Madeleine Smith/Lena

Wardle was frustratingly elusive. No complete copies of Marion's paper to Cornell had surfaced, and without Haverlock's diary it was impossible to test da Silva's claim that it was nonsense.

It was almost midnight when they left the restaurant and went their separate ways. When Kathy got home she stripped the notes and images off her wall, then had a long shower. Only then did she look through the mail she'd picked up from her box. Among the envelopes was a letter from the UAE. It contained an airline ticket, first class, to Dubai and a very brief letter. *Dear Kathy*, it said, *Forgive me. Please come and let me make it up to you. Love, Guy*. She threw it in the bin.

Later, as she went around switching off the lights, she fished it out again, and looked at it for a while. Then she put it on the table and said softly, "Oh, what the hell."

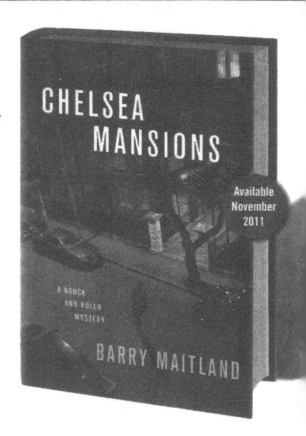